INTRODUCTION BY JULIE E. CZERNEDA

STRANGERS

TALES OF THE UNDERDOGS AND OUTCASTS

AMONG

US

STORIES BY

KELLEY ARMSTRONG
A.M. DELLAMONICA
GEMMA FILES
HAYDEN TRENHOLM
EDWARD WILLETT
A.C. WISE

AND MORE

EDITED BY SUSAN FOREST & LUCAS K. LAW

LAKSA ANTHOLOGY SERIES: SPECULATIVE FICTION

STRANGERS AMONG US

TALES OF THE UNDERDOGS AND OUTCASTS

LAKSA ANTHOLOGY SERIES: SPECULATIVE FICTION

Edited by Susan Forest & Lucas K. Law

LAKSA MEDIA GROUPS INC.
www.laksamedia.com

Strangers Among Us: Tales of the Underdogs and Outcasts
Laksa Anthology Series: Speculative Fiction

Library and Archives Canada Cataloguing in Publication

   Strangers among us : tales of the underdogs and outcasts / edited
by Susan Forest and Lucas K. Law ; [introduction by Julie E. Czerneda].

(Laksa anthology series: speculative fiction)
Issued in print and electronic formats.
ISBN 978-0-9939696-0-7 (paperback).—ISBN 978-0-9939696-4-5 (bound).—
ISBN 978-0-9939696-2-1 (pdf).—ISBN 978-0-9939696-1-4 (epub).—
ISBN 978-0-9939696-3-8 (kindle)

   1. Science fiction, Canadian (English). 2. Fantasy fiction, Canadian (English).
3. Speculative fiction, Canadian (English). 4. Mental health—Fiction. .Mental illness—
Fiction. I. Forest, Susan, editor II. Law, Lucas K., editor

PS8323.S3S77 2016   C813'.0876208353   C2015-907597-1
                                                      C2015-907598-X

LAKSA MEDIA GROUPS INC.
Calgary, Alberta, Canada
www.laksamedia.com
info@laksamedia.com

Edited by Susan Forest and Lucas K. Law
Cover and Interior Design by Samantha M. Beiko

FIRST EDITION
Printed in Canada

Susan Forest

To my parents,

Don and Peggy Forest,

Who shared with me their love of stories.

Lucas K. Law

To my parents,

Leonard & Florence Law,

For the joy of reading and love of libraries;

To my partner,

Tim H. Feist,

For the continuing support and love;

In memory of

Marilyn Lewis-Steer,

Who challenged me to tackle this anthology project

(instead of talking about it).

CONTENTS

FOREWORD

Lucas K. Law

My family loves to read newspapers, books and magazines, regardless of category or genre; reading, or rather, the quest for knowledge and information, must be etched in our genetic make-up. So, it isn't a surprise that the public library was my favourite childhood haunt. I was constantly flooded by my over-active imagination; I chatted with my imaginary friends, making plans, dreaming ideas and telling stories.

And let's not forget food, the cradle of my family's gatherings and kitchen conversations, constant in motion throughout my life: for, through stories, our mother's home-cooked meals offered a window into our past, present and future.

What do reading, imaginary playmates, and clan gatherings have in common to this book you are holding?

Family and friends, creativity and story.

All of us have special memories and favourite stories in our kin traditions, which we often share, even with strangers. But, for some of us, buried beneath those wonderful connections lurk secrets, fears and self-doubts. We wear masks to hide, shade or guard our shame and loneliness. Sometimes, we do it so well, even our loved ones have no clue about our misery, struggle and depression.

For some, family support provides enough strength to allow them to overcome their struggles and challenges in a positive way. Others are not as fortunate. They watch their lives crumble away, layer by layer, piece by piece.

Each of us has a story to tell. In the last few years, several of my relatives and friends have been struck with mental illness. I have seen their isolation, fear, confusion, job losses, insecurity, and anxiety. Mental illness continues to be burdened by stigma, and despite loving support, often those affected still have difficulty asking for help or talking about their experiences without feeling guilt and shame.

The idea for this anthology germinated as I was struck by the thinness of the line between mental health and mental illness. Mental illness can target any age group at any time. Mental illness can afflict a person for a period of time or become a life-long struggle. Mental illness can spring from many sources and manifest in many forms.

In this anthology, Julie E. Czerneda and nineteen authors come together to show their support for mental health through the written word. Susan and I are grateful for their Tales of the Underdogs and Outcasts, for the glimpses we are given into these fictional lives warn us not to underestimate the underdogs and outcasts: they have the resources to teach or save the world.

This book is for a special friend and fellow writer, Marilyn Lewis-Steer, who passed away on May 28, 2015, after a valiant battle with cancer. She gave me the inspiration and mental adjustment I needed to begin this work. I will always remember Marilyn for her kind words, her belief in lifelong education, her support for volunteerism—to pay forward and give back. To her, I needed . . . I wanted to say a final thank-you. This one is for you, Marilyn.

Please promote mental health and support your local charitable organizations. A portion of this anthology's net revenue will go to support the Canadian Mental Health Association.

—Lucas K. Law, Calgary and Qualicum Beach, 2016

INTRODUCTION

Julie E. Czerneda

Who are strangers?

People we don't yet know. We spot them, cued to their difference from the familiar-to-us by their look, by how they walk or talk or dress. We prepare for each new encounter, for you never know—do you?—with strangers.

Strangers. The harried mother who spares a fleeting smile . . . the tattooed boarder who gallantly holds the door . . . the executive bickering with thin air . . . the teen moving to music only she can hear . . . the blue-faced football fan who weaves and waves to everyone around.

Strangers. The child who doesn't meet your eye or smile back . . . the ancient who rocks and spits . . . the man who stalks by, swearing at passing cars . . . the huddled silent shape in a doorway, eyes fixed on air.

Strangers.

Our reaction, of course, depends on many things: the situation, our experience and expectations, how they seem to us at first glance. It's instinctive and often necessary to make a snap judgment: ignore, avoid, or greet. We don't come tagged with our inner truths. We can't tell by looking if that angry-looking stranger is angry at us—

Or at something only she can see.

Scary either way, isn't it? Such a disquieting awareness, that the mind can be ill. We know what to do about gashed skin or child's fever. We can see for ourselves when a wound is healed or a child is over a flu. The mind though. It's secretive, complex, powerful. When it's sick, we flinch, not knowing what to do, unable to see. There's nothing familiar to guide us.

Which is why stories like the ones gathered in this astonishing anthology are important. They put us inside the heads of strangers. They make us feel those inner truths. What is it like to be angry or afraid, to hear voices, to be unable to relate to another human being, to struggle and slip and struggle and wish—above all—to be understood. To strive when it's our minds—not crippled limbs or other ills of the flesh—that betray and hobble us. To do our best when society, family, friends ignore or dismiss us.

To triumph, as in these stories, despite that terrible solitude. Or . . . because of it.

As with any encounter, there's the chance you'll meet a stranger here who proves familiar; maybe someone you already know. Maybe yourself.

If you do, toss away experience and expectation. Ignore the differences. Dismiss pity and any preconception of weakness.

Instead see the potential. Feel the passion.

For we are all strangers to one another, locked inside our minds, healthy or not quite. We're each the unique sum of advantage, disadvantage, and living with both. As you read these imaginative, original stories, you'll discover what matters most of all:

What we choose to be.

—Julie E. Czerneda, Severn, 2016
Author of *The Clan Chronicles* from DAW Books

THE CULLING
Kelley Armstrong

We grew up with stories of how the Cullings saved us. Stories of the famines and the aftermath, a world that once grew grain and corn in abundance, the forests overrun with rabbits and deer, lakes and streams brimming with trout and salmon. How all that had come to an end, the water drying up and everything dying with the drought—the grain and the corn and the rabbits and the deer and the trout and the salmon. And us. Most of all, us.

Left with so few resources, it was not enough to simply ration food and water. Not enough to reduce birth rates. Not enough to refuse any measures to prevent death. We needed more. We needed the Cullings.

The Cullings removed surplus population by systematically rooting out "weakness." At first, they targeted the old and infirm. When that was no longer enough, any physical disability could see one culled. Even something that did not impair one's ability to work—like a disfiguring birthmark—was said to be enough, on the reasoning that there was a taint in the bloodline that might eventually lead to a more debilitating condition.

The population dropped, but so did the water supply, and with it, the food supply, and eventually more stringent measures were required. That's when they began targeting anyone who was different, in body or in mind. If you kept too much to yourself, rejecting the companionship of others; if you were easily upset or made anxious or sad; if you occasionally saw or heard things that weren't there . . . all were reasons to be culled. But the thing is, sometimes those conditions are easier to hide than a bad leg or a mark on your face. It just takes a little ingenuity and a family unwilling to let you go.

ᕕᕗ

"Who are you talking to, Marisol?" my mother says as she hurries into my room.

I motion to my open window, and to Enya, who had stopped to chat on her way to market. She says a quick hello to my mother and then a goodbye to me before carrying on down the village lane.

I murmur to my mother, "A real, living friend. You can see her, too, right?"

"I was just—"

"Checking, I know." I put my arm around her shoulders. Having just passed my sixteenth birthday, I'm already an inch taller and making the most of it. "I have not had imaginary friends in many years, Momma."

"I know. It's just . . . I've heard you talking recently. When you're alone."

"I argue with myself. You know how I am—always spoiling for a fight. If no one's around to give me one, I must make do." I smack a kiss on her cheek. "I don't hear voices, Momma. I'm not your sister. I have a little of what she did, but only a little, and I know how to hide it. I don't talk about my imaginary friends, even if they're long gone. I don't let anyone see my wild pictures. I don't tell anyone my even wilder stories. I am absolutely, incredibly, boringly normal."

She makes a face at me.

"What?" I say. "It *is* boring. But I will fake it, for you and Papa."

"For *you*, Mari. Our worries are for *you*, and yours should be, too."

"But I don't need to be worried, because I am very careful."

"The Culling is coming."

"As you have reminded me every day for the past month. I will be fine. I'll even stop arguing with myself, though that means you'll need to break up more fights between Dieter and me."

"Your brother will happily argue with you if it keeps you safe."

"It will." I give her a one-armed hug. "I'll be fine, Momma."

The Culling by KELLEY ARMSTRONG

Liar, the voice whispers in my ear. I squeeze my eyes shut, force it back and steer my mother from my room.

I have heard whispers that the Culling will be worse this year. Rumours say one of our two wells is running dry. The man who started the talk was a runner, one of those who carted the wheeled barrels from the well. The council called him a liar and a traitor. Said he'd been paid by another town to sow dissent. They executed him in the village square. But that hasn't stopped the rumours. If the well is drying up, this will indeed be a terrible Culling. And I must be prepared.

I do what I always do when I need a reminder. Because sometimes I do. There are nights and, yes, days, when the voice in my head says I shouldn't be so careful. I shouldn't need to be. That I should stand up and fight back. That I am a coward if I do not. But that is, I recognize, the sickness talking.

Fighting back is not an option. It absolutely is not, and it's madness to think it could be. I must remember that my aunt was the same age as me when she was culled. I must not comfort myself with my parents' insistence that my sickness is not as severe. Any defect—mental or physical—is cause for Culling.

I walk through the village square. At the far side is a wooden box, barely the height of an average person and even less wide. Inside is a man. He sits in the back corner, thin legs pulled in as he hums to himself. His hair is matted and filthy. His naked body reeks. We might not have the water to clean ourselves as we used to but we have adapted, and there is no excuse for this. No excuse other than that he does not care, is beyond caring, cannot even bring himself to let others run a damp rag over his skin.

He doesn't just smell of old sweat. There's the stench of urine and feces too. The notice beside his cage explains that he used to have a bucket, but it was taken away because the only use he made of it was to beat anyone who opened his door.

The man is here as a warning, lest we feel sympathy for something as harmless as talking to oneself. That was how his sickness started, the sign explains. As a boy who'd whispered to himself and then talked to himself and then shouted at himself, and others and the voices in his head.

This is you, that voice in my own head whispers. *This is what you'll become—naked and stinking in a box.*

I squeeze my eyes shut to silence it. It's quiet most of the time, like the girl in the corner of the class who rarely speaks, and you can almost forget she's there. Almost.

I come here to remind myself that she's there—that voice, that sickness.

My parents say my aunt never hurt anyone, that her voices never commanded her to do anything worse than draw wild pictures, beautiful and haunting pictures that she'd sketch in charcoal on wood slabs, before scrubbing them clean to reuse. My parents kept the last one she did, before she was Culled, and sometimes I pull it out and lose myself in it, and I weep because I see so much in them. Because I understand them—the fancies and the dreams and the nightmares within them, equally horrifying and beautiful.

I come here to remind myself of what I must keep hidden. Of how hard I must work to hide it. For my sake. For my family's sake.

Before I leave, I'll whisper to him and slide food between the bars, and feel guilty as I do so, as if I'm treating him like an animal. But it is all I can do. Repayment for the lesson he provides.

"Marisol?" a voice says behind me, and I turn to see Enya, market basket over her arm. She covers her nose with her free hand. "What are you doing here?"

"Reminding myself," I say.

Her brows rise. "Of what?"

"Of what the council protects us against. When the Culling comes, I will feel pity for those who only seem a little different and not at all dangerous. I'll remind myself of that." I point at the notice, which explains how he killed his entire family before being captured.

She nods. "It's hard sometimes." A wry smile. "Most times, I think, for anyone with a heart. But we must remember why it is done."

I say, by rote, "For the protection of all. So that we may be healthy and safe, and may bear equally healthy children who will contribute all that they can."

"Exactly," she says and loops her arm through mine. "Let's see if I can sell the rest of my wares, and we'll buy a treat and forget about the Culling. It does not concern the likes of us."

Oh, but it does, the voice whispers. *It really does.*

CR

The Culling begins with a physical examination. With my clothing off, two physicians inspect me from top to bottom. It doesn't matter if I've been undergoing this since birth. It is done every year in case some physical deformity, like a curve of the spine, appears as we grow into adulthood.

Next come the mental tests. These used to stop when we reached puberty, the assumption being that if we were slow of mind, it would have appeared by then. Now they continue until we are twenty, looking for signs of other mental impairment, the kind they believe might come with a sickness like mine. I have no such problems, though, and I fly through the tests.

The final stage is the psychological examination. That's the one I most fear. It's the one everyone fears. If we are quick to anger or sadness or even joy, might it be considered a sign of impairment? If we display the behaviour they call "obsessive" or "compulsive" or if our pattern of thinking is deemed to be different from the norm, might that be enough? Even to be overly anxious about the testing itself could see us labeled unfit.

My parents, using the example of my aunt, have trained me how to answer these questions. How to give the "normal" responses. I take a light sleeping draught for three nights before, to ensure my worry doesn't rob me of sleep. They feed me the best food available, a luxury even on their generous salaries. They give me half their rations of water. They brew teas meant to calm my nerves. In short, they do everything possible to ensure I am alert and happy and healthy and that nothing as small as being hungry and irritable might make the inquisitors take a closer look at me. I have always passed the tests with ease. As I do again this year.

I'm in the village hall with my brother, Dieter. No parents are present while the youth are being tested. It is allowed, but parents fear that even normal anxiety over their child's results could be misconstrued. So they stay out. Dieter and I are at the table together, receiving our results.

"Marisol Perret," the woman drones, not even looking up from her paper. "You have successfully passed this year's tests, as has Dieter Perret." She hands us two circles of paper. Both are yellow. "Please report to the next room to await further testing."

I look at my yellow circle and then at Dieter. He frowns and says to the woman, "But we passed. Our tests should be complete; our circles are green."

"There has been a change this year," she says, making a note in her book. "Those with a family history of impairment will undergo additional screening. You may proceed to the next room."

"But—" Dieter says.

She looks up sharply at that, cutting him short. "Do you wish to lodge a complaint, Dieter Perret?"

"No," I say quickly. "He's confused by the change, that's all. No complaint, ma'am."

She grunts, as if disappointed. A complaint is almost always accompanied by inexplicable test failure. I shoot Dieter a look. He mouths an apology, but worry clouds his eyes.

I lead him away and whisper, "I'll be fine. I always am."

Pure luck, the voice whispers. *And it cannot hold.*

CR

I sit across the table from the head inquisitor. I've never spoken to her before. I duck away whenever I see her coming in the streets. Now I keep asking myself what I've done to warrant her personal attention. Dieter is being tested by one of her underlings. But she came in especially for me.

I tell myself it's our family history and, since I am older than Dieter, I am more likely to show signs of the illness our aunt suffered. A simple matter of probability. Not suspicion. But as I sit there, watching her scratch in a notebook, having not yet said a word to me, sweat dribbles down my face and the voice whispers, *She knows.*

There is a cup on the table. She brought it with her. I thought perhaps she was bringing water, a subtle reminder to me of the danger we face as a village. Or a reminder of who she is, that she can drink so freely.

Yet she has placed the cup closer to me. I know it is not a peace offering. Not intended to put me at ease. I stare at that cup, and a drop of my sweat falls onto the table.

"Marisol Perret," she says finally, looking up. "Do you solemnly swear that all answers you have given in your previous interview are correct?"

I discreetly swallow before answering, so I don't stammer. Another trick my parents have taught me. I look her in the eye and say, "Yes, I do."

"Drink the contents of that cup, then, and we will be sure."

"What?"

"We have obtained a potion used by other villages to ensure honesty in the Culling interviews. Of course, we cannot afford to use it for everyone. But when there is a family history, combined with irregular responses in the interview—"

"Irregular?" My voice squeaks, and I struggle to deepen it before saying, "Irregular how, ma'am? I was told that I passed."

"Drink the contents of that cup, and I will re-conduct the interview."

"But—"

"Are you objecting, Marisol Perret?"

"N-no." *Control, Mari. Get it under control.* "I just . . . I don't understand. I'm not yet eighteen and if there is a change to the proceedings, my parents ought to be notified before I—"

"Are you objecting?"

"No, I—"

"Are you challenging the prerogative of the council?"

"Never. I just . . . I just want to understand."

"Drink the potion. Answer the questions. That's all you need to understand."

I hesitate just for a moment. She gets to her feet and calls to the guard posted behind her. "Please note that Marisol Perret has challenged the authority of this inquisitor and the Culling."

"No!" I leap up. "I never said—" I grab for the cup to drink, but she snatches it before I can.

"This interview is at an end. In refusing to participate, Marisol Perret has proven that she has something to hide. On that basis, she will be Culled at midnight tomorrow."

The guard strides forward and grabs me. I struggle as hard as I can, protesting that I didn't argue, didn't challenge her authority, that I'll take the potion, answer her questions . . .

He drags me out the door. The inquisitor is already gone.

See? The voice whispers. *You cannot win.*

ଔ

I am to be Culled. Not because of my sickness, but because they need to Cull more people this year, and I am as good a candidate as any. It is almost ironic, that after years of hiding my sickness, it isn't even that which damns me. It is a simple matter of logistics.

They need to reduce the population. My family has a history of sickness. I briefly questioned this new technique for revealing it. *Anyone* would have questioned it, feared it would reveal some hidden thread of sickness. We all worry about that in this world. We can't help it. We analyze every thought and emotion for the signs that could see us Culled.

I remember when I first started showing symptoms. My mother had tried to calm my fears. We all show "signs," she said, to some degree. We are sadder some days, more anxious on others. We have the occasional wild imagining. We may have a voice in our head that encourages us to do wrong or chides us when we do. It is a matter of scale. At the one end, yes, there are those like the man in the cage, where the sickness has eaten his mind. But they deserve care, not fear. And for the rest, like me, it is a matter of dealing with the symptoms as one would any minor ailment and allowing me to remain a productive member of society.

I don't know if I believe her. I've seen the man in the cage, and heard the words of the council too many times. I feared his fate was, indeed, my future.

Yet it is not. My future is to be dragged into the desert beyond the village and executed before I can consume any more precious resources.

My future ends at midnight.

Unless . . .

"We've bought the exemption, Mari," Dieter whispers outside my cell. He's snuck in. No one can visit those waiting to be Culled, but there are ways. Just as there are ways to avoid execution. My family has paid—dearly, I'm sure.

An exemption.

That does not mean I will be allowed to stay. Only that my life will be spared. That I will be freed once I'm taken to the place of execution. Freed to die in a barren desert wasteland. Because that's the only option, no matter how much desperate families convince themselves otherwise.

My family has paid for hope. And that's why I won't tell them to keep their money. However steep the cost, my mother still blames herself for not being able to scrape enough together when my aunt was Culled. My family needs that hope, to believe I have survived, found others who've been exiled, living like nomads in the desert. It is an impossible dream, but I owe it to them.

Once I'm freed, I'll find a quick way to die. It may not be as merciful as the executioner's axe, but it will grant me dignity. Choice.

I hug Dieter as best I can through the bars, and we both cry, but I tell him I'll be fine. I'm resourceful and determined. My sickness is far from debilitating. So, I'll be fine. Just fine. Better even, without the specter of the Culling hanging over me. I'll miss them all, but in the end I'll be better off.

Yes, the voice whispers. *You will.*

❧

We are taken into the desert at midnight. Taken far from the outer wall, so that no one traveling from the village in the days to come will stumble over our desiccated bodies. When we reach the spot, I see headless corpses stacked like cordwood, undisturbed from previous Cullings because there are no longer predators large enough to drag them away. The very sand around us is stained permanently red. Somewhere in that pile is my aunt. I turn away before I find myself searching for her.

The executioner works methodically. We are bound in a line, and he does not even free us from our ropes. We all kneel, still in that line, and he works his way down it. There are eleven of us. I know their names. Have spoken to them all before. In a village of two hundred, it is impossible not to have crossed paths. But here, we say nothing. We simply wait, resigned.

The executioner gets to the last three. I'm between the other two. The girl next in line will have an exemption. My family is well off; hers is wealthy. Sickness runs in it as well, the methodical sickness, with its obsessions and compulsions. I knew her in school, and had noticed those tendencies, but they were so slight they impaired her not at all. This year, that doesn't matter. This year, she was Culled.

She will have an exemption, though. That means the last three of us do. That's the logical way to do it, leave us for the end. Yet the executioner raises his axe and she lets out a cry, and I know she *does* have an exemption . . . and it doesn't matter. It never mattered. Wasted hope.

The axe falls, severing the rope binding her to the string of new headless corpses for the pile. Then it rises again and cuts the one between us. Another cut separates me from the young man to my right. We rise, shaking off the rope as the executioner efficiently tosses the new corpses on top of the old. We remain unmoving as he wordlessly begins the long trek back to the village.

"We should stick together," I say. "There's a chance we can survive if we—"

They run, in separate directions, leaving me alone.

What did you expect? The voice whispers.

 C3

I walk until I can't. Then I sleep. I need to find an easy way to kill myself, but nothing presents itself in this endless desert. I won't die of exposure. I just won't—that's a horrible way to go. Tomorrow I'll figure out a solution, even if it means burying my head in the sand and suffocating. For now, I'm too exhausted to even try that.

I wake in the night to a hand on my shoulder, but as I jump up, I don't panic. I think it's one of the other exemptions. They've realized I'm right—that we might stand some chance of survival together. He or she has tracked me down, not difficult through the sand. I'm a little alarmed by how eagerly I rise, just as I am by how disappointed I'd been when they ran. I might tell myself I don't hope to survive, but obviously I do. I cannot help it.

When I leap up, though, the face over my own is a weathered stranger's. He squeezes my shoulder and says, "Be calm, child. We have a place for you. A proper place."

A proper place.

You know what that means, the voice whispers.

An image of the man in the cage flashes through my mind. I've heard stories of this, of towns where they don't merely display one of the "sickened" as an example but where they have an entire menagerie of them for entertainment.

A proper place.

"Come," he says. "We'll—"

I lash out. I hit him hard, a blow to the stomach, and he falls back in surprise. I scramble up only to see two other shadowy figures. One holds a blade that glints in the starlight. I run at the other, who seems unarmed, but she knocks me down, and says, "We'll have to do it this way, then," and presses a noxious-smelling cloth over my mouth and nose. I still fight, I fight so hard, but my struggles fade and I fall into night as the voice whispers, *There is no escaping. You always knew that.*

I wake several times, enough to realize I'm in a cart, but I'm so groggy I fall straight back to sleep, lulled against my will by the heaviness in my head and the rhythm of the cart wheels. When I am finally able to open my eyes more than a slit, I'm no longer in that jostling cart. I'm in a darkened room on a pile of blankets, my head cradled on a pillow.

I rise and blink. It's a shelter of some kind, with fabric overhead. A tent? We've stopped to camp, then.

I blink to help my eyes adjust. Daylight seeps in through the fabric seams. The weathered man sits beside me. His eyes are closed, though. He's fallen asleep at his post.

I creep from my bed, my gaze fixed on him. He doesn't stir.

I make it to the tent flap and push it open. Light floods in, and I'm blinking to adjust again. That's when I hear voices—someone giving orders, someone talking, someone laughing. Voices from every direction.

I push my head out and see that I'm in a village. There are tents, like the one I'm in, but permanent buildings, too.

I curse under my breath. I've reached my destination. *My proper place.*

No matter. I can still escape. No one guards the door. I'll move carefully and, if I'm spotted and recognized as a stranger, I'll run. If I'm caught, I'll fight hard enough that they'll decide I'm not worth the effort and kill me. That will be better than any fate they have in store for me.

I slip along the tent. I can see people down the road. Two people walk and chat. A young woman hammers a board onto the side of a house a few doors down. A man heading toward her has some kind of device braced under his arm and his pant-leg hangs oddly, as if he's missing part of his leg. I stare at that, but I presume it's a recent injury and he'll be Culled next time, though it seems strange they'd waste the medical care required to treat such an injury. They certainly don't in my village. That keeps my attention and I walk out further than I intend.

Someone spots me—an older woman coming around the corner, talking to a man who seems distraught. She's assuring him everything is fine. I stare at that, too. Public displays of emotion are unwise—they could be mistaken for sickness. Perhaps she is his mother, getting him quickly off the street before anyone notices. She gives me a smile as she goes by, but apparently she's too caught up in her charge to notice I'm a stranger.

I look around. I can see a wall, like the one around our village, and I make my way toward it. As I do, a noise startles me, but it's only a thin piece of wood banging lightly in the breeze, a notice nailed to a building. I can't resist sidetracking to read it.

Village meeting next moon to discuss settlement at newly discovered spring.

Volunteer settlers may sign up for interviews at this time. Single, young tradespeople preferred but exceptions, as always, made for families.

The Culling by KELLEY ARMSTRONG

A new spring? Our village found one years ago, but decided it was too far to transport water. Why had they not considered this—relocating people to start a new village? Perhaps that wasn't possible and this was a trap—people would leave and never return, executed as a form of the Culling. Even as I think this, I know it doesn't make sense.

I look around. I see the man with the walking device has stopped. He's giving instructions to the young woman working on the building. She listens as he picks up a hammer and demonstrates, no more restricted by his impairment than I am by mine.

I look toward the distant wall and then back at what I can see of the village.

Is it possible this isn't what I thought?

No, I cannot believe that. I want it too much. Hope is a dangerous thing.

I continue toward the wall. That's when I see a picture on a building wall. A huge picture, taller than me. It's not *of* anything, not a literal representation. I see trees and storm clouds and lightning bolts, and it is magical and wondrous and terrifying. It reminds me of my aunt's picture, the one my parents hid. It reminds me of my own, too. Mine represented the maelstrom of my mind, the things I see in my head, equally wondrous and terrifying. And here they are, drawn large.

I'm seeing things. I must be. No one would show these things in public. No one would dare.

"Do you like it?" a voice asks behind me.

I turn to see my mother. It's then that I'm sure I'm dreaming. Or lost in my sickness, finally pulled under by that ever-threatening tide.

But it's not my mother. She's too young, perhaps around her thirtieth year. This woman looks like her and yet is not her. She looks like me and yet is not me. She's somewhere between the two and when I see her—really see her—a memory sparks deep in my mind.

"Hello, Marisol," she says. "It's been a long time."

I open my mouth, but my voice catches, a sob coming out instead. My aunt reaches for me and pulls me into a hug and says,

"You're safe now," and for the first time, the voice agrees. *Yes, now you're safe.*

DALLAS'S BOOTH
Suzanne Church

Dallas and his equipment waited for someone to dash into his phone booth and place a call. Any call. Trucks and streetcars screamed by while he squinted down at the sweet neon glow shining through the booth's plastic walls. The painted sheet metal roof had been defiled with a splat of white and green sludge—a Rorschach inkblot of defamation.

Damned birds.

He limped into the kitchen, channeling his rage into the knurled handle of his cane. His mother had presented him with the device when he'd still believed in the merits of physiotherapy. She'd found it at one of those conventions where people wore elf ears and talked in made-up languages. She declared it "cool." Said it would reduce the embarrassment factor. *Wrong.*

He grabbed a broken bucket from under the kitchen sink and filled it to just below the crack. Slopping and sloshing with every step, he walked back and heaved the water through his second-story window at the roof of his booth.

Problem solved.

Abandoning the bucket, he headed for the only seat in his living room: his lime-green leather chair. A throne in a cluttered kingdom of electronics.

He flicked the "On" switch for the lipstick-cam and turned the dial left, then right, then left once more to adjust the contrast for the live-feed video image of his booth's inner sanctum. Next, he activated the power bars for the computers, monitors, and the two banks of audio sensors and recording devices. Finally, he scanned the labyrinth of wires, particularly those leading to the parabolic microphone hidden behind the *Twice-the-Bargain Pizza* sign below his apartment.

All go.

Pleased, he removed the headphones from the chair's arm and waited for a Toronto denizen too stingy to own a cell phone. Or too paranoid to use one.

After almost two hours, the equipment auto-activated. He licked his lips at the sound of a coin dropping.

"Hi, Mom. It's me," she said.

With a glance at the monitor, he savored the voice of the brunette repeat-customer he'd nicknamed "Becky".

A pause, and she added, "He did it again."

The microphone didn't register the other side of the conversation. Tampering with a public phone was more illegal than Dallas's other, lesser indiscretions.

He squirmed in his chair, thinking of Becky's choices. *Why call your mother, when you should call the cops?*

Becky sniffled. She turned to face the hidden camera and the dark, swollen region around her eye conveyed her latest struggle. "On the face this time. He's not trying to hide the bruises anymore."

Dallas waited through another pause, as Becky's mother probably insisted she leave the guy. He twisted the headphone cord between his fingers.

She turned her back on the camera and played with the coin-return slot. "I can't. He went out for smokes and he'll be right back. I needed to hear a friendly voice, that's all."

Another pause.

"He'd find me." Becky sniffled. "He has people everywhere."

Dallas wanted to shout out the window, "Leave him!"

Live-feed-Becky shook her head. "Mom . . . I love you. Gotta go." She hung up.

The equipment recorded for five extra seconds as Becky opened the door and fled the booth into the humid summer air. Dallas grabbed his cane and walked to the window. He leaned back, in case she looked up, and watched her hurry around the corner.

He needed to catalogue the call into his "Becky" directory. Calling up the new file, he said to himself, "If the bastard ever uses my booth, I'll kill him."

He opened a digital photo of Becky he'd taken months earlier. In the profile shot, captured with a zoom lens, she wore a forlorn expression. He touched the computer monitor, yearning for the soft warmth of her skin. With closed eyes, he fantasized how he would brush her hair aside and place his hand under her chin. She would look into his eyes, helpless against his strength, and he would kiss her moist lips. Finally, her body would relax, safe in his arms.

℈

Dallas woke with a start, from a call in progress. He jammed on the headphones.

"I told you, two kilos." The spiky-haired punk-of-a-dope-dealer Dallas had nicknamed "Bob" glared in the direction of the hidden camera.

Dallas scowled at live-feed-Bob.

"Early Friday." Bob took a drag from his cigarette and then polluted the booth with his filthy habit. "Under the expressway. Put it in a duffel bag this time."

After a pause, Bob slammed the receiver onto the cradle and stormed out of the booth.

"Be nice to my phone, dirt-bag." Dallas sat in the dark, waiting for Bob to vacate the zone, before cataloguing the call. His stomach growled loud enough to wake the roaches.

"Better scurry or I'll squish you," he said to them as he entered the kitchen. He always opened the fridge without turning on the light so they wouldn't do their worrisome flee-and-hide dance. He slid two cheese slices from the package and loaded a plate with crackers from the cupboard. Un-wrapping each slice carefully, he folded them twice to make four perfect squares—the filling for eight cracker-sandwiches. Then he coaxed cold water from the tap into his mug with the chipped rim.

Each mouthful felt like a piece of his childhood, the processed cheese an orange window into lazy Saturday mornings filled with cartoons and bad sitcoms. In those days, he could sit cross-legged, ride a bicycle, and frolic in a park without a second thought, lucky enough to live the invisible life afforded only to the healthy members of society.

Once he'd finished his snack, he rinsed his dishes and set them in the rusty drain tray. The stove clock read 2:25 a.m. on his way to the bedroom. Leaning his cane against the night table, he sat on the unmade bed. The sheets felt slimy against his skin as he rolled onto his back. "I'll ask Mom to clean you more frequently," he told them. The sheets remained unimpressed.

"How can Becky stay with that guy?" he asked the ceiling. "The next time she uses the booth, I'm going down there to talk some sense into her."

Yeah, right, the ceiling jeered.

Because of his earlier nap, he couldn't find sleep. Instead, he lay on the bed with his arms crossed over his chest, fantasizing himself into a hero's shoes.

03

When he rubbed the sleep from his eyes, the sunbeam had passed the foot of the bed to shine on the filthy wall. Stretching his stiff muscles, he stood and walked to the closet. The scrawny guy with the mangled leg glared from the mirror with disapproval.

Mom's gonna be here soon. He grabbed his cut-off sweat pants from the pile on the floor and pulled them over his boxers. Yanking his last clean T-shirt from a hanger, he struggled to put it on with one hand while holding the cane with the other.

He skipped breakfast, choosing instead the lime-green chair. Mornings always dragged. Disasters requiring a payphone took time to develop. Through the window, a kid's screaming tantrum mingled with the screech of streetcar wheels against metal tracks. Before long, Dallas heard the unmistakable three taps on the apartment door.

"Dallas? It's Wednesday."

He turned off the booth's video feed, shuffled to the door, and said, "Hi, Mom."

She hugged him. "You're looking . . . well, I suppose. It's good to see you, honey." She picked up two bags of groceries and set them on the kitchen counter, leaving the door uncomfortably open. Dallas turned his back to the gaping doorway, anxiously waiting for her to bring the remainder of the supplies inside.

As she stowed the food in the kitchen, she yelled, "Drag the laundry bag to your room, would you? I'll stow your clean clothes after this."

"My leg's bothering me, today." The excuse sounded as weak as his self-esteem.

"Fine. I'll get it." She returned to the open door and hauled the big laundry bag through, catching dust bunnies as she dragged it along the floor. "I'll run the vacuum around for you, too," she added, as she closed the door with a reassuring thud.

"Thanks," said Dallas, as much for the closed door as the offer to clean. "Don't forget my sheets."

"I've started stripping them already," she called from his room. "Oh, and I bought cherry Pop-Tarts as your *special treat* this week."

Dallas winced. "Cherry's not my favorite. I'd rather you get blueberry."

She scowled, standing in his living room with a handful of soiled sheets. "That's the thanks I get for doing your shopping?"

"Sorry, Mom. Thanks, so much. For everything. *Really.*"

She disappeared into his room again. "Did you get that programming contract from that company? I noticed your computer's running."

"Yeah. But they won't pay me until the work's done. Could you lend me another hundred?"

"Transfer what you need." She sighed with the disappointed tone that Dallas despised. "You know all of my account numbers."

"Thanks."

While she scurried around the apartment, tidying, vacuuming, and giving him the *I'm-so-disappointed-in-you* stare, Dallas sat at his computer and pretended to work. He counted to a hundred in his head, seven times, and reached sixty-three before she finished.

She stood by the door, waiting for him to see her off, and said, "Why don't you go for a walk? It's a beautiful day."

"I don't want to."

"You can't hide in here forever."

"So you say."

She held out a business card.

He stared at it. "What is it this time, Mom?"

Holding the card up so he could read the print, she said, "Lizzie's daughter sees this therapist at the free clinic."

"I hate shrinks."

"She's a counsellor, not a psychiatrist. No drugs, just a sounding board. Besides, the exercise would help your leg."

"Nothing will help my fucking leg!"

"I'm sorry." She rubbed at her eyes, clearly holding back tears. "I'm only trying to help."

He bit his lip, crossed his arms over his chest, and said, "I'm sorry for losing my temper, Mom, but I *need* to get back to work."

"Sure. Whatever." Grabbing the full laundry bag, she added, "See you next week. I love you."

"Love you, Mom."

She closed the door behind her.

He squinted through the peephole, keeping his attention on her and avoiding the edge of ruin. She descended the stairs, traversing them as if her feet performed the easiest action in the world. Her ragged gray hair bobbed down with a rhythm of innocence, unaware of her peril. At any moment she could lose her balance, catch a toe in a rut, or fall headfirst over the side as the archaic railing collapsed under her grip. He opened the door and tried to say, "See you next week." But the sight of the stairs brought forth a terror that gripped his throat. Only a squeak emerged.

As he locked the door, his surveillance equipment auto-activated. He hurried to luxuriate in the first call of the day.

"Russell, it's me." A new caller. After donning the headphones, Dallas studied the video-feed. The newbie had dark hair pulled into a pony tail, long bangs obscuring his eyes, and a stocky build, likely from work that required his hands not his brain. "I locked the keys in the car. Can you meet me at—"

Dallas tugged the headphones off with one hand and set them on the chair. No point listening to a one-timer. Returning to the kitchen, he retrieved the Pop-Tarts. He opened a two-pack, broke off half of the top one, and headed back to his chair. He checked the equipment and gazed at the artificial too-red-for-cherry filling between the ragged edges of pastry.

As he squeezed the edges of the tart together, the jam oozed out, dragging Dallas back in time.

He looked past the subway stairs, at the blood pooled between the jagged bones erupting from his mangled leg. People shouted while the train barreled into the station.

He shook his head, forcing his attention back to reality. His cell phone rang. He dropped the pastry and picked up the receiver. "Yeah?"

"This is an automated call from the—" He hung up, avoiding the marketing spiel. The oppressive silence of the booth lingered. Despite the traffic streaming past his window, he felt alone in the world.

Except for Becky. She needed to escape from her husband, Doug, as Dallas had nicknamed the unknown asshole. Doug likely drank too much and downloaded porn. Doug was probably too stupid to hold down a job. In Dallas's mind, Doug watched hockey for the fights, smoked three packs a day with the milk money, and screwed prostitutes when he wasn't beating the life out of Becky.

The tiny fragment of Dallas's ego that believed he could man-up vicariously played out a scenario. *Next time she makes a call, I'll open the door and descend one stair at a time. Like Mom. Once I reach the bottom, I'll glide through the front door and pretend to wait for the phone booth. When Becky cries, I'll offer comfort.* His heart pounded at the thought of holding her, being the man that she so desperately needed. The stairs, demons of deception, snickered at his plan.

He shoved on the headphones, unable to block the mockery. He took slow, deep breaths, trying to control his fear as he waited for the world to wander into proximity.

CR

A caller shouted, "How could you be stuck in Niagara Falls?"

Drug-dealer-Bob again. The ass-hat looked as though he hadn't slept since Tuesday. Bob's unknown partner-in-crime must have woven one hell of a long excuse on the other end of the call because the drug-dealer didn't speak for three minutes.

"Get back here, quick. I need you for a Friday delivery." The Bob on Dallas's live-feed picked his nose and wiped it on the inside wall of the booth.

How the hell am I going to clean that off?

A pause.

"What about Saturday?" Bob picked his nose again.

If you wipe that on the glass, I'll come down there, and . . . you bastard!

The other person must have imparted a heap of bad news. Bob made a fist, pacing back and forth and kicking the door of the booth. Finally, Bob slammed the receiver. The equipment caught off-the-phone expletives in the five seconds before shutting off.

❧

The sunbeam had already caressed the foot of Dallas's squalid bed on Friday morning when his equipment auto-activated. *Did I forget to turn it off last night?* Dallas sprang for his cane. By the time he reached the lime-green chair, he could hear Becky's sobs.

"He's furious, Mom. I'm so scared. What should I do?"

Dallas screamed the thought, *Leave him!* in Becky's direction.

Her mother must have said the same words, because Becky said, "I want to. I do. But he'll come after me."

Dallas took a long, deep, encouraging breath, grabbed his cane, and headed for the door. The key hung where it always did, dusty and unused on the nail beside the frame. He stuffed it in his pocket, opened the door, set the spring lock, and yanked the knob behind him. He leaned against the closed door, glaring at the stairs.

Only two flights of eight.

Sixteen slippery, steep, worn-down, ugly steps.

His mother managed the trip every Wednesday. He'd done it himself, countless times, before his accident. Before his leg morphed into a dark-alley freak-show.

He inhaled, gripped his cane, and took a guarded step toward the staircase. And then one more.

After three hard swallows, and one hyperventilating fit— during which he experienced the acrid stench of the neighbour's curry—he forced his feet to move to the brink of the summit.

Looking down made his head spin, so he focused on the ceiling. The holes of peeling paint had grown bigger and more numerous than the last time he'd stood here. The remaining paint had faded from brown to gray.

He gripped the handrail. Remarkably, it felt solid in his hand and did not—as he'd expected—break free of the wall in a crumbling mess of rust and wood. He waited, motionless, staring at the pock-marked ceiling, remembering a time when he'd taken so many aspects of his life for granted.

Sixteen risers. Eight-and-eight repetitive movements of the feet, each bringing him closer to life outside of the roach-nest he called home. Anyone could do it. *Except for Dallas, the broken cripple.*

"Becky needs me," he told the stairs.

They didn't answer.

He moved his foot forward, bit his lip, closed his eyes, and pulled back in a panic. "I can't!" The sound of his admission echoed off the empty walls, pounding him with humiliation. Turning on his heels, he pulled out his key, fiddled with the lock, and stumbled into his apartment. The deadbolt flipped with a satisfying clunk.

Safe. Defeated.

Once his pounding heart slowed, he shuffled to his lime-green chair. Searching through folders for comfort, he played Becky's call.

"I'm going home, Mom." A pause. "Only a small bag, with enough for a couple of days."

"It's about-fucking-time," he said aloud to replay-Becky.

☙

Dallas spent the remainder of the day snacking on cherry Pop-Tarts and waiting for Becky to use his booth. To summon her mother for their freedom-ride. At two minutes after seven-thirty, his heart skipped a beat when she opened the booth's door. Fresh blood drizzled down her chin from her split lip, the bruise over her eye now dwarfed by deep wounds all over her face.

"Mo?" She sounded as though she'd stuffed cotton in her mouth. "E roke my yaw." She cried as she listened to her mother's advice.

Dallas gripped his cane with a surge of newfound strength and deeper, more intentional resolve. With the key still in his pocket, he charged out the front door.

Outside, with the door behind him, his surety faltered. The precipice so close, so *endless*. With thoughts of that poor woman, crying, broken, waiting in his booth for someone to save her, he gritted his teeth and stepped down.

One.

He panted there, exhausted. *Fifteen more. Three times five. My age on the night of my first hickey.*

He raised his good leg and stepped down.

Two.

The only even prime. The surgical floor at the hospital. He remained upright, safe from the stairs' games.

Moving another step down, he thought, *Three.*

The first odd prime. The number of pins in my leg. The grade I barely passed, the year my teacher kept me during recess to explain how Daddy's heart had attacked and killed him.

Dallas gulped some much-needed oxygen into his lungs, and took another step down. Then another. Three more.

Safe on the landing.

"I'm halfway," he told the stairs. Leaning on the windowsill, he celebrated the milestone while the sun beamed through the cracked window. He could still smell the neighbour's curry from above, now mixed with hints of lemony-fresh laundry soap from below.

Eight more.

Two times four. Two cubed. The number of strangers who donated their blood for me.

He limped toward the crest's precipice, clutching the railing. "You're good. Do it. *Now!*" Before he chickened out, he descended the entire flight of eight steps without stopping.

Gasping for breath, from pride more than effort, or maybe fear, he stood in the vestibule, eyeing the mailboxes. His mother had the only key. *Forget the mail, Becky's in imminent danger.*

He pushed the main door and faced the outside world. Fresh air. Smoggy air, in reality. Despite the exhaust fumes, he took a deep breath and held it for a long while.

Becky lingered in the booth. She turned her back on Dallas when she saw him staring at her, and covered her broken face with her hand. He limped to his booth and fumbled in his pocket, pretending to search for a coin. When the door opened, he looked up at her, and said, "Miss, I—"

Without making eye contact, or saying so much as a quick, "Hi," she dashed across the street, slipping between a streetcar and a cube van, disappearing into the *Quick-Stop Variety Store.*

Dallas held the door to his booth with his right hand and his cane with his left. His moment with Becky had been nothing more than a microsecond of awkward failure. Standing, exposed and defenseless on the street corner, he ducked into his booth for protection, picked up the receiver, and returned it to the hook. Noticing Bob's disgusting snot on the plastic wall, Dallas pulled a tissue from his pocket and tried to wipe the mess away. The flimsy thing only spread the goo into a bigger glob. With his thoughts on Becky, Dallas turned to leave his booth, and froze, standing face-to-face with Dope-Dealer-Bob.

"Are you going make a call, or what, dick-bag?"

"I, uh. . . ." He gripped his cane and started out of the booth, staring at his feet, mumbling, "Forgot the number."

Bob shoved past and closed the door.

Dallas waited outside, listening.

"Tomorrow's no good. I don't have . . . fuck. I'll call you back." Bob hung up and stepped out of the phone booth, looking past Dallas as though a mangled freak could actually be invisible.

Dallas turned to follow Bob's sightline. Becky stood frozen outside the variety store, staring at Bob.

"Get over here, bitch!"

She waited for a gap in the traffic and then hurried across the street, head down. She mustn't have seen the looming minivan. Its grill grazed her shoe and she stumbled to the ground next to them, safe but startled.

"Beat it, cripple." Bob shoved Dallas hard, sending him sprawling to the pavement.

"I yeeded shome. . . ." She reached into her bag and brought out a box of feminine protection products.

Bob slapped her across the cheek. Blood poured down her messed up chin. "Put it away. I hate girl-shit." Bob-the-Drug-Dealer was, in reality, Doug-the-Husband. One and the same. A wife beater *and* a criminal. The bastard used the booth for his office. Doug grabbed Becky by the arm. "Come on."

Still sprawled on the ground, Dallas crawled toward his cane. *You're not dragging her away*, he thought. *Not this time. Not ever.*

A silver Buick with tinted windows pulled over to the curb beside the quarrelling couple. The power window, on the passenger side, hummed down revealing a woman driver alone in the car. The plump woman's gray hair matched her wrinkled face, the creases so deep she looked as though she'd been carved out of clay. "Gwen!" she shouted from the car.

So that's Becky's real name.

"Get in the car." Her mother sounded firm and frightened.

"Fuck you, old bitch." Doug dragged Gwen away from the car.

Gwen dug in her heels, but Doug outweighed and out-muscled her. Dallas willed her to fight harder, kick the guy, do all that she could to get away, but she seemed to have given up. She looked like a broken doll being punished by the mean kid at recess.

As Doug hauled Gwen around the corner and into the quiet side street, her mom abandoned the Buick, leaving the door open and the engine running, to hurry after them. "Let her go. Right now!"

Gwen sobbed.

Dallas hobbled to his feet with the help of his cane. He couldn't allow Gwen to move out of sight.

The commotion caught the attention of a young woman smoking a cigarette on her front porch. She yelled, "Hey, leave her alone or I'll call the cops."

Doug held up a hunting-style knife and yelled, "Mind your own fucking business, bitch."

The smoker stubbed out her cigarette and disappeared inside.

Gwen's mother yanked her daughter's right arm, trying to wrench Gwen free. Doug held firm to the other arm.

Dallas lurched toward the conflict. A car sped past him, up the side street, honked the horn at the tug-of-war, and kept moving. Once Doug took Gwen home to the privacy of their apartment, her man would teach her the worst kind of lesson, ensuring Gwen never ran away again. *Ever.*

Doug kicked at Gwen's mom, to force her to release her daughter's arm. Gwen blocked him with her own body. The scene played out like a surreal crime drama.

A streetcar stopped and three passengers disembarked. They each stared at their cell phones, earbuds stuck deep, oblivious to the volatile situation unfolding a few feet away. Assured that no one would stop him, Doug punched the old woman in the chest, sending her flying.

"Awk," mumbled Gwen.

Close now, Dallas saw a spark in her eye, a flare he'd never seen before on his live-feed. Gwen pounded at Doug, her fists and shoes an explosion of fury, hitting more air than man, as though she'd stored every ache in a jar, and now smashed the glass and everything inside it deep into the source of her anguish.

Dallas raised his cane with both hands, holding it like a hammer people used to ring-a-bell for a prize. With sweaty hands, he called up every ounce of frustration that he'd felt for Gwen, for her mother, but mostly for Doug. The cane arched, smashing into the back of Doug's head.

He dropped. Dallas made contact again, screaming, "Damn you!" with such ferocity that spit flew from his mouth. For this blow, he used all of his contempt for every stair that had distanced him from the outside world.

Gwen and her mother stood motionless, watching. They stared at Dallas like a fiend and a champion, all stuffed into one crumpled package.

He smiled weakly, holding the bloody cane behind his back, ashamed of his brutality. "You're safe now B . . . Gwen. You should go with your mother." He pointed his head toward Doug. "I think he's done." Across the street, the smoker stood on her porch again, clapping.

"Ank ou." Gwen reached out a hand to touch Dallas, changed her mind, and pulled it back.

"Hurry," said Dallas. "He won't hurt you anymore."

The mom asked, "How do you know my daughter's name?" The two women supported each other with a hug-hold.

He shrugged. "You called her by name."

"What's your name? No, on second thought, I think it's best if we don't know." She guided her daughter toward the open car. Gwen climbed into the passenger seat of the Buick.

Dallas followed, waving goodbye. The car window hummed closed. He watched them disappear around the corner, and then returned to Doug, studying the man's chest for movement. He lay still. Dallas wanted to say something profound, some hero-epitaph that would torment Doug on his way to hell, but he couldn't put any meaningful words together.

He looked over at the smoker. She shouted, "Beat it. Before the cops come. I didn't see jack shit."

He grabbed the knob of his cane, his hand slipping on the blood. He thought about extracting a tissue from his pocket, but his hands had blood on them, too. He knelt down and wiped all of the mess onto Doug's shirt. The red stain looked vivid and hyper-real against the stark white T-shirt. Blood red, not cherry red. Would Gwen, her mother, or the smoker snitch? Would the cops take one look at Gwen's face and call it all justice?

No matter what, I saved her. She's free.

And so am I.

His stomach growled. He searched Doug's pockets, relieved him of his cash, and headed across the street to buy a box of blueberry Pop-Tarts.

WHAT HARM

Amanda Sun

Colin still remembered the night he was sold. Most four-year-olds would have questioned their father hitching the workhorse to the wagon under the moonlight, the stiff leather of the old harness creaking against the rusting buckles, the gelding stamping at the dirt path beneath his weary hooves. But Colin only pressed his hand against the horse's lowered muzzle, velvet and warm beneath his chubby fingers. The gelding's nostrils blew warm air against his cheek, the dark midnight world slipping away until it was just him and the smell of leather and horse hair and earth.

Most four-year-olds would have questioned why their father lifted them gently into the back of the wagon, the starlight and moonlight spread in stripes of dim white across the wooden boards, encrusted with sharp ends of hay. They would have searched the doorway and windows for their mother, standing there with a tallow candle half-melted onto the bronze holder. They might reach their hands out to her on the other side of the bloated glass pane as her eyes turned away, glossy as stones and cold as the night air. They might have wondered as her breath puffed against the flickering light, as the window went dark and the wagon lurched forward. But Colin did not wonder, because Colin did not know to wonder. He thought only of the horse's soft nose and the wagon wheels spinning, and he made not a sound, because Colin couldn't speak.

They rode in silence to the center of town, the hooves first thudding against the packed dirt as the farmland slowly passed, then clopping against the cobblestones, the world lit in the shadowed light of the lampposts that lined the abandoned town square. The earlier rain still glistened in tiny puddles that collected in the uneven stonework. Colin peered over the side of the wagon, watching the spokes of the nearest wheel as it whirred round and round. Not once did his father tell him he was leaning too far, that he might tip out the edge. Not once did Colin tug on the back of his father's jacket, or ponder his hunched shoulders as he gripped the reins, slack against the flanks of the gelding that snorted into the stillness.

The wagon jolted to a stop and the spokes stopped turning. Colin's father sat for a moment, then climbed down the spokes. There was a small splash as his boot heel landed in one of the tiny puddles, and Colin watched the drops spray onto the cobblestones, glimmering like dark beads in the moonlight. His father's warm hands pulled him from the cart, and the boy reached out for the horse's velvet nose. The gelding reached his muzzle toward the boy and whinnied into the cold air, but Colin's little hands couldn't reach him. The two slipped farther from each other as the boy's father carried him away to the curb by the stone bridge, to the quiet row of houses without a single candle in their windows.

All was still and quiet. The only light came from the tavern, where the murmur of a tune drifted into the square from the crack underneath the wooden door. The thick glass windows filled with shadows and shapes—dancing and arguments and bartering while candlelight flickered around all of them; warmth and crowds and conversation. Colin hated crowded places. He would cry and moan and beat his fists with his eyes squeezed shut.

His father left him on the curb of the damp stone bridge. He looked at him for a moment, his gaze distant and cold. Colin didn't notice, though, for he never looked into his father's eyes.

"Stay here a while," he told the boy. "I'll be back." And he turned to the tavern and closed the door behind him.

The midnight air was cold against Colin's thin coat. He sat as he was told, though he longed to return to the wagon and the waiting horse. He didn't question why he'd been left on the bridge in the night. As the moon lowered in the sky, he didn't question why his father didn't return. He merely sat and stared at the wagon wheel, remembering the way it whirred like a top when the gelding pulled it forward.

After two hours, when the chill had begun to shake Colin, his father burst from the wooden door, his face red and his eyes bloodshot. He seemed surprised, almost disappointed, to see Colin still sitting there. Colin did not run to him, or even look at him. He rocked back and forth, thinking of wagon wheels and velvet muzzles. His father looked from Colin to the wagon and back again, and he choked on a strange cough and blew his nose into the handkerchief he kept in the pocket of his dark green coat. Then he lifted the boy back into the spiky hay strewn across the wagon and slapped the reins against the horse's sleek flank. The wagon jolted forward and Colin squealed with delight, because the spokes spun like pinwheels in the springtime air.

They rode up the hill far past the town, to a stronghold darker than the last swell of water that slicks over a man's head as he drowns. Even the candles lit in the windows of that black stone fortress seemed to flicker with a dimmer light that drew shadows instead of expelling them. The horse tossed his head with each step, his mane spreading like the thick branches of the dark forest that closed in around them. He brayed low and wild as Colin's father encouraged him toward the iron gate, where a woman waited in a long silver dress of moonlight, her brown hair curled around her shoulders like a cloak against the darkness.

The wagon stopped, but Colin's father did not reach for him. Instead he spoke to the woman. "Please," he said. "He doesn't speak, and he's not right in the head, but he's a hard worker and he'll be useful."

"If he's useful, take him home," she said. But the father shook his head.

"I'm a farmer," he said. "The oats failed this year, and he's no good to apprentice as a blacksmith. Don't think me unkind. I struggle enough as it is without having another mouth to feed."

The branches of the dark trees pressed in around Colin, shadows gathering as the owls called to each other in the blackness of the night. The wheels had stopped, and the horse's eyes grew large as the dark puddles from the town square. He tossed his head wildly, fighting against the harness to back the wagon down the steep path.

Colin opened his mouth and began to moan, his cries getting louder as the horse began to rear up against the tightly locked wagon box.

His father grabbed the horse by the noseband, pulling him to standing still again, and then reached for Colin, grabbing his wriggling body from the wagon as he moaned and beat the stifling dark air with his fists. He fought back the shadows, but his father only saw him swinging at nothing, and shushed his moans, not knowing that they kept away the demons that lurked in the bare branches of the trees.

"He's only startled by the horse," his father said. "He won't do this all the time."

He held Colin tightly to his chest as the boy struggled. The horse reared up again and Colin broke free, rushing to the gelding's side. His moans stopped as he clung to the horse's leg, as the horse whinnied and wrapped his neck around the boy. Sweat and foam dripped from the horse's muzzle and trailed down Colin's arms, warm and familiar. Their breathing slowed and calmed, but his father yanked him away. "I've told you a thousand times," he snapped. "He'll trample you."

Colin whimpered. The gelding pawed quietly at the dirt.

"Please," his father begged again. "I can't return to my wife with him. There's no blacksmith for miles since the old one passed, and I've shod Lord Kiarak's horses for two years. I can turn the heads and hearts of the town to his rule. I'll refuse service to those who won't bend to the iron of his will. Please. I've been faithful."

The lady in silver nodded after a moment, her dress glittering in a gasp of starlight. "What harm can be done?" she said. "We can put him to use in the vault." She reached for a soft pouch tied around her waist and pressed two gold coins into Colin's father's hands.

They did not notice how the horse had calmed from Colin's touch, nor how he stretched out his muzzle now to blow hot breaths on the boy's fingertips. They did not think of anything but the dark trade they made in the name of charity.

The wheels spun wildly as his father raced the wagon down

the steep hill and into the darkness of the night. The lady pressed her slim fingers against Colin's shoulder, like tiny links of chain binding around his young frame. And though it was hard for Colin to concentrate, though it was hard for him to think outside of the pinwheel spokes and the horse's terror and the curl of the black branches filled with demons, he knew at that moment that the gold had been carried home instead of him, and that he'd been sold into the service of Lord Kiarak of the midnight valley.

℣

It was, in fact, five more years before Colin beheld the warlord Kiarak, the one those in the vault called the Black Scourge of the countryside. *He spreads like a plague*, they murmured to each other. Those who dared to stand up to him were cut down like men fallen deathly ill. He took the countryside, then the village, then the kingdom beyond the mountains. His reach grew and festered, but all Colin knew was the vault below his dark fortress of stone. He swept the cells and stacked the candles, emptied the chamber pots and polished the chains, and when the prisoners begged and wept for the keys, Colin never met their eyes or understood their deep cries for mercy.

"Don't bother," the older prisoners told the new. "He's as black-hearted as Kiarak."

"It's not that," others would say. "He's mute and stupid, and he lives in his own world of madness." Perhaps they thought he'd lost his mind in the darkness, or that he was too young to understand his part in holding Kiarak's enemies until the warlord made examples of them, in the pike and head sort of way.

"Here," the prisoners would say, "he won't spill secrets at least. What harm can a boy like that do? He's just a flea on Kiarak's backside."

But Colin grew in the shadows of the vault, his eyes downcast to the swept straw of his broom and the scuttling of spiders in the corners. And one day, the door to the vault was left open, and the light of the early evening spilled in like strands of gold. Colin hadn't much interest in going above—his world was ordered and organized, and had he been able to speak, he would've admitted to enjoying the mundane sweeping and emptying and polishing. But it was the whinny of a horse that drew his sharp ears, and the spinning of wagon wheels, and the thundering of hooves shredding sod and kicking into the air in a frenzy.

Colin ascended the stairs with his broom still in hand, the bristles whispering as they stroked the cold stone walls. The courtyard of the dark towers stretched out around him.

Kiarak had returned with his troops from a raid gone awry. A soldier slumped in his saddle, bent over the neck of his horse, crimson blood dripping down the tarnished silver rows of his chainmail. Horses cried out and reared and spun in circles as soldiers grabbed desperately at the reins. A legion of riders tumbled to the ground, the stamping hooves of their horses crashing down around them and sometimes on them, followed by haunting cries that shook even the prisoners in the vault below.

And amongst the chaos rode Kiarak, towering taller than the rest. The wounded soldiers crashed around him like waves around a looming cliff. They said Kiarak's father was a fairy of midnight dreams, for even in spite of the terror that exuded around him like an oily sheen, there was a majesty to him that made Colin unable to look away. The iron crown on Kiarak's head fastened down a headdress that draped around him, hiding his face from view. It billowed over his shoulders like a cape of night and stars as his stallion spun in circles and bucked, trying to unseat the Black Scourge of the midnight valley.

Colin didn't care much that Kiarak's face was hidden—he stared instead at the roan stallion that reared and brayed with a hoarseness that rattled in its ribcage. Foam dripped from the bit to the shredded sod of the courtyard. The horse's eyes were wide with terror, from whatever horror that could make Kiarak's army turn back from anything. A shadow beast from the island of mist, Colin thought, one that lurked only in sunlight and devoured men whole, but couldn't be slain, because how could you wound a shadow? Or a drake from the mountains to the south, one with scales of shimmering pearl that glossed away the danger of its sharp and poisonous fangs. But it didn't matter, for Colin could only focus on the blade that had dug into the horse's flank, the thin sliver of metal that gleamed in the fading daylight, that no other had noticed but him.

Colin stared at the fragment of a blade, his skin burning as if he, too, had been sliced open. He ran toward Kiarak, ignoring the looming, oily darkness that kept others a safe distance from the fairy-touched warlord. Colin ran toward the bucking, spinning horse, dropping his broom to the ground with a clatter, and reaching for the sliver of blade in its flank. It wasn't easy to grab, but Colin moved carefully with the stallion in its dangerous dance, ignoring the horse's sharp bite on his shoulder as he pulled the fragment loose.

He soothed the horse with gentle moans even as the blood ran down his shoulder. The stallion snorted, and the coughing and braying stopped. He lowered his muzzle, his breath warm and damp upon Colin's calloused fingertips. He nuzzled the cut on the boy's shoulder, and batted at him gently with his broad nose. The midnight valley fell silent as the sun slipped below the horizon and banished the pursuing shadow beasts until the sun could rise again.

Kiarak's voice was lead grating against stardust as he asked who the boy was. He asked why a boy who could tame the dark spirits of fairy horses was working such mundane tasks in the vault.

"Why have you kept such talent withering and wasting with the dead?" His voice dropped like granite from a cliff.

And, in a whirl of activity that overwhelmed Colin, his world changed once more. He rested his hand on the calmed horse until he was pried away, pulled backward by two of the soldiers.

"Another idiot to amuse the Black Scourge," one muttered, and Colin squeezed his eyes shut and moaned and beat his chest. The greasy warmth of the horse's muzzle was gone from under his fingers, and the men held him too tightly in their grip. "With the war horses of all things," the soldier said. "Put this pig in with the seed crop and then see what'll happen."

But the other sniffed. "He's harmless, that boy. Can't even understand what's going on around him."

He could, Colin thought. He just understood in a way the soldiers couldn't. The world was different to him. Darkness and shadow and light, small things casting huge shadows that he didn't care to look at.

But the world lightened, then, like the dawn after a fading nightmare where one can only remember the sweat and the heartbeat and the fear. Colin was surrounded by roans and bays and war horses of all types. Fairy horses, stallions and mares, majestic greys and Arabians, Percherons stolen from murdered kings. One of the stable hands gave Colin a new broom, spider webs woven between its bristles, and a flask of water, and directions to the wheelbarrow and the curry combs.

Colin's eyes lit up at the princely rows of horses in their stalls. He breathed in the greasy smell of them, the stale air close around him like a familiar blanket. And he thought of the clank of his father's hammer, and the sizzle of iron horseshoes plunging into water, and he felt a longing in his chest that he hadn't felt for five years. And then he felt a depth of love and affection toward the blackest of hearts; for Kiarak, son of midnight dreams, had given to Colin everything he had ever wanted.

CR

Colin stayed up all that first night, brushing each horse until it gleamed like oil and ink, working steadily down the rows until morning, without a care for sleep or water or food. He swept the aisles and laid down the soft shavings and breathed in the sawdust until he choked on it.

He didn't notice the eyes gleaming in the dark, watching him, nor the glint of metal in the shadows. He didn't notice anything but the elegant horses, their contented snuffles and the swishing of their tails. And it wasn't until he reached the last empty stall, when he bent to touch the tattered cover of a book half-buried in hay, that the girl grabbed him from behind and held the sharp gleam of a knife to his throat.

"If you try anything, we'll kill you," she said, and Colin said nothing, because he couldn't speak. The sharp edge of the blade bit into his throat and he moaned a low sound, and after a moment the girl saw that he was different, and helpless, and she wondered what harm a boy like that could do, so she let go of his throat and sheathed the knife as he beat his fists against his frightened chest.

The girl collapsed backward as Colin's moans rose like the tide of an ocean. She sat in the empty last stall beside her blanket and her buried book, and she rocked back and forth with her hands clamped over her ears. But she didn't look away from him, like the others did. She watched him with wondering eyes, and with sympathy, not pity nor disgust. Colin noticed this, as he noticed the little things that others missed. When his wailing stopped, the girl lowered her slender fingers and blinked at him with eyes the colour of lavender.

"You were sold, weren't you?" she said. Colin didn't answer, but looked at the side of the stall. He tried to concentrate on the sound of a gelding stomping at a fly, the muttering of a bay as he tossed his head from side to side. "We know," she continued. "We were sold too, to work in the stables."

Her voice was gentle now that the blade was gone. Colin wanted to ask her why she'd attacked him, but he couldn't, so instead he ran his hand along the soft grain of the stall wall and was careful not to look at her.

"There's something wrong with us," she said, and at first he thought she meant her and Colin, and maybe that was true. But she meant only herself. "The voices never stop," she said, twisting her index finger against her temple. "It's a curse from a gremlin, we think, on our mother's firstborn. At least that's what they said when they kicked her out of town. That's what she told the lady in silver when she sold us. So now we look out for ourselves. You can't trust anyone in the midnight valley." She flashed a glance down the aisle, but the other stable hands were nowhere to be seen in the middle of the night. "We're Alyx," she told Colin, and then Alyx reached out her hand to him.

Colin didn't take it. But he did try very hard to meet her eyes with his.

His gaze turned again to the small book beside her blanket, a rearing horse printed on the cover. Alyx saw his eyes fall upon the torn volume, and the guilt overwhelmed her. She lifted it gently in her hands.

"Do you like to read?" she asked him. If he could answer, he would've told her he hadn't learned how to read. But of course he couldn't answer. So instead Alyx shuffled aside in the stall, and after a moment Colin sat beside her, his eyes fixed on the printed rearing horse and then on the stall wall.

She opened the first page and began to read. And though he felt his mind drifting as she spoke of fairies and mares and knights galloping across valleys, Colin liked the rhythm of her voice. It was like the gentle clopping of the workhorse harnessed to his father's wagon—*clip clop, clip clop*—or the whirring of the wheels spinning the pathway into musical gold. It was comforting in a way his own mother had never been, a warm blanket of sounds and cadence and words, and he felt a deep gratitude in his heart to her, and to the Black Scourge of the midnight valley for giving his world this gift.

"Be quiet," Alyx snapped suddenly, breaking the music of her reading in two. Colin startled, for he hadn't said anything. "It's us," she explained to him. "She wants us to get the knife again. She doesn't trust anyone. But we won't listen to her, so it's all right."

Another time, she stopped reading and began to cry, rocking as she had when he'd moaned. He matched her rhythm in the rocking, and she noticed him then, keeping pace with her. The motion calmed her, and her lavender eyes dried, and she picked up the book and read once more.

"Maybe we're a good pair," Alyx said, when at last she finished many chapters. "The voices in our head never stop. And you never speak. There's enough noise in here for the both of us."

And Colin liked Alyx well enough, and she liked him, for he wasn't like the stable hands that looked at her with disgust or lecherous thoughts. He was harmless, for he couldn't speak or think complexly enough to look at her like that. And what harm can a boy like that do?

So they sat together for the rest of the evening and rubbed the saddles with oil and polished the bits until their fingers shriveled with dried soap and grimy leather. And the next day they rubbed down the horses and cleaned the stalls, and read together, and rocked and moaned and cried, and they did this for the next night and the next, until many years had passed and they were the closest of companions.

What Harm by AMANDA SUN

သ

Kiarak's iron grip on the lands spread like a plague, and kingdom after kingdom fell. Outside the midnight valley and the dark towers of Colin's world, the boldest of kings cried out in terror for a mercy that didn't come. They shrieked and drowned in blood and horror, and the gold and penance came in, and the coffers filled with tribute. All fell to the warlord whose father was the fairy of midnight dreams. None could stand against his army or his might. All shook before him, except Colin, who loved him fiercely for the companionship of Alyx and the horses.

Colin knew nothing of Kiarak's black heart; not even when his own village fell, not even when that tavern went silent, its windows shattered and pounded by rain. Colin's world was warmth and fur and cobwebs. It was straw and whinnies and barn cats that purred like the whirring of spokes. It was Alyx and spirited fairy horses, saddle soap and leather and polished bits and buckles.

And it would've stayed that way, had Kiarak not welcomed a shadow rider, traveling with begrudging tribute on the back of a shadow beast from the west. He stayed and drank too much of the stardust draughts from the kitchen, and he leered at the lady in silver who had paid two gold coins to Colin's father. He took the keys to the cells in the vault and he played merry tunes on the bars of the prisons as the men pleaded and reached for the iron keys to their freedom. He splashed kerosene about the hallways and lit the straw on fire and left the prisoners shrieking in the smoke, as the child who'd replaced Colin beat the flames out with the worn, patched apron tied round his waist.

For, while the son of midnight dreams was dark indeed, even midnight comes in shades, and the darkest black can be darker still than the eye can see. Kiarak did not do such things, for his cruelty always had purpose. This was a rider of shadow beasts, and atrocity was his plaything.

He wandered then to the stable, and he hobbled the mare in the first stall for sport. At the shriek of her agony, Colin leapt from the empty stall where he'd been paging through Alyx's book. He didn't panic at the sight of the shadow rider, for he'd seen many such terrors in his life and not recognized them as any darker than the midnight valley. He didn't even worry when he saw Alyx hiding in the shadows, for he knew she was safe there. But then he saw the panic and the anguish on the mare's face as she limped, and he began to moan in empathy and clench his hands into fists.

The rider's face twisted with delight, and he came at Colin to make sport of the boy, but Alyx and her knife tackled him from behind, and the shadow rider fell to the aisle where Colin's broom had just swept away the straw and the cobwebs.

The shadow lord grabbed the blade from Alyx and rolled on top of her, tossing the blade to the side of a nearby stall. He saw the beauty in her face as the others did, and he despised her for it, and the shades of dark swirled in his mind as he contemplated how best to destroy her. She saw the destruction in his eyes and she screamed, all of her voices at once, and Colin knew he must save her, but he didn't know how. And so he moaned in great wails that spooked the fairy horses and sent them rearing in a calamity of braying and smashing and chaos. The whole world shook with the hundreds of hooves moved by Colin's moans of terror, and he forced himself to unclench his fist and reach with shaking fingers for Alyx's knife. He gripped the handle as the shadow rider laughed with delight, as he towered over Alyx and the slow-witted stable boy. He grabbed at Alyx's neck and choked the screams from her, but the cacophony of hooves and moans brought the soldiers and Kiarak himself, bursting through the door, a manifest nightmare, his cape of stardust and midnight fluttering like the inky wings of a raven.

Alyx and Colin looked to Kiarak as the soldiers grabbed the shadow rider and dragged him from the stable. Alyx cried bitterly, collapsed in upon herself with relief. And Colin beamed at the stable wall, with Kiarak just in his view. The warlord had saved him once more, just as he had freed him from the vaults and given him the horses and Alyx.

Kiarak stepped forward and helped Alyx to her feet, and Colin's heart glowed with light, and it took him several minutes to realize that the son of midnight dreams was beating her.

And when he was done, Kiarak dropped her in the aisle,

bloody and whimpering, for Alyx had put her safety first, and had not protected his prized war mare.

Then Kiarak saw Colin staring with unfocused eyes and it grated against his patience. He stepped toward Colin and slapped the boy across the face with the back of his iron glove, and the sharpness of the metal was nothing to the sharp metal taste of blood that filled his mouth.

"Stupid boy," Kiarak spat, the words like flint sparking rock in a black desert cave. And he stalked out with his cape seeping starlight and unsettling dreams behind him.

When dawn came, the shadow beast of the rider galloped across the mountains, its stirrups swinging, its saddle empty. The rider was swallowed by darkness and never found, not even a single shred, of which, it was whispered, there were many scattered about.

And darker still was Colin's confusion and betrayal, for these things were all too complex for a harmless boy like him to understand. He stood with one fist clenched, the other loose, fingers still wrapped around the blade of Alyx's knife as she whimpered on his swept floor between the stalls. He looked at the blade as ideas and shadows and plots swirled in his troubled mind.

After a time, after the other stable hands helped Alyx up and dabbed her wounds with stained cloths from the tack room, after they ladled warm water from the trough into her mouth, Colin finally forced himself to move, the knife still gleaming between his fingers. But when every chore was finished, he dropped the blade from his hand, for after all, what harm can a boy like that do?

 C&R

No monarch could stand against Kiarak and his black hearted army. All the kingdoms had fallen but one, on the other side of the isle of shadow beasts, and the troops marched onward, ready to take the last in the resistance. An elven prince had risen there to guide the foolish in a massacre waiting to happen, for none could stand against Kiarak.

They still speak in that country of how Kiarak fell to the elven prince, how he fell to goodness and justice and the last spark of hope.

They speak of how the warlord charged forward, iron blade gripped in iron glove, and how the girth of his saddle snapped and dropped him to the feet of the army, how they surrounded him with spears, his cape spread out like a midnight of glittering stars.

They don't speak of the narrow gash across the well-cared-for leather, the jagged cut no longer than a dagger's length willfully dragged against the grain. They don't speak of how the leather stretched thin for hours like the bond between adoptive father and disowned son, until it buckled under the strain and snapped. For how could they know how such a small incision could bring down an army of darkness? It's simpler to give the credit to a regal elven prince and his cheering army of light, their golden banners arcing through the air.

For what harm could be done by a boy like that? What harm, after all.

HOW OBJECTS BEHAVE ON THE EDGE OF A BLACK HOLE

A.C. Wise

Maggie sat on the end of her bed and aligned the x-rays—three ghost-white views of her sister's spine, bruised dark with the cancer that had recurred after over a year of remission. A pink post-it note stuck to the topmost x-ray read: *I'm tired*. It wasn't much by way of suicide notes, but there wasn't much else to say.

Maggie slid the x-rays back into their envelope, keeping aside the business card mailed with them. Connor Barston, her sister's boss, director at the South West American Nuclear Research Facility—SWAN. He'd found the x-rays in Jan's office and sent them to Maggie as her next of kin.

Maggie hadn't cried yet. She imagined Doctor Parsons telling her that was perfectly normal—everyone processes grief differently. As if Maggie didn't know. She'd said goodbye to Jan a long time ago. The wound wasn't fresh, only a pale, faded scar.

Even so, that scar twinged.

Maggie moved to her desk, scrolling through her email to the last message Jan had sent her. The first in nearly a year, but possibly one of the last emails Jan had sent. Period.

Not a cry for help. Not even a goodbye. Jan didn't want to be talked out of her suicide. Once she'd made her mind up about something—whether it was her opinion of Maggie, or her decision to empty her bank account and book an appointment at an underground Death with Dignity clinic rather than face another round of chemo—she didn't change it. Not that Maggie blamed her; after her first bout with cancer, after watching their mother die slowly of the same, it was a reasonable choice.

But between Jan's death and her last email, it was the latter that interested Maggie more. A sound file and a single sentence: *Thought you might find this interesting.*

After a year of silence, after a lifetime of being strangers to each other, Jan had set aside her professional ego and reached out to Maggie.

That, more than Jan's suicide, shocked Maggie.

Since their respective graduations, their careers had run parallel. Maggie had chosen engineering, things that could be touched, quantified, and explained. She'd even been part of the design team working on the collider at SWAN, where Jan worked, but Maggie had never been to the facility in person. Her career and Jan's were truly parallel—never intersecting.

Jan had made her career in particle physics. Ghost science, as Maggie thought of it. Spending a lifetime studying what could only be observed indirectly by the effect it had on things around it.

So what Jan thought Maggie might 'find interesting', she couldn't imagine. The sound file was labeled *SWAN Recording - 10-14-31.* Maggie hadn't opened the file when Jan first sent it, but she played it now.

Her fingers crept to the back of her neck, tracing the patch that settled just below her hairline, covering the first few knobs of her spine. The patch that keep her dosages regular, her brain chemistry in check.

A slow, deep sound filled Maggie's bedroom. It had a stretched quality. Thin. Just above where Maggie's fingers skirted the edges of the patch, her skin puckered tight. A sound, a vibration, a note played directly into the bones of her skull—hauntingly familiar, and yet utterly strange.

The clip came to an end, and Maggie breathed out.

What the fuck had Jan meant by sending it? A problem she finally—at the end of her life—couldn't solve, but thought Maggie could give her insight on, somehow? Her sister had never followed up with an explanation, and now it was too late for Maggie to reply and ask.

Before giving herself time to fully think it through, Maggie booked a flight to Arizona, then sent an email to Barston, Jan's boss: *I want to see where my sister worked. I was part of the design team on your collider. I can get security clearances if you need them. My flight arrives tomorrow morning.*

Was this why Jan had sent the email, to intrigue Maggie enough that she'd cross the continent to see for herself what Jan had been working on? Or had she simply meant to needle Maggie one last time by sending her a puzzle without a solution? Maggie bit her lip, worrying chapped skin. Was there any chance sending Maggie the sound clip had been some sort of a strange peace offering? She'd never been particularly good at guessing Jan's motives. For anything.

She pulled a spiral bound notebook from the bottom drawer of her desk. On the first available blank line she wrote: *April 13, 2032: Twenty-one years, three months, and nineteen days. I am not being haunted by my sister's ghost.*

The same sentence filled every page, repeated daily, the date changing, but nothing else. There were notebooks before this one, an archeological record tracing Maggie's handwriting from her eleven-year-old block print, to the back-sloping experiment with cursive, to now—a hybrid mix, barely legible, even to her.

Maggie ran her fingers over the indentations made by the ink, tracing the shape of each letter, blushing her skin pale blue. She tucked the program from Jan's funeral between the pages, closed the notebook, and returned it to the drawer.

I am not being haunted by my sister's ghost. For the first time in a very long time, an inkling of doubt crept through the walls she'd spent more than twenty-one years building. Had the words ever been true?

☙

October 19, 2011

Maggie watched as the ghost placed her fingers precisely over indentations in the puzzle box that neither she nor Jan had been able to find. Real-Jan, at least. Ghost-Jan seemed to have no trouble. Because the ghost *was* Jan; Maggie had no doubt about that. Her sister slept peacefully in the bed beside hers, and her sister also sat cross-legged on the end of Maggie's bed, not denting the covers. One Jan in two places, both equally real.

Which meant it was okay to open the puzzle box. When Gran had given it to them, they'd promised to open it together. Ghost-Jan withdrew her hands, tilting her head to say, *now you try*.

Maggie fit her fingers exactly where the ghost's had been. A faint click, and the box slid open.

"What are you doing?" Jan sat up, glaring at her. "You opened the box. You promised you wouldn't."

"But you helped me." The words slipped out before Maggie could stop them.

Her sister narrowed her eyes; Maggie recognized the look, but she wasn't fast enough to explain—of course Jan had helped her, they'd opened the box together, couldn't she see? Jan lunged. Maggie pulled the box back, trying to protect it. Jan grabbed the edge, a tug of war between them, then the box slipped, catching Maggie in the mouth.

The light snapped on; their mother stood in the bedroom door, weary gaze moving between them.

"She opened the box without me." Jan spoke first, pointing an accusing finger.

Maggie opened her mouth to object, glancing over her shoulder so Ghost-Jan could back her up, but the end of the bed was empty. Panic gnawed at her. Her lip throbbed. She touched it, smearing her finger red.

"I'm bleeding."

Jan whipped around to glare at her, the word *tattletale* burning in her gaze. Maggie clapped her hand over her mouth, ignoring the pain. She didn't want to get Jan in trouble; it would only make things worse.

"Let me see." Their mother tugged Maggie's hand away from her mouth. "It's not bad. We'll put some ice on it."

Jan's cheeks flushed, her eyes bright—caught between anger and tears.

"I'm sorry." Maggie pushed the box toward her sister as she slid off the bed, but Jan shoved it angrily away.

"I don't want the stupid box." Jan turned her attention to their mother. "You always take her side!"

"I'm not taking anyone's side."

Jan followed them as far as the bedroom door and then slammed it the moment they were in the hall.

"I hate you!"

The words were barely muffled by the wood. Maggie flinched; she had no doubt they were meant for her.

In the kitchen, her mother handed her ice cubes wrapped in a tea towel. "This will make you feel better."

Maggie sat on a chair and dutifully pressed the ice to her sore lip, but if anything, it made her feel worse. Her eyes stung; Jan would never forgive her. She hadn't meant to do anything wrong. It made perfect sense at the time. Jan had helped her open the box while Jan was asleep in bed. But now, in the bright light of the kitchen, it all jumbled up in her head, putting a tight feeling in her chest, hitching her breath.

"Want to tell me what happened?"

Maggie shook her head. She pressed the ice harder against her mouth, trying to distract herself with pain.

Her mother crouched, her face level with Maggie's. "Maggie." Her tone was soft, but there was an edge to it; her mother expected the truth.

Maggie couldn't stop the tears this time. "I didn't mean to. I'm sorry. Jan's ghost helped me with the puzzle box, then Jan woke up and got mad."

Maggie wanted to lean against her mother's shoulder, but her mother held her at arm's length.

"You were pretending there was a ghost?" Lines creased the corners of her mother's mouth, and something flickered in her eyes that Maggie didn't understand, but it frightened her.

"No." Maggie shook her head hard enough to make her jaw hurt. "There was a ghost. Jan was sleeping, and she was a ghost at the same time."

"Maggie." Her mother kept the distance between them, instead of letting Maggie burrow against her, looking at her intently. Maggie wanted to squirm under the pressure of her gaze. "I need you to tell me the truth. No fibbing. No pretend. What did you see?"

"A ghost. I saw Jan's ghost." Maggie's voice rose, her breath stuttering in uneven gasps. "I'm sorry. I didn't mean to make Jan mad. I didn't mean to make you mad."

She fought to get her breathing under control, which only made it worse.

"Oh, baby. I'm not mad. Come here." Her mother's expression softened and she pulled Maggie close, but not before Maggie saw her frown deepen, worry creasing her forehead. It made her mother's next words sound even more like a lie. Maggie had seen Jan's expression; she knew her mother's words weren't true. "It's not your fault, baby. No one's mad at you."

ᏣᎡ

April 14, 2032: Twenty-one years, three months, and twenty days. I am not being haunted by my sister's ghost.

Maggie drummed pen against notebook as the plane whisked her to Arizona. Her free hand crept toward the back of her neck. Catching herself, she deliberately gripped the armrest instead.

The words she'd written were true. She knew they were true. But that didn't mean Jan's ghost wasn't real. Real in the sense that her brain chemistry showed her things that weren't objectively there. Or convinced her that her body didn't belong to her; someone else was controlling her, and if she could just find that person, everything would be okay. Or gave her the feeling of a void opening up beneath her, threatening to swallow her whole, until pain allowed her to focus and make it stop.

The patch kept all those things at bay, regularly adjusted and fine-tuned, checked by Dr. Parsons at each appointment. Maggie trusted in her diagnosis of schizoaffective disorder. She knew what happened without her medication. She knew the ghost wasn't—objectively—real.

But once upon a time, she'd known Jan lay asleep in the bed beside her at the same time as she showed Maggie how to open the box. And even now, twenty-one years, three months, and twenty days later, a tiny part of her still wanted both things to be true. Ghost-Jan had been kinder. She'd been patient. She hadn't hated Maggie for no reason.

Maggie rubbed at a tension knot in her shoulder. Twenty-one years, three months, and twenty days—she was still crap at deciphering her sister's motivations. Death hadn't changed anything between them. Jan was as much of a stranger to her as she'd ever been.

Maggie tucked the notebook into her bag, slipping her feet into the shoes abandoned during the flight. They'd be landing soon.

Once she'd gathered her bags, Maggie took a cab straight to SWAN. Connor Barston met her in the lobby himself. Maggie still had his business card tucked in her pocket. The way he stepped forward, hand out, ready to shake, pushed her guard up. The tight expression around his mouth and eyes didn't help him.

"I don't need the full tour. Just show me where my sister worked." Maggie ignored his out-stretched hand.

Barston faltered, but his smile came back too quickly. It was an effort for Maggie not to grin, watching the complicated contortions of Barston's expression.

"Follow me." Barston pivoted.

Maggie followed him to a hallway filled with identical doors. One bore Jan's name, and Barston unlocked it without stepping out of the way.

"I'll be fine from here. Thank you." Maggie pasted on her sweetest smile, making sure to show teeth.

Barston actually stepped back a pace, and Maggie saved herself from laughing by stepping around him into the tiny office and pulling the door closed. Jan's office was made smaller by book shelves lining two walls. An old-fashioned wooden desk dominated, topped by an old-fashioned computer surrounded by precarious stacks of paper.

At least they had one thing in common.

A corner of Maggie's mouth lifted, but the familiarity didn't last. Aside from physical paper, there was nothing else here to link her to Jan. No photographs on the walls, no personal effects at all, nothing to accidentally remind Jan she had a life outside this sterile building.

A sense of absence, of disassociation, haunted the whole room. But more than that, something felt specifically missing. Maggie's gaze settled on the corner of Jan's desk—a space conspicuously clear of paper.

The puzzle box.

Alone in the room, Maggie snorted a laugh. She had no evidence Jan had even kept the puzzle box, let alone brought it to work. Except the empty space at the corner of Jan's desk seemed to call for it. The box belonged there, like a pulled tooth.

Maggie opened desk drawers. Old-fashioned paper files, no sign of their Gran's gift. Supplies: pens, highlighters, paperclips. They both still liked to write by hand. Maggie quelled an impulse to reach for her bag and pull out the notebook. She quelled the urge to touch the back of her neck. Breathe. Stay calm. In and out.

She leaned against Jan's desk. Her hand brushed the mouse, another old fashioned touch, waking the computer screen. It wasn't even password locked. Maggie blinked, surprised. Maybe Barston had been in there before her, snooping around. Either way, the computer was open to her now. Maggie sat.

Sound files littered the desktop, all like the one Jan had sent her, but with different dates. Pulse tripping, Maggie chose one at random to play. Like the file Jan had sent her, it reminded Maggie of a whalesong, but less musical. Something bent and warped out of true. Something hauntingly familiar she couldn't place.

She turned the computer's speakers all the way up. The sound reverberated inside her skin, shivering her ribcage, pressing a hand to her lower back. Her jaw ached.

Maggie tapped the patch clinging to her skin—restless, tracing its edges. She played the next file, and the next. Her skin itched. There was something there, but she wasn't sure what it was. Not yet. Why the hell had Jan sent her the file? What did she expect Maggie to understand?

Maggie clicked on the next file. A video popped up. She hadn't even noticed the different file type, but Jan's face filled the screen.

Tired. Shadows bruised Jan's eyes—stubborn no matter how the light hit them—and lines etched the corners of her mouth. She looked like a woman who'd accepted death, but still walked, talked and breathed.

Jan's ghost recurring—pale, washed out, and stretched thin somehow. But this ghost's eyes weren't as kind. They weren't cruel, just weary. This Jan hurt, through and through, but rather than turning that pain against the world, she held it all inside.

A tremor started near Maggie's feet. She leaned back in Jan's chair, crossing her arms around her body, holding herself in, letting the video play.

"The sound showed up right after we fired up the collider for the first time."

On screen, Jan was framed by her office, sitting in the same chair where Maggie sat now.

"I wish we could call it a result, but there isn't anything conclusive to link the sound to the collider start-up."

Jan leaned forward. Though the webcam didn't show her arm, it was clear she'd opened one of the sound files. The sound washed through the speakers, doubly ghosted, a recording of a recording.

"We've captured three instances of the sound so far. There's no clear pattern. It could be a glitch in the equipment. It could be a flaw in the structure of the collider itself."

Maggie flinched. But Jan's words weren't directed at her. For once. They were simply the words of a frustrated scientist running out of time.

"So far, nothing we've done has predictably caused the sound to manifest. Maybe it has nothing to do with the collider. It could be pure coincidence. Fuck it. Maybe the goddamn building is haunted."

The recording cut off. Maggie let out a breath. She counted the files labeled sequentially on Jan's computer—thirteen in all. Plus one more video file.

Maggie played it. More of Jan's frustration. She nearly closed the last video without letting it play out, but Jan's words stopped her.

"The only theory I've been able to come up with . . ."

The recorded ghost of Jan paused, swallowing, then shook her head.

"I'm not going to rehash it. There's no point."

The video ended. Maggie stared at the screen. Rehash what? She spent the next few hours searching through Jan's computer. There weren't any other videos. If Jan had made other recordings, they weren't here.

Maggie yanked open the desk drawers again, stacking Jan's files atop the already dangerous piles. All that remained in the last drawer was a yellow legal pad and an old hand-held tape recorder. Jan definitely liked her antiques.

The recorder was empty. If Jan had used it to make other recordings, where were the tapes? A faint indentation remained on the notepad, words pressed into the paper before the top sheet was ripped off. Maggie traced her finger over the lines, thin as a scar. Holding the paper into the light and relying on touch, she could just make out the words — *The Mythology of Black Holes*.

Fuck. Another cryptic clue from Jan. More words, leading nowhere. If her sister could just make sense, for once.

Maggie tossed the legal pad. It skimmed over the precarious piles, taking several folders with it as it tumbled to the floor. Maggie's head ached. The absence where the puzzle box should've been continued to glare.

Fuck it. Even now, even after death, Jan tormented her.

Maggie spoke aloud to the empty room. "What the hell did I ever do to you?"

◌◌

September 7, 2017

Maggie lifted her hair away from the back of her neck. The electric razor buzzed in her other hand. She pressed it against her skin, made the buzz shiver through her skull. Honey-dark strands of hair hit the floor, curling like parentheses against the white tile.

Maggie set the razor down and ran fingers over the notch of stubble. The hair would grow back. The doctors would have to shave her again before the patch went in; Dr. Parsons had told her they'd treat the follicles in the spot to keep the hair from growing back. For now, she wanted to test the sensation, one tiny thing she could control on the cusp of everything changing.

The bristles felt strange and familiar at the same time. In another three weeks, the patch Dr. Parsons had prescribed would cover the spot — scarcely an inch wide, clever wires buried beneath her skin to monitor any changes and delivering a slow, steady release of chemicals. Schizoaffective—just like her mother before her, and her mother's mother before that.

"You're not special."

Startled, Maggie turned, dropping her hair over the shaved spot. The razor clattered to the floor. Jan stood in the doorway, her arms crossed. Her sister's eyes were hard. Maggie sorted responses, ticking them off like a mantra to bring her pulse back in line:

Shut up.

Fuck off.

Don't tell mom.

I know.

Nothing she could say would help. Jan had already made up her mind. She'd decided Maggie's silences, when she couldn't figure out what to say that wouldn't make Jan mad, meant she was stuck up. She'd decided Maggie trying to stay out of her way, avoiding conflict, sticking close to Mom and Gran, meant the three of them were part of a secret club that didn't include Jan.

"Leave me alone." Maggie kept her voice quiet, even. It didn't matter what she said; Jan would hate her either way.

She stepped forward and Jan stepped back, flinching. As if Maggie had ever hurt her, or shown even the slightest inclination to violence. Maggie closed the bathroom door.

"What the fuck?" Jan slapped the wood as Maggie leaned against it, holding it closed.

Each blow shook the door, and Maggie's body with it.

"Fuck you then." Jan gave the door a final kick. Maggie heard their bedroom door slam across the hall.

Maggie sat on the closed toilet lid, legs shaking. After a moment, she reached for her backpack. The orange plastic pill bottle rattled as she pulled it out. Three more weeks and she'd never have to take a pill again. Last chance.

She tipped today's dosage into her palm, then let it fall into the sink with a soft clatter, running water to wash it down the drain.

She waited, watching.

"Come on," Maggie whispered. "Where are you?"

For the past week, she'd been throwing her pills down the sink and the toilet. But Jan's ghost hadn't returned. Maggie dug her nails into her skin. The space behind her eyes prickled.

Only the frantic, sick, panicky feeling had returned. Only the feeling of a void trying to open beneath her had returned. But not Jan's ghost.

The unease picked at the edges, worsened by adrenaline. She hated it. Hated fucking with her medicine. But she had to. Because, what if Jan's ghost was real? What if the doctor was wrong? Just because her mother and grandmother were sick, it didn't mean Maggie was sick, too.

Maybe the ghost was real. Maybe opening the box hadn't been her fault. A mistake. Jan hated her for no reason. Not because Maggie was a bad person.

She squeezed her eyes closed. She imagined shaving off the rest of her hair. She imagined taking one of the pink plastic safety razors from the bathtub and opening a thin line on her skin. Something to help her concentrate. Something to hold the panic at bay.

She opened her eyes. The bathroom shone back at her—scrubbed clean corners, gleaming white tiles. Empty. No ghost. Maggie slammed a fist into the towel rack, and it clattered to the floor.

Tears, not just from the hollow behind her eyes. A hole—lined like a geode with jagged crystalline growth—stood in place of her heart and lungs. Breath turned into a ragged sob. There wasn't enough air.

Maggie reached into her bag again. Her vision smeared. She pulled out a battered notebook, writing on the first blank line: *September 7, 2017—Six years, eight months, thirteen days. I am not being haunted by my sister's ghost.*

A wordless yell twisted through her. She flung the notebook across the floor, ink-lined pages fluttering.

A tentative footstep in the hall, but no knock followed. The sound didn't come again.

Maggie crawled into the tub. She drew her knees to her chest, wrapped her arms around them, and pressed her spine against the ceramic.

Years passed. A moment passed. And a hand touched Maggie's

arm. She jerked, slamming her elbow against the side of the tub. Her mother's face hovered, barely visible through the blur of tears.

"Are you okay?"

Maggie shook her head. She couldn't manage words, sniffling and choking on a bitter laugh. Stupid question. Of course she wasn't okay.

"What's happening?" Her mother sat on the floor, leaning against the tub.

Maggie sat up, wiping tears with the back of her hand, smearing salt. Her gaze moved around the bathroom—razor, strands of hair on the floor, towel rack knocked from the wall, notebook.

Beyond the door, a floorboard creaked. Her mother had shut the door behind her. If Jan stood in the hall after sending her mother in, Maggie couldn't tell. She breathed in and out, an exercise her doctor encouraged in any stressful situation. It didn't work.

"I threw away my pills." Maggie didn't look at her mother, keeping her in her peripheral vision.

"How long?" Her mother's lips flattened—the slightest tremor betraying her.

"Only a few days. I'm sorry. I wanted to . . ." But Maggie's voice failed. How could she explain?

After a moment, strong fingers squeezed hers. Her mother didn't push, or ask for an explanation, and Maggie was grateful.

"Can I tell you something?" Her mother still held Maggie's hand.

Maggie glanced up through still-damp lashes. The thin-pressed line of her mother's lips turned into a frown, but not directed at Maggie. Her gaze fixed on the cabinet beneath the sink, though clearly not seeing anything in the room.

"When your father and I were getting divorced, before everything was finalized, he still had house keys. When things got nasty between us, he tried to mess with my pills—hide them, steal them. With everything going on—work and school and lawyers— I didn't notice right away. That was before the patch, or anything like that of course. It was the worst feeling in the world, going back to not knowing what was real, feeling like maybe I wanted to kill myself. I think that's what a sick part of your father hoped would happen."

The expression on her mother's face was one Maggie had never seen before—lost and hopeful and sad all at once. Maggie had a vague memory of walking into the living room—she couldn't have been older than five—and seeing her mother standing in front of the TV, ceaselessly flipping channels. She remembered wanting to watch cartoons, and being upset, then afraid. That memory had the quality of a nightmare now, the light from the TV making her mother look inhuman, and Maggie calling her and getting no response. Jan had taken Maggie's hand, led her to their room, and read to her from a picture book to calm her down.

Jan must have phoned their grandmother, though Maggie didn't remember that part. A year or two after Maggie had first been diagnosed, her mother told her how, before she was medicated, she used to think all the people on TV—in shows and commercials—would whisper terrible, awful things about her the moment she couldn't see them. But if she kept flipping and flipping, keeping her eye on them, it would be all right.

"I can't imagine ever making myself feel that way on purpose," her mother said, giving Maggie's fingers another squeeze before standing up. "So I understand whatever you're going through right now must be really bad. I'll make an appointment with Dr. Parsons tomorrow."

Again, there was that look of sadness, mixed with hope. The faintest of smiles touched her mother's lips as she paused at the bathroom door, a world of pain behind it. As her mother left, Maggie thought she caught a glimpse of Jan quickly closing her bedroom door across the hall.

∞

Maggie didn't bother to knock before barging into Connor Barston's office. She'd bullied her way past the flustered receptionist, and no one else had tried to stop her.

"My sister had a puzzle box on her desk. What did you do with it?"

"You can't be in here." Barston rose, his face shading to red;

Maggie cut him off.

"And you can't take things that don't belong to you. I have security footage showing you in Jan's office."

She held up a flash drive, her own, and blank, hoping Barston wouldn't call her bluff.

"Your sister was keeping her research notes in there. That's SWAN property."

Maggie couldn't help smirking. "You couldn't figure out how to open it."

The director flushed deeper.

"If there's anything groundbreaking, I promise to share." Maggie held out her hand.

Barston scowled, but after a moment, produced the box from the top drawer of his desk. He held it out, showing the corner that had chipped the last time Maggie had seen the box. Her pulse snagged. She snatched it, tucking it under her arm and pressing it close to her side to keep from trembling.

She pivoted on her heel, muttering, "Asshole," under her breath as she walked away.

CR

June 11, 2021

Maggie used the back of a kitchen chair for balance as she kicked off the stiff shoes her mother had insisted she wear to the church. A run laddered up the left leg of the stockings; her mother had insisted on those as well.

"Gran would have hated that service," Maggie said. "She only joined the church for the choir."

Jan stood by the counter, setting up to make coffee. She shot Maggie a look. Their mother only shook her head, looking weary. Another needling remark tried to rise to Maggie's tongue, but she clamped it down. Today, of all days, why was she trying to pick a fight? "I'm going to change," she said instead.

"Your grandmother's friends will be here soon." Her mother's voice followed her, as tired as her pinched expression.

"It's too hot." Maggie kept walking.

If she turned around, the space inside her might open up and reveal that instead of being hollow, it was full of stored up pain. Or she would say something else awful—sarcasm, antagonism, a shield against the hurt inside. Her head ached, not just from the still air of the church, or the cloying scent of the ostentatious spray of flowers draped over her grandmother's coffin.

The old bedroom looked the same. Her bed and Jan's, neatly made, sitting side by side. No ghost version of Jan perched on the end of her bed, but Maggie smoothed the comforter nonetheless.

"You could at least try thinking about someone other than yourself for once." Jan, Real-Jan, leaned in the doorway, arms crossed.

"Could you shut the door? I'm trying to change." Maggie reached for the duffel bag she'd brought from home. Jan didn't move, but something changed in her expression, catching Maggie off guard.

"I'm moving to Arizona. I've been offered a job." She'd never heard Jan's voice quite so hesitant before. Was Jan looking for approval? Looking for Maggie to tell her not to go?

"That's . . . far." Maggie swallowed, surprised to find a salty taste in her mouth.

To distract herself, Maggie unzipped her duffle bag. The puzzle box lay on top of the folded clothes.

"I guess I better give this to you now, then."

Maggie had brought the box with her from her small apartment. Until this moment, she hadn't decided whether to give the box to Jan.

"Why do you hate me so much?" Maggie hadn't meant to say anything at all, but the words slipped out as Jan's fingers closed on the box.

Jan's mouth opened in surprise, and something inside Maggie recoiled, a sick part of herself pulling back the moment Jan revealed a crack in her armour.

"Never mind. Forget I said anything." Maggie let go of the box.

Jan let go at the same moment and it crashed to the floor, a chip splintering off the edge.

"It's because you always ruin everything." Jan bent to retrieve the box, a quaver in her voice.

Jan straightened, holding the box against her chest, and Maggie was surprised at the brightness in her eyes, tears waiting to fall. Maggie opened her mouth, then snapped it closed. Something about Jan's posture, her expression, made Maggie think of a dam, cracking finally after years of holding back a flood. "Before you came along, everything was fine. Mom and Dad loved each other, and me, and we were a family."

Jan didn't raise her tone; there was no animosity. It sounded like a rehearsed speech, Jan finally severing the last ties between them so she could move across the continent with a clear conscience.

Maggie wondered whether her sister even believed the words.

"Dad was an asshole." Maggie's jaw clenched, heat behind the words she hadn't expected. "He tried to make mom sick during their divorce. He wanted her to kill herself."

The slap came too quickly for Maggie to avoid it—the crack of palm against cheek—and it left her ears ringing.

"You always take her side." Jan's nostrils flared. "You, and mom, and Gran. You and your little secret club. There was never any room for me. Dad was all I had."

Maggie gaped. Did Jan really think they'd tried to exclude her? A shared history of fucked up brain chemistry was just that, nothing more, nothing less.

The light in Jan's eyes cracked. The same hand she'd used to slap Maggie flew to cover her mouth, and tears slipped from her eyes. "Maggie." It was barely a whisper.

But it was too late. It had always been too late. They'd grown up in the same house, but they were strangers. The thought twisted inside Maggie's stomach, sour and hard.

"I liked you better when you were a ghost." Maggie snatched the duffle bag from the bed, slamming Jan's shoulder and throwing her off balance as she reached for the door. "I'm going to stay in a hotel. You can explain that to Mom."

℞

Maggie sat behind Jan's desk, the puzzle box in front of her. She had the door closed, a spare chair wedged under it in case Barston changed his mind and decided to intrude.

She stroked the polished wood, ran her fingers along the grain, thinking back. A Thanksgiving here and there, their mother's funeral, of course—Maggie could count on one hand the number of times she'd seen Jan in person since giving her the puzzle box. She ran her finger along the edge, pausing at the chipped corner.

Maybe she did ruin things, but so did Jan. Something else they had in common. Was that why it was so hard, why they'd never been able to get along? Deep down, they were too much alike, too stubborn. On the rare occasions Jan reached out, Maggie pulled back, and vice versa. They could have worked together, Maggie's designs informing Jan's research; Jan's research pushing Maggie's designs. They could have done something great together, maybe changed the world.

Maggie closed her eyes, calling up the memory of Jan's ghost, and placing her fingers against the puzzle box accordingly. There was a faint click. Maggie opened her eyes. Old-fashioned, half-sized cassette tapes filled the box. She slipped the first one into the recorder she'd found in Jan's desk earlier and pressed Play.

"The mythology of black holes." Jan's voice filled the small office space.

This time, when Maggie's hand wanted to creep to the back of her neck, she didn't stop it.

"All black holes are metaphors," Jan said.

Maggie glanced at the legal notepad, which she'd replaced on Jan's desk, mentally tracing the words.

"For instance, if one could observe an object moving toward a black hole, to the observer, once the object reached the edge it would appear to slow down. At a certain point, it would seem to stop, caught infinitely on the point of crossing the event horizon. However, to the object itself, time would move normally. It would cross the event horizon, and from that point, there would be no escape."

On the tape, Jan made a sound between a cough and a laugh. Maggie's throat tightened. No wonder Jan had kept these recordings separate. They were more like a diary than her research notes.

"So here's your metaphor. I'm falling toward the event horizon. That's the cancer diagnosis, in this case. Once I cross over, once I get the test results back, there's no escape. But from the outside, it appears there's still hope. I haven't fallen yet. From the outside, everything looks fine, and there's still time to make things right."

Jan paused. When her voice resumed, it was with a hitch.

"I always wanted to see a black hole. Stupid thing for a scientist to say, right? Right before we fired up the collider I was convinced, absolutely convinced, we would find evidence of a miniature black hole, something stable enough for our instruments to detect. But no dice. I guess I'll just have to be content with metaphors."

A click, and the audio ended. Maggie unclenched her fingers from her neck. Hands shaking, she slotted the next tape into the machine.

"Then, there's the sound." Jan's voice, picking up a thread in the middle of her one-woman conversation. A rustling as she shifted the recorder closer to the computer and played one of the audio files.

It was the same as listening to it in the video on Jan's computer—an eerie doubling between two recordings. An echo of an echo. Maggie's skin puckered. Her sister's ghost, finally talking to her now that it was too late. But talking nonetheless. Trying to tell her something.

"I don't understand." Maggie spoke aloud. On the tape, Jan continued.

"There's a theory—an object on the edge of a black hole, once it crosses the event horizon, is destroyed. Except a perfect copy is created. Or an imperfect one. Nothing can ever be created or destroyed, so the energy is spread across the surface of the black hole and stuck there, a copy made out of light, and the original is gone, burned up completely. A black hole is a factory for ghosts."

Maggie's hand skittered across the desk, an involuntary movement knocking the puzzle box to the floor. The remaining tapes scattered.

"So if we don't understand everything about black holes, if we in fact understand very little, which is the case, who's to say metaphor couldn't be reality? Maybe light and sound and time all bend out there in the deepness of space, and something comes back to us, unrecognizably changed. The original copy is destroyed, but something survives, different, but the same.

"I'd like to think that when I cross the event horizon, that maybe, just maybe the rules are malleable, and maybe some piece of me—the same, but kinder, more patient—will survive."

Maggie's hand went to her mouth. The tape clicked to an end, but the echo of it remained, Jan's voice, coming back to her from the other side of death. Jan's ghost, in audio form, bent and changed into something kinder, more patient. The same, but different. And what about Jan's other ghost? What if what Maggie had hoped—even knowing it was impossible—actually wasn't impossible at all? Both things could be true, her sister's ghost, both a hallucination and real. Light and time bending, and some fragment, some imperfect and kinder copy of Jan coming back to her years before she died.

There was so little sound in space, only the radio waves that came from the deepest parts in a cosmic roar. No one knew how sound might behave around a black hole. But if a black hole could bend gravity, light, then why not warp sound? Why not form a strange, imperfect copy as Jan had hypothesized and send her voice back to her—stretched, changed, completely unrecognizable?

Maggie shook her head, tears slipping free. The mythology, the metaphor of black holes—that was what mattered. Ghost science. It's how she had always thought of what Jan did—studying things that couldn't be seen except for the effect they had on what was around them. Even if Maggie never unraveled the sound Jan had been studying—and she would keep trying, even if it meant staying in this miserable climate for a while longer, and even working with Barston—she had this. Jan's ghost, real in a way Maggie had never suspected. Her sister's final gift to her: her words, kinder, gentler, coming back to her from beyond the event horizon. In a way, Jan had bridged the gap. If Maggie kept searching, it would be like they were finally working together after all.

ଓ

February 7, 2011

"When we grow up, we'll be scientists. We'll discover something no one else has discovered before." Maggie kept her voice to a whisper, glancing over her shoulder occasionally.

On the bed beside hers, Jan didn't stir. Maggie turned back to the ghost. Her solemn eyes were just like real-Jan's eyes, but kinder; she waited patiently for Maggie's next words.

"Maybe we'll find a new planet. Or a cure for cancer. I bet we could do it together."

It was a struggle to keep her voice low. She wanted to shake the real Jan awake. Wouldn't she be excited to know she had a ghost-twin? Three brains were even better than two, after all.

Maggie glanced back at real-Jan and bit her lip, changing her mind. Real-Jan wouldn't listen. She would roll her eyes at Maggie, or call her names. Ghost-Jan was safer. Maybe one day, Maggie would figure out how to talk to her real sister. But for now, she turned back to ghost-Jan, who continued to wait patiently for Maggie's words.

"We could even build our own rocket ship," Maggie said. "Like that movie about the farmer who built a rocket in his backyard. We could explore the farthest stars and find out what's on the other side of a black hole. What do you think?"

The ghost remained silent. Maggie glanced over her shoulder one last time. It was hard to tell in the dark, but as the real Jan rolled over in her sleep, it looked as if she smiled.

WASHING LADY'S HAIR
Ursula Pflug

"I heard you could get Rick Sutton's sculptures here," the woman said, "for half the Yorkville price."

Coiffed and slender, she wore an equally slim black suit that smelled like money. Feeling shabby, Karen wished she'd gotten properly dressed, but maybe her vintage flowered dressing gown, smudged mascara and vaguely matted hair could actually help. Shadow always said people came to the gallery just to feel they were a part of something.

"You can," Karen said. Maybe the woman thought if she had one of Rick's animals, her life might change, just a little bit. She might be right too: Rick's work was that amazing. Karen knew it wasn't just because Rick was her boyfriend that she thought so—his work actually sold, and not for pennies. Well, sometimes anyway.

"Show me," the woman said, and Karen had only to point to the ceiling where a manta ray, three feet in circumference, hung from a chain.

"It's six hundred dollars," Karen said. "Which is half of what you'd pay uptown. And it's his newest, so truthfully he wanted to keep it a bit longer, but . . ." She made an ingratiating gesture.

"I'll have to think about it," the woman said, "Not that it isn't gorgeous." She hesitated before asking, "Do you happen to know where I can get any Green?"

Karen just shook her head no, as Shadow had instructed. Green wasn't scheduled, but it wasn't exactly legal either. Shadow and Rick had both tried explaining the difference between selling and personal use, between synthetic and leaf, between last year and this year: a bristling confusion of facts that, just when it was about to cohere in Karen's mind, always chose to disintegrate instead. Like a sea urchin she'd just stepped on, but not before it poked her sharply in the soft sole of her foot.

The woman gave her a disbelieving look. "But I heard."

Karen just shrugged, returned to the desk, leaving the woman to browse. She opened the little metal box that served as cash register, sorted change into appropriate compartments. The box was dependable in times of power outage, which was often. Everyone was dumping their smart phones in favour of stacks of clipped together file cards, and email, no longer reliable, was out. *Green Magic* sported a meeting area consisting of a spotty Wi-Fi connection and more importantly, comfortable seating. There was no charge for use of the embroidered couch and the connection; people who met at the store sometimes ended up buying clothes or art.

Beside the couch, a metal stand housed fabric paints, mason jars of brushes and a stack of white tees Shadow had liberated from the dumpster behind a Spadina jobber. Karen took the top shirt and stretched it over a painting board. She'd let an arty customer try her hand at painting a shirt to take home the week before, and now Shadow charged people for the pleasure. Karen figured it was the first thing she'd come up with that her boss had approved of.

Karen sighed, staring at the shirt. People who had never dived could hardly be better painters than her; they didn't have a wealth of undersea imagery in their heads to draw upon.

The door chimes rang, startling her. The woman had finally left. Karen wouldn't tell Shadow; he'd complain she could have closed the sale.

No sea here. Karen missed the Pacific Ocean. Occasionally she took the streetcar to Cherry Beach, just to sit there looking at water. Lake Ontario was so big you couldn't see the other side, but there were no breakers and no jellyfish and it didn't smell of salt. Of course, the Strait of Georgia didn't have much in the way of breakers either. She'd grown up in Vancouver but she'd never spent much time on the island, outside of Victoria. Some friends of Rick's had told her it wasn't really the ocean till you'd built a bonfire on Long Beach, brought hand drums and tents or—if it was summer—just curled in a sleeping bag. No one else around for miles. It wasn't really Green till you'd done that. Back then, she still thought her life would change just by being with Rick. It had, too, but not quite in the way she'd hoped.

Still, they'd been in Toronto, now, for over two years, and some things were definitely better.

໙

Back in Vancouver they'd mostly sat in their east side basement apartment heating little pots of green paste on their hot plate. Once it was warmed, they rubbed the paste gently into each other's skin where it was thinnest: temples, neck, the insides of elbows and knees. Waiting for it to begin, staring into each other's eyes, smiles of delight deepening and widening. And there it was: a popping sound, like squelching through soft clean river bottom mud. But it was more than that; it was a popping feeling, her skin transmogrifying. Karen would look then, just to make sure what she felt was also what she saw: Rick's hand wasn't just a hand anymore but also a whale's flipper, the whale's flipper brushing her own, that of a green sea turtle.

Shape shifting. It was electrifying.

Rick never disappeared entirely when Orca arrived. Karen still felt the warmth of primate skin, the hardness of the bones within, the slender bird feet tendons. She knew if she pressed just so, his tendons would move, just a little, and at the same time she'd be touching skin that was slick and rubbery and wet, so alien it left her breathless. Cetacean skin.

Sometimes the change arrived mere moments after dosing, sometimes it took hours to achieve. They chanted and drummed to bring it nearer. They closed their eyes and tuned into the process with every scrap of energy and will, and—something like love. Definitely something like passion. Wasn't prayer in the end just that, an expression of passion for the divine?

Walking, they'd talk about everything that was wrong with the world. If it was up to Rick, he'd have been born as a pre-industrial revolution European peasant. Then, even if his land wasn't his and most of the products of his work, whether it was a lamb or a vegetable or a loaf of bread, went to the owner, well, at least he and his woman could sit on the broken back step peeling apples and looking at the moon. They'd tell folk tales to the little ones, and someone would get out an instrument and someone else would sing, and the apples would be organic because no one had ever even heard of pesticides back then, let alone invented them.

℘

Karen had shared Rick's daydream about a feudal existence with a *Green Magic* customer once and he'd told her she was romanticizing a brutal existence. Which was probably true but you had to hope there was a better life somewhere; maybe for some, the implausible fantasy lay in the future.

The present was no help at all.

Nowadays you had to work forty or more hours per week at a call centre, told how to dress and what to say. Everything mapped out bit by bit, piece by piece, all of it, until you got home and there was nothing left, no *you* anymore. Every part of you remodelled by them and for them, for the privilege of an evening can of soup or a box of take-out and a thriller on the DVD.

And there it was, her mother's life. To prove it, Karen noticed she'd painted not a whale or a turtle on the T-shirt as she'd intended, but a flower sporting Thelma's face.

Rick had always told her art was a kind of therapy.

Thelma stared at her reproachfully.

Why was her mother mad at her this time?

Why was she still so mad at her mother?

It wasn't Thelma she ought to be mad at, anyway, but Thelma's boyfriend Syd.

℘

Rick's manta ray sculpture swung just a little on its chain. She ought to wake him up but if she did he might just dive again. These days, Rick spent most of his time awake upstairs in the bedroom, diving. Not working on his art at all. It was worrisome.

Green wasn't addictive; many users said their physical and psychological health improved when they did a little Green now and again. But lately Rick returned to Green Lady over and over, withdrawing from real life.

Karen dabbed away at her mother's face. It had been Shadow's idea that she painted shirts. *Green Magic* didn't do much business; the weekends were their big days, but it still made sense to open during the week—you just never knew. If she painted "Greenstyle" T-shirts while she clerked she might make a little money and create additional stock for the store.

She didn't think the painting of the flower with her mother's face was "Greenstyle"—she ought to be painting visionary fish, sharks, manta rays, even jellyfish. Still, the likeness was better than she had any right to expect. She'd actually taken more art lessons than Rick ever had, and only now did she remember her instructor telling her she had a talent for portraiture.

∞

She'd painted Thelma with a mournful cast to her face, and while Karen definitely hated Syd she couldn't hate her mom. Even back in Van she hadn't blamed Thelma—she'd just needed to get out of harm's way. She understood why her mom would want to get tipsy on Friday nights, forget everything for a few sweet hours, even her daughter, who it was ostensibly all for. The supervisor with his creepy surveillance, the landlord who didn't fix the washing machines in the basement, the spiralling costs of gas and food and rent and insurance and fear.

"Relax, Thelma, just relax, I'm here. Take off your shoes, I'll rub your feet for you."

Karen felt ill, hearing Syd say that. But why should she deny her poor overworked mother a pleasure that, after all, Karen indulged in with Rick as often as she could?

Well, they used to, anyway. Nowadays Rick dove so much it had affected his libido.

"Darling, Karen hasn't eaten," Thelma said. "I'll just run down to the corner and pick us up a bucket of chicken. And then we can pick up where we left off."

Karen hated the taste of KFC; never mind that the cost of the bucket would've paid for a sack of organic brown rice Thelma could've made with vegetables: better tasting food that might just help to keep her encroaching cancer at bay. But who had the time, or the energy? It was Rick who had taught Karen about natural foods, how to make kombucha tea and grow herbs on the windowsill and sprout grains.

"Of course," Syd said, and grinned at Karen, meaningfully. She knew what was coming, and awful chicken was the least of it.

And just like the other times, she hadn't told Syd to stop. She'd frozen. She couldn't understand why; she hated herself for freezing. No, that was wrong: she actually had tried telling him to stop. He'd grinned at her, a grin with just the tiniest, shocking hint of menace in it.

There were footsteps outside in the hall. Syd stopped. Karen moved away from him and adjusted her clothes. He smiled: a weird mix of gratitude and again, menace.

Don't tell. He didn't have to say it out loud.

Thelma came in, looking happy to see them, but especially, it was unarguable, Syd. He got up and took the takeout bag from her and assembled food onto three plates. Thelma laughed and Syd kissed the top of her head. No, he buried his face in her hair and Karen watched in some horror as her mother melted, as if this was the one good thing that happened in her week. She'd never give it up. How could she?

Syd winked at Karen over her mother's shoulder and said, "It smells delicious."

"We'll sit and eat, the three of us," Thelma said happily, and Syd, serving the chicken, said, "I brought a movie over."

The chicken smelled rotten.

Everything had smelled rotten for a long, long time.

The part that, oddly, creeped Karen out the most was that Syd didn't even behave as if he were hiding anything. Maybe he thought it was normal, even fun, for the three of them to sit down together and watch the latest sex and violence thriller bordering on porn and eat chicken bred with no heads, right after he felt her up.

Did the chickens really have no heads? Karen wasn't sure if

it was true or Greenie apocrypha but it didn't really matter. It could've been true; if it wasn't true now, it would be soon.

It felt like it was true now.

She left without eating her chicken. She never told Thelma. She went to Rick's. Her schoolbooks were all in her locker at the high school. She wore Rick's clothes, and bought a few more at the St. Vincent de Paul, which was a lot cheaper than Value Village. She went on student assistance so she could help Rick pay his bills. He welcomed the windfall and spent a lot of it on art supplies. And Green.

Diving and phone calls were activities inimical to one another. And Karen wouldn't have called her mother once they'd resurfaced; after diving, sleep always seemed of the utmost importance, leaving pesky to-dos like letting family know you're safe to be left till morning. Anyway, Thelma wouldn't have worried, not right away; she'd have known Karen was at Rick's.

ભ

Problem was, she'd never called. And it was two years later.

Shit. No wonder Thelma was melancholic.

Karen picked up the store phone, looked at it.

Put it back. Shadow would hate it if she used long distance.

She left her painting to get up and re-arrange the crab in the window. It was slipping a little from its perch in a pink velvet Victorian armchair; if it fell forward to the floor it might break; papier mâché was hardly the most hardy of materials. Beautiful and rose-hued, the crab's huge claws were painted with an eerie life-like verisimilitude. Light-shadows of waves floated across its back as though it were underwater, and prisms swirled in its eyes. Most visionary art was wall art painted on canvas and the fact that Rick's was 3-D gained him an extra cachet. Even his early attempts back in Vancouver had been clearly better than average. It was why she'd crushed on him in the first place, more than his looks or his charm which were, truthfully, somewhat non-existent. Karen had still been living at her mom's, going to high school and hating her mom's creepster boyfriend. Dropping in at the café where Rick worked part-time and hung his sea creatures had been her one solace; the dreamy oceanic peace in his work implied another world was possible, in a way nothing else ever had.

ᘓ

Rick hadn't gone to Emily Carr. Green Lady, he used to tell her, earnestly mixing adhesive in their basement apartment, woke the neurons in his brain. He'd stay up all night studying and reading and making big slurries of smelly papier mâché. He spent their money on wire to make the armatures and flour to make glue. Karen wouldn't have thought it possible to burn through a check buying flour, the cheapest of all possible supplies, and he probably wouldn't have, if it weren't for the infestation. One day when she went to close the big twenty-five kilo bag of flour Rick had left open, she was greeted by the tiny smiling faces of countless little white wriggling worms. She didn't want to see what they turned into after they pupated, so she dumped the flour out in the alley, under the surprising winter-blooming hollyhocks, the uncollected pumpkins planted by forgetful guerrilla gardeners, caved in now and covered with the slightest dusting of snow.

Rick told her she was hallucinating.

"Hallucinating the faces, Rick, but not the worms."

She remembered looking at his sculptures and wondering whether she should drop in on Thelma and ask if her mother could get her a job at the call centre; she could work in the evenings after school. It might work except she already got so tired. Algebra seemed especially strange when they'd dived the night before, never mind the regularly scheduled day-after exhaustion. Maybe if she'd had a nutritious breakfast more often, she could've concentrated. Maybe if Rick had cleaned up the apartment now and again.

And that smell. It had rained for months on end and Karen told Rick she thought the half finished sculptures were rotting instead of drying out.

Smell pulled you back like nothing else. Was it just the Vancouver damp? Mould was supposed to be so very bad for you.

Mould. The smell had come from mould. But it wasn't mould

in the walls.

Gathering up the laundry after school one afternoon, she'd lost her footing and fallen into an unfinished orca sculpture, and the ghastly smell had suddenly been everywhere. Enveloping her, touching her, clothing her. The smell was like Syd's hands. It gave her the same feeling of shocked humiliation, as though the mouldy whale was raping her, as Syd, technically, hadn't. There'd been a knock at the door then; the landlord asking for the check.

"I thought Rick paid it," Karen said, looking down at the smelly goo on her sneaker. Syd's smell was suddenly still on her too, in spite of all the baths and showers she'd had in the interim. But there it unarguably was: the smell of lavender oil and alcohol and cheap cigarettes, intermingled with the smell of rotting papier mâché—a smell not entirely dissimilar to the smell of normally drying papier mâché but more sour, more vile, more loathsome, more Syd-like.

It was as if Syd's hands were still under her shirt while she waited for Thelma to come home, while she waited for Syd to notice he was crazy and offensive and stop.

While she waited.

While the landlord stared at her, smelling that smell.

Karen finally said, "No, Rick didn't give me the rent." Greenies always said one shouldn't spend too much time thinking about such bullshit, and the truth was, chronic divers were forever having their hydro cut off. Even in the rare instances when they had the money, they often forgot to pay.

Maybe welfare had found out she wasn't at school much anymore. She'd been cut off and that was why there was no money for food; it wasn't, as she'd thought, that Rick had spent it all on art supplies. Karen wasn't sure. She stood there blankly looking at the landlord, just as she'd sat there blankly while Syd felt her up.

Neither moment had any intention of ending; worse yet, they were merging. Maybe they'd go away if she swore at them. Karen was tempted, but she didn't. Both the landlord and Syd remained where they were. At least the landlord's hands weren't under her shirt.

The landlord stood staring at her goo coated foot and then he turned around and shut the door on her in a final sort of way, more or less as she had done to her mother that night. Karen sat down on the unmade bed and cried. She was afraid of being charged with welfare fraud.

Perhaps she cried, then as now, because she hadn't eaten or maybe because of the overpowering smell of mould and of Syd's breath which still, even now, clung to her.

Mouldier even than the mould.

They were given their eviction notice two days later.

Rick insisted Green Lady would fix things. She was magic, mistress of synchronicity, of providential solutions appearing as if out of nowhere to solve even seemingly insoluble problems.

"Why didn't Lady help us before?" Karen dared to ask. "We've never seen her, not even once." Green Lady was an aquatic goddess vision who appeared occasionally to divers. Rick and Karen had been waiting a long time.

"Because we didn't ask for her help before we dove," Rick replied, the perfect logic of it creasing his face into a delighted elven grin.

☙

Green Lady's hair. There had been so much of it.

They'd gone walking after their dive, thinking they'd resurfaced and it was safe to do so, oddly not exhausted as was usual, and saw her hair emerging from the sewer grates. It was made of weeds. Living weeds; dead weeds; grass with clumps of mud in it; bits of stones and seashells and the tiny legs of crabs' shed exoskeletons.

And really a lot of garbage.

Karen sat down on the street and plucked bits of broken glass and bits of Styrofoam, bits of plastic bags, bread tags and surprisingly many tiny oval fruit stickers out of the goddess's hair. The Styrofoam was the worst. Of course it didn't decompose, but why did it have to convert to pellet form? There were beads and beads and beads of it stuck in Green Lady's rampant hair, flowing now, not just along the gutters but over the curb and along the street.

Karen sat there for what felt like hours, cleaning Lady's hair. It felt like stringy mud in her fingers, muddy and slimy and maybe some of those clumps weren't mud at all. Her hair was coming up, out of a storm grate, after all, and the recent storms had wreaked havoc with the city's plumbing. Karen understood suddenly that the mould from the rotting carcass of orca and the smell of Syd's breath and Syd putting his hands on her all stemmed from this simple undeniable fact: they hadn't looked after Lady's hair, hadn't kept it clean.

Rick sat down beside her, crying and threading the condoms and syringes out of her hair, careful, so careful not to stick himself. In no time they had a big heap going. Rick doused it with lighter fluid. They burned it, burned all the garbage that had been stuck in Green Lady's hair.

"Thank you for helping," Karen said.

"I wouldn't even have seen it, if you hadn't pointed it out," Rick said. "It was here all the time, her filthy hair. She was begging us to clean it for her. I've walked past it a million times and never even dreamt it was there. Maybe now my life can change."

"How come we see the same thing at the same time, anyway?" Karen asked.

"That always happens on Green," Rick said.

"But we resurfaced hours ago," Karen said.

"Maybe this time it's real," Rick said, "Maybe it's the next level." He pointed at Lady's hair, which, now it was clean, began to move, sparkling and shining and flowing down the sidewalk, an endless green wave, smelling of beauty and the sea.

They stood there, holding hands by the little fire of burning plastic which made a worse smell, Karen had to admit, than Syd's breath and mouldy papier mâché put together. But at least they were getting rid of it at last, the pollution in Lady's beautiful hair and in their own souls, it felt like. And then they heard sirens.

"Let's go," Rick said, and still holding hands they ran down alleyways only he knew. Hiding in the unused entryway of a brick building, they waited and waited for the cops to find them, but they didn't.

The phone rang the second they got in the door to their basement flat. Rick talked for an hour. It was his friend Shadow, long distance from Toronto.

The Green thing was catching on. There were people who went dancing after they did Green; Green visionary art was needed to hang in the clubs. The sea creature sculptures were perfect; Shadow would introduce him to the club owners. But of course Rick was good; Shadow knew that. He'd always been talented. Those drawings he'd done in his binders at school instead of his chemistry; they'd been amazing: hauntingly beautiful and sad and masterfully drawn. "Greenstyle." It was clothes too; maybe Karen could get into that, or she could work in Shadow's gallery and clothing store, *Green Magic*. They could live upstairs.

Rick got off the phone and stared at Karen. "I told you so."

"What, what, what?" Karen asked, and so Rick told her all of it.

"I told you Lady would fix it up," he said, but not in a mean way, just as if he was a little boy who had finally met his fairy godmother.

My mother couldn't take care of me properly. I couldn't tell her about Syd. Thelma needed him too much and it was too weird, I just couldn't voice it, and maybe Lady will be our mother now.

"It's not even our mothers' fault," Rick said, "they did what they could, the world being what it is. Their own lives are so lost after all, lost from themselves, how could they mother us any better than they did?"

"You knew what I was thinking."

"Lady makes that possible," Rick said, it had to be admitted, a little smugly.

"I was so mad at Thelma for leaving me alone with him, for not noticing Syd was that kind of guy. She was so starved for anyone who'd be even a little nice to her. He rubbed her poor feet in real lavender oil," and Karen started to cry.

"Yes, but now it doesn't hurt so much anymore, does it?"

"That's true," Karen said, because it suddenly was. "Why?" she asked.

"Because we have a real mother now."

All moments go on forever, Karen thought, not one of them ever ends, either the bad ones, or, more usefully, the good ones.

She'd never told Rick about Syd, and about her mother before.

And he'd been kind.

CR

It was time to close. Karen, after taking out the garbage which smelled more than a little, locked the street door and turned out all the lights.

Slowly, she made her way up the stairs, wondering what to make for dinner. She should make rice and vegetables, but she was so tired. Maybe a can of soup. Almost anything, so long as it wasn't KFC.

For once there were no dark circles under Rick's eyes. Still, she looked at her boyfriend's sleeping form a little reproachfully and said, "What happened to my dreams?" She didn't ask what had happened to Rick's dreams, because, implausibly, they were coming true.

Maybe Karen didn't believe in Green Lady as much as he did. Or maybe she should figure out what her dreams even were.

It would beat a lot of the other things she had planned for tomorrow.

THE WEEDS AND THE WILDNESS

Tyler Keevil

"Always this bending process, this landscape gardening to make the mind more attractive."

—Henry Miller

There are vans driving around the city: large white vans without any markings on the bodywork. I saw the first one last week, can still see it in my mind. The paint was so fresh and bright it hurt my eyes to stare. I was standing in the garden, watering my marigolds, when it drifted by—smooth and silent as a shark. All the windows, including the windscreen, were tinted so the driver appeared as a vague and featureless shadow. It's hard to say what struck me most—its secretive nature or the predatorial efficiency with which it moved.

In the week since the first one, I've seen more and more of the same.

It's not the same van—it can't possibly be the same van—but I'm hard-pressed to spot any difference between them. They are all in immaculate, pristine condition: no spots of rust, no dents or grooves or scratches. The face of the driver is always similarly obscured. I never catch them speeding, but neither do they seem unhurried. Rather, they prowl about the streets with identical, mechanical purpose. What that purpose is I can't possibly say, but their very existence unnerves me. I can't help but feel as if this is the start of something.

CR

These days, I spend most of my time in the garden—if it can be called a garden. It's more of a jungle, a thriving tangle of grasses, heathers, evergreens, bulbs, corms, perennials, shrubs, ivies, saplings and flowers. This is the busiest time of year. Bluebells are popping open like tiny firecrackers. A multitude of crocuses, daffodils, tulips, and dog's tooth violets are coming into blossom—splashing the lawn and beds with paint-box colours. The next phase of perennials is starting to emerge: hot red bleeding hearts and gold-petalled leopard's banes, alongside the delicate blue and pink wood anemones. My shrubs flower early in the year as well: rhododendrons, magnolias, azaleas—the list goes on and on. Yes, my garden is running rampant. As is the case every spring, complaints come to me in the polite manner of neighbourly concern. They ask me: *Would you like to borrow my lawnmower, my trimmer, my pruning sheers?* Some even offer to do it for me. Since my retirement, I've learned that people in suburbia don't like things to be too different, too wild.

But that's their problem, not mine. I see my garden as a form of personal expression. Maintaining such disarray is a full-time occupation. I reserve evenings for my business dealings (I make a small profit selling organic fertilizers and lawn supplies over the internet) but my days are entirely devoted to my plants. With the countless hours I spend among them, feeding and watering, tending and trimming, it has been impossible for me not to notice these vans. So far, they seem content to go about their business, as I go about mine.

CR

I would like to make some enquiries on the block. If I weren't such a coward, that's exactly what I'd do. But even the thought of it opens a gaping pit in my stomach, brings a sheen of sweat to my back and a hot, allergenic flush to my cheeks. My garden is my refuge. The notion of venturing out, of interacting and engaging with people, unsettles me. It's nothing serious. I'm simply more comfortable in my own space, with my plants. I suppose that makes me an eccentric. I'm sure that's what they call me, anyway, behind my back. What of it? Every neighbourhood needs one. I give them something to talk about over dinner. The eccentric and his garden: wild, unkempt, madcap, bizarre, unmanageable.

Strange how gardens reflect personality. Though I've barely exchanged more than a few awkward words with my neighbours in as many years, I feel I know them. I know Mrs. Crenshaw, with her obsessively trimmed lawn and manically pruned hedges—squat and square as slices of frosted cake. I know, too, the young couple on the corner, who neglect their yard for months and then decide to attack it, apropos of nothing, with ferocious zeal. Grass clippings and leaves are left where they've fallen, covering a lawn devoid of style, care, or character—like a haircut executed by a drunken barber. And what do I know of Mr. Amonte and his brood? I know the first thing he did, upon moving in across the street, was to drown his yard in a sea of cement. The only lawn he has left is a small plot, about two by six feet, that rests in the centre of the patio like an unkempt and overgrown grave.

The thought of approaching these people, or most of the others, horrifies me.

There is only one yard, one person, on the block that I find interesting. Like myself, Jay is something of an anomaly. A weed. A thirty-something divorceé. Her husband was the gardener, studious and conventional. Since their split, she has taken secret pleasure in allowing his carefully tended beds to run rampant. The lawn hasn't been cut for months. It's become a raging meadow, filled with knee-high stalks of grass, dandelion heads, snowdrops, buttercup clusters, and chains of Michalmas daisies. Along the perimeter, fierce japonica shrubs vie with smoke bushes and holly trees for dominance. It is a garden to fall in love with.

I know Jay has gone back to school recently. I see her coming and going, head down, a load of books clutched to her chest. She would be worth talking to, and I've had the opportunity on occasion when she's ordered supplies from me (I offer her a discount). But whenever I deliver she is as reticent and tongue-tied as me. She's like a furtive jungle animal hiding out amongst all that foliage. Our very similarities make communication between us difficult.

It is impossible to say if she'd understand about the vans.

CR

I've developed a system. It is not enough to observe. I must also record, analyze, and assess the nature of the threat posed by these vans. Already I've had several breakthroughs. I've discovered they come only during the day, during which they pass by no less than two and (so far) no more than five times. There can be no doubt they wish to avoid drawing attention to themselves. Their ultra-quiet engines and alarmingly inconspicuous exteriors are proof enough of that, but today I noticed something far more menacing: the vans have no license plates. Or rather, the plates have been deliberately obscured. They seem to have been coated with some sort of reflective material, which catches the sunlight and cunningly foils any attempt to discern the lettering. There really is no way to differentiate among them. The only reason I can assume I'm seeing numerous vans, rather than the same one over and over, is the sheer number of sightings. They seem to be increasing by the day. Surely it can't go on like this? Surely— the authorities or somebody—will put a stop to it? We can't just have these anonymous, impossibly efficient vans cruising up and down the block, the neighbourhood, the city, unchecked. Yet, that's precisely what seems to be happening.

I jumped just now, at the sound of a distant car. They have me on edge, you see. But night is falling as I write, and with it comes the safety of darkness. At twilight, the grass whispers and the leaves mutter to one another. And the smells! It's impossible to describe the smells—a perfume of cherry blossom, honeysuckle, and magnolia. I know if I put down my pen and stepped off the porch, if I placed a palm on the dew-wet grass, I'd be able to feel the vibrant hum of nature, flowing like a current. This time belongs to things natural and pure. The thought of one of the vans suddenly appearing is not only abhorrent, but unthinkable.

CR

The Weeds and the Wildness by TYLER KEEVIL

Disturbing. That is the only word I can think of to describe what I saw today. I was in my garden—carefully pruning my clematis—when I heard the unmistakeable purr of an approaching van. I reached for my notebook (which I always keep at the ready) and jotted down the time, as per my custom. But I was to witness something new. Instead of cruising past, the van began *slowing down*. I watched in horror as it pulled to a stop in front of Mrs. Crenshaw's place, and two figures (I hesitate to call them men) clambered out. They wore white jumpsuits, like painter's coveralls, along with white hats, white gloves, and white boots. Surgeons' masks muzzled their mouths, and clear plastic safety goggles obscured their eyes. These goggles, like the license plates of their vans, seemed to constantly reflect sunlight, making it impossible to see anything behind the lenses. Petrified, I watched these men open the rear doors of the van and unload a large supply of everyday gardening tools. I found that more alarming than if they had pulled out an arsenal of weapons: machine guns, bazookas, crates of grenades. For they acted as soldiers, and it was this incongruity—between their military manner and the banal nature of their task, which unsettled me most.

The first one slipped a pesticide pack on his back and immediately set to dosing Mrs. Crenshaw's entire yard, like a marine spraying a flamethrower. Meanwhile, the other turned his motorized trimmer on her privet hedges, shearing the tops and sides with mercenary precision. Last, they attacked the lawn, which was cropped until it resembled a monstrous putting green. The whole incident seemed to occur in fast-motion, as if I were watching a film being played back at twice the normal speed. Before I could make a single note, the tools were disappearing back into the van. One worker slipped behind the wheel while the other deposited something in Mrs. Crenshaw's mailbox. Then the engine purred to life. Both doors swung shut, scarcely audible. Wheels turned silently on silky-smooth tarmac.

They were gone.

The world slipped back into real-time. The street was quiet, dead, save for the chirruping of a lone blackbird overhead. Nobody else had witnessed the travesty. I was shaken and stunned, almost shell-shocked, but I walked—as casually as possible—over to Mrs. Crenshaw's, and checked in her mailbox. Within was a quarter sheet of white paper. Plain black letters in a nondescript font read: *Your lawn has been serviced.* That was all. It was so shockingly absolute I dropped the paper as if it were infected, diseased, contagious. I rushed home, slamming the door and snapping the deadbolt behind me.

In my notebook I wrote: *They have stepped up operations.*

☙

The rest of the week has proved me right.

Just as the sight of cruising vans became familiar, so too have the sightings of men in white suits. A day doesn't pass when I fail to spot them, on our block or those nearby, wielding their vast array of weapons: lawnmowers, trimmers, clippers, hedgers, saws, power rakes, edgers, rollers. From daybreak until twilight they are busy, like swarms of ravenous white ants scrambling over the city. They fill clear plastic bags with grass clippings, weeds, twigs, moss, flowers, leaves—anything. Anything that stands in the way of their generic, pristine lawns.

This afternoon I had a harrowing encounter with Mrs. Crenshaw. In the middle of loading sacks of fertilizer on my flatbed for the weekly deliveries, I stood up to find her hovering nearby. Rake-thin, long-limbed, and hook-nosed, she had the look of a wingless, featherless bird. I forced myself to smile, even asked after her health. Perfectly familiar, perfectly friendly, even though all our previous conversations (or altercations) had been based around my unruly lawn encroaching on her pruned paradise.

Yet she had a smile for me, as well. Quite dazed. It matched the look in her eyes: as if she were gazing through me rather than at me. Encouraged by this congeniality, I asked her about the vans, and the men I'd seen. "Oh yes," she said, her smile broadening. "Them. I hired them, you see? I am weary of my lawn. It is so much easier to let them take care of it." I pressed her further, asking who 'they' were and how she had contacted them. To these queries, she merely waved her hand airily. She's not quite sure, she told me. Perhaps on the internet, or in the phone book.

Perhaps through a friend. It's even possible, it seemed to her, that she hadn't hired them at all. But what troubled me most was the dull, glazed expression on her face—like a lobotomy patient. As if she herself, like her lawn, had undergone some kind of treatment. She, oblivious to my suspicions, began to wax enthusiastic about 'them,' telling me I should consider hiring them to take care of my own 'yard problems.' She said 'them' like their service was some kind of a miracle cure, a new drug her doctor had prescribed. Soon it will be the talk of the town, she promised me.

Them.

CR

This week I have recorded other incidents that confirm my fears. The jottings in my journal are no longer concerned with which lawn seed to use in spring, or the best way to cultivate wisteria. No, it reads now like a military log for what I am beginning to think of as 'The Resistance.' The Resistance of one. In this way I have kept track of their activities. They are at the university, tearing up boulevards, yanking out shrubs, hacking down trees. They are down in the city's parks, laying generic strips of turf, slashing back hedges, gutting flower beds. They are on every corner, every street, shameless now, gaining momentum. Even as I write this I can hear them working on our boulevard. The harsh whine of their machinery rises in the air, like the buzz of swarming locusts. There is no foreseeable end to it. They won't stop until they've slashed every tree, lawn and hedge into submission, until they've eradicated all the dandelions, nettles, ragwort and thistle from the entire city. The vision comes to me now, like something out of Revelations. The lawns are perfectly flat and groomed: squares on a massive green checkerboard. Row after row of identical trees, stiff and monotonous as cardboard cutouts, stretch down each and every boulevard. There is no sense of disorder, no sense of life and chaos. It is a man-made apocalypse, Judgement Day welcomed with open arms. And this unnatural vision will come to pass unless we wake up from our general slumber, unless somebody—anybody—stands up and shouts, "Enough!" Out of unlikely necessity, it looks like that person may have to be me.

STRANGERS AMONG US

If I truly am the lone Resistance, I may as well resist.

CB

I waited until early evening, when their activities typically ceased for the day. Cool, waning sunshine fell like honey over lawns, sidewalks, lampposts. Armed with spade and shovel, I marched out to the boulevard. A fitting no man's land. A suitable place to begin. While the neighbourhood slept, 'they' had changed it into a perfectly groomed strip of grass, smooth and flat and straight as green ribbon. Gripping the spade firmly by both hands, I raised it over my head.

I struck a blow.

The turf was still fresh, and hadn't settled. Easy enough to peel back entire sections, roll them up like carpets. These were cast aside. Next came the planting. Using buds and bulbs and shoots and cuttings from my own stock, my own garden and flower beds, I dug and planted, sowed and covered. First, I laid down a fierce and aggressive vanguard: grenades of golden canopied achilliea, each one an explosion of yellow, dropped in next to brigades of Halberdleaf hibiscus, and battalions of kniphofias—their flowers jutting straight up like the bloody spears of a phalanx. I worked myself into a sweating, panting frenzy.

Halfway through my operation, I heard footsteps.

Imagine my surprise, in looking up, to see Jay approaching, heavy textbooks clutched to her chest. She smiled at me, and told me my display was beautiful. I thanked her, too spent to be properly nervous or tongue-tied. Moments passed. Then, in a quiet, hesitant tone, she asked me if, maybe, she might be able to help, possibly? In answer I gestured at the remaining bulbs, stalks, seedlings and stacks of stones. Of course I could use her help. Blushing slightly (she has plaster-pale cheeks, so the red stands out like circles of paint) she dropped her books and set to work. Without changing her clothes, without gloves or proper shoes, she dove straight in like a vole.

We worked together, in comfortable silence. What I remember most are her hands—her pale, bony hands, dipping into the earth, and the way the dirt stained her palms, gathered under her nails, smeared her forearms. Behind my fiery frontline, Jay selected calmer colours: some cream-flavoured marigolds, the soft, sundial shapes of osteospermums, and a sprinkling of white petunias. The stepping stones went in last, laid out flat, cool and grey as puddles.

We finished as the sun died. Shattered and sweating, we stood side by side in the spreading dark and gazed at our creation: the paler colours hovering like strange and beautiful ghosts, the darker shades playing shadow-tricks on our eyes. With the work done, my reticence returned. It had been so easy and comfortable while we were united by purpose. Now silence clung to us like spider webs. Jay reached for her books, muttered excuses about dinner, reading, working on her thesis. I stood and nodded like a bobble-headed doll. I said I had things to do as well: orders to fill, bills to process. But before she went, she seized me in a swift, impulsive hug—squeezing her bony figure against me, her arms tight on my neck.

And in my ear I heard: "I really appreciate what you're doing."

At that she withdrew, scuttling across the street. She seemed to know what I was up to—with my observation and my recording, my vigilance and my resistance—though I didn't know how. I wondered about that while I watched her scurry up her steps and slip inside her door, as silent and soundless as a mouse retreating to its den.

ಐ

There has followed a frenzy of activity, a veritable revolution. Across the city, wherever I can, I am fighting them. I perform spontaneous acts of creation on a daily basis, off-setting Their meticulous devastation. In the cooling dusk, with whatever tools are on hand, I (the Resistance!) am taking to the streets, riotous and seditious. An oasis of pink-belled Digitalis appears here, bursting clusters of fuchsias ignite there. The wildest, fiercest plants make the most effective allies: Russian vine, silver ivy, holly, rhododendron hedges. These and countless others push belligerently into Their artificial wasteland, recovering lost ground. And weeds: my secret weapons. Proliferate, burgeoning weeds.

Patches of buttercup bloom overnight, occupying manicured lawns. Bindweed creeps up on flowerbeds, overpowering them. Dandelions, sorrel, leafy sponge, dock, tansy, pokeweed — they are able soldiers all.

My workroom has become a place to plot, to draw up battle plans and manoeuvres. Which fertilizer can create the most havoc? Which seeds to scatter where? Those answers I don't know, I research on the internet. I do not have their numbers or their supplies, but I have nature on my side and the benefit of surprise. They never know where I will strike because I act at random. Disorder is my ally; chaos is my friend. I take inspiration from a blog I've stumbled upon in my searches; it is run by somebody called Narcissus, who posts messages and well-known quotations at least once a day. They are always uplifting and seditious. One of my favourites was Michael Pollen: *A lawn is nature under totalitarian rule.* Today it was a W.H. Hudson quote: *Rather I would see daisies in their thousands, ground ivy, hawkweed, and even the hated plantain with tall stems, and dandelions with splendid flowers and fairy down, than the too-well-tended lawn.*

The knowledge that there are others like me keeps me going, in this war of attrition. What I do today may be undone tomorrow. Squadrons of marching ivy, platoons of toeflax, armies of bullthistle: all can vanish in a single morning. For I have not stopped Them. I am only keeping Them at bay. But the idea that this is even possible, that I can slow Them down, has given me hope.

❦

Hope, too, I've found in our own, local struggle. During the evenings, Jay and I persevere. Following our initial efforts on my boulevard, imagine my delight to have her join me again, and again, always during those same hours. What began with that initial chance encounter has blossomed into a nightly ritual; she has joined my Resistance. This week we targeted the boulevard in front of her house. Now it looks like an extension of her garden: unchecked, unmanageable, unyielding. Stretches of geranium grope their way around segonia shrubs and pink-flowered azalea.

And in finishing, what could be more sensible than to continue? Up and down the block, spreading nature's anarchic vitality, gaining ground in inches and feet, ignoring our neighbours who now seem too dumb and dull to protest. From behind their windows they peer out, blinking myopically like bunnies trapped in glass cages.

Tonight, just now, as Jay and I stood surveying our latest masterpiece—a stunning display of ornamental grasses, ranging from Liriope to Little Bluestem, planted in front of the Amonte's home—something unexpected occurred. She asked me if I'd like to come in for a drink. A lemonade, perhaps, or something stronger?

I accepted, of course, and found myself following her across her lawn and into what I could only describe as a cave of books. Books carpeted the floor and leaned against the walls in precarious towers. Others lay across chairs, desks and tables, the pages spread open like the wings of exotic and dormant moths. She ushered me into her living room, wading through textbooks, fiction anthologies, poetry chapbooks, paperback novels, volumes of critical essays, collections of plays. She cleared a seat on the sofa for me before vanishing into the kitchen. I heard cupboards opening, bottles capping, liquid pouring. She returned with two glasses of vodka lemonade and sat next to me. The low-slung sun was shooting its last, blazing rays through her window, making our glasses glow like lanterns.

That kind of intimacy did not come easy to me; a familiar nervousness filled me like a fever. I cleared my throat, explained that I'd never been much of a reader. She glanced around, blushing, as if surprised to see all those books scattered about her living room. She explained about her studies, about her Master's degree. When pressed, she elaborated on her thesis: a project combining her twin loves of literature and horticulture. It must have been obvious to her that I didn't understand everything she said, but her patience allowed some of the concepts to filter through—like the relationship she perceived between plants and words, mother nature and human nature. Thoughts are like seeds, growing in the darkness of our consciousness. Cultured and nurtured, they sprout into ideas, grow into finished and complete structures. A poem, say. Or a story. But in hostile environments, smothered and suppressed, they die at the backs of our skulls, the stillborn babies of infertile imaginations.

And I, fascinated, listened to her as she opened up, a night flower unfolding in the dusk, her words evoking a heady, almost dizzying effect in me. Later, we took our drinks and chairs to her front window, there looking out upon our own creation: the wild, rambling boulevard. Stalks and stems stood out in stark silhouette, and flower heads seemed to float in the dark like will-o'-the-wisps. Jay swirled her drink, causing the ice to tinkle pleasantly.

Then she said, "Abram Urban said 'My garden of flowers is also my garden of thoughts and dreams. The thoughts grow as freely as flowers, and the dreams are as beautiful.'" She recited this in a low, mournful tone, as if reading at a funeral. I looked at her, wondering why I hadn't realized before. Narcissus. She was my Narcissus. And as if in confirmation, she brushed my forearm with her fingertips, her nails searing my skin. The sudden gesture—so natural yet so shockingly intimate—left my skin throbbing hotly, as if I'd been burned, or marked.

ଦ୍ୟ

They have struck back, as I knew they would.

We are dusk-mites, operating under the cover of darkness. Jay and I feel much safer doing our work during the evenings rather than exposed in the daytime. For in the day they are strong, and in the day we are vulnerable. Legions of vans swarmed the city this week, more than I have ever seen, redoubling their efforts. Battles are won in increments, in inches, and they're taking back the ground we've gained. Our beautiful grass collage? Gone. The rock and stone garden we arranged in front of Mrs. Crenshaw's? Vanished. For days on end the air in the neighbourhood has been thick with the reek of oil fumes, cut grass, pesticides, moss killer. This retribution, of course, is not unexpected. Yet they are pursuing other avenues—far more shocking and, I fear, ultimately far more dangerous to our well-being.

This morning there came a knock at my door. When I opened

it, I saw Jay standing there, looking perplexed. She had her book bag slung over one-shoulder, and in her hands was a slip of white paper. She held it out to me, asked me if I'd had a similar notice. I took it from her, my insides going numb, as if I'd swallowed ice water. It was easily recognizable, with its plain black lettering, its obtrusive font, its single declarative sentence, so minimalist and so menacing: *Your lawn is due for servicing.* I told her, no, I hadn't received anything like this. Not yet. She frowned and took it back from me, studied it while nibbling her lip.

"It must be some mistake, then. I'll call and explain I don't need it."

I tried to tell her. I babbled inarticulately about the seriousness of the situation, the effects of the treatment on Mrs. Crenshaw and Amonte; I stammered on about Them. But she didn't seem to understand, or want to understand. She laughed at my worries, kissed me on the cheek, said my concern for her was touching. "It's fine," she told me, adjusting her bag. "I'll be fine. You'll see." She wouldn't quite look me in the eye, though. I wanted to grab her, shake her, tell her she was fooling herself. Instead I stood there, silent and frozen, my tongue stuck like a fishhook in my mouth, as she trotted down my steps and hurried away from me, away from the truth.

CR

They came for her the next day. Or maybe the day after. It's hard to say, given what occurred. One thing I know for sure: she was at school, and helpless to stop them. Two vans pulled up and out sprang a handful of white minions. I stood at my window, paralysed. Impossible to describe what the sight of those vans did to me, glaring so whitely.

It was a massacre.

Through the glass I heard the scree of gas engines firing up, the helicopter thop of mower blades, the buzz of trimmers, the moan of hedge clippers. They came well-armed, well-prepared. Those sounds were awful enough, but far worse was what I saw: sunlight flashing off metal blades, black fumes spewing into the air. Stems hacked like tendons, branches hewn like bone. Petals scattering like chunks of flesh. Green froth spit and spattered across their pristine suits, the gory lifeblood painting dying patterns. I was safe, behind closed doors. But Jay. Jay. I knew that nothing would be spared. Nothing.

As I watched, I heard something else: a strange, keening cry. It was coming from my own throat. Then I was outside, acting without thinking. Grabbing a spade from my garden, I charged towards them—shouting over the roar of equipment, brandishing the tool like a sword. Engrossed in their work, eyes obscured by goggles and mouths hidden by masks, they ignored me until I stormed amongst them, threatening and shouting and cursing. Then, one by one, the engines died. My breath coming raw and ragged, I turned on their vehicles, swinging the spade like a hatchet against headlamps, windscreens, doors, and hoods.

"She doesn't want it! Leave her alone!"

They stared at me, impassive and inscrutable. Inhuman, alien creatures! I was vaguely aware of doors opening up and down the block, of a crowd gathering. I continued my tirade, screaming and bashing, my words and blows growing weaker and weaker, until I had nothing left but blind spots in my vision and a cutting pain in my chest. My knees bent; I went down. I fell in the field of butchered plants, the scent of death ripe in my nostrils. Quivering, twitching, nauseous and fearful, I lay there in a semi-conscious state.

Feet and voices surrounded me. "That's enough now," one said. "We'll take you home," came another. They were not Them (for They do not speak) but my own neighbours. Gentle and firm. The spade was wrested from my grip. Hands lifted me, supported me. Faces hovered on all sides. I recognized Mrs. Crenshaw and Amonte and the young couple and still others. Every one of them smiling sickly, emboldened by daylight and the proximity of the vans. En masse they guided me away from the scene towards my house, all the while keeping up their sinister murmurs: *Everything will be okay, now. Soon you'll see. It doesn't even hurt.* I was led (or forced) through my open door, stretched out on the sofa, my protests drowned out by the chorus of soothing, cooing voices. *That's the way. . . . Just lie down. Stay put.* And I obeyed, helpless to resist—as the world went black before my eyes. I heard fading voices, retreating footsteps, the gentle click of the door swinging shut behind them.

I remember the throb of motors coming to life.

℃

I am now lying in bed. Pale, lugubrious light is oozing through my bedroom blinds, leaking across the floor, and pooling in puddles on my bed. The sweat of troubled dreams has soaked through my sheets. It's been this way for days: days in which I've heard the constant passage of vans, the permanent haze of noise created by their machines. I have never felt so alone.

Jay, my Narcissus, is gone.

As soon as I recovered, I went to see her. But once I stepped out of my house, even in the darkness of evening, I knew all hope was lost. I could see the totality of their job. Where once there grew evening primrose, foxhollow, pink hyacinths and purple forget-me-nots—a wondrous jumble of greenery and colours—there is now only the same empty vacuum as in every other yard on the block. Flat, rectangular, soulless, expressionless. Lifeless.

Spurned on by perversity, or desperation, I went to see her anyway. The only sign of the morning's massacre was the faint, sickly sweet smell of freshly killed vegetation lingering in the air. I mounted her porch, knocked twice, stood standing and waiting like a salesman. And imagine my horror, my agony, as the door swung open, to reveal Jay, smiling blandly, her expression as fixed as a doll's: eyes dim, mouth slack, features blank. Behind her, in perfect order against the walls, like hundreds of soldiers lined up to be shot, were her books. It was too much. I began to weep, clutch at her. I tried to hold her. She didn't have the presence of mind to be scared, or angry. Rather, she seemed only confused and bewildered. She patted me affectionately, still smiling. "There, there. Everything is okay. What's all this fuss about? Come, now." I extricated myself, backed away, unable to take my eyes off her, still searching until the end for some semblance of the woman I knew. She stood still in the doorway, her body oddly limp: a cropped flower wilting in its vase.

So now I lie here, stuck among sweaty sheets with my painful memories. The heady stench of her sweat as we worked. A bead of blood glistening on her thorn-pricked fingertip. The tentative, breathy whisper of her voice. The touch of her fingers on my arm, like fire.

And outside, all the while, I hear Them working . . .

☙

I am up, now. Out of bed. Spurned on by the sound of something sliding through my mail-slot, something that brushed the carpet with a soft, serpent's hiss. I'd been expecting it, of course. Still, it was enough to rouse me. Throwing on a bathrobe, stumbling to the entrance hall, I saw one of their quarter-sized sheets of paper, nestled by my doormat. I refused to pick it up, fearful of its terrible, hypnotic power, fearful of being immobilized.

In writing this now, the utter hilarity of my position occurs to me. My lawn's disorder is like a last vestige of individualism amongst this utterly generic wasteland. My neighbours walk by it, refusing to look, avoiding it as if, through denial alone, they can will it (and me) out of existence. And who's to say they're not right? Soon my lawn will no longer exist. Soon I will no longer exist. Having taken the kingdom, They are ready to storm the tower.

And I've been as compliant, as submissive as the others: lying here, waiting for Them to come, waiting for the end. I've neglected my duties, stewing in my mire of depression, despair, and self-pity. But just now, for the first time in weeks, I've looked at Jay's blog. There, to my heartache and delight, I found a final message from Narcissus—posted just before the end, quoting Thoreau: *Gardening is civil and social, but it wants the vigour and freedom of the forest and the outlaw.* Until now my resistance has been pacifistic, while around me I have seen landscapes changed and minds reshaped. No longer. Jay has shown me the way.

The passive, civil resistance of gardening is no longer adequate.

☙

I am in a unique position. My storehouse is already filled with chemicals, with fertilizer, with everything I need. There are internet sites that offer simple instructions. A fool could follow them. All week I have been mixing ingredients, and loading my van with innocuous-looking packages. I've been going over my maps, and drawing up lists of possible targets. But I also plan to improvise. As ever, chaos will be an ally, and I can make deliveries wherever I see Them working, or at any address where They have already done Their damage, and the people are beyond saving. I know there are others out there who will understand, who may be waging their own battles and resisting this in their own way.

I know I am not alone.

Tonight, the night before the exodus, I am filled with a dream of tomorrow. No, it is more than a dream. It is a premonition. As I drive out of the city, I hear explosions and see towers of flame, like lances thrusting up from the earth. And the terrible aftermath! Vans torn and shredded. Billowing black columns of smoke. Helicopters circling overhead. Sirens wailing in agony. These sounds will create the swansong of the Resistance as we beat our final retreat. You cannot save people who do not wish to be saved. I head into the wilderness, for the wild. Far from this place we will meet again, those of us who still believe in natural chaos; who still believe there is beauty in the tangled snarl of vines around tree trunks, in the way weeds can crack apart pavement, in the riotous nature of blossoms and buds. There we will meet and find others like ourselves, others who abhor the sight of cropped grass, square hedges, symmetrical trees—precision and perfection. We will cultivate our beliefs, drawing strength from the land, waiting for the time when the city turns stagnant, when every lawn is uniform and every mind is unanimous, and the light of humanity begins to slowly go out like a gas lamp dimming in the dark. Only then will we return.

LIVING IN OZ
Bev Geddes

The door squeaked open. Old doors in old homes were the best for that. Freaked people out to no end. I never understood why. Old homes are old homes. That's part of the deal. Not so good when you're trying to sneak in past curfew or keep sleeping babies asleep. Now, the squeaky doors were useful to me.

The smell of soggy tissues and coffee hung in the air. He really should empty that wastebasket more often. It was a welcome place, relaxed and easy. I'd been here a few times. Before. I threw myself onto the worn couch and announced, "I'm here."

He didn't even look up from the papers he was studying at his desk, scribbling a note here and there with a half chewed pencil stub. The silence stretched. I waited. It sometimes took a while.

"I know you're there," he said, finally looking up. With a sigh, he pushed his glasses up onto the top of his head, hair shaved to a frosted stubble. He was slim and fit and had a smile that eased the tension out of the room. It wasn't a put-on kind of thing. Bernie wasn't that kind of psychologist. He never made you feel crazy. "It's been a while."

"Over here, on the couch." I waved, though I didn't know why. Hard to break old habits, I guess.

"I know," he repeated. "I'm just slow today. It's been a busy day." He pushed away from his battered oak desk and slumped down into the winged chair facing me, tucking his legs beneath himself. He didn't pick up the tablet of paper that had been thrown onto the end table beside him with obvious abandon. "You've been invisible again, haven't you?"

"Comes with the territory," I muttered.

"Not necessarily." He folded his hands across this stomach weaving his fingers together. He was settling in. "We've discussed this."

"Um hmm. And you still don't get it."

"Then why do you come here, if I don't understand your situation? That doesn't make much sense. Looking for a convert?" A slow smile curled into the corners of his mouth.

"Because you hear me." I folded my legs underneath myself too. It was warmer that way, and I was tired of being so damn cold. I spent my life being cold in a city gripped with snow and ice for six months of the year, and now I was still cold in this unfamiliar terrain. It wasn't right. There ought to be some advantages to being in my present state. "I need someone to really hear me. I don't know why."

"Lots of other people would hear you, if you'd let them." He paused and I knew what would come next. "They would see you, too."

I waved my hand at him, dismissing that last comment. It looked thinner . . . more translucent than before. I wondered how long I would have that hand.

"People don't want to see me."

"I think you're underestimating them. Friends and family at least."

I laughed at that. My laugh sounded harsh. The edges of it scraped the ear. It came from just below the surface, with no depth and no softness. Someone had once said that I had the best laugh, a belly laugh that seemed to fill my whole body. A laugh that could nudge smiles onto faces. It was real. I remember. Now it was just an echo.

"They were too tired." I made another useless gesture with my hand, indicating my body, "This was too much for them. I was a burden. I knew that. Even if they didn't use the word. That's why I left. It was the only option open to me anymore."

"You're wrong. It isn't too late. They can still see you. You're still you, just different. Trust them."

"Different? People don't do 'different' very well. If you don't fit into the box, they have no clue how to interact with you."

"Not all people. You have to try. Give it a chance."

"I've tried."

Bernie's eyebrows knitted together, and he got that intense look that would flit briefly across his face before he relaxed back into therapy mode. "You've tried? Tell me when? What did you do?"

"Today on the bus, as I was getting on, I saw a woman sitting there. Her face was so very sad. She was crying. She seemed embarrassed to cry. We're not supposed to let people know that side of us. It makes them uncomfortable. But I could feel her grief. It shone from her like a beacon. I sat behind her, trying to send all the warmth and comfort I could. To let her know it would get better, that the grief would ease."

But some grief doesn't just ease. It crashes over you like a wave or laps at your toes the rest of the time, always there ready to take you down. It doesn't go away.

"Grief is a storm," I said, nodding at this thought. It's more than a wave, more devastating, longer lasting. A wave hits and then recedes. Storms build, descend, wreak havoc, then scurry away only to circle back again. "The storms are different all the time. It's just a matter of degree."

My gaze drifted out the window, frost-etched patterns of silver blocking the view of the street. I didn't share the rest of my thoughts on grief storms but I counted out the ones that I knew so intimately.

The white-out of the blizzard storm where there is nothing but surge upon surge of driving snow. Each snowflake stings with memory and settles on the soul a grief so pressing the body screams beneath its weight. The world doesn't exist outside of this storm. Here there is no end.

Then there's the crazed thunderstorm full of fury and red-hot strikes that shake the earth below you. You scramble for cover knowing the storm will seek you out and there is no escape from the crackling stab of lightning.

The sudden north wind pain that rakes your face with icy fingers and pulls the breath out of you. This one sneaks up on you like rounding a sheltered corner only to be blasted back into grief with a single gust of wind.

The rich earthy storm of the fall that heralds the cold of winter is less overwhelming but, with the constant drizzle of days, it is grey and pressing. It wears down the heart slowly.

Finally, the dead calm of an August afternoon when the heat seems endless—and so does your life. When you feel nothing, and there is nothing. Nothing in front, nothing beside, nothing behind you. It's just an endless sheet of still water and your boat is sinking.

Grief is so many different storms.

"Sometimes words don't help," I said, looking down at the rug, a mottled richly hued old Indian one that Bernie had found on the boulevard a few years back. He was so proud of it. I could tell by the way he uncurled from his chair and rubbed his feet along its thick warmth, allowing a smile to wrinkle his eyes into a half-moon.

Bernie leaned forward and scratched his nose. I could hear his fingernail rake the skin and I was surprised he didn't have welts from scratching too hard. I knew it meant he was choosing his words carefully. "No, you're right. Words don't always help. But sometimes just letting someone know you're there and it matters that they're struggling is enough. Sometimes a hug or a touch is good. A day, a week, a year, three years later. Always."

I nodded quickly. I knew this. He had said this to me before.

"I did. I touched that lady's shoulder. Squeezed it as I left the bus. I wanted her to know someone cared."

"And?" Bernie's eyes were bright. "She saw you then, didn't she?"

He deflated as I shook my head. "She looked up, but no, she didn't see me."

There was a part of me that wished she had, that someone could. Being like this was like watching the world through a slightly distorted pane of glass, wavy and indistinct. I could see people carrying on, laughing, falling in love, fussing about bills, eating food and really tasting it, complaining about their kids or jobs or spouses. All, so simple. So taken for granted, the basic act of continuing to live.

Somehow I had lost the ability to carry on. Bernie had said it was something that got messed up in my brain that day, something biochemical. It was like a light switch turned off or on, depending on your perspective, and nothing was the same anymore. I wasn't the same anymore. Nothing made sense.

I lowered my head and rubbed my hands along my thighs. It seemed as though the outline of my legs had faded further into the red plush of the couch. Was I fading faster than I thought? The process of leaving this world had been so slow. How I wished it would end and the final wisp of whatever I had become would be gone; sucked into the breeze like the smoke from a chimney in the autumn chill. Then I could remain in the Other—for good.

I could feel myself trembling. "I haven't got the strength. I'm not in Kansas anymore," I whispered.

"Bullshit!"

My head snapped up at the sharp tone of Bernie's voice. It hadn't been a loud expletive, but his tone shocked me into attention. He had never spoken to me like that before. I felt my eyes widen. "What?" I stammered.

Bernie didn't move, but I could see his jaw working. He was wrestling with himself about something. We held each other's gaze as the web of silence stretched between us.

"You're looking for proof that you're in this world. That doesn't come from other people. Sometimes you're just stuck in some nightmare place that you can't wake up from, like Dorothy in the *Wizard of Oz* finding out she wasn't in Kansas anymore. There's no escape from this. You have to re-learn how to live in the world. Our world. This world. Not Oz." He ran his fingers across his stubbled head, knocking his glasses. They tipped precariously over one ear. He didn't seem to notice.

"It *sucks*. It's fucking hard."

He looked dispirited suddenly, spreading his hands out in front of himself, palms up. "You have to decide every day that you're here. Every single day. Wake up in the morning and say to yourself, even if it's just for today, I am."

I turned away for a moment. There was something he missed. Something he couldn't understand. Something only those who have been to this hell understand. We are here, but we are not here.

The tornado that ripped me out of my life was a massive funnel cloud of roiling black that billowed out of the west and then dropped out of a clear blue sky. It was sudden, unexpected. I had no warning. One moment I was standing in my kitchen, laughing, and the next I was thrown into that heaving sky. Even the birds didn't have a chance to go silent in front of this storm. It came. It obliterated. And then it pitched me into a world that had no sense of familiarity, no foundation, no home.

"You have to choose. Only you can decide."

The deep ache in my chest throbbed. I could feel the darkness that swirled, like that funnel cloud, filling the space where my heart had once been.

"I died that day, Bernie," I whispered. My voice sounded like the wind soughing in the trees. I wasn't sure he could even hear me.

"No, you didn't. You're here in front of me. Your son died that day."

I shook my head trying to clear the image that flashed in the front of my brain endlessly. Over and over. My body twitched as though a shock of electric current had been shot through my veins. The agony cut through every corner of my body, slashing and searing. Branding me. It was physical and all-encompassing like no other pain I had ever endured. Even sleep provided no escape as nightmares rolled through the dark, one after the other. I wept for my son, for the life he would miss, for me. My tears formed a river that dragged me under its raging current.

"When I cut my son down from the rafters, my heart died with him."

Bernie moved over to the couch and I could feel his arms circling my shoulders, squeezing, bringing me back to the present. To the moment. To the only place I could breathe.

"Just stay. You'll never be the same, but we need you here."

"What's the good of having a body if you haven't got a heart?"

Bernie barked a laugh. "It seems to me that even the Tin Man managed to make a difference, heart or no heart." He squeezed me tight and returned to his chair across from me. His eyes glowed with warmth. "But you have to let people hear the truth. You have to help them understand what you carry every day. What many people carry every day."

"But people don't want to know."

"So what? It's time for everyone to listen. The more we talk about it, the less frightening that Wicked Witch becomes." He grinned again. "Since we're talking about Oz, maybe you need to become Dorothy instead of the Tin Man. She was the brave one. She was lost but kept on going. That's courage."

The tightness in my chest eased at the memory of my favorite childhood story. I stood up, my legs trembling, and tottered over to the window. I breathed out slowly, the warm, moist air forming a mist on the window pane. I sketched out a heart in the fog with my finger tip. I said nothing as the outline of the heart slowly filled in and then melted away.

Strange how that story seemed to fit. I had thought about it for a long time but, as with so many things, the pieces snap into place in their own good time. It had been the tornado of my son's death that ripped my life from its foundation and dropped me in a place that was nothing like home, just like Dorothy. Somehow she managed to find her way down a long, treacherous road. There were no signposts or directions and the path led through horrible places. I sighed deeply and turned, one final thought whispering through my mind, like a spring breeze that holds the promise of better days—it was a story of courage and hope and friendship. It was a story of returning.

I raised my eyes to meet Bernie's gaze. I felt a tug of warmth behind the pain like the glow of a porch light through the dark of a summer night. The light was flickering. Faint. It would take everything I had to keep the storms from blowing the tiny spark out. There were no guarantees. But I had seen it. It had come from inside of me, and that was a beginning.

"So I guess I'm living in Oz," I whispered.

"For now."

"And I need to find my way home." I glanced out the window again at the quickening twilight.

Home.

One ruby-slippered step at a time.

I COUNT THE LIGHTS
Edward Willett

Selvan Hori, Terran Ambassador to Prevaria, paused on the stairs that spiraled around the Tower of the Silent God and peered anxiously at the pool of shadow in front of him. One of the green lights that gleamed eerily every nine steps had just gone out, vanishing as he stepped away from the previous light, and between the darkness and the black stone, it looked disconcertingly like the next dozen or so steps had entirely disappeared. Since he was currently some two hundred feet above the cobblestoned courtyard of the Temple complex, that was not a comforting thought.

The air around him moaned with the constant song of the Tower, carved here and there with complicated openings that turned it into a giant organ pipe, played by the sea breeze by day and the land breeze by night, so that only in the stillness of dawn and sunset did it fall completely silent. The complex chord engendered awe and tranquility in Prevarians, apparently, but it contained enough subsonic frequencies that the dominant human response was faint terror.

The steps haven't gone anywhere, he told himself. The light has just gone out.

But he paused anyway, partly to gather his courage, partly to give his pounding heart a chance to slow and his breathing a chance to steady.

∞

"I count the lights."

Alfred Kelvas, Head of Security for the Terran Diplomatic Mission to Prevaria, tapped the soundbud in his right ear and glanced at the flexible screen on the underside of his left wrist. The datalink status indicators glowed green. As far as the AI back in the Embassy was concerned, that had been an accurate translation of the short squeaking phrase the blue-skinned Prevarian monk hunched on the stone bench before him had just uttered.

Maybe the translation had been faulty in the *other* direction. Kelvas decided to try again.

"I'm sorry, I think the translator may have malfunctioned," he said, while the speaker concealed in the breastplate of the body armour he wore under his dark green uniform squeaked like a demented mouse. "I asked your name."

The monk splayed his three-fingered hands and turned them rapidly from side to side, the Prevarian equivalent of a vigorous nod. He squeaked again. "I count the lights."

Kelvas forced down his irritation. Two days ago, Ambassador Selvan Hori had fallen from the three-hundred-foot Tower of the Silent God, the central feature of both the Temple and the capital city of Prevaria. Support for the painstakingly negotiated trade agreement between Terra and Prevaria was plummeting as fast as the late ambassador had.

Kelvas's superiors were demanding answers, the Prevarian Motivator, roughly equivalent to the Terran Prime Minister, faced revolt from the hard-core isolationists on her Council of Satraps, the Navy was making contingency plans for a complete withdrawal . . . and somewhere, the planetary pillagers who lurked in the shadows between the civilized stars were gathering their mercenary forces in anticipation of moving in and taking over. Prevaria stood on the brink of invasion, conquest, and environmental ruin, though its politicians didn't seem to grasp that reality.

All of that meant increasing pressure on Kelvas to find some answers. He didn't have *time* for malfunctioning translators.

Nor did he have time for the cheerful tri-tone bell that now sounded in his earbud. "Excuse me," he said to the monk. "I have an incoming communication."

"I count the lights," the monk said . . . possibly.

Grimacing, Kelvas stepped off to one side. He tapped twice on his earbud to accept the call. "What is it, Simon?"

"I'm sorry to disturb you, sir," Simon's deep voice came back, "but Tyrone Boynton is in your outer office. He's been there since this morning. Five hours and counting."

Kelvas closed his eyes. "With Eve, I suppose?"

"No, sir," Simon said. "By himself."

Kelvas's eyes flew open again. *That* was new.

Eve Boynton had been after him for weeks to find a job for Tyrone in the Embassy. Kelvas liked Eve. He'd known her back on Earth; she'd come to their house in Bozeman for dinner once or twice, on weekend jaunts from the Diplomatic Corps Training Centre in Geneva; Kelvas's wife, Annie, had liked her, too. Eve had barely mentioned her brother then—he and Annie had gathered Tyrone still lived with his parents, and was attending some kind of special school, but Eve hadn't said exactly what kind of school or why he needed to attend it.

But then, a few weeks ago, Tyrone Boynton had showed up *here*, on Prevaria, to visit Eve. He'd arrived on the regularly scheduled Navy supply ship, taking advantage of the rule that allowed family members to visit staff on station, at least in locations where nobody was shooting at each other. By the regulations, he was due to return to Terra on the next ship headed that way, in about a fortnight. But a week ago Eve had come to Kelvas, Tyrone in tow. They'd sat in his office, Eve stiff and upright in one of the leather-covered chairs in front of his desk, Tyrone in the other. No taller than Eve—and Eve was not a tall woman—he had an oddly unfinished look, his facial features soft and doughy. He sat with his eyes downcast, rocking slightly in his chair, his hands, too big for the rest of his body, gripping his knees tightly the entire time.

Eve had told Kelvas why Tyrone had come to Prevaria: the siblings' parents had died and she'd begged the authorities to send him to her. He couldn't live on his own, she explained. If he'd stayed on Earth—or if he returned there—he would be institutionalized. Eve, her voice breaking, had begged Kelvas to allow Tyrone to stay.

The trouble was, the Diplomatic Corps rules were clear: to live on Prevaria in the Embassy compound long-term—and draw a Diplomatic Corps paycheck—Tyrone had to have a job . . . of which there were none suitable to someone of his limited mental capacity. Kelvas explained all that. Eve begged. He finally got rid of her by agreeing to "see what he could do," but in fact he hadn't given it another thought—certainly it hadn't crossed his mind since the Ambassador's death.

He wouldn't have been particularly surprised to hear that Eve was waiting in his outside office, hoping to press her case further, but Tyrone by himself? That made no sense. The young man hadn't said a word when he'd been with his sister.

"What is he doing?" he asked Simon.

"Sitting. Staring at the Persons of Interest screen. Rocking back and forth," Simon said. "Special Agent Eston is the Officer of the Day. I could ask him to come take Tyrone away but . . . I think that would frighten him."

"Probably," Kelvas agreed. "I assume you've called Eve?"

"I've tried, sir, but she's on duty in the comm centre, and you know how crazy things are there since the . . . incident. She'll be out of touch for another couple of hours."

Kelvas sighed. "And I presume you've told Tyrone I won't be back for hours . . . if at all . . . today?"

"I tried, sir. I'm not . . . I'm not sure he understood."

Kelvas shook his head. He *really* did not have time for this. "Then let him sit there as long as he wants," he said, aware he'd let his irritation into his voice, and not really caring, either. "Once Eve is off duty, have her come get him." *And then have her make sure he's on the first ship home,* he wanted to add, but didn't. *There's no place for someone like him here. Especially* now.

"Yes, sir."

"Anything else that needs my attention?"

"Mr. Kimblee would like to meet with you."

Kelvas sighed again. "Let me guess. He's champing at the bit to organize the withdrawal of the Embassy staff."

"He did indicate that contingency planning of that sort would be the purpose of the conversation," Simon said carefully.

John Kimblee, Kelvas's second-in-command, had never had a good word to say about Prevaria in Kelvas's hearing: he clearly resented being stationed on a primitive new-contact planet without access to the many pleasures of the Core Worlds. He would have closed down the Embassy the second they'd heard about the Ambassador's death if it had been up to him.

Fortunately, it hadn't been.

"Tell Mr. Kimblee I will speak to him at my earliest convenience, and leave it at that," Kelvas said. "Anything else?"

"No, sir. Sorry to have bothered you."

"Just doing your job," Kelvas said. "No need to apologize." *But don't bother me again*, he wanted to say, and he suspected that, too, seeped into his tone of voice.

"Yes, sir," Simon said. "Simon out."

The tri-tone played again, in reverse order.

Kelvas took another look at the screen on the underside of his wrist. All datalinks remained green. He turned back to the waiting monk. "All right," he said. "Let's try this again. What's your name?"

Big-eyed like a lemur and with a snout like a dog, the monk looked up at the Tower of the Silent God, looming over the courtyard, and pointed with the longest, central finger of his left hand. "I count the lights!"

☙

Ambassador Hori leaned against the black stone of the Tower, breathing deeply of the cool night air. He'd had no choice but to make this ascent. Prevarian tradition insisted that no treaty could be finalized until the negotiating satraps had ascended the Tower, both to meditate upon the agreement and to show their commitment to upholding it before the Silent God.

The climb was made along this staircase, bereft of any guardrail, which spiraled around the spire's exterior. Every nine steps glowed a dim green crystal lantern, set above a carved face, each face an Aspect of the God, each unique: some smiling, some frowning, some howling in rage or fear, some slack in sleep or death. Believers offered a silent prayer as they passed each Aspect. Ambassador Hori was not a believer in the Silent God, but he was a somewhat-lapsed Catholic, and now, as he waited to regain his breath, he offered a prayer of his own, to the Archangel Gabriel, patron saint of diplomats, that he could make it to the top of the tower without suffering a heart attack.

He dared not fail. To do so could well sabotage the trade agreement he had been working on for six long local years—almost eight Earth years.

He knew well enough there were plenty of Terrans for whom that would be the ideal outcome. For that reason, he was ordinarily accompanied everywhere he went by two bodyguards in constant contact with his head of security, Alfred Kelvas. But the High Deaconness who presided over the Temple Complex had made it clear that no weapons could be carried up the Tower, and since his bioengineered bodyguards were weapons in and of themselves, their presence on the Tower could and would have been seen as sacrilege, and used to derail the impending agreement. And so, over the strong objections of both his bodyguards and Kelvas, whom he had formally absolved of all responsibility for whatever might happen to him during the climb, he had left his men stationed at the foot of the steps, and ascended on his own.

His heart no longer pounded and his breathing came more easily now, and that lessened his disquiet. He was at least two-thirds of the way to the top: he could surely make it the rest of the way. There's life in the old man yet, *he told himself, smiling — it was something his wife liked to say to him. He took a fresh breath and, staying close to the Tower wall, stepped cautiously into the pool of darkness.*

෴

Kelvas glared at the monk, who was still pointing uselessly at the Tower, then gave his head a frustrated shake, turned, and strode across the courtyard to where the High Deaconness watched and listened with her handmaiden, a young Acolyte. The two Prevarian women stood in the shadow of the Tower, swiftly lengthening as the sun sank toward the saw-toothed mountain range in the distant west.

"Is there a problem?" the High Deaconness said. Though her simple shift was the same plain white as the monk's loincloth, several jeweled gold bracelets on each arm and a gold circlet on her brow marked her rank as the highest non-secular authority on the planet.

"Yes, High Deaconness," Kelvas said, "I'm afraid there is. Your so-called 'witness' will only say one thing. 'I count the lights.'"

"I'm sorry," the Deaconess said. The translator rendered her squeaks as calm and slightly amused. "I thought I had made it clear that Brother Lodolo is one of the Holiest."

"Yes, I heard that," Kelvas snapped. He wondered if the translator would accurately render his irritation, and decided he hoped it did. "I thought that meant he would have special knowledge of the Tower. Why does he keep repeating that meaningless phrase?"

"But it is not meaningless," the Deaconess said, now sounding puzzled. "He is one of the Holiest. The Holiest are those closest to the Silent God, for their minds are uncluttered."

"Uncluttered?" Kelvas said blankly. Then he understood. "You mean . . . *empty?*" He glanced back at Brother Lodolo. "Oh, that's just wonderful," he snarled . . . under his breath, but of course the translator passed the phrase along.

"Is it not?" the Deaconess said. "To be able to concentrate on worship without the distraction of more mundane concerns . . . the Holiest are the most fortunate of the God's children."

Lodolo, clearly agitated, suddenly stood and strode across the courtyard to Kelvas. He jabbed his finger upward at the Tower. "I count the lights!"

Kelvas's irritation swelled to the point he had to clench his jaw to keep from saying something so undiplomatic to the Deaconess it might provoke a worse crisis than the one in which they already found themselves. *Who am I kidding? It* couldn't *get any worse.*

But he needed *answers.* He needed a *witness,* and he'd thought that was what he'd been promised. Instead, he'd been presented with the village idiot.

"Thank you," he said to Lodolo, though gratitude was the farthest thing from his mind. "I'm done."

He turned away.

Lodolo grabbed his arm. "I count the lights!" he cried. "I count the lights!"

Startled and annoyed, Kelvas pulled his arm free, so hard he tugged the monk off-balance. The little alien stumbled and fell onto his bare blue knees.

Kelvas barely noticed. "Who else?" he demanded of the Deaconess.

The handmaiden hurried forward to help Lodolo to his feet. Kelvas belatedly realized the gravity of his error as the Deaconness's ears flattened—as bad a sign in a Prevarian as in the dogs they vaguely resembled.

"You will talk to Lodolo, or you will talk to no one." The Deaconess' squeaks had a sibilant hiss that the translator didn't need to interpret: he had deeply annoyed and offended her, and he couldn't afford that. If any answers were to be found, they would be found here, at the Tower of the Silent God, where the Ambassador had met his gruesome fate, so close to where Kelvas now stood that he would be walking in the man's blood if it hadn't been scrubbed from the stones.

The guards the Ambassador had left at the base of the stairs had heard the impact from halfway around the tower. They'd run to the scene. One had spent the next few minutes throwing up while the other, of stronger constitution, had frantically called Kelvas. Meanwhile the monks had also come running. As their religion demanded, they had immediately set about removing the Ambassador's scattered parts and ritually cleansing the place where he had died. By the time reinforcements arrived from the Embassy, the Ambassador's remains had already been burned to ash in the furnace of the central altar, the smoke of his immolation rising up the chimney at the heart of the Tower, completing the ascent his body had fallen so fatally short of.

The fact the Prevarians had disposed of all evidence before the Terrans could even begin their investigation had not inclined the anti-trade forces among the Terrans toward granting the benefit of the doubt, and in turn their accusations of assassination were rapidly driving those few Prevarians still on the fence about the wisdom of trusting the Terrans toward their own anti-trade camp.

If any answers were to be found, it would have to be with the help of the High Deaconess; and so, though it grated on him like fingernails on steel, Kelvas forced himself to say, with as much sincerity as he could manage, "I apologize, High Deaconess." He looked at the monk, who stood hunched over, rubbing his knees. "Brother Lodolo." He turned back to the Deaconess. "I am feeling the stress of this grievous death, and I allowed it to sharpen my tongue in a most undiplomatic way. Please forgive me."

The Deaconess's ears flattened further for a moment, and he thought he had ruined everything; but then they slowly rose. "Apology accepted," she said. "This is a difficult time for us all."

I Count the Lights by EDWARD WILLETT

I doubt it's as difficult for you as it is for me, Kelvas thought uncharitably. *Although if the Navy withdraws and your precious Temple is flattened by scavengers* pour encourager les autres, *it will be.*

He turned back to the Brother Lodolo, who had straightened and folded his arms. He rocked from foot to foot. "I count the lights," he said, the translator giving his voice a pleading tone. "I count the lights. *I count the lights.*"

"I'm sorry," Kelvas said. He knew the apology sounded stiff, but he did the best he could. "I'm sorry, but I don't understand."

"Is your translation link broken?" the Deaconess said behind him.

"No," Kelvas said.

"Then how can you not understand? Lodolo counts the lights."

"But . . . why?" Kelvas turned back to her. The handmaiden who had helped Lodolo had taken up her eyes-downcast post at the Deaconess's left hand once more. "*Why* does he count the lights?" *And how the hell is that of any use?* he wanted to add, but didn't.

"I told you. He is Holiest. His mind is uncluttered, giving room for the presence of the Silent God. He counts the lights because that is how the Silent God has told him to worship."

This is going nowhere, Kelvas thought again. But diplomacy insisted he continue the charade a little longer. "But . . . what lights?"

"The lights of the Tower." The High Deaconess pointed up. "There are five hundred and sixty seven steps on the outside of the tower. Every nine steps, there is a light: sixty-three lights in all. Sixty-three is a holy number, for the holiest number is three, and sixty-three is three threes."

Three threes? Kelvas frowned for an instant, then understood: because the Prevarians were three-fingered, they calculated in base four, in which the highest digit was three. The numeral 333 in base four equaled 63 in base 10.

"Every night," the Deaconess continued, "Lodolo walks around and around the tower. He counts the lights, from bottom to top, then from top to bottom, then from bottom to top. He does this sixty-three times, one for each light. Then he ascends the Tower, counting again from bottom to top; and descends, counting from top to bottom. Thus does he worship the Silent God. And something he saw, as he performed this act of worship two nights ago—the night the Ambassador fell—has troubled him deeply. Offended him, I would judge."

But he can't communicate it, Kelvas thought. *Great. Perfect.*

Kelvas felt a cautious tug at the sleeve of his uniform. He looked around. Lodolo hastily stepped back, as though afraid Kelvas would knock him down again. *That was an accident,* Kelvas thought, but now that his irritation had subsided . . . slightly . . . he felt guilty. "It's all right," he said to the monk, keeping his voice as calm as he could. "What is it?"

Brother Lodolo, short even by the standards of his people, stood, child-like, only as tall as Kelvas's chest, which made it hard for Kelvas to remember that in fact—as the Deaconess had told him as she guided him to the monk—he was twice Kelvas's age. The Prevarians lived longer than humans, and Lodolo was elderly even by their standards. He didn't repeat his single phrase this time: instead he pointed at Kelvas, then up at the Tower.

"I don't understand," Kelvas said, again. He was getting very tired of that phrase. He *hated* not understanding. It was his job to understand: to understand the ramifications of the deteriorating diplomatic situation, to understand the society of the planet on which he served, and when things went horribly awry—and nothing in his long career had gone as horribly awry as things had gone here with the Ambassador's death—to investigate *until* he understood. He glanced at the High Deaconess. "Do you know what he wants?"

"He wants you to ascend the Tower with him," the High Deaconess said, the Translator rendering her as astonished. "It is a great honour. Without precedent."

A great honour? Kelvas thought. He looked up at the black stone spire. How many steps had she said? Five hundred and sixty-seven?

He sighed. Still, he followed Lodolo the short distance to the base of the Tower because, with the High Deaconess watching, what else could he do? *And anyway,* he thought cynically, *I could use a little divine favour right now.*

But as they approached the long staircase that wound around and around the tower, Lodolo held up a three-fingered hand and then pointed to a bench built into the wall.

"Now what?" It was impossible not to be irritated all over again.

"You cannot climb the Tower of the Silent God while the sun is above the horizon." The High Deaconess and her handmaiden had followed them, and now she spoke as if the truth of what she said was self-evident. "It is not a place one goes to see the sights of the world, but to see inside one's own soul. You must wait until twilight."

"I'm not—" *climbing it to worship your non-existent God,* Kelvas almost said, but fortunately thought better of it. Instead he paused, glanced at his watch, and said, "Very well."

Though the climate in the Prevarian capitol, tempered by the nearby ocean, varied little, the days still grew short in the winter, and the solstice was only a few tri-days away. Technically, Kelvas could have returned to the Embassy for an hour, but that might have meant facing Tyrone Boynton or John Kimblee, and he didn't want *that.* So instead he sat on the bench next to Lodolo, who, fortunately, did not continue repeating "I count the lights" over and over again as Kelvas half-expected. Instead, the monk rocked silently. Like Tyrone.

Kelvas wondered if Eve's brother were still sitting in the outer office, staring at the Persons of Interest screen. The images and videos that cycled endlessly on that screen were of known troublemakers, terrorists and criminals. All Diplomatic Corps security headquarters were required to display the POI feed in prominent locations: the modern equivalent of a bulletin board covered with wanted posters. Kelvas had never heard of anyone being apprehended because someone had seen his or her image or video in the POI feed, but regulations were regulations.

Which reminded him again of Eve's request that he bend those regulations for her brother. He sighed. Much as he sympathized with her plight, bending regulations risked an official reprimand, and that, in turn, risked a black mark on his record just before retirement—which could impact his pension.

Of course, failing to solve the murder of the Ambassador he

was charged with protecting would be an even bigger black mark. He glanced at Lodolo. Was this rocking blue alien with the "uncluttered" mind really his only lead to what had happened?

Apparently, God help me. He glanced up at the Tower. *Any god.*

He turned over his wrist to expose the datascreen and spent the remaining time until sunset reading messages and sending several variations of, "The investigation is proceeding apace and a resolution is expected shortly," which was a flat-out lie, but at least bought time.

I'm chasing wild geese, he thought as he sent the last message. He glanced at Lodolo, who had stopped rocking and now sat motionless, eyes closed. *And sooner or later those wild geese are going to turn into pigeons and come home to roost.* Despite everything, his mouth quirked. *I must be worried. I'd never have come up a mixed metaphor that ugly if I were thinking clearly.*

He sighed. He'd almost taken early retirement from Diplomatic Corps Security three years ago, and if he had, he and Annie would currently be fishing in the mountains of Montana and hoping against hope their daughter would find someone with whom to give them grandchildren. But the opportunity to be head of security at a major new embassy on a newly opened planet had seemed too good to pass up. The pay was very, *very* good. Though Annie hadn't made the trip out here with him, she'd visited a couple of times, courtesy of the free-transportation program that had also landed him with the Boynton problem.

I guess we can still go fishing after I'm cashiered out the service, he thought wistfully. *In a much smaller boat. Wearing a disguise. Which will also be useful for panhandling for loose change on weekends.*

He sent a final note to Simon, updating his secretary on where he was and what he was doing. If he fell off the Tower like the Ambassador . . . well, it would end all hope of a trade agreement, for one thing, but what really concerned him was that he not simply vanish without Annie ever knowing what had happened.

Almost without his noticing, the sun had slipped behind the dome of the Temple. The lengthening shadows vanished completely a few moments later. In the deepening twilight Lodolo finally stirred, and looked up at the Tower. "I count the lights," he said helpfully.

"So I've heard." Kelvas got heavily to his feet. "Let's get this over with."

The High Deaconess had left them during the hour they waited, but she reappeared now, striding across the stones of the courtyard on bare three-toed feet. "I will wait here for your return," she said. "To learn what you have found."

Or to make sure they clean up the blood promptly, Kelvas thought.

The eerie green bioluminescent lights of the Tower had come on as the day faded. As the evening land-breeze sprang up, the Temple began to emit a low organ-like chord that made the hairs on the back of Kelvas's arms stand up. He knew the Prevarians felt peace and awe when they heard it, but considering what had happened to the Ambassador, he thought the human fear-response might be more appropriate.

Lodolo began to climb. As they passed the first light he said, as Kelvas expected, "I count the lights"; but then, for the first time, he said something else. "One."

Another nine steps. "I count the lights. Two."

And again. "I count the lights. Three . . ."

They climbed onward. The steps, worn and slightly rounded, sometimes even sloped down, away from the tower. Kelvas kept as close to the wall as he could, trailing one hand along it. The last light slipped from the sky. Darkness surrounded the base of the Tower: all illumination in the Temple Complex was shielded to prevent it from spilling upward. Only outside the Complex wall did the ordinary bluish illumination favored by the Prevarians appear, and even that was sparse: the Prevarians had better night-vision and what they considered brilliant illumination was more like what Kelvas associated with the kind of restaurant where the ambiance was more important than seeing what you were eating.

Lodolo strode confidently up the middle of the stairs, seemingly unconcerned by the ever-deepening abyss to his left. "I count the lights. Fourteen . . ."

Kelvas was fit for a man in his late 50s—he had to be, in his position—but he still found the climb wearing on him. The ambassador had *not* been particularly fit—he *hadn't* had to be, in *his* position—and Kelvas found himself impressed Hori had undertaken the climb at all. *He really believed in this trade agreement,* he thought. *He really cared about this planet and its . . . people.*

"I count the lights. Twenty-eight . . ."

Kelvas had never cared very much about any of the worlds on which he'd served. His heart was always back on Earth. He didn't *hate* the various aliens he'd met, and he'd done his level best to understand their societies, but not out of real interest: only so he could do his job and identify potential threats to the diplomats he was charged with protecting. He didn't think of aliens as people so much as *things* that he had to deal with efficiently in order to do his job.

"I count the lights. Thirty-two . . ."

Like this simpleminded monk. Kelvas gulped more air and kept climbing, trying to ignore the growing ache in his calves.

Around and around. And then . . .

Just like that, Lodolo stopped. He didn't say, "I count the lights." He didn't say . . . what number were they up to? Forty-six? Instead, he made a low, unhappy moan in his throat. He tugged at Kelvas's sleeve, and pointed. Kelvas, who had been climbing with his head down, concentrating on putting one foot after the other, looked up.

He couldn't see any reason for the delay. They stood two steps below one of the green lights, casting what seemed to him a paltry pool of illumination, though no doubt beautifully bright to Lodolo. An Aspect of the God, smiling beatifically—although even that had a slightly demonic look to human eyes, given the strangeness of the Prevarian face—stared out from the wall below the light. The next light glowed some five metres away.

Kelvas looked at Lodolo. The monk, still moaning softly, had begun to rock back and forth again, for no reason Kelvas could see.

Kelvas resisted the urge to say "I don't understand." He resisted the urge to say, "I count the lights. Forty-seven." But he couldn't just stand there all night, either. He took a step forward, and then another. The monk's moan deepened.

As then, as Kelvas passed the smiling Aspect of the Silent God, the next light, number forty-seven, went out.

To Kelvas's eyes, it was as if the steps disappeared completely, swallowed by the darkness. Their black stone barely showed even in the green light of the bioluminescent lamps. The stars glimmering overhead had no hope of reflection.

Lodolo plucked at Kelvas's sleeve, as though trying to stop him from advancing. But Kelvas pulled free, barely noticing, mind racing. Was this where the Ambassador died? Had Lodolo seen this interruption in the lights as he walked around the Tower, counting the lights?

But why had the light gone out? And what lurked in the darkness?

Kelvas turned and looked out over the city, trying to get his bearings. The Embassy glowed on the horizon, its Terran lights brighter and whiter than anything else in sight. The Ambassador had fallen from the side of the Tower facing the Embassy . . . a fact that the anti-traders insisted pointed to a Prevarian murder plot.

It could have been right here.

It *had* to have been right here.

But how did that help him?

He couldn't send a forensics team up here to investigate: the High Deaconess had made it clear that would not be allowed. The Prevarians lacked the technological know-how to even attempt to gather samples, and in any event, the steps were ritually washed every day, the only time anyone mounted the Tower while the sun shone.

If he were going to discover anything, it would have to be now. He took the flashlight from his belt and unfolded the collapsible framework that allowed him to attach it to his uniform cap so he could keep his hands free. Once the lamp was firmly in place, he reached up and switched it on. Lodolo cried out in distress and flung his blue arm over his big eyes at the flare of bright white light.

"Sorry." Kelvas started back up the steps, head down, studying each riser and runner in turn. A trip wire, perhaps? But no, not if the steps were washed daily: someone would have discovered it.

He looked up at the wall as he approached the spot where the next lamp should have gleamed.

There it was, its crystal sides reflecting his torch, but devoid of even the slightest green glow. Below it, the Aspect of the Silent God: in this instant, in sharp contrast to the Aspect he'd just left, screaming in apparent terror, mouth wide, eyes bulging, the perfect embodiment, for a human, of the Tower's constant threatening moan.

He looked down at the steps again, and leaned forward to get a closer look at the step right in front of the burned-out lamp.

ᛣ

Just enough light came from the stars glittering above that Ambassador Hori could make out the shape of the dark lantern, and the indistinct Aspect of the God below it. He came abreast of it.

Something slammed into his side. He toppled left. The steps were only a metre wide, and sloped downward. His upper body fell into nothingness, and dragged his legs with it.

Prevarian gravity was very close to Earth's. Ambassador Hori had just over four seconds to stare up at the whirling stars above him before, for him, they were blotted out forever.

ᛣ

"I count the lights!" Lodolo shouted—*screamed*. Then the monk slammed into Kelvas from behind as something else shot over his head, brushing against his shoulder. Kelvas thudded to the steps, gasping, then rolled over.

In the light from Kelvas's torch, Lodolo struggled for balance on the very edge of the precipice, giant eyes enormously wide in terror, arms flailing. He tipped backward—

Kelvas lunged forward.

He grabbed the monk's blue-skinned ankle, jerking Lodolo back onto the steps even as he toppled.

The monk slammed down on the black stone harder than Kelvas had, and lost his breath completely, gaping soundlessly as his face purpled in the light from Kelvas's headlamp.

Kelvas whipped around again, searching frantically this way and that for their attacker.

The circle of light slid over black stone.

Nothing on the steps.

Nothing on the—

No—there!

A flicker of movement, in the gaping mouth of the Aspect of the God.

He raised his light. A round black ball, contracting as he watched, settled silently into place. An instant later the darkened lamp glowed back to dim green life.

Kelvas got carefully to his feet and drew the weapon he wasn't supposed to be carrying on the Tower, a tiny personnel stunner. He jammed it into the opening and triggered its powerful electric jolt. The thing in the mouth of the carved face sizzled and popped, then dropped to the steps. It rolled toward the edge of the sloping stair.

Lodolo shot out a three-fingered hand and grabbed it. "I count the lights!" he gasped out, as he allowed Kelvas to slip the ball from his palm. It weighed far more than its size suggested: it would have to, since it had to have mass enough to force a grown man from the steps.

"Indeed you do," Kelvas said. "And you do a very good job of it." He slipped the ball into his pocket to examine later, then held out his hand to the monk, who gripped Kelvas's five fingers in his three and let Kelvas help him to his feet. Kelvas took a deep breath. Adrenaline had left him feeling a little shaky. "Let's go down," he said.

But Lodolo, releasing his hand, tilted his head left then right then left again, the Prevarian equivalent of a human head-shake. "I count the lights." He moved to the wall and touched the lamp, fully alight again. "Forty-six," he said. And then he turned away from Kelvas and resumed climbing. "I count the lights," he said nine steps farther along. "Forty-seven."

Kelvas hesitated. He put his hand on the heavy ball in his pocket. He looked down the steps for a moment. Then, moved by some strange and unexpected impulse, he climbed after Lodolo, following him all the way to the top of the Tower of the Silent God.

CR

Four Prevarian tri-days later, Kelvas sat in his office at the

Embassy, his back to his desk, looking out over the city through the office's single large window. In the middle-distance, the Tower of the Silent God pointed at the sky. The sun had almost set, and already the green lights were beginning to glow along the five hundred and sixty-seven steps.

The black ball he had recovered had quickly revealed its secrets. Both it and the dousing of the light were triggered only by the presence of a Terran. It had been planted very specifically to kill the Ambassador . . . or any other human who happened to climb the Tower. But no human other than the Ambassador ever had, or had been expected to.

It was clearly not Prevarian technology, but tracing it to its human source might have proved impossible had a lead not been forthcoming from a most unexpected source.

Hence the visitors whose arrival Kelvas awaited even now.

The tri-tone chimed in his earbud. He tapped it twice. "Yes, Simon?"

"Eve and Tyrone Boynton are here," Simon said.

"Send them in," Kelvas said. He turned to face the door, and stood as Eve and her brother entered. He nodded to Eve, whose face bore an interesting expression of mingled hope and pride, but when he rounded the desk, he went straight to Tyrone. "Tyrone," he said. He held out his hand. Tyrone looked at it.

"Shake his hand, Tyrone," Eve said.

Tyrone looked at her, then back at Kelvas's hand. He held his hand out hesitantly. Kelvas took it and shook it firmly. "Thank you, Tyrone," he said. "Without your help, we never would have solved Ambassador Hori's murder."

"Mr. Kimblee . . . meet with bad man," Tyrone said in his high-pitched voice, soft and lilting as a child's. "I saw him." He pulled his hand back, and turned around and pointed at the office door. "Out there."

"I know you did," Kelvas said.

He had returned from his climb of the Tower to find Tyrone and Eve waiting for him in his outer office, under the watchful eye of Simon. Simon had leapt to his feet as he entered. "I'm sorry, sir," he'd said. "I called Eve as soon as she came off-duty, but she couldn't get Tyrone to leave, either."

"I'm sorry, Mr. Kelvas," Eve said, and he heard the worry in her voice; he knew she was afraid Tyrone's strange stubbornness would convince Kelvas once and for all there was no place for her brother on Prevaria. "All he'll tell me is that he has to talk to you. Over and over again."

Over and over again, Kelvas thought. *Like Lodolo.* And so Kelvas did what he would never have done before, and sat down next to Tyrone and asked the boy what he wanted to say.

And Tyrone pointed at the POI screen and explained, in his halting fashion, that he had seen Mr. Kimblee talking to one of the people on that screen. He pointed out the man when his image rolled around again: a certain Peter Lagat, with known ties to one of the criminal syndicates bankrolling some of the more notorious of the planetary pillagers.

Tyrone, it turned out, liked to walk around the Embassy compound late at night. "He doesn't sleep well since Mom and Dad died," Eve had explained. "He walks to make himself tired."

I wonder if he counts the Embassy's lights? Kelvas thought in passing, while he busied himself with sending messages, and arranging an arrest detail. A little over half an hour after Kelvas's return from the Tower, John Kimblee was in custody and under interrogation.

As Kelvas's second-in-command, Kimblee had been fully aware of the Ambassador's plan to ascend the Tower of the Silent God. A thorough forensic audit of his assets revealed that he had also been in the pay of Legat's syndicate. His enjoyment of the luxuries of the Core Worlds had not been feigned: he'd enjoyed them so much, during his last visit there, that he'd been massively in debt until he agreed to work with Legat to sabotage the Prevarian trade agreement.

Of course, although the murder device had been of human manufacture, it had not been *placed* by a human: that had been the work of one of the *Prevarian* anti-trade factions: one whose own links to the waiting scavengers had been uncovered by the . . . *forceful* . . . investigations of the Prevarian government. The faction had made a deal to rule the planet on the scavengers' behalf once the trade deal was dead and the Terran Navy gone. The sacrilege of Prevarians actually daring to climb the Tower of the Silent

God in order to commit murder had shaken Prevarian society to its core, just as the corruption revealed on the Terran side had shaken Earth—and destroyed several fortunes, reputations, and political careers.

The new Ambassador, Kuzue Akamatsa, even now awaited the descent of darkness so that she . . . and her entire staff . . . could ascend the Tower. Once that had been done, the trade agreement would, at last, be formalized. Kelvas had spent the day making the security arrangements for the signing ceremony to be held the next day in the Great Hall of the Prevarian People, out of sight on the other side of the Embassy from his office.

But that was for later. "You did a good job, Tyrone," he said. "A very good job. Would you like to work for the Diplomatic Corps permanently?"

He heard Eve's gasp, but he didn't look at her, only at Tyrone. Tyrone's brows pulled together. "Perm . . . permanently?"

"For good," Tyrone said. "Work, and stay here with your sister. For good. "

Tyrone's face split into an enormous grin. "Yes, Mr. Kelvas! Yes, please!"

Kelvas glanced at Eve. "He'll work as a night watchman. He'll walk the grounds just as he has been. He'll report anything out of the ordinary he sees." He returned his gaze to Tyrone. "Can you do that? Watch carefully every night? Report anything you see that you think is strange?"

Tyrone nodded vigorously. "I see things," he said. "I see when things are different. That's how I saw Mr. Kimblee and the bad man. I can do that."

Kelvas held out his hand again. "Then welcome to the Terran Diplomatic Corps."

This time, Tyrone shook his hand without prompting.

"Take him to HR and get the forms filled out," Kelvas said to Eve. "They're expecting you."

"I stay, Eve!" Tyrone cried to his sister. "I stay!"

Tears glistened on Eve's cheeks. She hugged Tyrone tightly. "You stay!" She smiled over his shoulder, rather wetly, at Kelvas. "Thank you, sir, thank you!"

"You're welcome," Kelvas said softly.

I Count the Lights by EDWARD WILLETT

Eve led her brother out of the office, and Kelvas returned to his chair. He turned to look out the window once more. Darkness had descended at last. The new ambassador would be beginning her ascent of the Tower of the Silent God.

Though he couldn't see all of them, Alfred Kelvas began to count the lights.

THE DOG AND THE SLEEPWALKER

James Alan Gardner

To the Dog, the starship's bridge was quiet. He'd been told there was actually a din of chatter in the minutes leading up to a warp jump—members of the crew constantly calling out readings. But the noise was restricted to the brain-chip connections that linked everybody else. The Dog had no augmentations, so all he heard was the soft shifting of people in their seats on the rare occasions when they had to push buttons with their actual fingers instead of just doing it with their minds.

After a long period of silence, the captain cleared her throat. "Mr. Bok," she said aloud, "are you ready for jump?"

"Yes, Captain," said the Dog.

"Very good," she said. She looked to make sure the Dog's hand was hovering above the insultingly large red button that was the one and only feature of the Dog's control console. She nodded and said, "Jump in three . . . two . . . one . . ."

The captain's body went slack. So did the bodies of everyone else on the bridge.

Except the Dog.

Whatever warp-space was—and whenever the Dog asked, crew-members answered, "It's hard to explain"—whatever warp-space was, it played hell with electronics. And with fancy nanotech particles. And hormone implants. And all the other add-ons that 99.9 percent of humans were now augmented with, beginning before they were born.

All augs had to be shut down an instant before a jump, for fear they'd blow a gasket and injure or kill their hosts. That meant everyone went unconscious—people depended so much on their built-in devices, they went comatose without them.

Except the Dog: he had no devices. He was an un-retouched human with no role in the world except to hit the red button that would restart every person and gadget on the ship when the jump was over.

He didn't push the button. He settled back onto his jump-couch.

Now the bridge was totally quiet. The crew were still breathing, but nothing more.

The ship's systems were shut down too. No gravity. None of the faint sounds that usually filled the background: the distant hum of the engines, the whisper of the ventilators. Everything off.

The room wasn't totally dark, thanks to light-emitting diatoms in transparent sea-water tubes that ran across the walls and ceiling. Their glow was as dusky as twilight, but the eyes of the crew had amplifiers that let them see as easily as if everything was under floodlights.

Or so the Dog had been told. His own eyes were simply accustomed to the dark.

He pulled his zapper out of his pocket. It was nothing more than a battery with two metal terminals on top. In the normal universe, pressing a button made a blue electric spark arc between the terminals. When the Dog pressed it now, the result was a flat orange ribbon that rose from one terminal, a little like a candle flame. The other terminal surrounded itself with a cloud of utter blackness.

Okay. The ship was still in warp-space. Whatever that was.

CR

When he started this job, the Dog had been told that less than one percent of warp-jumps fell short of completion. "Up and out in no time at all" . . . that was the phrase everybody repeated. A starship left normal space and returned several light-years from its starting point with no time elapsed during the gap. That was the theory—what crew-members believed.

In the Dog's experience, almost every jump took longer. He pictured warp jumps like jumps in skiing: skiers came down those ramps then soared into the sky, sailing, sailing, till they hit the bottom. Starship crews believed they jumped flawlessly, touching down exactly where they aimed. But usually, they didn't; they landed short, then had to coast the rest of the way to where they wanted to go.

A ship might only need a few seconds to settle out of warp-space and back into the normal universe. Then again, it might take longer. Hence the need for the Dog: someone who wouldn't press restart until he knew for sure that the ship was back in safe normality.

Ship designers had tried alternatives: hundreds of automated tricks intended to eliminate the need for Dogs. The tricks never worked reliably; warp-space had a knack for causing malfunctions in human-made devices. Either the ship would restart prematurely, in which case most of the crew died in agony as their body-mods went haywire . . . or the ship never booted at all, in which case a boatload of comatose crew-members eventually froze or suffocated because the ship's life-support systems never came back online.

In the earliest days of warp travel, someone joked they should just train a dog to push a big red button when the reboot time came. But no one trusted a dog enough to risk an entire ship and crew on canine judgment. Eventually, humans were used instead—humans who for one reason or another didn't have augmentations. Such people came to be known as Dogs, even if no one ever used the name to their faces.

Crew-members seldom talked to the Dog at all. Talking was a dying skill; children still learned to do it, to encourage the development of their lungs and their sense of hearing. But most people stopped speaking aloud when they reached adulthood. Every voice the Dog had ever heard was raspy with disuse.

Except for the simulated voices of computers. Computers could talk just fine . . . and they did it to keep the Dog company. Actual humans were edgy around him—he was outside their comfort zone. People tended to treat him as if he were stupid . . . maybe even dangerous. "Different" meant "Can't trust him." There'd been incidents where Dogs suffered emotional breakdowns from lack of personal interaction.

So computers had to fill in the gaps. They chatted and provided connection. It worked . . . mostly. Virtual intelligence software was almost good enough to simulate human contact—good enough that the Dog seldom thought about how lonely he was.

Not while the computers were running. Which they currently weren't.

The Dog tried his zapper again. It still produced the orange ribbon and the black cloud. This jump was shaping up into a long one—if the ship didn't slip quickly back into normal space, the wait was often substantial.

The ship's clocks, of course, would register zero time, as would the internal clocks of the crew. They'd congratulate themselves on another perfect jump. No one would ask the Dog otherwise.

CR

He unstrapped himself from his jump-couch and floated out of the bridge. Every hatchway was open, as per standard jump procedure. Normal space always came with the risk some meteor pebble would punch through the hull; you had to keep all hatches closed so any air loss from the breach was confined to a single section of the ship. But warp-space had nothing in it—no pebbles, no matter at all. The greatest danger during a jump was going too long with life-support off. A place like the bridge, where a dozen unconscious people were breathing in a relatively small space, could run into problems. Opening all the hatches let everyone share the full supply of oxygen.

Even so, without active ventilation and CO_2 scrubbing, the bridge got musty fast. The Dog liked to go elsewhere if the lag-time looked lengthy. It meant one less person breathing the bridge's restricted air.

And what did it hurt if the Dog roamed the ship? No one would know he was gone.

CR

By the light of tubes filled with glowing plankton, the Dog floated down a corridor. He knew the ship well; he'd been its Dog for ten years. There was no point transferring anywhere else—career advancement didn't exist for Dogs.

Years ago, Dogs carried out other duties besides pushing the restart button. Gradually, however, such assignments were discontinued. Regular crew-members complained that Dogs mishandled every chore. The Dog didn't believe it—more likely, the crew were just ill-at-ease with Dogs working beside them. But it meant that a job on one ship was exactly the same as another . . . so why would the Dog go elsewhere?

Without augmentations, he was just a Dog. And he couldn't get augs because . . . well, when he was young there'd been medical reasons, but now it was simply because he was needed the way he was. Dogs were valuable, even if they weren't valued. If the Dog got augmented now, he couldn't compete with people who'd been amped since they were in utero. Rather than be an inadequate version of everyone else, he'd rather just be a Dog.

He drifted down to Engineering. It was the biggest space in the ship: a cube three stories high, with lighting tubes thick on every surface to give a bright clear view of the machinery. Lots of light. Lots of air. When a warp-jump went long, the Dog amused himself by zooming about in zero G. Metal pipes and computer columns formed towers throughout the chamber, giving the Dog an obstacle course he could weave around. He could fly like a weightless bird, while down on the floor, crew-members stayed earthbound, strapped in their seats.

That's how it usually went . . . but today when the Dog arrived, he discovered a sleepwalker.

℣

Crew-members often moved during jump-sleep. They pushed imaginary buttons or lashed out at monsters in their dreams. A few spoke slurry words, saying more than they did when awake. But in all the Dog's time on the ship, this woman was the first who'd managed to unstrap herself from her jump-couch.

She was broad in body and face, but her hands were slim and

wiry — apparently the ideal physique for engineers, since everyone else in Engineering had a similar build. The Dog had run into the woman on numerous occasions . . . sometimes almost literally. All crew-members walked around with an air of distraction, ignoring their surroundings as they mentally conversed with each other or scanned schematic diagrams that the ship transmitted into their brains; but this woman stood out from the rest for her strength of preoccupation. Several times, the Dog had been forced to dodge into hatchways to avoid her: as if she were sleepwalking even when she was awake.

Now she really was sleepwalking: eyes open but gaze blank. The woman moved as if in a dream . . . but that dream seemed to involve dismantling the ship.

She'd been at work for several minutes before the Dog arrived: reaching into machines and pulling out component pieces. Some of the pieces still floated close by her; others had drifted away in the absence of gravity, getting caught in the room's tangle of equipment or else bouncing lazily off the walls.

When the Dog saw what she was doing, he launched himself toward her. He grabbed her shoulder and tried to pull her away from the access panel where she was silently taking things apart. She howled and fought his grip, shouting sounds that weren't words.

She was strong — stronger than the Dog. He'd never had muscle enhancements. On the other hand, he was awake; she wasn't. She was also accustomed to having every single action fine-tuned by chips and implants. With her mods shut down, she was uncoordinated. She flailed, all her movements off balance. The Dog took a clout to his jaw, but he got her away from the equipment. He pushed her clear, sending her floating toward the ceiling.

That gave him time to catch his breath. And to rub his jaw. His bones were weaker than hers — especially his jaw versus her knuckles.

The Dog surveyed the circuit-boards and other components caroming in all directions thanks to his tussle with the woman. More than a dozen machine parts were flying loose around the room. With every system safely shut down, the ship might not have been damaged by having its bits pulled out; however, restarting the ship was out of the question until everything got put back in place.

If the woman had only pulled out one or two pieces, the Dog might have tried putting them back himself—square pegs would fit in square holes, right? But with so many parts yanked free, there was just too much chance of mistakes. Every piece had to be returned to its proper location; and the job had to be done fast, before everyone ran out of oxygen.

The Dog muttered, "Never wake a sleepwalker." Wasn't that the old saying? But in this case, he had to make an exception.

င

The Dog didn't know how much the crew understood his job. They treated him . . . they treated him like a dog. A dog whose only trick was poking a single button.

He had more tricks than that. Given the number of starships jumping around the galaxy, anything that could possibly go wrong had already happened on some other ship. A ship that survived an emergency did so because its Dog found a way to cope. Old Dogs talked to new ones and passed on their solutions, so if a problem happened again, every Dog could be prepared.

This wasn't a secret—not exactly—but the social disconnect between Dogs and crews encouraged deliberate ignorance. When was the last time a regular crew-member asked the Dog about his work? Never. Nobody on the ship wanted to know how much they depended on the Dog to keep them safe.

For example, the dog always carried a stim-shot: an auto-injector that held enough stimulant to overcome someone's warp-jump coma. It didn't need much juice—unlike with a real coma, crew-members weren't deeply unconscious. They were just shut down a little, so they wouldn't face the trauma of being offline. They'd rather be anesthetized than deal with who they were without augments.

The Dog hoped the sleepwalking woman wouldn't have a nervous breakdown just for being woken prematurely.

He had no difficulty reaching her. She'd stopped flailing—zero

G was relaxing once you got over the initial strangeness. She was still grabbing at objects that only existed in her dreams, but she looked relatively peaceful.

Until the Dog slammed the injector into her neck.

ↂ

Perhaps he used too much force. He'd never done this before; he didn't know how hard to press. And he was nervous about being near her, considering how much his jaw still hurt. He wanted to get close as quickly as possible, inject her, then jump clear.

But when he hit her with the injector, she didn't strike back— she screeched. Then she curled up and moaned. She bounced off a wall, but didn't notice. Like a billiard ball, she coasted from surface to surface until she bumped into some machinery and continued to moan in the middle of the room.

From a safe distance, the Dog said, "Hello? Uhh . . . hello? Can you . . . sorry, this is important. Please calm down."

She uncurled a little from her fetal ball. "I can't hear you!" she wailed. "I can't see!"

"I don't think that's true," the Dog said. "You're just offline."

"I'm blind," she said, looking straight at him.

"You're not," he told her. The Dog could see the woman's eyes were focused on him. "It's just that your augs are turned off. We're still in warp-space. I think. But even if we've dropped back to the normal universe, we can't restart till you fix the ship."

"What's wrong with the ship?"

"You . . . uhh . . . you were sleepwalking. By the time I found you . . ."

The Dog gestured at the components drifting around the room. The woman squinted at them; she blinked, then widened her eyes as if she was trying to find a way to make her vision work properly. She said, "I couldn't have . . ." then looked at her hands, moving them closer to her face then farther away as if she couldn't focus. Most of the pieces that she'd handled were just clean electronics, but a few had been moving parts, covered with grease or oil. The Dog could tell she was seeing the residue on her fingers. She could probably smell it too.

"Oh," she said. "Oh damn. I dreamed I . . ." She began to curl up again.

"Hey, no!" the Dog said. "Please, no. We have to fix things. Before we run out of air."

"I can't fix anything," the woman snapped. "I don't know where the pieces go."

"Then tell me who does know," the Dog said, looking at the other engineers strapped on their couches. "I've got another stim-shot. I can wake anyone we need."

"Nobody knows," the woman said. "It's all on computer. Why would we memorize schematics when we can just look them up?"

"What happens if the computer breaks down?"

"We look on another computer. Everything here has at least five-fold redundancy."

The Dog sighed. "No, it doesn't. But maybe we have enough." He waved at the floating components. "You gather those up. I'll be back in a minute."

"Where are you going?"

"To my Kennel."

෪

It really was called the Kennel . . . unofficially, of course. Officially, it was just Bunk-Room C7, its only distinguishing feature that it wasn't located in the same part of the ship as all the other bunk-rooms. The Dog had the space to himself: just him and the many emergency supplies that nobody wanted to know were there.

Including a complete set of starship construction manuals. On paper.

In the starship's official records, the manuals were "Carbon Storage Sinks". That wasn't a lie—paper was a long-lasting material that sequestered carbon and kept it out of planetary atmospheres. At least it was a good enough storage medium to satisfy government requirements . . . and if you were going to manufacture paper anyway, you might as well print something useful on it.

(The Dog suspected that someone had played fast and loose with regulations to make the manuals possible . . . but you don't look a gift horse in the mouth. The manuals had been in his Kennel when he first arrived on the ship, and he never asked where they came from.)

Nine hefty books. The Dog had once thumbed through them, but they were completely over his head. He was a Dog, not an engineer; if the manuals were ever needed, he wouldn't be the one using them. He'd just wake someone with the right expertise and say, "Here, hope these help." He didn't even know which manual he needed now . . . so he threaded them all together on a spare jump-couch strap, then he slung it over his shoulder. With gravity still at zero, he had no trouble dragging all the manuals back to Engineering.

CR

By the time he got there, the Sleepwalker had corralled the floating components. She'd taken off her uniform jacket and used it to wrap the pieces so they didn't drift away again. She was shivering in just her shirtsleeves—with life-support off, the ship was beginning to cool. But when the woman saw the Dog, she tried to hide her shivers. She put on a neutral expression and asked, "Are those really books? On paper?"

The Dog nodded. "Schematics and repair instructions."

"Paper books," the woman said. "This'll be like making fire by rubbing sticks together." But when the Dog offered her the books, she took them and started flipping pages. After a moment, she made a face. "This is ridiculous. We'll freeze before I find the right information."

"One of the books is an index," the Dog said. "That might help."

The woman scowled, but found the index book and searched through it. The Dog wanted to ask if he could help, but decided against it—she would just say no. Nobody ever thought that Dogs had brains. He waited quietly as she paged through the index, then through another book. Eventually, she reached a complex-looking diagram; the dog saw her move her fingers across it, unthinkingly making the gesture that increased the size of a picture on a display screen. When nothing happened, she swore, squinted hard, and swore again. "This isn't going to work!"

"Wait," the Dog said. "I have a magnifying glass."

"A what?"

The Dog's uniform had numerous pockets, and each was stuffed with knick-knacks he might need in a pinch. He pulled out his largest magnifying glass (he had three) and offered it to the woman.

She looked at it dubiously. The Dog moved closer and held the glass over the page. "See what it does?"

"Oh." She took the glass and moved it up and down, back and forth, above the paper. "Better," she said. "Primitive, but workable." She floated toward the access panel where she'd pulled out all the components. "Let's get started."

CR

Several pieces went back easily, locking into connections that other pieces didn't fit. But this left six electronic circuit-boards to fit into six identical sockets . . . and while the boards didn't look exactly the same, they were close enough that they couldn't be distinguished by looking at the diagram, even with the magnifying glass.

"Aren't they labeled?" the Dog asked.

"Of course, they're labeled," the Sleepwalker woman answered. "With RFID tags." She pointed to a tiny metal fleck on one of the boards. "If my internal systems were working, I could wave my finger over that and tell everything you'd ever want to know about the board. Make, model, serial number, date of manufacture . . ."

"But the board doesn't have a visible label?"

"Visible labels can be misread," the woman said dismissively. "And the writing can flake away or get damaged. And you have to actually look at them rather than just wave your finger. Besides, if you can't read RFID, you have no business being in this . . ." She stopped and avoided looking in the Dog's direction.

The Dog asked, "What the worst that could happen if we plug a board into the wrong slot?"

"I have no idea," the woman answered, "but it won't be good. Each of these circuits contains logic chips with millions or billions of coded instructions. If you put one in the wrong place, most likely the board will recognize it's not connected properly and just do nothing . . . but that's bad if the ship relies on it to do the right thing."

"I thought everything on the ship has five-fold redundancy. If something's hooked up wrong, won't four back-up systems just take up the slack?"

"Maybe," the woman said. "But restarting after warp shutdown is . . . delicate. Since a jump takes zero time, some systems are designed with the assumption that nothing could possibly have changed during the gap. They boot up assuming that everything is working the same as before the jump. They don't start checking for possible errors until everything is back online."

"Oh," the Dog said. "That sounds . . . ill-considered."

"It's stupid is what it is," the Sleepwalker said. "But if you want to slam an entire starship from drifting with every system off to every system running fully, and do it so fast that nobody notices an interruption, you have to take shortcuts. Once in a while, that bites you on the ass. Especially if some idiot goes ripping out pieces . . ."

She stopped and turned away. The movement started her drifting across the room, away from the Dog and the machinery. "Uhh," the Dog began . . . but what could he say? It's not your fault? The woman must know that already. But she blamed herself anyway.

After a few seconds, the Dog said, "We need to figure out which circuit-board is which. So we need to read the tags, right? How does RFID actually work?"

The woman remained turned away, but she said, "Basically, you hit the tag with radio waves. That causes a sort of resonance inside the tag's circuits; they echo back a signal filled with digital information."

"So we need a source of radio waves, and something to read the echo?"

"Essentially."

The Dog pulled out his zapper. When he triggered it, a blue spark jumped between the terminals. "Okay, good news: we're back in normal space-time. Our equipment should work." He pushed the trigger again; it made another spark. "And I'll bet this little gadget produces radio waves. Moving electricity does that, doesn't it?"

"Usually," the woman said. "Probably enough for our purposes."

"So all we need is a reader." The Dog tried to remember if he had anything like that in his emergency supplies. No. Everything was deliberately low-tech. "I don't suppose you'd have some kind of battery-powered reader?"

"Why would we?" the woman said. "We all have readers built in." She brightened. "But if we've really settled back into normal space-time, I can just boot my augmen—"

"Don't!" the Dog interrupted.

"Why not?"

"I've heard it's not good to boot up in a vacuum. I mean, when no other systems are working. Because your augs will try to sync with everything else around them, and if they can't . . . things go wrong."

"Like what?"

"I've just heard stories from other Dogs. If your implants try to connect, and nothing answers back, some of them just . . . wait. Meanwhile, other augs do start on their own, but they assume that everything else is running too, so they start pumping out hormones or whatever they do, and it's all . . . it can go bad very quickly. Like a machine where half of the pieces start and half don't, so they grind against each other."

The woman grimaced. "I get the picture. And it's ridiculous." She sighed deeply; the exhalation started her moving backward. "Don't get me wrong, I believe what you're saying. I'm an engineer. I know how short-sighted machine designers can be. Someone says, 'We don't have to worry about weird situations that can't possibly happen.' Then the situation happens and someone's brain explodes." She looked at the Dog. "That's what you're talking about, right?"

"Probably not a literal explosion," the Dog said. "But . . . imbalances. Maybe very bad."

"Always?" she asked.

"It varies. You all have different implants . . . different natural metabolisms . . . it's unpredictable."

"So if I reboot, I might be okay."

The Dog didn't answer. He had no idea what the odds were for "okay" versus "dead", or anything in between.

The woman took a breath. "All right. Look down there." She pointed to one of the other engineers, strapped unconscious on his couch. "If I can't finish this myself, he's the person to wake up next. He'll know what needs to be done."

"We could wake him now," the Dog said.

"No. I know what needs to be done too. And I got us into this mess."

"You didn't. It just happened."

The woman gave him a thin smile. "Nice try. If this works, the drinks are on me."

She reached both hands behind her head and rummaged through her hair. Augmented people always had reboot switches, but the locations varied; the Dog felt relieved that the woman didn't have to undress to reach hers. After another moment of rummaging, she said, "Ah, there." She gave the Dog a look, then her whole body jerked.

She jerked again.

She started swearing like someone who's just gashed her finger . . . but she didn't stop. She kept going, words shooting uncontrollably out of her mouth: a flow of profanity in multiple languages, all shouted at the top of her lungs. She gave the Dog an embarrassed look, as if she wanted to apologize but couldn't— some wild part of her brain had seized her voice, and the rest of her brain had no access.

At least the woman hadn't died immediately; on the other hand, brain dysfunction was bad. The woman must have realized the same thing because with a lurch, she turned back as quickly as possible toward the access panel, wanting to get the job done while she was still able. An involuntary jerk sent her floating away from the machinery—like her voice, her body was developing a mind of its own.

Tics. Spasms. She looked to the Dog for help, even as she threw curses in his direction.

He flew to her side and put his arm around her waist. She

continued to convulse, but didn't fight his grip. He guided her back toward the machinery.

The six unattached circuit-boards were tucked into the pages of the manual books. The books themselves were tied by their strap to a pipe beside the access panel. The Dog took one of the boards out of the book that held it and offered the board to the woman. She reached out, but couldn't control her hand enough to do anything useful. The Dog took her hand gently and moved the RFID chip beneath her shaking fingers.

After a moment, the woman thrust her hand toward one of the empty sockets inside the panel. Carefully, the Dog inserted the circuit-board into the slot.

ଓ

They did the same thing five more times. The Dog found the process painful . . . not holding the woman's warm body, but having her scream in his ear and seeing her twitch in frustration as she tried to control herself enough to get the job done. Her voice had become ragged with continuous yelling. And the Dog could feel her tiring from so much exertion—weak trembles underlay all her other spasmodic movements. When the final board snugged into place, the woman's body seemed to slacken even though she continued to writhe and curse hoarsely.

"Is it fixed?" the Dog asked her. "Can I restart the ship?"

She shoved him toward the exit door. The room was getting stuffy—the woman's shouts and exertions had used up a great deal of oxygen. But the Dog still took the time to guide her to her jump-couch and secure her thrashing body in the straps. He hoped she wouldn't twist free in the time he took to get back to the bridge. If she was spinning around the room when the gravity came back on . . .

The Dog didn't have time to worry about that. He was getting dizzy from lack of oxygen. He'd been exerting himself too.

ଓ

Back at the bridge, almost unconscious, the Dog hit the big red button. Within a second, everything resumed as if nothing out of the ordinary had happened.

Almost.

CR

The Dog ran back to Engineering. By the time he got there, the other engineers had already unstrapped the woman from her couch—she was still shaking and screaming. As they hurried her to the sick bay, they gave the Dog hostile looks: what are you doing here, gawking at our friend?

The woman herself seemed too dazed to notice. The ship coming back online would have jolted her hard: some of her augmentations would suddenly reconnect, disrupting what remained of her metabolic balance. The Dog wanted to follow her to sick bay and hear what the doctor said . . . but then the captain called him to the bridge to explain numerous anomalies detected after the jump.

Such as nine heavy "carbon storage sinks" dangling from an open access panel in the Engineering room.

CR

Reports had to be filed, then carefully hushed up. It was bad for morale if the crew were forced to acknowledge how deeply they relied on an unaugmented nobody. Even the captain seemed eager to put it out of her mind.

CR

When things finally grew less hectic, the Dog went to sick bay to see how his Sleepwalker was doing. By then, she was under sedation; the doctor said she would stay in that state till the ship reached a planet with a full-service medical center.

"She'll be all right, won't she?" asked the Dog.

"Eventually," the doctor replied. "We've reached the point where we can replace pretty much any part of the body that gets damaged."

"Even her brain?"

"Sure. We take full brain backups whenever people sleep. We'll restore everything as of last night—she'll lose less than a day of memories."

"Oh," said the Dog, "that's all right then. I guess that's good."

He went back to his Kennel.

The captain would call when they needed him again.

CARNIVORES

Rich Larson

Finch pried himself out of the autocab midway down Jasper Avenue, where Carnivor gastro-bistro, the city's most exclusive new eatery, skulked between concrete high-rises. He'd read up on the restaurant's architecture when he and Blake first started planning the heist, so he knew it was a collaboration between a Bolivian artist and a decaying engineering AI, and that the swooping ridges of the façade, together with its calcium-spike stalactites, were meant to evoke the maw of an animal. For everyone with neural implants synched up to fine dining augreality, the restaurant's name was slashed into the air in bright red.

Finch thought it was a bit kitschy. Blake, his partner in crime, thought it was bleeding edge haute couture and required Finch order a new suit that was not bleeding ugly. The Armani jacket already felt unpleasantly tight around his bookcase shoulders and thick-ribbed chest—a problem Finch was well used to. Not many stores catered to Neanderthal hybrid proportions.

The autocab squawked for payment. Finch licked his massive thumb and stuck it against the reader, then held the taxi in place by its door frame while he checked his appearance in the window. He ran a hand over his slicked red hair and adjusted the Full Windsor noose around his neck, wondering if the tattoos clawing out from under his cuffs looked professional enough in cobalt blue or if he should have masked them completely.

Finch let the autocab skitter back into traffic. It didn't matter how he looked. The darknet CV Blake had done up for him was a bullshit masterpiece, and Carnivor's proprietor, if her hacked pornstream was any indication, had a Neanderthal fantasy not uncommon among professional women. Finch inhaled. The cold air smelled like exhaust and something almost as pungent that his nose, tuned to Blake-imposed veganism, took a moment to recognize as cooking meat.

He made his way through the dilating doors into a mirrored entryway, where he was stopped by a bouncer who seemed to be mostly composed of HGH-pumped muscle and hair gel.

"Slow up, Red." He tapped the neural plug set into the shaved side of his head, making his starched Mohawk wobble slightly. "I don't see you on the facebook. In this *modern* day and age, you need to make a reservation, you know? And at Carnivor, we backlog up to three months."

"I'm not a guest," Finch said, sizing him up on old instinct. Scarred knuckles, crooked nose, probably fancied himself a boxer. The nametag scrolling down his breast pocket read Vick. "I'm here to see Ms. Carrow." He tapped his own plug, down behind his ear, and shuttled over the Carnivor-red interview request.

A briefly hurt look flashed across Vick's face before he regained his pre-set smirk. "Have to frisk you down, then," he said, cracking his fingers. "You're awful pale. Must be Irish, right?"

Finch stood scarecrow as the bouncer frisked. "Not that I know of. You?"

"You in the gravity gym a lot? What do you squat on standard?" Vick slapped one of Finch's tree-trunk quads. "Big old haunches on you. Big veins, too, I got tiny veins, shitty circulation—"

Finch snagged the man's hand tight enough to feel tendons rasp up on each other, then slowly moved it away.

Vick turned his grimace into a grin as he yanked his fingers back. "Your kind aren't much for conversation, are they? More used to grunting."

"You done?"

"Yeah, I'm done. Left your club at home, obviously." Vick nodded toward the interior. "Right this way."

Finch ran through a few ways to snap Vick's neck as he followed him across a gleaming obsidian floor, past copses of smartglass tables and spiny organic sculptures. He watched a gaggle of Ghanaian businessmen wearing fashionably gashed suits put in their order while what appeared to be 2010s slaughterhouse footage played across their table. Finch shook his head. Kitschy as fuck.

While Vick was distracted by the swaying hips of a neon-lipped server, Finch scanned for fire exits, motion sensors, and small black cameras nestled in the ceiling corners. What he took to be the private dining alcoves were hidden behind a noise-cancelling black shroud.

Caught up in sending Blake the footage, Finch brushed against one of the shuddering sculptures and received a blast of hot peppery breath full in the face. He swore loud enough for Vick to turn around and give a hyena giggle. His eyes stung all the way though the silver-white labyrinth of Carnivor's kitchens, where cooks doing prep-work shouted to each other in a thick blend of Tagalog, Somali and English. The smell of meat hung heavy, almost dripping.

Finch was still blinking away tears when they arrived at the door to Ms. Carrow's office. Vick pointed him in without speaking, suddenly sour-faced, then stalked away.

"Thanks, Vick," Finch called after him, flipping the bird to his turned back.

ℂ℁

Ms. Holly Carrow was in virtual conference when Finch stepped inside and closed the synthetic oak door behind him. Her dim-lit office was partially overgrown, with a faux-skylight shafting artificial sunshine onto the artful twists of branch and vine sprouting through the glass floor. Very envirochic, very expensive. It matched up with the utterly obscene amounts of anonymized money Blake had found flowing into Carnivor's accounts, which in turn seemed linked to a mysterious bi-monthly delivery from a Brazilian medi/pharma company.

Very envirochic, very expensive, very warm. Finch did not do well with warm. Wasn't built for it. He could already feel sweat prickling along his hairline as he approached Carrow's desk. She was reclined in an orthochair, her dark head tipped back in its cradle. Neural plugs pulsed at her chemically smoothed temples. Her lips looked like a line of dried blood and her jawline was wide and perfectly angled.

Finch touched his own with some measure of jealousy, rasping his thumb along the coarse beard that helped obscure his Neanderthal lack of chin. As he stepped through the dappled light, a spindly-looking chair unfolded itself opposite the desk and blinked an inviting green. Finch sat gingerly; he'd done in their apartment's cheap folding chair that morning halfway through Blake styling his hair.

Finch put his hands on his knees to wait, and realized the roll of his trousers looked like a miniature chub. Right as he was smoothing out his crotch, the restaurateur's eyes flicked open. People always came out of a deep slice at the most inopportune moments. Finch tried to move his hand in a natural path to his knee.

"Sorry for the wait." Carrow's sea-green eyes tracked the movement like a laser. She gave a faint smile. "I hope it wasn't making you . . . squirmy."

"Not at all."

"Good." Carrow's chair reconfigured, sliding her upright, and she extended a hand to make it all one sinuous motion. "Mr. Finch, I presume."

Finch took it, finding it drier than he'd expected and strong. "Pleasure."

"You have a very impressive CV, Mr. Finch." She looked at the girth of his knuckles with more than faint interest—Finch remembered a few favourites from her pornstream and tried not to let it show on his face. "Private security coordinator for EpiGen. Paramilitary service in Pakistan and India. Very impressive."

Finch blinked. "I do what I'm good at, I suppose."

"Yes." Carrow's eyes roved down his chest, lingered a millisecond too long at his hips. Her cheeks tinted with a near-imperceptible flush Finch knew to look for. "We all play the cards we're dealt. Genetically or otherwise. But I do wonder why a former CEO bodyguard wants to work security at Carnivor."

Finch squeezed his kneecap. Blake had made the CV too perfect. He had that tendency. "I'm at the point where I need a position that's longer term and lower risk." Finch paused, then played the trump card. "We don't live so long as you. Thirty-three is middle aged, for a neo. Cell decay will set in soon."

The restaurateur leaned forward. "You're a survivor from the original batch, then? From the Bangkok biolabs?"

Finch didn't have to lie on this point. "Yes. Number 23."

"I knew it," Carrow breathed. "Well, ah, suspected. I've always wanted to meet . . ." She trailed off, trying to re-establish herself. "What they did in those labs was an atrocity. The experimentation. You should know I was a fervent supporter of the Diaspora Act. Referendum 88, as well. Neo rights are a bit of a passion of mine."

"I don't follow the politics." Another thing he didn't have to lie about.

"You don't feel a certain responsibility to—"

"I'm me, first," Finch cut her off. "Anything else, second. Including neo."

Carrow's dark red frown reshaped to a sheepish smile. "I'm sorry. I must sound like a paleochaser who's side-windowing the wiki."

"Not at all," Finch said, sliding the polite veneer back over his voice. "I can tell when someone's reading the wiki. You know, 'you must have been so happy on August 16, 2055 when clone-grown Neanderthal-human hybrids gained full citizen rights.' Shit like that."

"Terrible." The restaurateur rose; her orthochair reluctantly put its massage pads away. "I've been in virtual all day, Mr. Finch. Walk with me." Finch creaked off his own chair and shadowed her over to the twisted trees. She wrapped her fingers around a moss-slick branch. "These aren't real," she admitted, sliding her hand up and down the length. "Real would have been too cheap."

Finch shrugged, ignoring the phallic tableau. "They're nice."

"Sometimes people have trouble with real and not real," Carrow said delicately, releasing the branch. "Sometimes mere illusion is offensive enough to make people take real action. An all-meat eatery, whether it's vat grown or not, attracts its share of critics. That's part of the charm, of course. Being contentious. The restaurant business is all about novelty."

"I tend to eat vegan, myself."

"So do I." Carrow smiled as she wiped her hands together, then turned serious. "For the past month, Carnivor has been receiving anonymous vitriol from an individual, or perhaps a small group, who take issue with our mode and aesthetic. They think it trivializes the horrors of the defunct livestock industry. Or something. I wasn't much concerned with them until they started making threats against our clientele's safety."

Finch remembered the late nights with Blake, composing anti-meat rants and credible bomb threats over a bottle of Luna vodka and hash. They'd gotten quite good at it.

"We attract an influential clientele," Carrow said, leaning back against the tree, managing to exaggerate the camber of her back with relative grace. "Movie stars, moguls, athletes. Bookings for our more exclusive offerings are often made months in advance." She paused. "We take the privacy of our guests very seriously. While most come here to be seen, others come here for the opposite. That's why I'm looking to improve Carnivor's security. I'd like to ensure no dining experience is interrupted by anti-meat radicals or celebrity chasers. The only man we have now, Vicky, is a bit . . . unreliable."

"I feel qualified to do that, Ms. Carrow," Finch said, lowering his voice to a controlled rumble as he stepped closer. "Though I would, of course, like to negotiate upward on the salary."

Carrow smiled again, the flush coming back stronger. "Well, we haven't discussed a benefits package yet, have we?"

☙

Finch couldn't resist unzipping his trousers once he was out the door, then doing them up again, noisily, on his way past Vick, whose face turned taut and ashy in a way that almost made Finch feel bad for the prick.

"She doesn't fuck in her office," the bouncer snarled.

"Doesn't fuck you, you mean. Maybe it's the haircut."

Vick's response was guillotined by the arrival of a designer-swathed couple smelling like cheap pheromone spray and expensive liquor. He checked them against the facebook with his jaw clenched tight, and gave a smile that was more grimace as a server led them off.

"Once she does fuck you, she'll fire you," he said. "She just wants some neo cock. Then you're back out on your ass. She loves her little ironies." He preened his Mohawk in the mirror wall, deadly serious. "And don't even think about hurting her. I've always wanted a go at a caveman."

That word still sliced into Finch's stomach, even after all these years. He felt the tips of his ears redden.

"You'd have to buy me a drink," Finch said. He looked Vick up and down. "Several drinks. And that's saying something, since my gut's got no enzymes to process alcohol. Pre-agrarian and all that."

"What the fuck are you grunting about?" Vick smiled like a shark; he had a nose for blood in the water. "Caveman."

Finch was squared to him without realizing he'd moved. "Say it again."

They stood toe to toe until the air was all but stinking with testosterone, or maybe just the sliver of vat beef caught in Vick's teeth. For a moment Finch was ready to throw the whole job, the weeks and weeks of prep, just for a chance to bash Vick's face in. Then a notification flag popped up in his peripherals. He opened it.

Unit, you get the job or fucking what? I'm dying metaphorically over here. Save me.

Finch scrolled Blake's message up and down, allowing a smile to ghost onto his face. He turned on his heel and headed for the LRT station.

∽

The dark apartment was mercifully cold when Finch let himself inside. Blake said his hardware ran faster near zero, and affinity for low temperatures was one of the reasons they'd got together in the first place. That, and a mutual talent for petty crime.

At the moment, Blake was sitting cross-legged in the middle of the carpet, surrounded by a maelstrom of biodegradable moving boxes, congealing cartons of Mai Pet Pad Thai, Finch's magnetic dumbbells, and the remains of the snapped folding chair from earlier that morning. Finch switched on the solar lamp, throwing stark shadows onto the white stucco walls.

Blake didn't so much as twitch his close-cropped head, heavy lids half shut, lips half parted. His neural implants gleamed white against black skin, carving channels up his spine and all the way to his temples. Blake looked almost holy when he was sliced in deep. Like a monk, apart from the drool wending down his numb chin and dripping onto his Adidas trackies.

Finch peeled off his suit, deciding to burn off the last of his fight-or-flight adrenaline on the pull-up bar. Blake had nixed the squat rack due to space concerns. Most of the floor was taken up by their two foam mattresses, currently slung into opposite corners despite their tendency to migrate together in the evening. Blake's was strewn with the colourful viscera of his half-unpacked wardrobe; Finch's was bare.

After fifteen wide-grip pull-ups, Finch dropped to the carpet with the veins across his shoulders blue and bulging. Blake was still sliced in, seeing only code, so Finch used one of the hacker's many shirts to sop the sweat from his springy red hair, then went to wipe the saliva from his companion's chin.

Blake's teeth snapped together.

Finch jerked his fingers back, dropping the shirt. "Fucker."

Blake's eyes winched fully open, beetle black. "Unit, you should have messaged me you were home." He looked down, blinking. "Why's my shirt wet?"

"You were drooling again."

Blake sniffed at it suspiciously as he stood up, making the implants in his back click and clack. Then he broke into a grin and offered his fist for a congratulatory knock. "Carnivor's new security consultant," he said. "I'm so proud of you, Unit. Overcoming your checkered-as-fuck past. Wearing a slick-as-fuck suit. Which you have since discarded."

Finch's hand was a spade compared to Blake's. "I could have shown up like this and still got the job," he said, bumping fists and then enveloping Blake's slender wrist.

The hacker grinned. "She was a paleochaser, huh?"

"Big time." Finch tried to keep his voice light. "You homo sapiens. Trying to breed us out of existence all over again."

Blake ran a playful hand down Finch's arm. "Who can blame her, though, right? Your biceps look cancerous right now." He plucked at the muscle. "You work out too much, Unit. Self-improvement is a short hop to, you know, self-obsession."

"Try a chin-up. Maybe you'll like it."

"I hate sweating," Blake said, moving to wipe the drool off his pant leg. "Shit's undignified." He gave Finch a sly look, then stepped out of the trackies entirely, leaving them pooled on the carpet. He rubbed one slim calf against the other. "You know, neither one of us has a uterus, so breeding you out of existence is pretty improbable. Chance you're willing to . . . ?"

Finch cut him off with a bruising kiss before they maneuvered to the floor, managing to miss both mattresses entirely.

CR

After five days at Carnivor spent standing straight-backed and stern-faced in the entryway, or else circulating the restaurant to search for the early signs of aggressive drinkers, lovers' spats, and general shitfuckery, Finch would have been ready to quit under normal circumstances. He'd cased out the place as best he could within the first few shifts, meaning most of his mental energy was spent tolerating Carrow's increasingly unsubtle come-ons and Vick's increasingly unsubtle jealousy.

But on the sixth day, when the delivery chime shivered through their implants, Vick's face turned cagey. "I've got this one," he said. "Remember, you don't talk to guests unless they talk to you. And don't call anything . . . kitschy."

Finch messaged Blake, a tingle of anticipation finally worming up his spine. *Special delivery. Think tonight's the night.*

The suspicion was all but confirmed when Vick returned in high spirits a half-hour later. "High-end stock fresh out the vat," he announced. "But now what happens to the older cuts still taking up valuable freezer space?"

"You sell them on MeatSpin," Finch guessed.

"I take them home, get out the griller, and feast like a fucking king all week long," Vick corrected, grinning widely. "Me and the Somalis in the kitchen have a deal all worked out." His smile shrank a few molars. "But I did let Cuaron cook one up for your supper. To celebrate your first week or some shit. So if you want to go eat, you go now. We're going to be limelight tonight. Busy-busy."

Finch unfurled Blake's reply in the corner of his eye: *Make sure, Unit.*

"Alright," he said. "Back in twenty."

Vick was already back to his customary scowl. Finch split for the kitchens, winding his way through the smartglass tables, slaloming the quivering sculptures, swapping nods or knocks with harried servers. When he pushed his way through the doors with a practiced elbow, he realized he'd got used to the smell. In fact, his stomach was squelching hungrily.

Finch maneuvered through spurts of steam and bilingual conversation, stopping at a bubbling pot where Cuaron whisked meat stock into briny liquid. She gave a start when she looked up, eyes wide and nervous. Some people never got comfortable around Finch.

"You just got a delivery, right?" he asked.

"Yeah. Yes. Just did." She chewed at her lip. "Why?"

"Vick says to double-check the freezer door sealed. Says it's been finicky." Finch shrugged. "Last door on the right, isn't it? I'll go."

"I'll go," Cuaron said. "*I'll go.* You should eat. Plated you something." She pointed a pinky finger back toward the battered white counter where a covered dish leaked steam in a long ribbon.

"Thanks."

Cuaron called a sous-chef over to the pot, then darted away toward the freezer alley. Finch followed at a distance, leaning into the chilled corridor long enough to see her go to the one windowless door at the end that none of the staff seemed to ever look at. Then he doubled back to retrieve his supper.

The cutlet was beautiful, perfectly-seared, and the urge to eat meat had been creeping back to him over the past week. Blake still held that the ideal diet derived protein from almonds and kidney beans, but Finch didn't have the same digestive equipment, did he?

Juice seeped from the meat as he cut into it, and Finch felt a responding spray of hot saliva under his tongue. Feeling only slightly guilty, he wolfed it down and headed back to his post.

CR

It was near midnight when the restaurant expelled its last diners into a chilled evening, and well after by the time the kitchen staff followed. Finch and Vick finished their final sweeps and activated the alarm system. Vick sealed the doors behind them with his thumbprint, then swaggered off to his waiting autocab.

Once the red tail-lights swished away, Finch buried his hands in his pockets and rounded the corner. Blake was waiting in the alley, geared up, trailing wires from his spinal implants and through his sleeves. He was already wearing a woolly balaclava, with a hole cut at the temple for his one neural plug, but Finch could tell he was grinning underneath.

"Time to find out what these fuckers are hiding, Unit," he said, tossing the other mask over.

Finch rolled the wool beneath his fingertips. "Special sauce recipe, probably."

"Ha." Blake slotted a stray cord into his smartglove, wriggling his fingers experimentally. "My bet's still on tetrameth. Imagine how much you could fit in a cow carcass."

"It's vat meat. They don't grow the whole cow." Finch pulled the mask over his head. "Ready?"

Blake solemnly offered his gloved fist, then remembered the delicate circuitry and swapped it for the other. Finch knocked, and they slunk back out of the alley with the static of a hacked police scanner fizzing in their ears.

Entry was easy. Finch stood watch for less than a minute while Blake, squatting in front of the door, performed a quick viral strike on the alarm system and snuffed the CCTV while he was at it.

"Some of the footage is encrypted," he said, touching a finger to his neural plug. "Downloading it now. How much you want to bet they scramble the backdoor cams on delivery day?"

Then he pushed his smart-glove's thumb up against the door to trigger the lock reset, and they were in.

It wasn't their first break-and-enter, but Finch's nerves prickled, and his breath came hot and fast inside his hood as he led the way. Through the main dining area, into the metal maze of kitchens, down the row of freezers to the windowless door. It had a physical lock, for which they had a prybar, and it came unsealed with a dull echoing crack. Cold air slithered out from underneath, billowing around their ankles. Finch shoved the door open and the lights flickered on.

Nothing out of the ordinary met them. The walls were furred with frost, and dark stains had seeped into the concrete floor. Six porpoise-sized slabs of pure vat meat, covered in filmy membrane, dangled from ceiling hooks. Finch sealed the door behind them, relishing the rush of cold.

"This must be the right freezer," Blake said. "It's the only one with a Faraday mesh." He shook his head like a wet dog. "Fucking feels like someone stuffed steel wool in my implants. Can't touch my cloud. Whatever's in here, they don't want anyone transmitting camfeed of it." He folded his arms across his chest and shivered, breath coming out in a puff of steam.

"Guess we start opening them up until the candy falls out." Finch stepped in close to the first slab, spun the prybar in his hand, and swung. Instead of cracking against frozen meat, the prybar sank several inches deeper into the gluey membrane than seemed possible. Finch yanked the tool free with a sucking noise and let it clatter to the floor. Then, digging into the top of the membrane with both hands, he peeled it away in sticky ammonia-smelling ropes.

"Bust it, Unit," Blake said through chattering teeth. "Dig that shit."

Finch grunted in reply, working himself into a rhythm, breathing clean cold air. A shape was emerging beneath, something vaguely familiar, and then —

The lights flicked out.

Blake turned his yelp into a nervous laugh. "Oh, fuck, Unit, that scared me," he said. Finch heard his hand scrape against the wall, and a second later the fluorescents sputtered back on. "Someone put the timer to five minutes. I'll dial it back . . ."

Finch blinked. Hanging from the hook in front of him, with the last shreds of membrane dangling off it like tentacles, was a plastic-wrapped human body.

Blake fell silent for a second, then put both hands on his head. "Fuck me," he muttered. "So she's doing mob work. Shit, Unit, this is bad shit. Maybe we should gut check. Maybe we don't want to blackmail someone who does disposal for a family."

Finch barely heard him. There was something unnervingly familiar about the slope of the shoulders, the shape of the skull. He only had to peel a corner, letting a tuft of red hair escape, to know. But he kept peeling until the face came clear. A wider nose, a thinner brow, maybe. More or less, it was what he'd seen in a mirror at fourteen, back in the biolabs where he'd played host to all the viral and pharmaceutical trials that would have been illegal to perform on a full human. The clones who died and were sent for dissection looked an awful lot like this on the gurney.

Finch thought back to the black-shrouded alcove. The restaurant business was all about novelty, Carrow had said. She loved her little ironies, Vick had said.

"The cameras." Finch swallowed. "Is there any footage from the private dining?"

Blake blinked stupidly, still staring at the hanging Neanderthal. "Uh. Yeah. Yeah, it's that encrypted shit. I'm just putting it . . . together." He squeezed his eyes shut, working his neural plug. His mouth wrenched downward. "Unit, I don't think you want to see this."

"Show me." Finch's voice came in a rasp he barely recognized as his own.

Blake wordlessly spread the fingers of his smart-glove and set a flickering projection against the blood-stained floor. Finch found himself looking down at a half-dozen diners wearing designer fashions and party masks, most of them drinking too quickly from their flutes, laughing nervously. The smartglass table, unwatched, was playing out a snowy scene with small black figures.

All the masked heads turned as two white-clad servers wheeled in the naked upright corpse of a neo, limbs spread like the Vitruvian Man, muscles waxed and airbrushed. They'd used a nerve clamp on his face, giving him wide eyes and a feral grin. The recording was soundless, but Finch could imagine what the server was saying as she highlighted a pectoral, a thick thigh, a denuded cock. All excellent cuts. Finch realized he already knew what it would taste like when cooked.

He managed to yank the balaclava off before bile spilled up his throat and sinuses and out, searing hot. Blake hopped backward to avoid the splatter. When it was over, Finch breathed in. Deep. Blew a clotted chunk out of his stinging nostril.

"Unit, you alright?" Blake's voice was wavery as he switched off the projection. "That's so fucked. So pure fucked. You eat something with cheese today? That's probably why you hurled so hard. Fuck."

Finch clutched at his abdomen like he might be able to claw it out entirely. He spat again and again, but supper's aftertaste kept coming back.

"I mean, all the old labs got shut down, right, but that genome's still floating around, right? That company in Sao Paulo, must be a front for some scuzzy black market operation, some warehouse thing." Blake had pulled off his own mask, was running an anxious finger around his plugs. "Sticks them into the system as medical cadavers, ships them up here. Neo a la carte, right? Brazil hasn't done up Referendum 88 yet. It might even be legal there."

Finch gathered himself, looking from the steaming puddle to the hanging body to Blake, who was shifting foot to foot, clutching himself against the cold. For a moment, the air seemed to shiver and warp.

"I've got the snaps." Blake tapped his temple. "Recorded you being sick, too, just because, you know, it makes it seem more real. This is so fucked, Unit. So, so fucked."

Finch slowly nodded. His head was coming clear, the heat in his stomach replaced by a ball of black ice. He was going to murder Vick. He was going to murder Carrow, too.

Blake's next words jarred him out of the revenge fantasy. "Unit, think how much Carrow will pay to keep this quiet."

"What do you mean, keep this quiet?" Finch croaked. "This isn't some money laundering thing. She's butchering them. Us. For meat."

Blake put his ungloved hand on Finch's midsection, knowing better than to try for the out-of-reach shoulder. "Finch. Unit. I didn't see this coming. I swear." His voice turned wheedling.

"But we have to remember the plan, Unit. This is ideal blackmail material. This could be a kingmaker."

Finch jerked him toward the open freezer, harder than he'd meant to. "Look at him, would you?"

"It looks like you," Blake conceded, wresting his gooseflesh arm away. "But it's not you. Hundreds of people look like you, Finch. They're not you. For all we know, this one had its brains blunted as soon as it came out of the exo-womb. It could be a frozen fucking vegetable."

"Doesn't matter," Finch said. "Doesn't matter. Carrow's getting fucked for this."

Blake moaned. Stamped his foot against the concrete. "Unit, you don't care about politics. You care about your gravity gym, and your beard, and getting laid, and getting paid. Right? That's what we're getting out of this. Paid. She'll cough up a fortune to make this go away. A fortune."

Before Finch could form his slip-sliding thoughts into a reply, a voice came from the door.

"Bullets are actually pretty fucking cheap." Vick had managed to stuff his Mohawk into the camosuit, but it flopped limply across his scalp as he pulled off the hood. His head floated over a vaguely man-sized shimmer in the air. A handgun hung suspended in front of it. "Supper didn't agree with you, Finch? Can't believe you actually ate it."

Finch was halfway to his throat before Blake wrapped around his arm from behind, clinging like a bird.

Vick grinned. His lips were tinged purple. "This your little fucktoy? No wonder Ms. Carrow couldn't get a rise out of you. Maybe that's the real reason Neanderthals went extinct, huh?" He drifted the gun from Finch to Blake and back. "Personally, I think we just hunted you all down like animals."

Finch swallowed. "Your boss loves neos so much she could just eat one up, is that it?"

"She's a fucked-up woman," Vick admitted. "And too trusting when it comes to knuckle-draggers. I knew you were shifty from day one. Hands on the wall, both of you."

Finch's swirling head was finally beginning to crystallize. Things seemed clear and bitingly sharp as he crossed to the wall and pushed his palms up against it. The cold stung his hands red. Beside him, Blake followed suit. He was shaking.

"I'd put that gun down if I was you," Blake barked. "Everything in here is uploaded to my cloud. Soon as you pull that trigger, it's everywhere."

Finch didn't have time to warn him before Vick smashed his face into the wall. When Blake brought his head back upright, his eyes were cloudy and blood bloomed from his nose.

"Faraday mesh," Vick said. "You can't send shit from in here. Now, in Ms. Carrow's absence, I'm going to make an executive decision and pulp the two of you."

"You really just camped out here in camo on the off-chance I was planning a robbery?" Finch asked. He saw Vick's handgun wobble slightly in his peripherals.

"I told her you were shifty." The handgun steadied, but Vick's teeth were half-chattering when he spoke. "Told her you were from some radical fucking Neo Rights paramilitary. Told her someone must have tipped you off about Carnivor."

Blake's forehead was pushed hard against the cold concrete and he was licking blood and snot from under his nose, tears tracking slowly down his cheeks, but Finch forced himself to laugh. "That's what you think? Paramilitary? I'm a criminal, shithead. We thought your boss was muling meth, and we were going to blackmail her."

The handgun trembled again when Vick shivered. "Then you're a fucking idiot for not figuring it out sooner. Caveman to the core."

"How about you and me go bare knuckle?" Finch suggested. "You always wanted a try, remember? Anyone can put a slug in a skull. Not anyone can say they fist-fought a neo. Come on, Vicky."

Finch was ready for it when a forearm slammed the back of his neck. "I'm going to eat you, caveman," Vick hissed in his ear, burrowing the gun under Finch's shoulder blade. "I'm going to eat your corpse. Think about that. Maybe a bit stringy. I'll still eat it."

"Vicky," Finch repeated. "She call you that when she throws you around in bed? Does she make you dye your hair red and get your skin bleached?"

The gun slid up to knock against the back of Finch's skull. He tried not to shudder. Blake's beetle black eyes were wide and he was mouthing what looked like *shut up, Unit, shut the fuck up.*

"You'll never be a real caveman, though," Finch said. "Poor circulation. Good luck in the Ice Age."

He slammed his hand backward into Vick's wobbling wrist, flinging himself away from the wall. The gun went off; he felt the sonic clap like a bludgeon to the skull and for a wild moment he thought he'd been shot. The lights flicked out—Finch remembered they were on a timer, remembered Blake had dialled it back—then his hands found Vick's neck and he forgot about everything but crushing his trachea.

A leg hooked him down and they fell to the floor; his sole slipped off the frozen vomit, and his kneecap cracked against the concrete. Metal bounced against his elbow and skittered away—the gun was gone. Vick scrabbled at his hands, clawing with manicured nails, but Finch held tight and tighter until the kicks became sluggish and Vick made a ragged vibration deep in his chest and the cartilage finally gave way. The puff of dead man's air caught Finch in the face. He retched.

"Unit, you going to throw up again?" came Blake's brittle voice, swimming through the fading keen in Finch's ears. "He dead? I been sitting on his legs. Unless that's you. You dead?"

"No. You?"

Blake's fingers found Finch's face in the dark; Finch found Blake's numb lips and kissed them softly.

"Unit," he mumbled. "Vomit breath."

൦ൠ

They left Vick crumpled on the freezer floor and stumbled their way to the fire exit, Finch limping, Blake stubbornly trying to support some of his weight. The street outside became a silent movie as Finch's hearing slipped away again. He could mostly hear his breathing, and blood swirling in his inner ear as they staggered down the block. Blake's voice was tinny and indistinct. It took him a while to realize what he was saying.

"It's uploaded, Unit. The clone in Carnivor's freezer. Those cams from private dining. Everything Vicky said. All in my cloud now." Blake raised his gloved hand and pressed a fingertip to Finch's plug. "Look."

Finch shut his eyes and saw the events of the past half hour race past in digital. Peeling back the membrane. Watching the smart-glove projection. Vick's disembodied head. The gun. He found his good leg trembling.

"All you have to do is disperse it," Blake said. "If that's what you want. I figure blackmailing someone as psychotic as Carrow is a shit plan anyway."

Finch hesitated for only a second before he selected dispersal and watched the web traffic begin to swell. The snaps and captions and visual/audio recordings began to expand outward, link by link, blooming like argon across forums and news recyclers. By morning, it would be everywhere.

"Of course, we need to get the fuck out of Dodge, now," Blake admitted. "Unless you think you can stand up to, you know, legal scrutiny and shit. We can swing down to the coast. San Diego again. You go back to bouncing, I leave off net scamming and try to find something legit. No more B&E, no more blackmail, no more getting mixed up with units who kill units." He paused. "You know. Boring shit."

"West Coast might not be far enough," Finch said, opening his eyes. "We'll be famous after this."

"Unit, I know." He blinked. "Autocab's on its way. It'll meet us up on the corner."

They staggered on in silence. It had rained while they were inside; the sidewalk was slick. The lampposts flickered on in sequence as they passed underneath.

"Brazil is pretty far," Finch said slowly, watching their shadow hobble along on long dark stilts. "Sao Paulo."

Blake stared at him, incredulous. "You mean go find that illegal clone factory, right? You trying to be a hero or something? Going paramilitary on me?"

Finch exhaled a long plume of breath into the cold air as the autocab pulled up to the curb. "That list you made. The things I care about. You should have been on it."

Blake fixed him with a piercing look. "Yeah?"

"Yeah. Up near the top. Beard-level, maybe." Blake laughed; Finch tried to grin. "And under that, I think it's time to make room for some other shit."

"Hero shit, you mean," Blake said, leaning back on the autocab.

"I'd view it more as self-improvement."

"I'll think about it, Unit. No promises."

Finch opened the door, Blake bypassed the payment screen, and the cab slid off into the night, flashing nearby attractions and restaurant suggestions on the upholstery. They watched in real time, without speaking, as Carnivor dropped off the list.

TRIBES

A.M. Dellamonica

Ling Yuan was the only one who saw the bird.

He had glossy jet-black feathers, a sharp beak, and a necklace made of clamshell and crumpled tinfoil. When he flew through the Science Room, gusts raised by his wings tore the spectral cobwebs off the teacher.

From beak to tail, he was as big as a shopping cart.

Just another ghost in a haunt-crammed school. Ling turned back to the window. Out on the lawn her own spook, Xian, was waiting. They'd been playing Faces. Ling mugged—faking joy, sorrow, silliness—and the ghost struck poses that copied her mood.

Resembling for the most part a just-grown doe, Xian had the tail of an ox, the sturdy hooves of a pony, and a bay coat shot through with gold and turquoise strands. Her head was recognizably that of a deer, with placid brown eyes and splayed ears. Hidden within her muzzle, though, were the razored teeth of a wolf.

Ling aped exaggerated surprise, mouthing the word 'Boo!' Xian sprang upward, then wobbled around weak-kneed, faking panic and its aftermath.

A sudden wave of stench—smoke, burning hair—interrupted the game. Coughing, Ling scanned the room. Marianne Schroeder and one of her Prettygirl minions were singeing the ends off Stacy's braids. A marble gargoyle—like Xian and the bird, invisible to the others—was egging them on.

Mr. Rupert shook free of his chair. "Shouldn't we all be in our assigned seats?"

A sigh ran through class. Gretchen pocketed her lighter and

released Stacy's hair. Ling joined a wary group of fellow-students at a table; it was her, Marianne, Roger from Yearbook, and a hulking kid named Brett who mostly hung out in Shop.

As groups of friends broke apart, the haunts in the room shifted uncomfortably, unsure who to shadow. Several glided off, no doubt headed for other classrooms where the lines of allegiance were clearer.

Talons clicking, the bird bounced up to the front. To Ling's surprise, Mr. Rupert looked straight at it.

"Who are you?"

"New Student," it cawed.

Ling covered her left eye—her *seeing* eye. The haunts vanished, and instead of a big bird perched on the edge of the teacher's desk, she saw a boy of about sixteen, with feathery black hair and red-brown skin.

"Say hello to Jake Raven, everyone," Mr. Rupert said, triggering some half-hearted mumbles. "Jake, tell us something about yourself."

"Glad you asked," Jake said. "I created the world—feel free to thank me later—and stole the sun, stars and moon to light it. I found the People in a clamshell . . ."

"Very funny," Mr. Rupert interrupted. "I was so hoping we'd get another comedian. Take a seat, please."

Birdboy hopped over to an empty chair. Two seconds later, Eddie Cojo showed up.

Eddie had been gone for two weeks, but he looked like he still belonged in a hospital. Stitches criss-crossed his face, and his arm was entombed in a cast. Running from fingertips to elbow, the plaster was—like everything that got within range of Eddie's pen or carving blade—enlivened with hand-drawn doodles, traditional Haida figures, skewed and altered into capering cartoons. He wasn't walking so much as shuffling, moving as if every step hurt.

Eddie spotted 'Jake' perching on a desk near the window.

Clack of beak, ruffle of feathers. "Hey, cousin," Jake said. He sounded friendly enough.

All he got in return was a scowl. Eddie pointedly tapped his sling with one finger before picking an empty seat on the opposite side of the room. Hunched over the broken arm, he began to draw.

He'd sit there for the rest of the day, if he could, outlining and inking without saying a word.

But nobody got left alone, did they? Two weeks before, the boys' basketball team had surrounded Eddie in the schoolyard. Ling saw their team spook, a kraken, hissing encouragement and gliding among the ball players, who cheered as their star center, Mike Shaughnessy, stomped and kicked Eddie. Blue scales glinting in the sun, the water-serpent swam through the grass like it was water, undulating through the sod.

All the students had been out in the yard, clustered into clubs. Marianne and her Prettygirls were up on the bleachers. The best view from which to preside over the slaughter, Ling had thought, helpless and furious.

Ling's sister Polly had told her that the haunts took a student each year, sometime between First Term Finals and Club Day. It was inevitable, Polly insisted—sighted or not, there was nothing the Yuan girls could do but make sure it wasn't them.

And maybe that was true, but Ling had decided to try protecting Eddie. She'd tried to show him what the school was, to make him *see*, to save him. It hadn't worked; all she'd done was embarrass herself.

So she'd thought, anyway. Then two weeks ago, as Mike raised his boot, as the kraken licked its chops and all the spooks moved in to witness the end, Eddie straightened from his curled, hands-over-head position on the ground. "Can't you do something?" he'd said, lips dribbling blood as he spoke, each word oddly calm and measured. As if he wasn't getting the crap kicked out of him. As if he wasn't about to die.

Did I do it after all? Ling wondered, at the time. Can he *see*?

A raven dove off the school roof then, cawing, buzzing the Basketball Boys. Flinching away, they gave Eddie a chance to lurch clear of their circle. Leaping the school's boundary wall, he'd staggered into the street . . . only to get pasted by a westbound car.

Now here he was, stitched and plastered, glaring at Jake, so pissed Ling didn't think he noticed the predatory grins of the Basketball Boys.

Tribes by A.M. DELLAMONICA

"Good to have you back, Ed." Mr. Rupert was on his feet, passing out booklets and peering at faces. Mostly teachers didn't notice *anything* that happened at MacKenzie Secondary. If they got free of the cobwebs and happened to catch you misbehaving, they'd send you to Detention. The study cubicle outside Miss Marino's office was where the haunts' power was at their strongest. An hour there was enough to make kids start eating their own hair; half a day could give them heart failure.

"As you know, class, there's been some violence . . ." The title of the handout was *Student Guide to Talking Through Conflict*.

Eyes glazed. Kids yawned. The Prettygirls reached for their phones. But before text messages started flying, a spider dropped down from the fluorescent lights and began webbing Mr. Rupert up again.

The teacher wandered back to his chair.

There was a relieved murmur as everyone shoved the booklets aside and returned to their friends. Stacy, clutching her singed braid and a recent exam, begged her way into the circle of Honours students. Three girls from the Drama Club clustered around Ling. At MacKenzie Secondary, safety lay in numbers.

The kraken flicked Jazinda a threatening glance as she settled next to Ling. Xian immediately leapt through the window, landing between Jaz and the kraken. Head lowered, she pawed at the ground, threatening to butt. The kraken undulated backward, sinking into the floor until only the tops of its eyes were visible.

Ling closed her left eye and the haunts vanished. Everyone was watching the new kid. Nobody else—well, except maybe Eddie—could tell he was a bird.

If he had really been a boy, it would have been hard to guess where Jake fit. He looked stringy and agile, possibly right for the track team. He was cute, but his clothes weren't expensive enough to get him in with the Liberty Heights kids. Maybe the jazz band?

He smiled at her, head tilted.

Ling opened both eyes, making him a bird again. Xian reappeared, along with the others—the gargoyle, Marianne's blonde prince, the spider, still working on Mr. Rupert, and the leprechaun who hung with the Honours students.

Jake hopped across the desks toward Eddie.

The kraken hissed and Mike Shaughnessy feinted in Jake's direction, lashing a foot out at ankle-busting height. The bird hopped sideways, delicately blowing a feather through the kraken's leering jaws and down its open throat. There was a snap, and the intended kick went into a chair. Mike turned purple; the kraken reared back as if slapped.

Jake winked at Eddie, who glowered and kept cartooning. Feathers fluffing, the bird sat beside him.

Coughing up the feather violently, the kraken circled the room. It wanted someone to chew on; Ling could feel it.

Seconds later, a Goth Princess turned on one of her own, slapping the boy beside her with a velvet-gloved hand, then shoving him forcefully away.

The outcast, Andy Holmes, sputtered a weak protest as the kraken coiled around his feet. The Basketball Boys started up a low, rhythmic taunt: "Homo Holmes, Homo Holmes, fag, fag, fag."

଼

At lunchtime, Ling sent Xian to watch over her fellow Drama Queens before heading down to Props, a musty warren under the gymnasium stage where the school stored its theatre costumes and set pieces.

She had used a couple of screens to wall off a niche for herself, a corner that held a faded red recliner and an old brass candleholder. The space was no bigger than a closet, but she could doze, read scripts by candlelight, or eat her lunch in peace . . . all without *seeing*.

She was working her way through a damp tuna fish sandwich and Ionesco's *Rhinoceros* when the trapdoor into Props squeaked. Ling quickly blew out the candlelight. That was too close.

Eddie's voice echoed down. "I saved your ass, man. You let that car hit me."

"You're not dead, are you?" The other voice was a low croak — Jake.

"Yet," Eddie said.

"Meaning?"

Click! The overhead lights blazed to life. "See these memorial plaques, Jake? A student goes nuts or gets fucked up or mostly just dies, every year just before Club Day. It's because of these ... spook things ... all over school. Isn't that right?"

"Obviously."

"Can't you get rid of them?"

"Rid? No. Stop 'em, maybe."

Ling pressed her right eye to the crack between the two screens. But for Eddie's injuries, they looked like an ordinary pair of boys. Jake was dusting the plaques with his sleeve.

"Your school's divided into factions and territories," he said. "Gym belongs to the kraken, zombie hangs out in the parking lot with the stoners, the qi-lin lives here on stage—"

"Qi-lin," interrupted Eddie. "The Drama spook—the deer?"

"Ling's deer." Something about being named scraped her skin, like a cold butter knife dragging over her flesh.

"So?"

"One sacrificial student a year," Jake murmured. "Spooks here, sleeping. I wonder why they're awake now?"

"You're asking me?" Eddie said.

"I'm not asking you, actually." Jake turned his head, looking straight into Ling's peering eye.

Dammit. He knew. He was of the spirit world, and he was asking her.

Reluctantly she emerged from her corner.

Eddie whirled, startled, his good fist raised and the plaster cast crossed protectively over his chest. It wasn't much of a threat, but suddenly Xian was galloping down the steps, placing herself in front of Ling, head lowered to butt as she pawed at the floor. The pose sparked a dim urge within Ling to shove Eddie. Kick his ass off our turf, part of her whispered.

"It's okay," Ling said softly to Xian, who snorted in disbelief. She ached to touch the gold and turquoise mane; instead, she kissed the air between the big deer eyes. The qi-lin's expression softened. Ling's urge to protect Props faded.

Eddie peered behind her screen. "This is where you vanish to?"

He did notice when she wasn't around. Ling fought a smile.

"Flirt on your own time, kids." Jake stretched his talons.

Eddie bristled. "We aren't—"

"Come on, Ling. Cough up."

"My sister sees, same as me," Ling interrupted. Her face was warm, and she locked her eyes on Jake. "It's a family thing. She went here before me. Marianne Schoeder's sister Ellie was her best friend."

Jake let out a little rattle. "And . . .?"

Ling made herself go on. "Ellie had a stone. It's smooth and round, like a mooncake. Someone found it, way back. Maybe thirty years ago?"

"Way back," Jake said. "You newborns."

"The grade twelves say one student keeps the stone, and before they graduate they have to pass it on. The keeper of the mooncake stone is protected. Their spook is strongest."

And solid. She looked at Xian, imagined touching her, and her eyes watered.

"They never get caught up in the warfare?" Eddie asked.

"No. Not them, not their friends. The Prettygirls rise above it all."

"And they decide who's the human sacrifice each year," Jake grunted.

Ling shook her head. "The spooks use us to fight each other through the first term, until winter break. When we come back to classes in January, whichever haunt's won, whichever group's strongest, they take an outcast . . ."

"And eat him?" Jake asked.

"This year, it's Boys' Basketball." She shivered. Their kraken had been drooling over Eddie from day one of the school year. "To stay off the menu, you need to have a spook of your own. You have to qualify to get into a club."

"Qualify," Eddie repeated.

"Rite of passage," said Jake. "Standard spirit stuff."

Eddie frowned at Ling. "When you kissed me last month, the week before the accident—"

Ling interrupted again; she wasn't going to talk about that, not in front of Jake. "In Drama, you audition for a show. That's how you get Xian to protect you."

"Your sister told you this?" Jake asked.

"She wanted to be sure I'd join a club," Ling said. "Polly's naturally outgoing, popular."

"I get it. She was afraid you'd end up dead because you're shy?"

Eddie laughed. "Shy? Her?"

"She's hiding in the school basement, kid."

In the fall musical, Ling had played Queen Victoria. Now she wrapped herself in that royal persona, raising her chin, as if the boys were nothing, fleas on the carpet. "Polly never knew where the spooks came from, Jake."

"Oh, that part I know." The bird pecked at a cheap plastic totem pole. "I put 'em here."

"You?" Eddie said.

Jake nodded. "Couple hundred years ago, these spirits were overrunning the forest, complicating life for the People."

Ling said. "What people?"

"*The* People." Eddie pointed from a doodle on his cast—a stylized Native bear—to his red-brown skin, so like Jake's.

"Ah," she said, embarrassed.

Preening his chest feathers, Jake continued, "The spooks traveled here with settlers from overseas. European ghosts, Chinese ones, Japanese, African. When they landed, though, the spirits didn't have proper holy sites. No ancestral homes, no power places. They were drawn to ours. They scared off the fish during the salmon run, lured women over cliffs, brought dead warriors back to life . . ."

"Enough, we get it," said Eddie.

"The People came to me. 'Raven, they said, can't you oust these bums?' I might've said no, but I'd just convinced this juicy frog to jump down my gullet, only to find out he was magic. Enchanted prince, some bullshit. Down in my belly, he's yelling to get out. Swears the next time some girl kisses me—and girls do kiss me—" he purred to Ling.

"Girls kiss all kinds of people," Eddie grunted. Ling, still playing Victoria, ignored him.

"Imagine getting kissed with an enchanted prince in your gut. He turns into a man, you get blown up from the inside out. I'd

had to puke the frog up. I was hungry, pissed off, inconvenienced
. . ."

"Yeah," Eddie said. "Your life's a vale of tears."

"Is heckling me your way of asking for help, Cojo?"

"Helping? Letting me get hit by a car?"

"Wah wah. Off the sacrificial altar and into a tiny collision. You
came out ahead, kid."

Ling broke in. "What's this have to do with school?"

"Back then this was part of the forest." Jake smiled, and it was
an old man's smile, his skin wrinkling like her grandfather's. "It
was a hollow in the hills, with cedars like a roof over top. The
tallest tree for miles stood here, and I had a nest in it. A holy
place. A lodge."

"So . . .?" Ling leaned against a prop sofa.

"I invited the invading haunts to a potlatch. My valley was
the kind of place that drew 'em; most came figuring they could
wrestle it out from under me. I fed them salmon and berries and
venison steaks, offered them smoke, opium—everything they
wanted. Gave 'em presents, got 'em laid . . . it was one stupendous
party. Finally they got tired. 'Hey, Host, where we gonna sleep?
The forest floor's covered in rocks and hunks of wood.'"

Eddie curled up, cross-legged on the floor, wrapped in the
story.

"I had to provide, eh? I rolled up a section of the forest floor, and
underneath was a layer of soft soil. 'Here,' said I. They curled up,
and kept right on complaining. 'Hey, Host, we're cold.' So I shook
off some feathers to give 'em a blanket. Were they finally happy?
'Course not. Wah, wah, these stars are too damned bright. 'Lie
down and shut your eyes,' I said, and when every troublesome
piece-of-shit myth was on its back, eyes shut, I rolled the forest
back over top of them. Made it nice and dark and warm. They
started to snore. All I had to do then was lay out a square of rocks
to hold down the edges of the land and leave them to sleep."

"But now?" Eddie asked.

Jake shrugged. "I'm guessing there's a hole in the seam around
the blanket. A mooncake sized hole, if what Ling's saying is
true. Twenty-five years ago some kid pried up one of my rocks,
and now there's a little light and noise creeping in. Those Van

Winkling gods hear you kids, trapped and bored, tearing into each other. They're drawing power from the warfare."

"You're saying it's our fault?" Eddie scoffed.

"I'm saying we find this stone and put it back, they'll doze off again." Jake tilted his head, eyeing Ling. "Can you get it from Marianne?"

She imagined school without the haunts. An ordinary school with ordinary classes. Teachers, petty fights and a safer place.

But Xian. . . . She looked into the qi-lin's eyes, felt the love there.

Maybe . . . maybe she didn't have to give up Xian. Maybe, with Jake around, the dying would stop.

"Ling?"

She shook her head.

"Suit yourself, toots. But remember—you dragged me into this."

Her? How? By kissing Eddie and giving him the sight?

With one thunderous wing flap, Jake vanished upstairs, leaving them alone.

Eddie looked at her through narrowed eyes, his sliced, stitched face wearing the critical frown he turned on his cartoons.

Ling shifted. He was between her and the staircase. "So . . . you saved Jake's ass?"

He nodded. "There's this story. Raven was cheating on a man. Um . . . doing it with the guy's wife. Husband came home, caught them, beat the crap out of Raven. Mashed him flat, broke his bones, tossed him down the outhouse."

"Ewww."

"Supposedly he didn't mind that much. In the tales, he's very philosophical about lying in sewage . . ." He spoke slowly, as if distracted, examining Xian. "Anyway, I'm at my grandfather's place, just after that Friday—well, I'd seen some weird things around school that afternoon. After you . . ."

"I remember," Ling said hastily. "Go on."

"Between you kissing me and Mike smacking me pretty hard at lunch, I thought the ghosts I'd seen, at school, were hallucinations. But when I get to Grandpa's, I hear the toilet singing."

"Singing?"

"Yeah. Guess who's down there?"

"Jake? Does that mean he cheated with ... your grandmother?"

"Let's not go there." He shuddered, raising the plaster-clad hand to his ear. "Raven talks me into putting a hook on Grandpa's fishing rod. I flush it, reel it back, and up he comes, mashed flat, stinking so bad I pass out . . ."

"Gross," Ling said. "And when you woke up?"

"Gone. I didn't think I'd see him again." Eddie rubbed the line of stitches on his cheek. "But when the Basketball Boys went after me, he turned up and buzzed 'em."

"He didn't save you from the car."

"Whatever doesn't kill you, right?"

"I hate that saying."

"Sorry." He wasn't really listening; his good hand drifted up, as if to brush her chin, or cheek.

The bell rang.

"Sorry, gotta go." Pushing past Eddie to the stairs, Ling made a run for it, Xian at her heels.

CR

Weeks passed. Tensions climbed. Gretchen pushed Fat Melissa down the stairs and Jake caught her in mid-fall. Then Marianne turned on one of the other Prettygirls, Irina, supposedly over her boyfriend. Irina almost caught a wickedly spiked volleyball with her face that day, but Jake flapped a wing and gusted it off-target.

The kraken and the Basketball Boys had switched their attention to the outcast Goth, Andy Holmes. Even with Jake running interference, the taunts of 'fag' kept coming.

"Kraken wants Andy now, doesn't it?" Eddie asked one day, looking worried and guilty, but Ling walked away without answering. After that she avoided everyone, spending her breaks reading plays, playing Face with Xian, cutting classes with the other Drama Queens and using the time to rehearse the spring musical.

Not seeing was all she could do. Raven would keep saving people. Or he wouldn't. And if he didn't, it wasn't her fault.

Weeks passed. Nobody died.

Tribes by A.M. DELLAMONICA

One afternoon when she had the stage to herself she and Xian danced, the two of them whirling around each other without quite touching. The deer's hooves struck against the wooden stage, sending off sparks, a fiery stream of gold that drifted between Ling's fingers and through her hair as she spun.

She couldn't give this up. It was *seeing* that had caused their mother's breakdown, when Ling was only ten. Polly saw the death in everyone she touched. Their younger sister screamed so much and spoke so little that Daddy had put her into a school for autistic kids.

But Xian loved her. The qi-lin made seeing bearable.

Collapsing in a panting heap to the stage floor, she was startled by the sound of clapping. Jake was perched up on one of the stage lights, watching.

She fought to still her breath as Xian glared up at him.

"If you got the stone from Marianne, Xian would be solid," he said.

"Her prince spirit wouldn't let me near her."

"So you have thought about taking it from her?"

"Why don't you grab it, Jake?"

"You think being a visionary's hard to deal with, kid? Try being at ground zero if a couple of us Old Ones go at it beak and claw. The whole damn blanket will come tearing up."

"You've been keeping everyone safe."

"Just bartering for time." He caught a ghostly spark with his beak, adding it to the clamshell necklace. "The spooks need that death every year, Ling. It's fine for you kids to fight and never resolve anything—you get out of here eventually. The haunts can't leave. Xian can't leave."

"You don't know what they can do!"

"They're stuck in a nightmare. You wake 'em up in the fall with your noise and your lust and your angsty pubescent hum. They jockey for position, they play your games, but winning means nothing if there's no prize. Bloodshed siphons off enough tension to put them to sleep while you're gone for the summer . . ."

"It's your spook garden, Jake," she interrupted. "You planted them here."

"Who gave Eddie the Sight?" His eyes were dark as storms.

"You dealt yourself in the game when you decided to save him. You want to play god? Get the stone, Ling Yuan."

"Get it yourself, asshole." With that, she ducked into the girl's shower room.

CR

Club Day was a mummery, a day-long orgy of boredom: in the morning, each school club did a presentation for the students and staff. The morning run-through was just a rehearsal. In the afternoon, all the parents and the School Board showed up for the real thing. This meant the whole school sat through the entire mind-numbingly dull show twice.

But it was anything but boring for Ling. No one had died. Yet. And the spirits would take that death today, unless Jake could keep them all safe.

The Yearbook Club opened the festivities with a slide show before yielding the stage to the Debate Society. Then—just before everyone slipped into boredom-induced coma—the Basketball Boys thundered out, each player doing a lay-up before gathering around their Regional trophy for a photo. The kraken swam amid their legs, eyes glinting.

As the band began honking its way through a Souza march, Ling saw people getting restless. Haunts glided through the gym, hungry and watchful. Blood was in the air.

The tension eased off when Eddie and Andy Holmes showed up, late, walking beside the Vice Principal, whose cobweb veils had thinned to crepe. A tiny wisp of a haunt trailed behind them, its small shape so dim Ling couldn't make out its features. Andy was holding a crudely lettered sign, orange posterboard with blue letters that read, "MacKenzie Secondary Comedy Club."

An anxious murmur ran through the assembly.

Miss Marino glared everyone into silence. "Right. We have a new club today. Ed will tell you about it."

Eddie shuffled up to the microphone. It howled feedback, and he fumbled it off. "Anyone can join," he said. "You have to tell a joke. It can be the dumbest thing you ever heard. It can be 'Why did the chicken cross the road? To get to the other side.' See, I'm done. Knock-knock jokes, whatever. That's our initiation."

Andy stepped up, reading from a printed page, some joke about a parrot in a freezer that had been making the rounds on the internet.

The wispy haunt became more substantial, and Ling saw it was a white hound, a puppy with reddish ears.

"Wonder what's that supposed to be," she muttered.

"Hunting dog of Arawn, I think."

She jumped. Jake Raven was behind her, body canted forward so his beak was inches from her ear.

"Arawn was the Welsh god of the underworld. Okay guy, I guess. Kinda morbid. Eddie's grandfather—the fellow with the cute Haida wife and the short temper—is from Swansea."

She tipped up her chin, retreating behind her Victorian lady face again.

"This is bogus!" the basketball captain bellowed.

"We got a club form from the office and we got an initiation," Eddie shouted, over a rising wasp-hum of student voices.

Suddenly, Emily staggered out of the bleachers, clutching her oft-burned hair. Hoots and growls rose around her, and someone threw a paper coffee cup. Latte sprayed out, staining her dress.

"Emily!" Eddie waved her over.

She ran to the stage, mounting the steps two at a time. "How many teachers does it take to screw in a light bulb?"

The voices rose to a howl, drowning out the punch line. The white puppy got larger.

Another kid got ejected from his pack—tripping down the bleachers, propelled, no doubt, by a shove. He crashed to the floor at Coach's feet, shaking him momentarily out of his webbed-up doze.

Students pushed new outcasts onto the gym floor, and Eddie kept taking them. Soon they didn't bother going onstage; they started telling jokes the second their friends turned on them. People were screaming, the din of panic amplified by the gym's echoey acoustics. Each time a group rejected one of its own, the kid would run to join Eddie.

There was nobody unprotected, nobody the kraken could kill.

The gym floor was bumping up and down under Ling's feet,

like a blanket with fighting cats underneath.

Now, all at once the other Drama Queens were pummelling Jazinda. Jazinda, who was always late for rehearsal, who could never get her lines right or sing on key. Jazinda, who'd been included at Ling's insistence, but who hadn't really worked out. They were seizing the chance to get rid of her.

"Stop!" Ling threw her arms around Jazinda's neck.

Xian was nearby, pawing at the floor, bucking. She reared, eyes wide and beseeching, and Ling was almost overcome by a sudden urge to shove Jaz away.

"No!"

The qi-lin danced in a harried circle, as if something was nipping at her flanks.

"They all need that death," Jake murmured. "Xian too."

Ling looked away.

The Prettygirls' haunt, an elegant blonde prince, glided out of the bleachers. Striding up to Miss Marino, he whispered a few words before wisping away the last of her cobwebs.

"Edward Cojo," Marino shouted, and the screaming stopped all at once. "Nobody said you could start a riot. Report to the study cubicle outside my office!"

Detention. A relieved murmur ran through the gym.

Eddie's mouth dropped open as Marino's lacquered nails closed on his shoulder. She dragged him into the hall, the white hound trotting anxiously behind. The other haunts followed: the kraken, the prince, the gargoyle, the nine-tailed fox, the Valkyrie. Xian gave Ling one cool glance before clopping out too.

Going for the kill.

For a second the only sound in the gym was panting, as if everyone had been sprinting. Then a shriek tore into the silence. The effect was instant. People slumped forward and sighed. A few girls buried their faces in their hands, sobbing in relief.

Marino clacked back in, fully shrouded and covered in busy spiders. She plucked the clipboard out of the Principal's hands. "Next club!"

"I guess that's that," said the low voice in her ear.

"No!" Ling jumped to her feet, whirling on Jake, seizing one black wing so he couldn't fly off. "You're going to save him."

"No mooncake stone, no miracle. Someone's dying today or the whole blanket shreds." He hopped back, eyes flinty, slipping out of her grip. The handful of feathers in her hand turned to a crumpled piece of paper. On it was a cartoon doodle Eddie had done: her and Xian, dancing.

"He's one of your People," she pleaded. "You owe him."

"Don't you get it, kid?" His voice was almost fond. "Eddie don't want someone else to die in his place."

Her eyes misted. "You could—"

"I'm letting him choose," he said. "Letting you choose, too."

Another shriek from the hallway.

Nothing there, she thought, nobody who can hurt him. It was a rationalization. Some of the dead kids had fatal seizures; one had hanged herself.

The world blurred.

"Take your seat, Miss Yuan," Miss Marino said.

Ling wiped her nose. The Drama Queens were sagging, weary and scared. Jaz tugged her hand, silently begging her to sit. Without Xian watching over them, they looked oddly vulnerable.

All the haunts were in Detention with Eddie, Ling thought suddenly. Watching the show. Waiting for death.

"Miss Yuan!"

She shoved her way to the gym floor, sprinting for the Prettygirls. Ignoring a burst of gasps and nervous laughter, she grabbed Marianne's purse, hauling with all her weight. The strap broke, and Ling went tumbling as she clawed for the zipper.

With a bellow, Marianne tackled her. Ling rolled, holding the purse to her chest, rooting through its contents even as she dodged Marianne's flailing claws. Lipstick and a wallet dropped out, along with a wrapped tampon and a couple of pens. A cellphone clattered across the floor.

"Give it back!" Marianne yelled.

Eddie screamed again.

There. A silk-wrapped weight, the size of a mooncake. Ling's fingers closed around it. Planting her foot against Marianne's belly, she shoved hard. Marianne fell back on her ass; Ling scrambled for the fire exit.

"Miss Yuan!"

She found Eddie on the floor inside Solitary, encircled by haunts, moving in spasms. His eyes were glazed, his mouth foamy. He had his carving blade in his hand and was chopping into the wrist of his plaster cast, shredding its doodles and signatures. He'd almost reached flesh.

Haunts were crowded around him, moaning and crooning, their voices mixing in terrible ways.

"Xian," Ling said, and the qi-lin turned to face her.

The deer's frame had filled out. She was full-grown; her hooves and teeth were made of gold. Strong and huge, she was indisputably in charge now. Her teeth glinted and the gold and turquoise in her fur shone.

The qi-lin came to her, bumping Ling's chest. It was a solid bump, not a mime. Ling gasped. Affection shone in the dark brown eyes. The sparks streaming upward from her hooves were bright multicoloured motes, streamers of fire that chimed like bells and didn't burn.

"Sweet thing," Ling crooned, putting both arms around the shaggy neck. Xian smelled of spring air and jasmine. She saw gold-lacquered doorways and crimson palaces, all the places they might explore, together . . .

All she wanted to do was stand here and hold on. But . . .

She forced herself to let go, to kneel beside Eddie and catch his flailing hands, throwing the knife away and dragging him out of Detention. The spooks followed, still whispering, hissing, moaning. The kraken headed up the pack. Marianne's prince, less handsome now, glared at her balefully.

Eddie screamed and spasmed.

"Back off," Ling told the spooks. "I don't get hurt, my friends don't get hurt. That's the deal!"

"Ed's not your friend," Jake said. He was smaller than before, a bigger-than-average bird perched up on the edge of the cubicle. "You run in different crowds, Ling. Only *Eddie's* protector can help him."

She looked at the stone in her hand—then at Xian, who drummed her hooves on the floor, inviting Ling to dance.

With a sigh, Ling pressed the stone into Eddie's hand.

Xian collapsed onto her forelegs, as if she'd been shot. She shrank to her former size, her head thrown back as if she was in pain.

Eddie's spectral puppy grew into a massive hound. Snarling, it snapped at the other ghosts, ears flopping as it drove them back.

Eddie's good hand lolled, the silk-wrapped stone loose in his palm. Ling closed her fingers around his, holding the stone in his grip. The dog began licking Eddie clean, healing his wounds with its tongue.

Eddie seemed taller now, more handsome. The stitched-up gash on his cheek became a mysterious twisting scar. His eyes opened. The cast fell away like a husk when he climbed to his feet.

The whole school was out in the hall.

People shifted. The outcasts who'd joked their way into the Comedy Club fell in around Eddie. Ling was nudged back, away from the people who mattered. The hound dog stood in front of the Comedians as they gathered. Head held high, it thrust its chest out proudly, lips curling in a doggy smile.

Eddie's eyes fell on the basketball team.

The kraken moved in front of the ball players, head weaving, teeth bared. Haunts lunged at it, testing its defences.

Andy Holmes grinned. "Payback," he muttered, and others repeated it, almost chanting. Big Mike Shaughnessy suddenly looked afraid. "Payback, payback, payback."

"Everyone, go back to rehearsal," Eddie said, and though he spoke softly, everyone filed back toward the gym.

Eddie caught Ling's hand before she could retreat. Her pulse raced. Was he going to—

He turned to Jake, holding out the stone. "What do we do with this thing? How do we stop it?"

"The stone wall around the school follows the line of rocks I'd placed to hold down the forest floor," Jake said. "There is a piece missing."

Eddie nodded and headed outside, leading them single-file: his spirit dog, Jake, then Ling and Xian.

"We don't have much time," Jake said. "The haunts still need a death today. People are confused, but the kraken's hungry."

"Split up?" Eddie suggested, and Ling nodded. He walked

to the nearest point on the stone wall and began examining it, feeling the stones with his good hand, working with the same intensity he had when he was drawing.

Ling looked at the cartoon portrait Eddie had drawn, her and Xian caught in mid-step, in perfect synch with each other, dancing in an upward stream of sparks.

Heart heavy, she turned to Xian and did a quick mime, playing a detective with an imaginary magnifying glass. "Where's the gap?" she asked.

The qi-lin raised her chin contemptuously. Queen Victoria.

"What am I going to do? Stay forever? Fail to graduate and hide in the basement, reading scripts?"

Xian drooped into her Sad Face pose.

"If Jake's right, you can go back to sleep." Tears were running down her face. "You won't have to cope with . . . with all this anymore. We'll both get out."

Just not together.

Xian didn't move right away. She stood, blinking her golden eyelashes, watchful and assessing. Finally she paced to the corner of the school grounds, out by the tennis courts where Eddie was nearly kicked to death.

Following, Ling looked over the wall. "I don't see . . ."

Xian pawed at the ground.

"Here?" Bending, she scraped at the dirt at the base of the wall, finding a thin slot where the stone should be. Digging with a finger, she exposed a mooncake-sized gap. A sour smell belched out of the exposed opening, a mix of whiskey breath, tobacco smoke and old fish.

"It's here," she shouted. Then she slumped down against the wall, pulling a sleepy face. Xian lay beside her, close as she could get without actually touching. Nose to nose, they stared into each others' eyes.

Goodbye, goodbye.

Raven lit on the wall above them.

"This is it," Eddie said. He bent to the hole, tracing its outline with his finger once before sliding the mooncake stone into place.

A feathery shiver ran through the ground. The whiskey and fish scent thinned and the air freshened. There was a jolt, so loud

Ling thought the stone wall itself had cracked.

"What's that?" Eddie asked nervously.

"Napjerk." With that, Raven began to sing. His voice wasn't sweet, but he beat his wings in a thrumming rhythm, low and regular. It was a soft croon, a soothing song, a lullaby in a language Ling didn't know.

Spirits drifted out through the school wall, heading across the lawn. They swirled and twisted and lost their shapes, drawn through the mooncake stone and down: Marianne's prince, the nine-tailed fox, the gargoyle, the leprechaun, the minotaur, the spider, the yeti, and—bringing up the rear, long tail lashing—the kraken.

Xian got to her feet, turning as if to run. She gave Ling one last glance, one last head-bob.

"Thank you," Ling whispered, still crying as the qi-lin drooped and dispersed, followed by Eddie's red-eared, white-bodied hound. When the dog was gone, Jake flapped down and pecked at the stone, wedging it in more firmly.

A long buzz—the noon bell-blatted out from the school building.

"You don't vanish too?" Eddie's voice was strained.

"Me? Was I even ever here?" Jake said, "Well, kids, don't blame me if this doesn't make your lives better. People your age, locked up all day with each other."

"We'll survive," Eddie said.

"Crazy fucking idea . . ." Raven shook out his wings. With a bow in Ling's direction, he flew straight up. She had a brief glimpse of green-filtered light and a very tall tree. Then she was just staring at the sky.

She scanned the schoolyard, which was filling with students and nothing else—no spooks, no spectral qi-lins. She closed one eye, then the other. Finally she opened them—both wide—and looked at Eddie.

"So," he said. "That Friday when you came up and kissed me."

Her cheeks warmed. "I was trying to help. I thought if you could *see* . . ."

"I'd hook up with a protector?" He stepped closer. "Join your club, maybe?"

She felt herself smile. "We *are* always short of boys."

"I can't act," he said.

"Neither can Jaz," she said.

He ran the back of his hand over her tear-smeared cheek. "What if I kissed you back?"

She put her hands on his shoulders, like before, and leaned. His mouth was ready this time, not just a surprised 'O'. His lips tasted of tart apples, and he didn't push her away this time, didn't stammer "Don't," and then flee.

"It'll fade," she said. "The *seeing* was only ever borrowed."

"I'm not sure I'd know the difference now." He looked around. "Place looks normal."

She closed and opened her left eye. "There's always something."

"Are you sure you didn't just want to kiss me?"

"Maybe. We'd have to try it some more. To be sure."

"Let's do that," he said, but before he could kiss her again they saw Miss Marino patrolling the school grounds, clacking around on her high heels with no cobwebs to slow her down.

"Step into my office and we'll talk about it." Tucking her hand into his with a smile, Ling led Eddie around to the side door of the school, heading for the privacy of the Props room.

TROUBLES

Sherry Peters

"Big day for you, Melanie, so it is," Dr. Taylor said, walking into my hospital room.

It was about time. I'd been waiting more than an hour. "You're late."

"Yes, well, there have been some troubles," Dr. Taylor said.

"Troubles?" That could be anything from mundane pickets to the more likely riots, though riots were rare in west Belfast in September. "Who is it? Protestants or Catholics?"

"Protestants, here in the neighbourhood." He handed me my meds and watched me swallow them before sitting next to me on the edge of my bed.

How many burnt out cars had my parents had to pass on their way here? "Are my parents all right?"

"They're fine; they're here and they're excited to bring you home."

I was more than ready to get out of here. The acute care unit of Belfast Mater Infirmorum was only three kilometres from my home, but I could have been on the other side of the world, I'd been that isolated. No one had come to visit me except my parents, not even Dawn. I couldn't blame her. She'd witnessed one of my freak-outs at school, yelling at the voices and everything. She hadn't acted weirded-out by me but . . . maybe she just hadn't wanted to upset me more. As long as she didn't hate me, I'd be all right.

I stifled a yawn as I dutifully accepted several bottles of tablets and Dr. Taylor's instructions on my new daily routine of self-medication. I smiled and nodded enthusiastically, promising to not go off my meds.

I had no intention of keeping my promise. I would've been happy to stay on the pills if they worked, but they didn't. Nothing worked. Not the different types of medications, nor the increasingly higher dosages, or the extreme measures of electroconvulsive therapy they'd attempted out of desperation. The voices had become louder, clearer, after that. They became real, no longer in my head. They were outside the hospital; in the streets, humming, singing, issuing orders I couldn't quite understand.

They were real. They were, I was certain. But they weren't human.

I was tired of the doctors using me as a guinea pig. I didn't belong in the psych ward. Well maybe, probably, I did, but I wasn't dangerous and I felt perfectly fine, except for the voices.

I couldn't blame my parents for sending me here. They'd talked about it for ages, well after my teachers told them I responded to questions no one had asked. My parents were convinced I needed help after an unfortunate outburst during my GCSE exams, when I was sure everyone was talking, and I yelled at my classmates— Dawn in particular—to quiet down.

My parents only wanted the best for me, but I wished I'd kept my mouth shut.

I didn't know better then. Since being here, I'd learned what to say and do, to keep from raising suspicions. I would be fine, as long as I didn't *respond* to the voices. They usually talked to each other, not me, anyway.

Once Dr. Taylor finished his instructions, I gathered my things and he walked me to Admitting where my parents waited. I waved good-bye to my fellow patients who were mostly gathered in the common room watching Hollyoaks on the telly. Everyone on my ward was either chronically depressed, bi-polar, or an emerging schizophrenic like me. All our conditions were easily managed with medication. Except for mine. But I wasn't going to tell anyone they'd failed to cure me.

It made me think schizophrenia wasn't a fitting diagnosis.

True, the voices were many, in my head and all around me, but I didn't see who was talking and they weren't talking directly to me. Of course, if that wasn't what was wrong with me, I didn't think I wanted to know what was.

"Melanie, Love," Mum said, hugging me. "You look exhausted. Are you still not sleeping?" She looked at Dr. Taylor, ready to send me back to the ward.

"I'm fine," I said. "Excited about coming home, that's all." And anxious about seeing Dawn.

"Melanie has made some very good progress, Mr. and Mrs. Macaulay," Dr. Taylor said. "She has her instructions and her routine. Keep an eye on her, but as long as she's taking her medication regularly, she will be fine. Give her a bit of time to adjust back to home life. Melanie, take it easy for a few days. Enjoy being home with your family. All being well, I will see you in a few months for a check-up."

"Thank you, Dr. Taylor," I said. I smiled and extended my hand to shake his. I was getting good at pretending to be normal.

⋐⋑

I lay in bed, curled up under my blankets thinking about the crowds we'd seen gathering at the corner of Tennent and Crumlin Road on our way home from the Mater. Some were wee ones as young as five, getting ready to riot. Flash-riot by text. That was usually how people heard about them these days. Our car had barely driven through the converging mob when police lines formed behind us. The Good Friday Agreement had been seven years ago; that was supposed to mean the worst of the violence was over. I was only a kid then, but even I could tell not much had really changed. Political tension was as high as ever, and riots were all too common.

Shouting started up outside my window, making me jump. By the sound, a crowd must have filled up the street like a big block party. Their words, though, were anything but party-like. They were bleak, full of hate and reminders of wrongs done. The people sounded like the hard men of the paramilitaries, except their voices weren't quite normal. They were singing or whispering at the same time they were shouting. These were not the paramilitary leaders; these were the voices, and they were the loudest I'd heard them on any night other than July 11:

bonfire night, the night we celebrated King Billy and the Glorious Revolution, the night before Protestant Northern Ireland marched to celebrate British rule.

I got out of bed. I'd looked out into the streets many times before, believing I could see who was talking. I'd been unsuccessful then, so I didn't know what made me think I would be successful now. Maybe it was because there were so many of them, they were so loud, so clear. They had to be real. Maybe that was it. I needed them to be real so I could justify leaving the hospital and telling everyone that I was fine now.

I pulled back my curtains.

There were men out there! Real men! Were they the voices?

I blinked a few times. Why was this time different?

I thought back to one of my last electroconvulsive therapy treatments. It had felt like something in my brain had clicked together, like puzzle pieces had been rubbing against each other before snapping into place. Dr. Taylor had said that was the relief I was supposed to have from my illness. That had been the moment the voices left my head completely and were more real than ever. I'd looked once or twice out my hospital-room window, but I'd only ever seen the brick wall of the neighbouring building.

I wasn't at the Mater now. I was at home, and I could clearly see there were men out there, though they were blurry, only half-solid. Around a dozen of these men hovered outside the bedroom windows of the brick semi-detached two-up-two-down houses on my street.

Hovered.

They had *wings*.

Big black wings made of some kind of webbing that shimmered in the light of the streetlamps. They looked like giant, man-sized, black butterflies.

That couldn't be.

I stepped back from my window and rubbed my eyes. Had I imagined the wings?

I looked again. Winged men. Like fay—only fay were mythical. They hovered outside the second-storey windows, whispering and singing. I pinched myself, hard. I was wide awake.

One man walked up and down the street, his wings tucked

back, barking orders to the others. He pointed at the twenty-foot green metal security gate at the end of the street, closing us off from Springfield Road and the Catholics on the other side.

"Remind them that their tradition has been stolen," he bellowed.

His words stirred a fuzzy memory of the time my primary school was attacked by an angry mob—Catholics—throwing stones at us as in the playground. A wave of fury surged through me.

"They're being punished because the city built the wall on the wrong side of Springfield," he raged. "They're being blocked from their birthright."

The whispers of the others changed; they repeated the rhetoric of the bloke on the street. These were the same lines we'd been fed every year during Parade Season, especially when the Orange Order wanted to march through the security gate and up Springfield to the Whiterock Orange Lodge. The words had been poisonous enough then. Now, they carried a lethal combination of weight and induced obedience. I shook my head, trying to dislodge their toxicity.

It was as if these winged men expected a parade. Soon.

But what parade? The Whiterock parade was supposed to have been in June, but the Parades Commission had said the Orange Lodges had to march up Workman and through the old Foundry site behind my place. The Orange Order had protested and gone into negotiations with the Parades Commission. I'd gone into the Mater and I thought the parade had gone on. Mum and Dad hadn't said otherwise.

The fellow on the street—the boss, I figured—opened up his wings then, and with a bit of a push, was up and walking along the razor wire topping the security gate.

Dream? Hallucination? I'd already pinched myself—

I wanted a better look.

I needed binoculars.

Dad was snoring. Now was my chance. I crept downstairs, stepping as lightly as possible. Every stair creaked a little and I prayed Dad wouldn't wake up. I retrieved the family binoculars from the kitchen drawer where Mum kept them to watch the birds on the clematis bushes that covered the section of Peace Line that made up our back fence.

I stopped to look at the calendar Mum had tacked to the wall by the phone. *Melanie home* was written faintly in pencil. Dad's trip to see the Glasgow Rangers play the Celtics was in pen with stars around it. The same with the Orange Lodge meetings, and Mum's volunteer shifts with the Lodge. And there it was: the Whiterock Orange Lodge parade, the one that had been originally planned for June 25, was there: Saturday, September 10. Two days away.

That fit with what I'd seen outside my bedroom.

Back in the privacy of my room, I parked myself at my window, binoculars pressed to my eyes, focused in on the nearest winged man outside the neighbour's window.

The boss was back on the narrow street, standing on top of a blue Vauxhall outside Dawn's house, two doors down. "The Orangemen must be allowed to march. The police are not on their side. The army is not on their side. The government is not on their side. Authority must be destroyed." Again, threads of fury wove through my thoughts, urging me to fight. I pushed them back.

Even with the help of the magnifying lenses the boss didn't get any clearer. A hallucination wouldn't get clearer with binoculars. *Crap.* The edges of the red bricks of the house were distinguishable, down to the occasional tiny crack and crevice. He remained only partly there, translucent. I could see the bricks and white window frame right through him.

Who were they? *What* were they?

The boss stopped and looked up at me. He cocked his head to the side, watching me.

He hopped off the car and walked toward my house, toward me, cautiously, as you would approach a wild animal, so as not to frighten it. He maintained eye contact with me even after I lowered the binoculars. My heart raced. My hands trembled.

With grace, he flicked his wings and rose up to my window. He was calm, interested, like he hadn't expected anyone to be able to see him, but like it was a common enough occurrence that it didn't surprise him.

I should have been creeped-out that this man, in his forties at least, was staring at me though my bedroom window, and me in my Justin Timberlake emblazoned sleeveless top and shorts for pajamas. I wasn't. He wasn't looking at me like that. There was a kindness, recognition, in his eyes. He knew what was happening to me, and it wasn't strange. Not to him. "Has Oisin sent someone to talk to you?"

Who? Wha—

Oh my God. He was talking to me—

He must have sensed my fear. He nodded. "It's all right," he said, his tone soothing, musical. A feeling of calm washed over me. "You're not alone. Oisin will be happy to hear about you. "

Oisin?

"Don't be afraid," he said.

I watched him return to the street, and speak with someone else, a fay woman. He pointed up at my window, at me. She glanced up and nodded. I snapped my curtains shut, sank to my bed and curled up under my McFly duvet.

These men were not hallucinations. They *were* real. *He* was real.

They had been real all along. It had taken the shock to my brain—the ECT treatment—to make it possible for me to see them.

If I *didn't* have schizophrenia—what was happening?

ଓ

I ventured downstairs, humming McFly's "Five Colours In Her Hair." In the snippets of sleep I'd managed, I'd dreamt I was the girl in their video, living in a black and white world, reaching for their full-colour world. Instead of the band reaching for me, it had been the winged man outside my window.

"You're up early, Love," Dad said. He stood at the front door, packed lunch in hand, ready to leave for work.

I shrugged. "Aye, well, sure the Mater had me on a strict schedule, so they did. It's habit now."

Dad flinched when I said 'Mater'. It was an embarrassment to take sick time unless you were actually on your deathbed. To have to admit anyone he knew was in the hospital because they were touched in the head, well that was just mortifying. Maybe I shouldn't have mentioned it, but I'd said it to show I was committed to getting better.

Though after last night, I wasn't so sure I was improving, or even if I had anything to improve from.

I wished I could talk to Dawn. Before I'd gone into the Mater, we'd told each other everything. If she thought I was mad from talking to invisible voices, she would think I'd lost it completely if I told her I'd *seen* winged men. Fay.

"Good on you." Dad kissed the top of my head. I knew, despite my tarnish, he wanted me to be well.

The front door opened. Mum walked in, hanging her cardigan on the peg. "Morning, Melanie."

"Where were you?" I asked.

"How is it out there?" Dad asked.

"Happy it's my last day, so I am," Mum said, putting her bag down on the table by the door.

"That bad?" Dad asked.

"Aye. Be careful. Come home as early as is right."

Dad kissed Mum and left for work.

"What's going on?" I asked. "Where were you?"

"Protesting," Mum said, walking into the kitchen. "Dawn was with us."

That wasn't like Dawn, to get involved. But then, I hadn't thought she'd abandon me, either, and she'd basically done that. But protesting? I trailed after Mum. "Like what was happening on Tennant yesterday?"

"No, no, just blocking traffic on Springfield during rush-hour to protest the re-routing of the parade." Mum poured us each a bowl of Muslix. "Several of the ladies from the Lodge. We've been taking shifts blocking Springfield Road for the last few days. The riots are picking up now. We should get to Tesco today and stock up on groceries to get us through the weekend."

"Is it really that bad? Should Dad be going to work?"

"Dad will be grand."

I thought of the fay out on the street last night, and I wondered if any of their words, their poison, had touched Mum and Dad, or Dawn, in their sleep.

"Anyway," Mum continued. "How are you this morning? You look tired. Did you not sleep well?"

"Sure, it's just a bit strange being home, so it is," I said brightly, hoping it wasn't too obvious my smile was fake. "I'll sleep better tonight. Do you mind if I go on the computer for a bit this morning?" I had to see what I could find on the winged men.

"Let's do our Tesco run first, then you can go on it as long as you like."

Tesco run. Being normal. "Sure." Being normal was what I needed right now.

After we finished breakfast, Mum and I walked up Workman Avenue and headed toward Woodvale Park. The moment I stepped out the door, I felt like someone was following me. I looked over my shoulder but there was no one, or, I guess in my case, *nothing*, there. Just the red- or brown-brick semi-detached houses. An ordinary, working-class street.

The military was already moving their armoured vehicles into the fenced-in property of the old Mackies Foundry, lining the road through the lot where the Orange Order bands were to march.

I shuddered, remembering how the fay boss said, "Authority must be destroyed." It didn't take much for me to imagine the parade turning into a slaughter-fest, killing the soldiers before they knew what was happening. Especially if the powerful words of the fay had any effect on the people sleeping behind those windows.

"Them soldiers should be protecting us, not them'uns over the wall," Mum said, jerking her chin in the general direction of the Peace Line and the Catholics on the other side.

For half a second, I swore the young soldier nearest me had his throat slit. I wanted to warn him, but I couldn't tell the soldiers winged men were compelling the neighbours to destroy them.

It took a minute or two to get the image of slain soldiers out of my mind. By then, Mum and I had entered Woodvale Park. The sense of being followed was stronger now. More stuff I couldn't tell Dawn, or anyone, about. She was better off without me as a friend.

We walked along the shrub-lined pavement, passing the two bowling greens just inside the park entrance. Faint humming came from behind me, like wind through the bars of the park fence, but higher.

Mum stopped, digging in her bag. "Where's that list of mine?" she muttered, distracted.

"Hiya," a woman said coming around to stand in front of me. I drew in a short breath. It was the fay woman from last night. Was she manipulating Mum's mind? Distracting her? "My name is Orla."

"What is it, Melanie?" Mum looked up, her forehead creased and her eyes narrowed. "Are you hearing them again?" she whispered.

Be normal. Be normal. "What? Oh, no. I'm fine. I just realized I've missed the entire summer. Shocked me a bit, that's all." It was a pathetic excuse, but thankfully Mum bought it.

"Och, Love. I am sorry about that. You do know we had to do what we did, don't you?"

Not even Mum could say they'd had me committed.

"Oh, aye. I was thinking that the parade tomorrow is going to have to be my twelfth." I tried to ignore the fay woman.

"Sure, why don't we have ourselves a wee bonfire in our back garden tonight?" She started walking.

"That would be brilliant, Mum."

"My brother Eamon, the fella who spoke to you last night, he asked me to talk to you," Orla persisted.

I faltered in my steps. If I moved forward I would walk right into her.

"Melanie?" Mum asked, stopping several paces ahead of me.

"Tripped over my feet is all." I scuffed my trainers on the path and pretended to straighten out my faded blue-jeans and pink sleeveless T-shirt. I never took my eyes off Orla. *Please move.* I willed the message to pass through the look I gave her.

"Come on, Love," Mum said.

I tried to side-step Orla.

"You don't have anything to fear," Orla said.

Mum was watching me as I just stood there, frozen to the spot. I saw her expression. She was going to commit me indefinitely. I stepped forward, bumping into Orla. "I'm sorry," I muttered.

Mum grabbed my arm, spinning me around. "Clearly it is too soon for you to be up and out. I thought you were taking your tablets."

"You're on tablets already?" Orla asked, like it was a bad thing, like I'd crossed some invisible barrier and it might be too late for me to get back.

"I am, Mum." I pulled my arm out of her grip. "I'm fine." I had to get out of here. I had to act normal.

Mum gave me a studied stare. "You're not. I'm taking you home, and tonight, I'm watching you take your tablets."

I should have stayed in my bedroom this morning. Maybe if I took my tablets like I was supposed to, I might still hear the voices, but at least I might not see who they belonged to.

"It's all right," Orla said. "We're going to help you."

"Come on," Mum said. We turned around and walked briskly back through the park. "If the tablets you're taking aren't the right ones, then we'll keep trying until we find the right help for you."

Orla had no trouble keeping up with us. "They think you're schizophrenic, don't they?" Orla asked, though it wasn't really a question.

I gave a tiny nod. I hoped Mum thought it was for her.

"You're not," Orla said. "Not exactly. To them, to humans, you are."

She wasn't helping me. My heart raced, and I wanted desperately to burst out of my skin, to get home and lock myself in a dark closet forever.

"For some—like you—" Orla continued, "what humans call hallucinations, are not in your head. I am very real. There are other liminal beings that are real. You've seen and heard them, haven't you? Not just me and Eamon. Don't respond. Think about it."

The fay—they were real.

I wanted to believe it. God, I wanted to believe it. But . . .

I counted out my breaths, trying to slow my heart. I wished her voice had the same soothing melody as Eamon's had last night.

"You are what we call a druid," Orla said. "A human who can see and hear us. A bridge between our worlds."

I smothered a gasp. Druids were Irish mythology. Us Ulster-Scots Protestants didn't go in for that kind of fairy-tale thinking.

"Druids are our spiritual guides and teachers, as they've always been in Celtic tradition. It is in the blood-line. We used to find new druids all the time, but now there are too few of you. We're losing so many to the mental hospitals."

No. No, this was too much. It would be better to be schizophrenic than whatever was happening to me. I would go back to the hospital and tell them the truth this time. Dr. Taylor would find the right treatment for me.

I let my breath out slowly, as I'd been taught. This was the right decision. It had to be.

But I could still see Orla's worried face peering into mine. I wanted her gone. When we reached our house, I rushed to my room and slammed the door. I hoped walls could keep her out.

"Melanie?" Mum had run up the stairs behind me, but stood outside my door.

"Ring Dr. Taylor," I called. "I want to go back. Take me back there. Now! Please!" I pulled my rucksack out of my wardrobe and started packing.

Fingers tapped my window, like rain pelting it. I looked up. There was Orla, hovering like Eamon had last night. "Open up, please, Melanie."

I closed the curtains.

Downstairs, the front door clicked open. "What's going on?" Dad was home early.

"She's not well." Mum's words outside my door were low, muffled. "She wants to go back to the hospital."

Dad's heavy footsteps thumped up the stairs. "What happened?"

"I'm not sure," Mum said. "We were walking to Tesco, through the park, and she stopped. She started talking to—nothing."

Orla banged on my window.

Dad swore. "Melanie, we'll ring the hospital, but everything is shutting down. There are carjackings in the city centre. There are crowds gathering. I was sent home from work early today. We're not going anywhere until after the parade tomorrow at the earliest. We might not get out until Monday. Are you listening?" Dad asked, knocking on my door.

He was knocking and talking; Orla was knocking and talking. I pressed my hands over my ears and curled up on my bed. Druids and fay—real or not, I wanted them to leave me alone.

"Melanie?" Mum's voice, worried.

My tablets were right there, on my bedside table. If only taking them shut my ears and eyes to the liminal world. They might, if I took enough. Maybe they could undo the effects of the ECT.

I lowered my hands from my ears as Mum came in and sat on my bed, wrapping me in her arms.

"It's stuffy in here," Dad said, coming in, too. "Let's open the window, get some fresh air. You'll feel better."

I know he thought he was helping me. He didn't see Orla out there. "No! Don't!"

"It's all right." Mum held me close as Dad pushed aside the curtains and cranked open the window.

"There is nothing outside." He waved in the general direction of Orla. "No monsters. I promise you, you are safe," he said, the way he used to when I was a kid and he had to check for monsters under my bed before I'd go to sleep.

No monsters, just *feckin' fay!* I curled up tighter in Mum's arms as Orla flew in and landed beside my bed.

"I'll call Dr. Taylor." Dad escaped down the stairs.

"Have a wee lie down," Mum said, stroking my hair off my forehead. "I'll come get you when it's time for your tea." She pocketed my tablets and left the room with one last reassuring, pitying smile.

Orla sat where Mum had just been. I scooted away from her.

"I didn't mean to frighten you with talk of druids and liminals." Her voice was soft and kind. "This must be so strange and a bit scary for you, especially if you've just been diagnosed with schizophrenia. Because most humans can't see us, they don't understand that you can."

I trembled, pushing myself further back.

"Don't be afraid of us, Melanie. Your ability to see and hear us makes you very special."

Special? Not weird, or sick. I shook my head. This was madness.

"Yes, it does," Orla said. "This is a good thing. I understand why you're afraid. You've grown up believing we're nothing but stories and myths. Of course it's going to be a shock to find out we're real. Most humans don't want to accept that there are people like you, who can see not just what everyone else sees, but our world, the liminal world, too. So they call it mental illness, and lock you up. You're not sick, Melanie. You're special. There are others like you, here in Belfast. We *need* people like you."

I'd never considered hearing voices, and now seeing who, or what, they belonged to, as useful. She waited for me, letting what she'd said sink in. I thought about the ward at the Mater, how I'd known all along that I didn't belong there, how none of the treatments Dr. Taylor tried had helped me. They hadn't worked, because they couldn't block out reality. I couldn't deny that Orla and the fay from last night were real. I heard them. I saw them. I could touch them. They weren't just body-less voices in my head anymore. I'd hated being drugged and experimented on. I didn't really want to go back there, did I? Sure, I'd be free of the judgment of the neighbours, of Dawn, but, what if there was something to this? What if I didn't have to go back into the hospital? What if I could be useful instead of some doped up zombie walking the halls of the mental ward for the rest of my life? Wouldn't it be worth looking into?

"How?"

"Liminal means in between. We are stuck between this world and the Other world. We're a part of both, and yet we are not fully in either. Druids are our anchor into this world. We live here, yes, but over time, we have lost many powers we once possessed. Druids still have those powers, to intervene on behalf of the humans when the gods are angry, and you help us care for this land we live in. We depend on you to barter with the gods, to perform rituals to save this earth, and to protect us."

"That's not possible," I whispered.

"It is, Melanie. Not right away, of course. It will take you years of study in the Druid Enclave, under Oisin, head of the Druidic Order. He and the others will teach you the stories and rituals. I understand this is overwhelming. Seeing us is the first step. A baby step."

Overwhelming was an understatement. I huddled there, mulling over her words, trying to make sense of it all. Orla patiently waited.

As unbelievable as it all sounded, her explanation made more sense to me than Dr. Taylor's diagnosis. Another puzzle piece fit into place. "So, I'm not sick?"

"Not to us, no," Orla said. "To your parents and other humans, you very much are. But no amount of medication will help you, and when the doctors figure that out, they are going to put you in the hospital indefinitely. We need you out here."

I sat up. Orla was very real. The winged men on the street last night had been very real. Fuzzy, but real. "The fay who were on my street last night, what were they doing?" I asked.

"Stirring up trouble for humans," Orla said. "Us liminals live at night. It's the lingering after-effect of our ancestors having been trapped under the hills for a thousand years. We were once nearly as human as you are, before we were exiled. We escaped the hills centuries ago but we still can't co-exist with humans, not really. We usually only go out at night. Talking with you as I did today, that's an exception for me. We have found we can survive if we give humans free reign during daylight, and free up the night for ourselves. My people figured out the easiest way to claim the night as our own was through creating conflict which made humans all too afraid to go out at night."

Oh, good God! More puzzle pieces snicked into place.

"You're responsible?" I asked. "Decades, centuries of violence in Northern Ireland—everyone living in fear, too afraid to go out because that's when the bombs and riots happen—it's because of fay?"

Orla sighed. "I'm afraid so, more or less. It's not something I agree with. Eamon and I have very different opinions on it. He sees the conflict as necessary to our survival. I'm working with the druids and a few others in the liminal community, to convince Eamon, and others who think as he does, that it isn't."

"As a druid, would I be helping Eamon or you?"

"Both, at first. Though I hope you will want to help me should you have to choose."

I was more than intrigued to think that what others thought of as my mental illness, might actually be useful in stopping the violence. "If I want to look into this druid thing instead of going back to the hospital, what do I have to do?"

Orla's smile was kind, caring, maternal. "You need to find a way to the Enclave. It isn't some weird-looking place. It looks like any other house when you walk past it. Oisin will be expecting you. He and the others will take you in. I promise they will teach you everything you need to know."

My bag was half-packed already. Mum and Dad were trying to ring Dr. Taylor. If what Dad had said was true, I had a day or two at most to consider this before I would be sent to the Mater permanently. "Where is this place?"

"Fitzwilliam Street," Orla said. "Number 63. Do you know where it is?"

I nodded. I had no idea how I was going to get myself there.

"I'll leave you to think on it," Orla said. "I'm going to tell Oisin that your family wants you to go back to the hospital. Hopefully he will find a way to get you, but he can't come and take you. He has to be careful. Please, find your way to Fitzwilliam Street."

"I'll do my best," I whispered.

I took a few minutes to collect myself, fix my hair and my clothes, then went down stairs to the computer. Mum and Dad were in the kitchen, at the table, talking in low voices over tea and biscuits. I slipped into the front sitting room without them seeing me.

Instead of going to my usual Sugababes fan forum—I had so much to catch up after having no computer access all summer, but that would have to wait—I opened up Google and typed in 63 Fitzwilliam Street. It came up as "Care Home for the Mentally Ill." In the corner was a picture of a square Celtic knot. I clicked on it and a new page opened up, welcoming me to—

The Druidic Order of Belfast.

I wondered if anyone who searched the website could see that image.

Or just people like me.

CR

Mum and I sat on our front step watching people gathering on the street in anticipation of the parade that would pass in about half an hour. The security gate cutting Workman off from Springfield had already been adorned with Union Jacks and a white sign saying, "Equal Access Denied Once Again."

Though the red, white, and blue paint on the curbs hadn't been refreshed in several years, it was still prominent, even in its faded glory.

I wondered if Dawn would come out to watch. It was possible she was with her mum at the Whiterock Orange Lodge helping get the lunch set-up for when the marchers arrived. What would I do if I saw her? What would she do if she saw me?

"Are you sure you want to be out here?" Mum asked.

I nodded. Other than feeling a little groggy from my tablets, anxious about this whole druid business, and desperate to appear normal, I was all right. "I want to cheer Dad on when he marches by," I said. I'd lain awake again, most of the night, thinking about what Orla had said to me. All the puzzle pieces were now in place, and the picture made sense in its full-colour glory. *I* made sense. I was a druid. I could find others like me, and I could be useful, if — and it was a big "if" — I could make contact with Oisin.

In the periphery of my vision, I noticed several fay standing on the roofs of the homes on my street looking down on us.

Orla stood in the neighbouring garden. She stepped over the low brick wall dividing our property. "How are you? You had quite a shock yesterday," she said, with a lilt in her voice.

Though I'd eaten breakfast not long ago, my stomach rumbled. I looked at Orla, wondering if it was the subliminal lilt that had caused my hunger. Orla merely winked at me.

"We need nibbles," Mum said. "Would you like some crisps, Love?"

"That would be brilliant. And maybe a sandwich? Thanks."

Mum kissed the top of my head before going in. I could tell she was still worried about me, but I was doing much better at acting normal today.

"You gave me a lot to think about," I muttered to Orla. I turned a bit to my right so I could keep an eye on the intersection of Workman and Forth, where the bands would be coming from, where some of the hard men of the paramilitaries were gathering, watching the rest of us.

Eamon hopped from rooftop to rooftop. He stopped on top of the house across the street from me, turned to me and dipped his head in a bow, acknowledging that I could see him. I returned the gesture. He joined the other fay on the rooftops closer to the security gate.

"I thought you said the fay don't come out during the day," I said.

"Parades are different." Orla stood next to me, arms crossed, shaking her head as Eamon and his soldiers settled into their places above us. Suddenly, she stifled a cry. "Oh, goddess. Dawn, no," she whispered. "She's not supposed to be here. She was supposed to be on holiday this weekend."

I followed her gaze. Dawn and her mum stood in their front garden, flags in hand, ready for the parade. I waved. She smiled and waved back. Her mum spotted me and, scowling, quickly turned Dawn around. Dawn turned back and mouthed, "I'm sorry."

Orla lifted into the air, then settled again, clearly agitated.

Dawn's mum. Huh. So that was it. That was why Dawn hadn't visited me in the hospital, or come to see me yesterday. She hadn't . . . abandoned me. She was still my friend. "You know her?" I asked.

"She's . . . oh goddess." Orla pressed her hands to her temple. "Of course. He made it so she'd be here. That's why he's doing this." She lifted into the air again, craning at Dawn as if trying to see better.

"What do you mean? What's going on?"

Orla took a deep breath. "Dawn. She's my daughter."

"What?" I spluttered. Dawn had a mum — .

Orla landed and paced the narrow patch of cement that made up my front garden, her eyes never leaving Dawn. "Eamon took her from me just after she was born. He gave her to this family." She waved in the direction of Dawn's home, her mum. "He destroyed any connection she might have had to our world, to me."

Good God! "What kind of evil is he? Why would he do that?"

"Politics." Her pacing increased, and she absently pounded the brick wall in front of our garden with her fists as she roamed. "He wants me to suffer because I oppose him." She stopped. "He must have manipulated her family into staying for the parade. He knew he was going to start a riot today."

The fay song *had* manipulated Dawn into protesting. "But, he was nice. He told you about me. Why be nice to me?"

She whirled, her eyes pleading with me. "Because we need you. We need druids. Not even Eamon can deny that." She turned back to the innocent scene before them, grabbing her hair with clawed fingers. "But to him, Dawn is expendable."

I was having some serious second thoughts about wanting to be a druid and helping the liminals. They were more messed up than the human world. "Go. Help her."

"I can't!" Orla cried out, agony inflecting her voice. "I can't touch a human!"

Mum came out of the house carrying a tray with a couple of Fantas, bacon sandwiches, and packets of Tayto Cheese and Onion crisps. "Everything all right?" Mum asked.

I stared at Mum. *Be normal. Be normal.* I helped myself to a sandwich and Fanta. Dawn was now standing on the curb with some other neighbours, chatting laughing. She had no clue what was going on around her. "Aye, grand," I lied, chomping down on my sandwich. If only Mum was still inside so I could keep on talking to Orla. Why was Eamon so duplicitous? Orla would explain it to me if I could just ask her.

The small clusters of neighbours chatting broke up as more and more people gathered on the street. Several waved small Union Jacks. Across the street, too far for me to hear, one woman sang to her baby in a stroller, marching in place and waving her flag to the beat of her song.

The fay began to sing. Celebration and discontent nudged at me from the periphery. Though I knew the emotions were caused by Eamon and his soldiers, I still struggled to push them aside.

Orla flitted over the wall and stood by Dawn, softly humming a soothing melody, edging out the discontent. Her song calmed me and a few others in close proximity.

Drum beats and the first notes of the flutes announced the arrival of the parade. The first pipe and drum band rounded the corner, led by their banner carriers, representing the Whiterock Orange Lodge.

I got up. Discontent niggled at me but Orla's song was strong enough.

Mum grabbed my arm. "Melanie, stay here, with me."

"It's all right, Mum," I said with a reassuring smile. "Come with me."

Reluctantly, Mum followed me out onto the sidewalk. I edged closer to Dawn. Orla used her magnificent black-webbed butterfly-like wings to balance along the waist-high wall that defined the boundaries between garden and sidewalk.

More bands rounded the corner. Lodge members in their bowler hats and orange sashes marched between each of the bands. Three more lodge bands passed before I could cheer my dad marching by. He waved and tipped his bowler to me, a smile cracking his concentration. A couple of the fay hovered over a handful of the younger marchers, cawing their discordant song. Thankfully, they left Dad alone.

The tail end of the parade disappeared down the street. Before Orla and I could complete our sighs of relief, a small group of marchers, the ones the fay had paid the most attention to, broke off from the parade and returned. They carried their banner and beat their drums in front of the security gate.

"Melanie." Mum tugged at my elbow.

A police Land Rover pulled up to the corner of Forth and Workman and the crowd, maybe two hundred in total, pooled around it.

"Melanie—"

Other fay stood next to the vehicle. With every dissonant note the fay sang, the police officers tensed.

A few young men climbed up onto the security gate and hung their Orange Lodge banner over the razor wire, dangling it on the other side. There must have been Republicans over there because moments later a handful of rocks and an empty wine bottle were thrown over the gate.

The volume of the fay song rose. So did Orla's, but Eamon drifted over, directing his song at Dawn, one eye on Orla. Dawn stepped off the curb.

"No! Dawn!" I cried out.

Orla rose into the air, singing desperately to her daughter, trying to worm between Dawn and Eamon. Eamon shoved her away.

Dawn drifted towards the crowd, beyond the reach of Orla's soothing song.

"Dawn!" I yelled.

"Dawn!" Orla's song broke off in a screech, and Dawn disappeared into the crowd.

"Melanie!" It was my Mum. "Get home, now!"

I pulled my elbow from Mum's grasp and ran onto the street into the crushing masses. Mum called after me but I ignored her.

The crowd moved in slow motion toward the security gate. The top of Dawn's head was still visible at the back of the crowd. The fay song was loud. I couldn't hear Orla. I had to rely on myself to suppress the anger they stirred in me. *They're manipulating me*, I repeated to myself as I got closer to Dawn.

The marchers, the instigators, pounded on the metal. The ones on the gate tossed debris over to the other side. Others fell in around me, pushing me further from Dawn. If they got any closer to the gate, Dawn was going to get crushed.

I pushed harder, shoving, elbowing, kneeing, whatever was necessary to get to her. The press of the surging crowd nearly picked me up off my feet. An errant elbow narrowly missed my nose, landing squarely on my forehead instead. It stung but I had to keep going. Dawn had flung a hand into the air, and her fingertips were still in my sights.

I'd never say I was the slimmest of girls, but I was thinner than most around me. I bent low and did my best to squeeze between the bodies. Someone stepped on my foot. My ankle twisted.

"Orla! Help me!" I could only hope she heard me. I didn't even know where she was.

By the time I reached Dawn, she had fallen. Her eyes were filled with terror.

One of the younger marchers was trying to use her as a stepladder to climb the gate. I pushed at his knees with everything I had. He lost his balance and fell into someone else.

I grasped Dawn beneath her arms and pulled her up. The crowd shoved us against the gate, mashing me into Dawn and forcing the air from my lungs.

There was no way out—

Then the crowd changed direction.

Orla. It had to be. I couldn't quite tell because of all the shouting, but the fay song of Eamon and his soldiers had ceased.

There was a tiny space in the confusion as a touch of sense returned to the people around me. I could breathe. Dawn shifted, scrabbling to keep from falling.

A new song started, off-key and harsh. Most of the protesters turned back toward the police Land Rover, and part of me wanted to push in that direction. Dawn tugged against me. She couldn't hear the song, but it was having its effect on her.

"Dawn!" I shouted in her ear to be heard above the cacophony. She could fight the influence of the fay, but she had to have something to focus on. "Your mum, Dawn. She's worried sick."

Dawn blinked at me, then her face cleared and she nodded.

There was enough of a momentary break for us to get our footing. Locking arms, Dawn and I fought our way back through the sea of people, swimming across the current of their determined push toward the police vehicle.

A glass bottle shattered on the ground, and oily blue paint spattered over our trainers. Dawn and I shrieked.

A second song interrupted the first. Orla, dueling with her brother. But how could she hope to overpower the songs of all the fay?

The back half of the crowd surged towards the Land Rover, sucking Dawn and me with them.

I stumbled over someone's feet, and fell to my knees. Dawn tripped and fell beside me. We huddled together, unable to rise against the trampling rush of people.

Again, Eamon's song stopped for a moment.

Orla sang anew, her voice over-powering all attempts by the other fay to battle her. Enough of a calm settled over the mob to allow a gap to open in front of us.

I grabbed Dawn's hand and, keeping our heads down, we shoved our way through the last of the crowds and back to the safety of my front garden.

We were panting. Dawn's trousers were torn. My hands were cut and bruised, and both our faces scuffed. But we'd broken free.

Mum pulled me into a tight hug. I looked down the street to the mob. Orla fluttered from the top of the Land Rover and headed our way.

Dawn's mum—human mum—was there too, hugging her own daughter. Letting go of Dawn, her mum said, "You saved her life. Thank you, Melanie."

I blinked. I had, I guess.

"It happened so fast." Dawn drew in a ragged breath, the impact of what had happened growing on her face. "I didn't know what was going on."

Orla flitted to Dawn's side, looking her over. "She's all right."

"Want to come over tomorrow?" Dawn asked. "We have so much catching up to do."

"I'll be there," I said, grinning. I'd make sure I didn't lose this friendship again. Oisin would have to let me keep it.

It was all surreal. I was the only one who could see or hear the liminals, and . . . for the first time I felt like . . .

It was all right.

I was all right. I was living in a full-colour world.

"Where's Dad?" I asked Mum as we went into the house.

"Safe at the Whiterock Lodge, thank goodness," she said, hugging me again. "He texted to say the army is blocking anyone from getting in or out of the neighbourhood right now, so he's going to stay there for a while."

In the hospital I'd missed Mum's care and affection, but after today, I knew I couldn't stay here anymore. The marching, the fay, the Troubles. Parades like these had too much potential for violence. I had to get to the Druidic Enclave. I had to become part of the solution.

"I've been thinking about yesterday," I said to Mum, falling into a chair by the kitchen table. "I don't want to go back to the Mater."

"Melanie . . ." Mum said.

"I know I need help," I interrupted. "I was on the internet yesterday and I found a site for a wee residential centre. Here in Belfast."

Mum bit her lip. She slipped into the chair beside me and took my hand.

"It's just on Fitzwilliam, close by."

Mum nodded slowly, her cheeks wet.

"I can live there, and get the care I need, without being hospitalized. When Dad gets home, I can show you both the website. It looks grand."

Mum took me in her arms and held me for a long time. Then she pushed me back to look into my eyes. "Are you sure?"

"I am." I smiled.

I was.

FROG SONG

Erika Holt

"Head for the water, Woof." Ruby clung to the long fur around her friend's neck and urged him to go faster. For three hours they'd been eluding their pursuer—a concerned dog lover intent on "rescue." Such were the risks of visiting the city. Out in the countryside, as long as a dog didn't appear to be suffering, people would leave him to roam. But some city-dwellers were relentless in their heroics. Woof's tongue lolled out to the side and he panted heavily. Ruby felt him slowing down.

Woof plunged through the undergrowth at the edge of the neatly constructed wetland they'd used more than once as an urban bolt-hole. As soon as he set foot in the murky water, Ruby slid off and with two easy strokes of her webbed feet reached the safety of the deep. On land, her weak, misshapen hind limbs were capable of no more than crawling, but water was her element.

"Go!"

Woof skirted the pond's edge and bellied his way under a chain link fence—no easy task for a sheep dog—before disappearing into a thicket. Ruby sunk low so that just her eyes poked from the surface, unblinking. Though she was somewhat larger than a frog, her marble eyes more than twice the size, never once had she been spotted in the water. People only saw what they wanted to see, or what they expected, and this woman was no different, her gaze skipping over Ruby like a flat stone across the surface.

"Come here now, boy! I won't hurt you!"

Ruby snorted, causing burst of bubbles to rise up. What did this person know? Woof did just fine. Certainly better than if he was locked away in a cage or forced to wear a collar all day like other dogs Ruby had seen. When the woman looked away, Ruby splashed her and was gratified to hear a surprised shriek before she dove. The woman was lucky. At least this water was clean.

CR

The next day they were back in the city, but not for sight-seeing. Ruby had business there. The pair hunkered down between a dumpster and a wall, waiting for Aaron to wake up. He had that smell, the rotting sweet breath that meant he'd had too much to drink the night before. It could be some time before he came to, but it was best to catch him first thing in the morning, so they waited. Ruby scratched behind Woof's ear and patted his head. If the smell was bad for her, it must be way worse for him.

Aaron was only the second human she'd ever spoken to, though she'd eavesdropped on many. Amitola—or "Rainbow" as the woman had preferred to be called, saying it made her "dates" smile—had been her first and best friend, but Ruby hadn't seen Rainbow in over a year.

But Aaron and Rainbow shared some similarities, which was what had drawn Ruby to him. They were both outside-people, who kept to themselves mostly, and showed small kindnesses to critters around them, like sharing their meagre food with Woof with no expectations of getting something in return. And, like Rainbow, Aaron seemed invisible to his fellow humans. Ruby had once asked what his name meant. He said, "screw-up" but when Ruby asked if that's what she should call him he stayed quiet.

She leaned against the wall, pulling her long legs into her chest. That she was part human herself was a certainty. Her upper body and shoulders were undeniably human shaped, as were her arms, and her perfectly formed, little hands, with eight fingers and two thumbs tipped by ten hardened nails. Her legs hadn't come out as well, more frog-like than human, but not as functional. Others like her, strange hybrid creatures, had been born of the soupy swamp behind the grey brick building—a baby-making clinic, Rainbow had told her—though most had been too malformed to survive more than a few days or weeks, and some had simply withered when the swamp was drained. At thirty-odd years old, Ruby was positively ancient, and now seemingly one of a kind. But despite her part humanness, she felt little kinship with these creatures who sped around in metal contraptions spewing fumes and noise, paved the world in black, and bustled in and out and in and out of revolving doors all day long. Like ants. An ant-human hybrid would be terrifying.

A deep engine roared in the distance, followed by the sounds of clanging and banging metal. The garbage truck. She squeezed with her legs and Woof rose, standing over the snoring man a moment before licking his face.

"Mmmrrrr," Aaron swatted at his unseen attacker and rolled over.

Woof pawed at Aaron's arm until he stirred again, finally opening his bloodshot eyes.

"Whaaattt? Oh. Hey, Ruby. Hey, Woof." He pulled up to a sitting position, tipping his head from side to side to stretch his neck, which cracked loudly. "Woo, feeling a bit rough this morning."

Though she'd learned to speak, it wasn't easy and her voice was soft. She felt as though she was shouting when she said, "I gathered everyone yesterday, told them you were going to help us. But you didn't come."

"Yeah," Aaron stared off down the alley. "Yeah, sorry. I . . . I got busy. I'll come tomorrow, okay?"

"We need you now."

"I've got my own stuff going on." He fished around in his nest of blankets, retrieving an empty glass bottle. He peered at it, frowning, as though not believing it could be empty.

"Three more floaters this morning. You said you had a plan."

Aaron sighed, scrubbing at his scalp with dirty fingers. "My plans don't tend to work out. In case you hadn't noticed."

He got like this sometimes. Negative. Surly.

"How will we know unless you try? Come. We'll take you, so you can see." Ruby turned Woof around and motioned for Aaron to follow.

For a moment he just sat, staring at the ground. Finally he said, "Fuck it," and hauled himself up, stuffing his blankets into a green garbage bag, which he tucked behind a grease recycling bin. "How far is this place again?"

"Not far." It was pretty far, but if he knew that, he wouldn't come.

They kept to the alleys, mostly, and the dead spaces below underpasses and around industrial areas. A longer route, but safer; especially now that the sun was up. Once on the outskirts, they ducked through a few culverts under the highway. Aaron grumbled about getting his boots wet, though his feet, along with the rest of him, could use a good soaking.

Usually, Ruby skirted the buildings bordering the slough she called home, but today she directed Woof into the heart of the complex. Aaron had to see everything.

Hulking metal skeletons of dilapidated buildings baked in the sun, mint green paint faded and chipped, giving way to rust, smearing the sides like blood. That was, where they weren't covered with graffiti, hastily scrawled doodles and hearts and names, and symbols only intelligible to their writers. A network of pipes—arteries and veins—zigzagged between and up and down the walls. Weeds fought to reclaim the gravel pad on which the structures sat. They were winning. Given enough time, would this place be swallowed up? And what would happen to the swallowers?

Woof carefully picked his way around broken glass, until Ruby brought him to stop.

"Wow," Aaron said looking around. "Is this place abandoned?"

A lone red-winged blackbird perched atop a stack, intoning its melodic call, but Ruby knew Aaron was referring to people. "Kids come sometimes in the summer. They make fires." They also drank a lot of the same sort of stuff Aaron drank.

"It's nice out here. Peaceful. Could be my country estate."

Aaron grinned and Ruby frowned. Not the reaction she'd expected.

"Just wait," she said.

They snaked around the buildings and headed downhill toward the water. When she'd first found this place five years ago, it had smelled alive, like peat and muck and algae-green water. Those smells were there still, but interlaced with a chemical undertone, and, depending on the direction of the wind, the stench of rotting flesh. She and Woof pulled bodies from the water daily, but could only take them so far.

As was her habit of late, Ruby scanned the pond's surface for floaters, spotted a minnow, its bloated white belly exposed to the sky. If not dead yet, it soon would be.

A vibrating croak cut off abruptly when they were spotted. The silence lasted only until Ruby was recognized, and then a chorus of voices burst forth, competing to be heard. Not in the ribbits or croaks that would be discernable to Aaron's human ears. The frogs spoke to her in their secret language, an undetectable, low frequency humming. Eggs failing to hatch. Malformed tadpoles. Metamorphoses gone horribly wrong. Burning skin. Foggy eyes. Paralyzed back legs. Is this the human who will help?

It seemed too much to relay to Aaron, so instead she pointed to the latest casualty. "There."

He approached the dead minnow and bent over, examining it. "Huh. So, stuff's dying you said?"

"Yes."

"Wonder why?"

"Follow."

They circled around to the west side of the pond where a jumbled pile of badly rusted barrels sat, a couple in the water. Ruby and Woof stayed back. They'd already tried everything they could think of, plastering the leaking cracks with mud and grass, pushing on the barrels. Nothing had worked.

Aaron moved closer to investigate. "Looks like somebody had a good time." When Ruby just stared, he added, "Those kids you mentioned? Bet they tipped these and rolled them down the hill. But yeah, this looks like the source of the problem. Wonder what's in them?" He kicked one on the water's edge, and a hollow echo sounded. Empty, or nearly so.

"I could try to find some gloves somewhere. Move them maybe. At least get them away from the water." He grabbed an edge of one, but though he could rock it, he could not tip it up to stand. "Or maybe not."

"You can do your plan. Your other plan. The one you mentioned last week, that worked for a pig. 'Some pig.' Remember?"

"I was blasted when I said I had a plan. It's . . . it's totally stupid."

"You said we just needed to get people's attention."

"Jesus, Ruby. My 'plan' isn't even real. It's from a stupid kids' book. I mean, here I was, talking to you, and you're on a dog for God's sake, and you're this . . ." He stopped. "And it just struck me as funny, you know? You're asking me to help, to convince people that you were in trouble, to save you. It reminded me of a story and I came up with this stupid idea. It was just a joke, Ruby. A dumb joke. I'm sorry."

"Aren't jokes supposed to be funny?"

"Yeah." As he reached around to pull up the hood on his jacket, Ruby saw his hands were shaking. "I gotta go." Gone were the grins and chuckles.

"Can you bring help to move the barrels?"

He mumbled something about having burned his bridges, and started back up the hill.

ʘʘ

For three long days Ruby waited for Aaron to return with help. How could he not, after what he'd seen? He'd seemed anxious and agitated by the time he'd left; the dead minnow and leaking barrels must've made an impression.

But, by the fourth day, she knew he wasn't coming. Or, if he was, he would be too late.

Ruby fiddled with a green and yellow woven string bracelet around her wrist, so tiny Rainbow had worn it as a ring until giving to her. When Ruby brought Rainbow a perfect, pink water lily in return, that was the only time she'd seen her friend cry. Rainbow wore it in her hair all day.

Maybe if Ruby gave Aaron something, a gift, he would do his plan as a gift in return.

Over the next several days, she and Woof made trips into the city. It took a while to find him, for Woof to sniff him out, as he'd changed alleys, now making his home in a concrete nook next to a chain-link fence. Ruby could see the appeal—the concrete soaked up heat, and warm air gusted from a metal vent above. But it was also a dead end, making visits, particularly daytime ones, risky. And so they came at night, bringing every sort of thing she could find and that Woof could carry in his mouth. A lily, of course, but also a sparkly stone, a shoe, part of a newspaper, and Woof's contribution—his favorite stick, thoroughly chewed. Most times Aaron wasn't there, although once he was sleeping and incoherent, but they just left the stuff at his feet for him to find in the morning. Still he didn't come back to the pond.

She saved the best present for last. A glass bottle, with two inches of the amber liquid Aaron prized so highly still left in the bottom. For this, they risked a daytime trip. She had to be sure he got it and knew it was from them. There was no lid on the bottle, and Woof seemed not to like the feel of glass against his teeth, so it was slow going to make sure none spilled.

When they arrived, Aaron was already awake, bending over and emptying the contents of his stomach onto the asphalt. After he was finished, Woof carefully placed the bottle down beside him. Aaron slumped against the wall and wiped his chin with his sleeve. He stared glassily at them for a moment, then shifted his gaze to the bottle.

"What's this?"

"It's gift for you," Ruby replied. She waited for a smile. Joy. Or tears. Happy ones.

Aaron sighed and banged the back of his head into the wall. "Fuck. You don't get it, do you?"

"Rainbow said friends give gifts."

"I don't have friends. Not anymore."

Ruby wouldn't have thought it possible for words to sting, but a sharp prickle stabbed deep in her belly. She tugged on Woof's scruff to move him back a step or two.

Aaron made a sort of growling sound and slammed his head into the wall again. "Look, I'm sorry, okay? Thanks." He picked up the bottle, sniffed, and recoiled. "Jesus." He threw it against the opposite wall and it shattered, spraying the liquid they'd so carefully safeguarded everywhere. "It's piss." He started to laugh, body shaking until tears streamed down his cheeks and dammed up at the edges of his scraggly beard.

These emotions Ruby couldn't read.

After a couple of minutes, his mirth subsided. "Aaaahh, thanks, guys. I haven't had that good a laugh in ages."

"What about the other things?" Ruby asked, gesturing to the shiny stone. "Do you like those?"

"Oh, that was you? Uh, yeah, yeah, sure." He picked up the stone, examined it a moment and set it back down. "Listen, I gotta get going." He stood and kicked some gravel, including the shiny stone, over the puddle of vomit.

Ruby dug her heels into Woof's sides, sending him springing forward to block Aaron's path.

She drew herself to her full height. "You didn't come back."

"I told you. I can't help. If you knew me you'd. . . . Just forget it, okay? Find someone else."

He jammed his hands into his pockets and looked at the ground. After a few seconds of waiting for direction, Woof made his own decision, padding over to the wall to retrieve his stick then pulling a U-turn to head for home.

Ruby didn't bother looking back.

They'd almost reached the alley's exit when a man appeared. His eyes were wide and his mouth hung open strangely, revealing missing bottom teeth. Sores pocked his face and bone-thin arms.

Woof stopped and Ruby hunkered low, hiding herself as best she could in his long fur. Woof watched the man who stared back at them with a blank, wild look. A low growl rumbled in Woof's throat. Sometimes that worked to scare people off. Not this time.

The man didn't say anything, didn't try to win Woof over with gentle words or placating gestures. Instead he approached slowly, arms extended, knees bent and poised for action. Predatory.

Woof bolted, nearly sending Ruby flying. She yanked his fur to right herself and Woof yiked. Distracted by that momentary pain, Woof caught a vicious kick from the man, square in the ribs. He crashed to the ground, sending Ruby sprawling on the pavement.

The man bent slightly and stared in her direction, squinting as though he didn't understand what he was seeing. Woof snarled and sprang back to his feet, lunging at the man and sinking his teeth into his calf. The man swore and jerked his leg. Woof maintained his grip until the man landed a solid punch to his back. Woof stumbled. Ruby dragged herself underneath the dumpster, the skin of her inner thighs tearing on the rough ground. The man stomped on Woof's paw and Woof yowled in pain. The man drew his foot back for another kick. Before it landed, Ruby heard, "What the fuck! Leave him the fuck alone!" Aaron's voice.

Instead of replying, the man made a sort of grunting, growling noise that Ruby had never heard a human make.

Then the sound of running, grunts and a scuffle, fists landing on flesh. All Ruby could see from beneath the dumpster were feet jockeying for position. Then the man fell and Aaron was on top of him, pummelling his face until it was a bloody mess.

"Stop!" yelled Ruby in her loudest voice.

Aaron held his next blow and rolled off the man. He walked over to the dumpster, got down on hands and knees, and peered at her. Then he stood, kicked at the wheels to unlock them, and rolled the dumpster a few feet until she was exposed. "Oh my god. Are you okay?"

"Yes. Please check on Woof."

The dog lay panting. As Aaron approached, he made as though to stand but yelped and collapsed. He whined softly.

"Shit, I think that fucker broke his leg or something."

Aaron crouched down beside Woof. The dog raised his head and snarled, drawing his injured paw in to his belly.

"Come on, boy. Let me help you." Woof continued to pant, drool wetting the fur around his lips, but finally turned his head away in a gesture of acquiescence.

Aaron threaded one arm between Woof's front legs and scooped up his hind-end with the other. With some effort he rose to standing, her friend in his arms. "God damn, you're heavy."

"I'll get him to the Humane Society and come back for you." He shifted Woof's weight, then shuffled off, disappearing around the corner.

But he'd neglected to reposition the dumpster, leaving her out in the open. The sounds of the city reverberated off the towering buildings, seeming to grow louder by the moment. Her wounds burned. Though the dumpster was the closest cover, the man would look for her there when he woke up—if he woke up. So far he hadn't moved. Using all her strength, she hauled herself over to Aaron's scant pile of belongings and covered herself with a filthy, stinking sleeping bag. Once again she found herself waiting, tried not to think about what might happen if Aaron didn't come back.

❧

Several hours later, Aaron finally returned. The man was gone. Ruby had watched him get up and stumble off, either forgetting she was there or hurting too much to care. Aaron staggered a bit but had the presence of mind to check around the dumpster.

"Over here," Ruby called.

Aaron spun and when he spotted her, relief washed over his face. He plopped down heavily beside her.

"Where's Woof?"

"Foot's broken. They're going to patch him up. He'll be okay."

"Why did that man attack him?"

Aaron shrugged. "Meth, probably. That shit wrecks people. He probably didn't used to be such an asshole."

"When will Woof come back?"

Aaron stayed quiet. Then, "Shit, how are you?" Gently, he pulled the sleeping bag back. "Wow. Okay I . . . I can't take you to the vet, or, er, the hospital. But. . . . How about I take you home, huh?" He emptied the contents of a cloth bag. "Can you . . . climb in? Or should I . . ."

"Where is Woof?"

Aaron sighed. "They won't let me take him, okay? You should have seen the way they looked at me. They thought I did it. Like I would ever! They think I can't even take care of myself, let alone a dog." Then, more softly. "He's gone, Ruby. I'm sorry."

Again he invited her into the bag, positioning it beside her and opening it wide, but she ignored him, curling in a little ball. It was like this when Rainbow disappeared. A heaviness pressing the air from her lungs, only then it had built over time. This felt like someone had dumped a load of rocks on her all at once.

She didn't resist when Aaron gently scooped her up and settled her in the bag. Nor when he mostly zipped it closed. In other circumstances the swaying movements of his walk might have been soothing, but instead every step jarred her raw insides until she thought she'd be sick.

At some point the movement stopped, and fresh air gusted in as Aaron unzipped the bag, setting it down carefully at the water's edge.

"Here we go. You're home."

Ruby didn't have to look to know there were more floaters. She crawled from the bag into the first few inches of water.

"Say something, Ruby."

A chorus of amphibious voices clamoured for her attention, but she didn't answer, just watched as the dried blood from her leg wounds formed a little cloud around her.

"How about that plan? My plan? Maybe we can get started." Aaron patted his bag, seemed to locate what he was looking for. He pulled a shiny metal rectangle from a pocket and brought it to his lips. As he exhaled, a long, reedy note sounded. He played a short tune unlike anything Ruby had ever heard. Unnatural, but slow and melancholic.

He stopped and shook his head. "Nah. Funeral song," he muttered.

And then another tune, completely different from the first. Fast and staccato. Cheery. An off-note sounded and Aaron stopped. He turned the instrument over in his hands, examining it.

When he didn't go back to playing, Ruby said, "What are you doing?"

"Trying to play 'When the Saints Go Marching In'. But I'm out of practice. Anyway, it's pretty hokey." He tapped the instrument on his knee. "Ha! I wonder if I can still even do it."

He began a new song, trying and failing a few times before seeming to catch the rhythm. The notes alternated back and forth from high to low yet a discernable tune soon emerged as he picked up the speed. As he continued to blow through the combs, Ruby could see the light of a smile in his eyes.

"Woo! Still got it. I think we should use that one. The opening riff's perfect. It's called 'Sweet Child O' Mine'."

A nice enough song with a nice enough name. But she still didn't understand how this had anything to do with his plan.

Aaron must've guessed her thoughts, because he said, "So, this is a totally whacked idea, but I though I could teach you and your . . . friends . . . a song. Like, the tune. Do you think they can learn?"

Ruby pondered the strange notion for a moment. "They are desperate. So . . . I think they will try. But what good will it do?" She gestured in the direction of the leaking barrels, the ever-expanding slick on the surface.

"We'll put on a show! I'll invite people . . ." He thought for a moment. "My sister. She'll come. And maybe I can convince her to bring her husband and her friends. It'll blow their minds to hear frogs—frogs!—singing Guns 'N Roses! They'll have to do something. It'd be, like, a miracle!"

Ruby failed to understand why a song, a "miracle," would be more compelling than the bloated, stinking bodies spiralling on the surface. But Aaron seemed so sure.

"Okay," she said. "What do you need me to do?"

"Translate. Explain."

At first the frogs were confused. What sort of help was this? Why was this human shattering the pond's tranquility with this awful noise? Why wouldn't she listen to tales of their suffering? Of lives lost since she'd be gone? Where was her furry friend?

Patiently and gently, Ruby answered their questions. She would listen, but later; she was so very sorry for their losses. If they hoped to survive, they needed to sing for him, with him. Woof was gone. Over and over she said these things until the eldest frog, an eight-year-old male—Papa—who'd recently lost the use of his right front limb, called for silence. With difficulty he swam near to where Aaron was sitting on the bank, and waited before him. A few others followed suit, until an army of ten male frogs grouped in front of him.

"Whoa," Aaron said. He clutched at the ground as though he wanted to get up and leave.

"It's okay. They will listen. They will try. Please, show them your song."

He played his metal box for about a minute before seeming to realize he'd have to go slower. Starting again and exaggerating each breath, he sounded the first eight notes and then stopped.

"Copy those sounds," Ruby instructed.

The frogs all tried to comply at once, resulting in a cacophony. Also, it was clear to Ruby that they couldn't hear the higher notes.

She asked whether Aaron could lower the pitch. He said he could but needed a different harmonica. When he returned the next day, Ruby explained to the frogs that they would have to coordinate; that each would be responsible for only select notes. When singing their own songs, they were accustomed to taking turns, so caught onto that concept quickly. Getting the key just right was harder. The larger individuals with deeper pitched songs took the lower notes, and smaller ones took the higher. After a couple of hours, the slightest hint of a tune emerged. A human tune, anyway. The females hummed in confusion at the garbled and disorderly din emanating from their male counterparts.

"Yes!" Aaron clapped and laughed. Ruby had never seen him so animated.

She was more than a little surprised when he showed up the next day to continue practice, and the day after that, though his notes weren't as careful as they had been on the first day, nor his speech as clear.

But after about a week he proclaimed them ready. "Becky isn't going to fucking believe this. I'm going to try to get her to come on Saturday—that's two days from now. So tell your friends to practice! They can't screw this up for me."

Ruby promised they'd be ready.

CR

The atmosphere over the slough on Saturday morning was heavy with nervous energy, as the frogs and later Aaron waited in anticipation—and some fear—of their human audience arriving. It was mid-morning before a woman appeared at the top of the hill, face expressionless beneath a hand used to shield her eyes from the sun. She had the same dark brown, curly hair as Aaron.

"Hey, Becks!" called Aaron.

"Hi," she replied after a moment, tone clipped.

More people emerged at the top of the hill; seven or eight maybe.

"Wow! You brought everyone! How's it going, Chuck?"

Chuck and the others murmured subdued greetings.

"Oh, hey. I don't think we've met." Aaron extended a hand to a man in a pale blue, button-up shirt and crisp dress pants. The man shook Aaron's hand.

"Edward Burke," he said, still grasping Aaron's palm and placing his other hand over-top.

Aaron pulled away. "Okay, so, I've got something amazing to show you all. Seriously. You guys won't believe this. Gather around."

The assembled crowd glanced at each other uneasily but moved a little closer.

From her position in the reeds, Ruby hummed to the frogs. Told them to be ready.

Aaron gave the pre-arranged signal. "One, two, three, four!"

The chorus began. But the frogs were nervous. Making noise around humans went against their every instinct. Some came in too early, and others too late. Notes were missed. It sounded bad, not like what they'd practiced, or even a song at all.

Aaron's triumphant smile faded to incredulity. Becky's head drooped and she crossed her arms.

He turned toward the slough. "You guys! Come on! You have to show them!"

"Jesus," one of the men muttered.

"Aaron," said Edward Burke, "I don't know what you think's going on here today or what you expect to show us, but your friends and family have their own reasons for coming. They're concerned and they love you and they're here to help. I'm an addictions counsellor at the Willowbrook Recovery Center. We'd like to talk to you today about your addiction to alcohol and how it's affected these people who care about you very much."

"No, no, no." Aaron's face blanched and he put up his hands. "Ruby! Get them to try again!"

Ruby complied, soothing the frogs, encouraging them. After a shaky start they began to hit the proper notes and in the proper time, even picking up speed as they gained confidence. The unmistakable strains of "Sweet Child O' Mine" rang out over the slough.

But the humans weren't listening. Instead, one after the other, they pulled scraps of paper from their pockets and read to Aaron, while others looked on and cried . . . *Nicola waited for two hours for you to pick her up from school. . . . Do you want to end up back in jail? . . . and you didn't even come to the hospital to say goodbye, didn't even come to his funeral. . . .* One sullen looking teen boy, almost a younger version of Aaron, stormed off.

When the song ended, Ruby surveyed their audience to gauge the impact; saw none. She told them to start yet again, louder, as loud as they could. They stretched their vocal sacs to bursting, amplifying their singing for these humans to hear, really hear, this song that would mean so much.

Then, silence descended. All eyes, both human and amphibian, remained on Aaron.

"Didn't you hear that?" he said.

"Don't you hear us, Aaron?" Becky shouted back. "This is it for you! We're not doing this again. Mom took money out of her RRSPs to pay for this. She didn't even want to come because she doesn't believe you'll change. Don't you care what you're doing to her? Even after dad died? To us? Just thirty days. You can give us thirty days, can't you? After all we've put up with?"

Aaron looked at the ground and everything was still.

Then Becky approached and hugged him, which seemed to take Aaron by surprise, as for a moment he didn't move. And then he did, folding himself over her and breaking down in sobs.

"I'm sorry," he said, over and over. She held him and stroked his hair, tears also running down her cheeks.

"Okay," he whispered. "Okay."

The release of tension in the group was palpable; a few people even smiled. They turned to leave, Becky's hand on Aaron's back.

"Wait!" Ruby called. "Please! Come back!" But her voice was too soft, carried away by the breeze rustling through the leaves.

⊗

Ruby lay on a log in the shade, as she did most days now, trying to stay out of the poisoned water as much as her semi-permeable skin would allow, ignoring the nausea and headaches that plagued her most of the time. A duck flapped weakly in the shallows, finally exhausting itself and becoming still for a time.

Two weeks after Aaron had gone, after many more creatures

had perished, including Papa, she'd told the frogs to go. They could hop. Try to find a better place; a puddle in a ditch, or a farmer's dugout. Somewhere to rest in torpor until things got better. A new pond, if they were lucky, clean and pure. Ruby tried not to imagine them as dried-out corpses, run over by cars or landlocked in the middle of a dry, barren field.

Leaving hadn't been an option for the minnows, of course. A few still darted beneath the water's surface, but not many. Leaving hadn't been an option for her, either, not without Woof.

For a while the water birds had helped to keep the loneliness at bay, but save for the dying duck, even they had gone, replaced by scavengers—gulls, magpies, and ravens, hurting her ears with their grating cries. She wished they'd just go, but that wouldn't happen until everything was dead, her included. Every day they watched her with shining, beady eyes, venturing closer and closer as though to test whether she still had strength to move. She swatted them away, but more often now wondered why she bothered.

At first when she heard the footsteps, she didn't look up. Moving made her head swim. But then came a familiar voice, calling, "Ruby? Ruby, are you there?"

Aaron.

She opened her eyelid membranes but otherwise didn't move. He spotted her and swore, running around the bank and taking a few steps into the water near where she lay.

"Ruby," he said softly, "are you okay?"

Not knowing how to respond, she just said, "I'm glad to see you."

"God, I'm so glad to see you too."

He looked different. Clean-shaven and like he'd slept and eaten well. Definitely smelled a lot better, no trace of the sickly-sweet stink on his breath or sour, unwashed stench on his body.

"Is it okay if I help you? Pick you up?

Ruby nodded.

He scooped her off the log and set her down on the grassy shore. From his bag he pulled a bottle of water and poured it over her, cool liquid washing toxic residue from her skin.

"Wait here. I've got a surprise." He sprinted off like he was being chased.

Ruby propped herself on an elbow.

When a huge sheepdog appeared at the top of the hill, she sat bolt upright, heart pounding, almost unable to believe it could be real. Woof.

There was no mistaking him, in spite of his strikingly clean and fluffy coat, gleaming in the sun. He sniffed this way and that, then came bounding down to her side with only a slight limp, big goofy grin stretching from ear to ear. Knowing better than to lick her bitter skin, he instead nudged her with a wet nose. Had Ruby been capable of crying tears of joy, she would have done it in that moment. Instead she reached out and pulled herself onto his back, hugging him and burying her face in his fur.

"Told Becks a dog would help me heal," Aaron chuckled as he walked up. "Teach me responsibility. She's going to be pissed when I tell her I lost him, but it's worth it. One more little screw-up's not going to matter in the grand scheme of all my screw-ups, especially if I stay sober."

"And I'm going to, this time," he continued. "I have plans. I'm moving to the suburbs to live with my cousin. He's lined up a lawn-mowing job for me and I registered for school."

Ruby raised her head to look at him. "That sounds nice. And thank you for bringing Woof back. I—" She felt an unaccustomed squeezing in her throat.

"What's wrong?"

She pointed.

A pained expression crossed Aaron's face when he saw the duck sprawled awkwardly in the muck.

"My family has gone," she said. "I'm alone here."

"I'm sorry I couldn't get them to listen. I heard them singing, Ruby. They were amazing. And you know what? It gave me hope. That I could do something like that, that you believed in me enough . . ." He cleared his throat gruffly. "I'm going to get the barrels cleaned up. It might take time, but I promise you, I won't stop until I get someone's attention."

Ruby looked around. There was beauty in this place. It could live again.

"I have to go."

"Yeah," replied Aaron softly.

They both stayed quiet a while, aware that the time of their parting was near.

"I want to give you something." From her wrist Ruby untied the bracelet, beckoned Aaron closer, and fastened it around his right, pinky finger. "There."

"Aw—Ruby—" He closed his fist around it and drew it into his chest. He reached out with his other hand to scratch Woof behind the ear. Ruby felt Woof's body sway as his tail started up.

After a minute or two Aaron stepped back, and Ruby took that as her cue to go. With a last nod to her friend, who nodded back with a slight, wistful smile on his face, she urged Woof into a walk and then a run, heading east, the way her family had gone.

WRATH OF GAIA

Mahtab Narsimhan

Jai stood atop the crest of the hill looking for the quickest way back to Base Camp. The stillness of the rainforest had disturbed him from the moment he'd arrived. Nothing moved—not a peepal leaf, not a crow's wing nor a wild pig or deer, foraging for food. The only "wild" thing was his GPS. It had started giving incorrect readings as soon as he'd entered the forest a couple of days ago, when he'd been assigned the task of evacuating remote villages. His GPS still hadn't recovered and Jai'd had to search the territory assigned to him, using a map. But he wasn't too worried. He'd memorized a few landmarks coming into Kushal and was sure he could find a shortcut to get back to civilization.

A foul stench of rust, ruin and decay rose from the swamplands, which lay to the right of a large banyan that dwarfed the surrounding neem, mahogany, and sal trees. The banyan's fluorescent-green roots, hanging from its branches, descended into the soil, tethering it firmly to its spot. For hundreds of years, this area in southern India had been the hub for electronic waste from around the world; the burial ground for billions of computers and televisions after being dismembered by the locals. Lead, copper, microchips, and miniscule amounts of gold were extracted for resale. The rest was scrap—burned and dumped into the water or left out in the open till rust devoured the metal and the ground swallowed the plastic. The evidence was everywhere: keyboards, shattered circuitry and blackened wire guts littered the ground, like ugly confetti after a drunken party.

Skirting the banyan was the road in and out of Kushal. Everywhere else the foliage was dense and would need serious elbow grease to cut through.

Kanika's shrill voice shattered the silence. "Where am I? Who brought me here? I want to go home!"

Jai bit back the urge to yell at her. Even though he'd seen no sign of tigers, known to inhabit this part of the forest, he couldn't let down his guard. There could still be plenty of dangerous beasts around them.

"Quiet," he called out softly, hoping his voice would reach the two women at the base of the hill where he'd suggested they set up camp for the night.

"She can't help it," Tanvi yelled back. "Her memory is not what it used to be."

Jai took a deep breath. Of all the villages he'd scoured, he'd found only corpses—and just these two alive. Where were all the people? What was going on here?

As the sun brushed the tops of the stunted trees and the shadows lengthened, he detected movement near the banyan; but by the time he whipped his head around, all was still. Backlit by the sun, the trunks glinted with a plastic-like sheen, and the shrubs and ground cover shimmered with an unnatural metallic gleam. It creeped him out.

Jai walked across the narrow spine of the hill with a distinct feeling he was being watched.

Something burst underfoot, spewing silvery goo that splattered his leg.

"Shit!" His bare skin burned, and the stink of rotting meat and copper filled the air. One of the bulbous pods of a sickly-grey bush was crushed under his foot, and splashes of a metallic substance ate tiny holes in his socks and shoes.

He poured some water from his canteen onto the shoes and backed away, making sure to avoid the pods. What the hell kind of plant was this? The pods looked like computer mice. He was seeing more strange stuff in these last few days than he had in his lifetime.

Now he could appreciate his commander's words. "The forest is toxic and the poison is spreading. We have orders to burn it to the ground as soon as you and the others are back with the surviving villagers. I would have preferred to send teams of two to bring back the stragglers but I don't have enough men. Be careful, Jai, and get back to Base, *fast*."

One of the survivors, Tanvi, came up to join him, holding aloft a flaming branch. "Is there a problem? Did you see something odd?"

Jai tried to mask his repulsion at the sight of her, hating himself for it. The right side of her face was paralyzed and she could barely move her lips when she spoke. Jai had to make a conscious effort to look at her. "No." He didn't add that she and her grandmother were the oddest things he'd seen so far. "Will you both stop jumping at shadows? You're safe with me." He tapped his machine gun lightly. He'd already caught her eyeing the hand grenades and dynamite in his bag, which he would use if required. "I have all this equipment to help us get out safely."

Tanvi held the branch up higher, smiling. Her soft brown eyes, reflecting twin images of the setting sun, looked like they belonged in a much older face. "Fire is the only thing that'll protect us from Gaia now. You should have left all this equipment back in the village like I suggested."

In spite of the grotesque smile, Jai found he was unable to look away. "And Gaia is?"

"The earth, the forest, the water. Gaia is all around you. We have disrespected and angered her. And if we're not careful . . ." Tanvi's voice fell to a whisper, her eyes gazing steadily into his, "she will hurt us."

Jai shook his head as he stared into those young-old eyes, trying not to laugh at her naiveté. Tanvi looked perfectly sane, and yet here she was spouting superstitious nonsense.

"Come on down," she said finally. "And please—"

"Humour your grandmother," he said, cutting her short. "We should have left *her* behind if you ask me. We'd have reached Camp faster."

Tanvi slapped him. It was so sudden, he didn't see it coming.

"If you *ever* suggest leaving Granny behind again, I'll smash your head while you sleep and throw you into the swamp." Her features were even more contorted with fury, her chest heaving under the short cotton tunic she wore. "You're here to help us, not abandon us."

He bit back the hot rage that sprang to his chest at the arrogance of her slap, resisting the urge to shake her. Of course, she was right, but—God!—he couldn't bring himself to say it. He glared at her, instead. Yes, his reason for being here was to bring survivors to safety—including the weird and deformed, which Tanvi and her grandmother certainly were—but—

He took a breath.

It was the eeriness of the forest. And of these two odd ducks. It had him on edge.

Soft clicks and whirrs disturbed the silence. Jai turned around and scanned the forest. Night had descended on them with the suddenness of someone throwing a cloth bag over his head. He saw no one.

"Who's there?" he barked.

"Now who's yelling?" Tanvi gave him a black look. "Learn to follow your own advice."

Jai was about to reply when they heard a shrill cry.

"Leave me alone! I'm not going anywhere with you."

Kanika.

They raced down the ridge together.

Tanvi's seventy-year old grandmother was huddled by the fire. She'd wrapped her dupatta around her head and was rocking back and forth, each movement taking her dangerously close to the flames.

"Watch out, old woman." Jai pulled her back by her sleeve just as a tendril of flame tasted the wiry grey hair circling her head like a halo.

Tanvi threw the burning branch she was holding into the fire and hugged the old woman tightly, murmuring in her ear. "It's okay. We're safe. This man will look after us." She stared at him over her grandmother's head, as if challenging him to contradict her.

Slowly, Kanika unwrapped the dupatta from around her face, looking around fearfully.

"There is no one here but the three of us." Jai was damned if he was going to humour these women's belief that the forest was alive.

"Who are you?" Kanika stared suspiciously at him. "Where did he come from?" This last was addressed to Tanvi.

"Granny, this is Jai from the military." Tanvi, stroked the old woman's hair. "He's going to take us to a safe place. We're getting out of here and never coming back."

"Shhh," said Kanika. "Gaia can hear us. She's cruel. She won't let us leave. "

"Let's eat, Granny," said Tanvi, tugging at Kanika's kurta. "I'm so hungry."

The old woman took Tanvi's face in her palms and kissed her forehead. "Yes, my beautiful child."

Jai snorted in disbelief. How could these two have survived when stronger, healthier villagers had died? One had a serious case of Alzheimer's and the other was just too ugly to be. They wouldn't last a day in the city on their own.

But orders were orders. He couldn't leave two defenseless women in the forest. The sooner he completed his mission, the sooner he'd be rid of them. It was two days' hard trek back to civilization, three if they couldn't keep up, and then he'd be free.

On a makeshift stove of stones, Kanika heated a dry chapatti, flipping it over with her wrinkled hands. As he waited, Jai noticed the ground in the immediate vicinity didn't have the slightest bit of grass or foliage, and the patch of bare earth seemed to be getting wider. He couldn't recall the clearing being this large when he'd suggested earlier that they stop for the night. Had the grass moved away from the flames?

Keep it together. One of them had to have their wits about them.

"I have a battery-powered stove." Jai, shrugged off his backpack.

"Don't bother," said Tanvi. "She's had enough of electronic gadgets. It's the reason we're in this mess today."

Jai joined them at the fire. "Didn't you make money from salvaging? Reclaiming heavy metals from electronics has got to be less back-breaking than farming."

"We thought so." Tanvi poked the fire with a stick. "We had food in our bellies and we didn't care whether it rained or not. Unlike crops, the computers still yielded their guts to us." She dropped her stick and turned to him. "But we got greedy. We asked for more and more e-waste but we didn't safely incinerate what we had. We just dumped it."

Kanika's sobs became audible over the sound of the crackling flames.

"We poisoned Mother Earth," Tanvi said. "Now she's exacting revenge on us."

Kanika wiped her eyes and blew her nose into her dupatta. Jai tried not to barf as she picked up a hot chapatti without washing her hands, wrapped a green chilli in it and offered it to him.

Jai looked into her rheumy eyes. Just how many rooms were vacant up there? Or was her skull one vast hall with the wind blowing through? Did she really expect him to eat that crap after she'd smeared it with germs?

He was about to refuse when he caught Tanvi's eye.

He took the proffered meal, taking care to avoid any contact with the old woman. Hell, he knew her mental state wasn't contagious. He knew he was being stupid, but he couldn't help it. He'd been orphaned as a child and the military had embraced him. He'd grown up in the company of men and any contact with women, other than to satisfy his physical needs, made him uncomfortable. These two made him *very* uncomfortable.

Kanika sucked on the cigar of her chapatti, gazing around, happily. She seemed to have forgotten the earlier outburst. "I used to play here as a child you know," she said. "The swamp was a lake then and we'd swim in it. It was clean. Coloured fish swam in it. Then we'd take the shortcut to the next village to buy sweets. That ugly banyan wasn't there. "

Jai chewed on the dry morsel trying not to think about what was on it, chasing it down with a swig of water. "Judging by its size, that tree is more than 200 years old. It was there even before you were born, Kanika. You must have forgotten." *Like just about everything else.*

"It wasn't there!" she wailed. "I tell you, it wasn't."

Tanvi threw him a dirty look, exhaustion etched on her face.

"Okay, *okay*. I believe you." He didn't want to incite the old woman any more.

Jai fished out a couple of ration bars from his backpack and offered them to Kanika and Tanvi. They declined. He shrugged, unwrapped one and chewed on it as the stink of the swamp wafted into the clearing. Crap. When people in developed nations recycled their electronics, they didn't have a clue that recycling really meant *rerouting* the trash to a poor country. They just dumped. Out of sight meant gone. And developing nations colluded. Their poor needed the e-waste to survive droughts and other calamities that climate change brought. Extracting metal from electronics was the only livelihood, for some. But now, here they were. *This.* All the army could do now was to relocate the survivors and treat the contaminated area till it could be used again.

Jai threw the ration bar wrapper into the fire. It was too bad. These poor women. They weren't blameless, but it must be hell to lose your house, your community. Everything. "Why didn't you travel with the other villagers?" he asked. "A group of twenty showed up at Camp a few days ago."

"Granny wasn't strong enough," said Tanvi, stifling a yawn. "Some days she can barely walk. The village elders knew we and the *special* ones would slow them down. They said they'd send help when they got out. At least they kept their word."

Kanika mashed up the softened chapatti with her gums making loud smacking sounds. She swallowed, wiped the sweat from her face and looked around, her eyes clouded in confusion once again.

"Special ones?" said Jai. "There was no one in Kushal except the two of you. Every other village was deserted." *Except for the corpses.*

"Special is a *kinder* word for deformed." Tanvi's voice was hard and bitter. "Children born with physical or mental challenges. We poisoned Gaia and she repaid us by poisoning our parents' bodies. We are the result. Useless in a normal society."

Jai took a swig of water, staring into the darkness. Hadn't he thought the same thing a while ago? But, truth be told, the village elders were right. Was it sensible to risk the lives of so many to save a few who would probably die along the way or be a huge burden on the already strained healthcare system in the city? He said nothing, but when he glanced at her, he was sure Tanvi knew what he was thinking. He looked away, ashamed of himself. *He couldn't help it.* Illness and deformity of any sort made him sick.

"I know the way," Kanika said. "I could've shown them the

way out of here."

Jai snorted.

Tanvi glowered at him.

That was a load of crap. And if it was true, what the hell was he doing in this stinking place? "So, if Kanika knows the way out, you two could have left at any time," said Jai. "Why didn't you?"

"Granny knows ayurvedic medicine. She was trying to save some of the villagers. She couldn't. Just as we were making plans to get out, you showed up." She looked into the flames. "Truth is, it's wiser to travel in a group or Gaia will get you. I'm glad you are here."

"*Gaia will get you*," echoed Kanika, cackling with laughter. "But I know places to hide. She won't get me or my Tanvi! Oh no, she won't!"

The old woman was talking nonsense. Yet—

He could feel something in the air. A crackle of electricity. A certainty that something was watching them, and waiting.

He stood up and started to pace. These two, with their stories of Gaia, were messing with his head. It was probably a summer storm brewing. Climate change had made the weather unpredictable—sunshine one hour and a downpour the next. That was the only explanation.

No way was the earth *alive.*

⊗

Tanvi and Kanika insisted on sleeping in turns. Kanika became hysterical when Jai suggested that both she and Tanvi sleep and he would keep watch alone.

"No!" she shrieked. "Who is this strange man giving me orders? Tell him to go away."

If only Jai could slip away and leave them to fend for themselves. But no. His commander was depending on him. And these helpless women would die without him. But he had to get them all back to Base Camp before he ended up strangling this old woman who could remember the colour of the swamp-water from years ago, but couldn't remember who he was and why he was here.

"All right!" He spoke softly, spreading his hands.

The diminutive figure in the mud-splattered kurta-pajama sobbed like a child, scrubbing her face with her fists.

"We'll do exactly as you say. Okay?" He plastered a smile on his face.

The old woman wiped her face with her dupatta and stood still, gazing into the distance.

Tanvi gathered more wood, moving slowly, stumbling over roots and stumps. She placed the fuel in small piles around the periphery of their camp. Jai thought he heard a soft scream as Tanvi put a match to each pile of wood but her expression remained blank as she lit them, one after another. Jai said nothing. If she didn't hear it, then surely his ears were ringing.

When all the fires—in the centre and around the periphery—burned brightly, Tanvi spread a threadbare blanket and made Kanika lie down. "Rest, Granny. I'll be watching and the fires will keep us safe."

For a while. If Tanvi expected the fires to burn all night, she'd collected a woefully small pile of fuel.

Kanika kissed her granddaughter's forehead, then knelt clumsily and prayed, tears sliding down her face from under her eyelids. Jai felt a pang. Kanika was so old and yet so childlike. He hoped he'd never live to see this age, or this illness.

He'd try to be gentler with her.

"Help me keep the fires burning through the night," said Tanvi, yawning till her jaws cracked. "And don't let me fall asleep, *please*." She untied her headband and shook out her hair. It was thick and black, cascading over her shoulders to her waist—the only beautiful thing about her.

"You look tired," said Jai. "A couple of hours sleep would do you good."

"No!" said Tanvi, sharply. "You city folk have no idea what you're dealing with. If you get killed, there'll be no one to help me get Granny to Camp. Gaia is watching and at the first opportunity, she will strike."

"I've heard all the stories about this place, but that's *all* they are," said Jai. "Toxic e-waste and carelessness have destroyed this forest, but you cannot seriously expect me to believe it comes alive and kills people."

"So you think everything you've heard is made-up?" She slumped heavily to the ground beside the fire.

"Yes." It felt good to respond honestly.

"You believe what you want and let me do the same." Tanvi yawned so hard, her eyes closed. After a moment, her head began to nod.

"Tanvi?" said Jai,

Tanvi's head shot up. "Sorry." She shook herself and walked about, staggered and almost tripped over her grandmother.

"Sit down and talk," ordered Jai. "It'll keep you awake."

Reluctantly, Tanvi sat on the ground.

"How long has your grandmother been like this?"

Tanvi stared into the fire. "Three years. Give or take."

"And how did her dementia start?" While she talked, Jai patrolled the area just beyond the clearing. The fires burned bright, shredding the darkness with orange spears of light. He kept his back to the flames so as not to degrade his night vision. By now this place should be alive with nocturnal creatures but there was not a single yowl, roar, or screech. The silence was deafening, unnerving. A gaunt yellow moon hung in the sky, tinging the landscape in a sickly light. The air smelled and tasted foul, like something from the belly of a rusted machine.

"Help!" someone called out.

It was so faint, Jai barely heard it at first. He walked a few steps away from the clearing and listened hard.

"Help!"

Jai couldn't tell if it was a man or woman but someone was in trouble. Could it be a villager he'd somehow missed?

No, he was sure he hadn't—

Wait. The only reason he'd heard the cry was because of the silence.

He walked back to the clearing. Tanvi was fast asleep, curled up in a foetal position on the ground. There were dark circles under her eyes and she looked dead to the world.

Crap. There was no point in trying to wake her.

"Please help me!"

Jai turned and ran.

The voice came from somewhere nearby. The women would be fine for a few minutes. He had to bring the other survivor back to the campsite.

Even as he hurried in the direction of the swamp, dread grew in him. He shook it off. This was just a forest. Nothing but trees, bushes, and a swamp. No witchcraft, or ghosts.

He reached the edge of the water. It was shimmery and viscous in the light of the yellow moon—like molten green lava. Bubbles rose to the surface and popped, releasing a stench so foul, Jai almost gagged.

"Who's there?" he called out, jamming his nose into the crook of his arm, taking shallow breaths. "Tell me where you are and I'll come get you!"

"Welcome," a voice whispered.

And then someone shoved him from behind.

"Hey—" He fell, twisting to try to save himself, onto the surface of the swamp. He sank, his skin burning as the muddy water rushed over him.

He managed to scream just once before he went under.

Scorching mud seared Jai's nose, his ears, oozed between his tightly-closed eyelids. His body convulsed as an electrical storm of images assaulted his brain—crying babies, a woman's gang-rape, snarling dogs, a recipe for roast chicken, a group of men dressed in orange decapitated on a lonely beach, an earthquake, an air-crash, a tsunami—as if he'd been plugged into a gigantic mainframe downloading millions of terabytes of data into him all at once, erasing his own memory—

Jolts of electricity pulsed through him. An x-ray image of the banyan tree imprinted itself on his neural network: millions of lines of code flowing down through leaves, trunk, roots, and into the soil and swamp, seeping through the earth for miles around.

God.

Kanika and Tanvi had spoken the truth.

He'd been the fool. Gaia was—just as they'd described her—intelligent and malevolent.

How? How . . .?

And Gaia provided the answer to his question.

Over the years, Jai, remnants of data from improperly discarded computers seeped into the land. My land. Me. I absorbed it. Assimilated it. Put it to use.

A few more seconds and his brain would short-circuit. He couldn't remember his own name.

The harder he thrashed, the more data barreled through his head. His skin was on fire. His lungs burned from holding his breath.

Don't be scared, Jai. Relax. It will be over in seconds.

No! I don't want to die. Let me go!

Be a man, Jai. Join us.

And in the background were a cacophony of sounds: mouse clicks, whirring of camera shutters, bits of songs in various languages, and hundreds of cell ring-tones. If only he could plug his ears—but he could barely move his hands through the viscous mud.

He flailed about and caught something solid.

His brain lit up with an image—the skeleton of an elephant. He let go, choking back the urge to scream. More skeletons, human and animal, buried in the mud, surrounded him.

Something with form but no substance grasped his right arm and twisted. Pain ignited his bones.

With every ounce of strength in him, he clawed at the mud to reach the surface.

Tidal waves of data crashed over, in, and through him.

His heart slammed against his ribcage and blackness gnawed at the edges of his consciousness.

Then—

He thrashed free of the mud and raised his good arm above the surface. It connected with the tip of something hard.

"Hold on to the branch!"

Tanvi's voice, barely audible over Beethoven's Fifth Symphony.

"Jai!" Tanvi yelled louder. "Grab the branch."

Gritting his teeth, Jai raised both arms and clasped the branch. His right arm throbbed and his skin felt freshly-ironed.

He held on and was pulled forward.

❧

Jai's head popped above the surface and he took a deep breath. The foul air had never tasted sweeter. He could barely open his eyes.

His ears rang. But he focused on the words he wanted, *needed*, to hear.

"Hold on, Jai." Tanvi's voice was close. "Don't let go."

Jai swiped the mud from his eyes and managed to crack them open.

Tanvi and Kanika stood at the edge of the swamp, barely a foot away, trying to haul him in.

Mud sucked at him, like long, grasping fingers, trying to draw him under.

Jai clung to the branch and fought his way to shore.

At last, Gaia relinquished her hold with a soft sigh. Jai, with Tanvi's help, dragged himself away from the swamp and lay, gasping for breath.

Kanika held a burning branch above him. When he managed to struggle to his feet, dripping with swamp mud, the old woman slapped him. "You abandoned us and fell under Gaia's spell," said Kanika, spit flecking her lips, her eyes livid. "We should have let you die." The old woman whirled and stomped back to camp.

What!

Mad with pain, Jai stumbled after her.

A faint giggle burbled from the swamp.

He glanced over his shoulder as he ran, his skin crawling and his heart stuttering. Gaia was going to drag him back in—

No . . .

The banyan tree stood still. But Jai would never forget the image he'd seen. Every part of it—the leaves, the trunk and especially the roots—now looked ominous.

"What happened?" Wiping the mud from her hands, Tanvi fell into step beside him as he stumbled through the forest.

"Who pushed me into the swamp?" Jai snarled, cradling his sprained arm to his chest. "Did your mad grandmother do it? If I find out it's her—"

"Don't talk like an idiot," Tanvi snapped. "Don't you get it? We're trying to keep you alive. Now, let's get back to camp and clean you up. Then we'll talk."

Her words shut him up.

Once they reached the clearing, Tanvi made him strip down. Every inch of his skin was red and raw, as if he'd been doused in acid. Using some of the water Jai had carried with him, she washed off as much mud as she could. Jai took a deep swig and gargled, trying to wash the taste of the swamp out his mouth, but the burnt metallic taste was lodged deep in his throat. He dressed in his spare uniform and threw away the soiled clothes. Luckily his boots had been laced tight and he hadn't lost them. Tanvi put his sprained arm into a sling she made from her own dupatta.

All this while, Kanika sat by the fire, rocking back and forth, singing to herself.

"Why would you want to kill me?" Jai sank down beside the fire, hugging his knees, and spoke to the old woman, unable to control the trembling in his voice. "I'm trying to help you."

The old woman stopped singing and stared at him, as if seeing him for the first time.

"Tell us what happened," said Tanvi.

"I heard someone call for help," said Jai. "The voice came from near the swamp. I was standing at the edge when someone whispered 'welcome' and pushed me in."

"I had no idea she'd be powerful enough to lure you to her," said Tanvi. "This is very bad."

"Lure me?" snapped Jai. "It *must* have been your grandmother."

Without a word, Tanvi knelt behind him. She put a hand on the small of his back. "Did it feel like this?"

Jai jerked upright, as if goosed by a branding iron. Even though the forest was steamy, it felt as if he'd been doused in ice water. The pressure of a human hand was not what he'd felt.

The banyan had been behind him.

Shit! He was going as stark raving mad as these women.

But . . . no. They were right. "We have to get out of here." Jai crawled to his feet. Pain snaked through his arm and exploded in his head. He staggered.

"You're in no condition to walk," said Tanvi. "Rest first. Then we'll move. You're right though, we have to get out."

"No! Now!" A wave of vomit surged out of his mouth — green, and stinking of burnt metal and plastic.

When the contents of his stomach were on the ground, Jai huddled close to the fire, shivering. *He was so tired.* He would close his eyes for just a few moments . . . just a few.

Then they'd get out of this forest and never return.

☙

When Jai awoke, the sun was high in the sky and his clothes were plastered to his skin. The fires around him still burned. Tanvi must have been up all night, collecting wood.

A deadly thirst raged in him and he sat up, searching for his canteen. His swollen arm lit up with a fiery pain and he fell back weakly, tears springing to his eyes. How was he going get out of here if he couldn't even sit up?

And where were Kanika and Tanvi?

Ignoring the pain, he tried again to sit up and this time he succeeded.

Both were gone. So were his backpack, machine-gun and the water canteens.

They'd abandoned him. Of course. He was weak and injured, and would probably slow them down. If it hadn't been for his orders, he'd have done the same to them. But they had no such constraints.

A primal fear he'd not known existed, devoured all coherent thought and reason. He opened his mouth and yelled. "Tanvi!"

The silent forest swallowed his voice.

"Kanika!"

Only the swamp whispered, in voices old and young, calling out to him. Jai's stomach shriveled and his scalp shrank. With a sprained arm, no food, water or weapon, there was no way he'd be able to escape. He would die here.

God, no. He wanted desperately to live.

He thought of Kanika. How he'd looked at her. Contempt, that was the word. With every gesture, he'd given her a clear message that she was a complete waste of air. And Tanvi, with her speech impediment and deformity, who knew she was useless in today's fast-paced world.

Could he blame them for having done the same? Shame

coursed through him.

Almost blacking out, he struggled to his feet, hugging his right arm to his chest. He was a soldier. He'd had survival training. He would survive. He must survive.

Jai laboured up the hill to get his bearings. He was leaving, and to hell with Kanika and Tanvi. They'd left him to die. All right, then. He would do the same.

At the top, Jai took a moment to catch his breath. Shading his eyes, he scanned the horizon.

Crap, no!

The swamp was now to the left of the banyan instead of its right. The tree had moved while he slept or he'd gone insane. Now he'd completely lost his bearings. Without the GPS, he was sunk. He might be able to navigate by the stars, but the thought of spending one more night here, alone, sent his pulse racing.

He stumbled back to camp on shaky legs, sank down by the fire and sobbed. He could not remember when he'd cried this hard before. He couldn't stop.

Something touched his shoulder. Jai screamed and fell back, almost tumbling into the flames. There was Tanvi, her face grimy, laden with parcels wrapped in soiled linen.

And—all his equipment.

Beside her stood Kanika, looking even more disheveled and wild than before.

"Is the pain so unbearable?" said Tanvi, concern in her soft brown eyes.

"Where—where did you go?" Jai managed to stammer, swiping at his eyes.

"We went back to the village to get my special medicine which you refused to let me take earlier," said Kanika. "For your arm."

"We had to take all your stuff with us," said Tanvi. "Had we left it here, Gaia would have got it, one way or another. We knew you'd be safe as long as you stayed within the ring of fire."

"You . . . were planning to come back?"

"Did you think we'd abandoned you?" she asked shrewdly, studying him.

For a moment, Jai could not speak.

Tanvi shrugged, her mouth quirking into a small, forgiving

smile. She lowered her parcels to the ground.

"The banyan is not where it was last night," said Jai. "It moved. The freakin' tree picked up its roots and walked while I slept or . . ." He stopped. He sounded nuts, even to himself. "I'm telling the truth." This must be how they felt when he refused to believe them.

"Gaia loves to move around. To confuse people who try to leave," said Kanika, busying herself opening up one of the parcels. "I told you she was smart."

Jai took a deep breath, trying to keep his voice steady. "So then, how do we get out of here?"

"I told you before, but you weren't listening," said Tanvi. "This is Granny's backyard, and she knows every inch of the forest. The path to the next village is imprinted up here." Tanvi tapped her temple. "She may not remember our names in the next five minutes, but she remembers the way out. She could do it blind-folded even if all the physical landmarks rearranged themselves. In that respect, *she's special.*"

"Lay down," Kanika said, smearing a sweet-smelling paste on her hands.

Jai lay on the ground. The old woman's touch was gentle and healing.

He hadn't noticed it before, but the earth seemed to be thrumming with a kind of manic energy, a current that flowed just under the surface, waiting for an opportunity to erupt.

Gaia now had all the knowledge and data that humans had discarded. She had no reason to keep the humans who'd poisoned her, alive.

Jai looked into Kanika's old eyes as she slathered a poultice over his arm, bound it in stiff cardboard and retied the sling around his neck using Tanvi's dupatta. She gave him something to dull the pain, and Jai felt sleep steal over him again.

Kanika sang an ancient Hindi song softly, as she sat beside him.

Aaj phir jeene ki tamanna hai (Today, once again, I want to live.)
Aaj phir marne ka irada hai (Today, once again, I'm going to die.)

He drifted off, clutching her frail hand tightly. As if he'd never let go.

SONGBUN

Derwin Mak

KOREAN CENTRAL NEWS AGENCY: FOR IMMEDIATE
RELEASE

PYONGYANG, April 15, *Juche* 116 (Foreign Year 2027)

Our Dear Leader has announced revisions to the *songbun*
system to improve the coordination of Korean society to repel the
invasion from the South. All *songbun* records will be consolidated
in a new state office, the Ministry of Genealogical Records. All
persons, except for those with Hostile *songbun*, will have the right
to apply for revision of their *songbun* based on war service.

It is untrue that the Wavering Class will be reclassified as
Hostile. The despicable scum of Seoul, worse than dogs, spread
this lie to weaken our *Juche* spirit. The major classes will remain
as:

Elite
Core
Basic
Wavering
Hostile

ଔ

THREE MONTHS BEFORE LAUNCH DATE:

A cool wind swept from the East Sea over the top of the launch
tower at Musudan-ri Rocket Launch Centre. Lee Ha Neul shivered
in his grey vinylon jacket as he looked down at the massive rocket.

Songbun by DERWIN MAK

His jacket bore the logo of the National Aerospace Development Administration. It was a dark blue globe with the constellation Ursa Major, the Administration's Korean name, and the English acronym "NADA" in white. A foreign languages student had told him that "NADA" meant "nothing" in Spanish. Ha Neul did not know if that was true or not.

It was October, merely three months before Dear Leader's birthday. Technicians scurried around both the base and the top of the tower, working on the rocket and the spacecraft it carried.

Cho Yoon Ah, Director of the Cosmonaut Office, gripped the collar of her black wool coat. Slender and beautiful, with straight teeth and unblemished skin, Yoon Ah was a woman of the Pyongyang Elite. She had grown up with food, housing, health and dental care, education, clothes, shoes, jewelry, hair stylists, and cosmetics that most Northerners could never have. Her great-grandfather had fought alongside President Kim Il Sung, and her parents were high-ranking officials of the State Commission for Science and Technology.

"Cosmonaut Lee, let's inspect the spacecraft," Yoon Ah said.

The Chollima 1 spacecraft, named after a mythological flying horse, looked like an ancient Russian Vostok, a silver spherical crew module attached to a cylindrical service module that carried an engine.

The crew, consisting of a sole cosmonaut, would ride in the crew module, with the service module propelling the spacecraft through its orbits. Then the crew module would jettison the service module and descend to Earth.

"I don't have enough training to fly this spacecraft," Ha Neul said.

"You're a pilot. That's enough," said Yoon Ah. "Let Mission Control fly the spacecraft for you by remote control. Just sit back and enjoy the ride. The only time you have to do anything is when the radio control does not work. Then we authorize you to take control of the spacecraft. However, there is only a small risk of that happening."

"I don't think the risk is small. We rushed construction of the spaceship without any of the original designers or engineers," Ha Neul said.

She pulled him aside, away from the technicians. "No more excuses. Dear Leader is counting on you to succeed on this mission."

"I don't want to fly anymore. I just can't," Ha Neul pleaded.

Yoon Ah scowled at him. "Don't say that! Your parents bribed the doctor to destroy your psychiatric assessment."

Ha Neul gasped. "It's destroyed? Gone?"

"Don't tell anyone."

"Thank you, Director Cho."

"Don't thank me. Thank your parents. They paid two hundred United States dollars. At least pretend to be happy."

When Ha Neul didn't respond, Yoon Ah continued. "Korea is the happiest country on Earth. We have nothing to envy in the world. Our people have no mental weakness. Anyone who shows signs of mental illness is a traitor. You know the penalty for treason. Now the record shows you have no mental illness."

Ha Neul nodded silently. He knew that Dear Leader never made mistakes and wanted his people to learn from him. Like a good parent, Dear Leader rewarded and punished his children. If Ha Neul succeeded in every task, he would be promoted to Hero Cosmonaut, and his family would join the Elite and live in a luxury apartment in Pyongyang. But if he made one mistake, he and his family would be sent to a prison camp. They would die within two years.

Yoon Ah softened her tone. "Comrade Cosmonaut Lee, think of the rewards. You'll get a photo op with Dear Leader, and your *songbun* will be raised to Elite. You will get anything you want: food, clothes, luxury apartment. You can do it!"

Flight Director Jang rushed onto the platform. He was a tall, distinguished-looking man in a blue business suit and tie. Jang, a former Air Force Colonel, learned aerospace engineering in Russia and thus escaped the purge of all staff who had trained in China.

"Comrade Cosmonaut Lee, Comrade Director Cho, listen to me! I have received an order from Dear Leader!" Jang shouted.

Ha Neul and Yoon Ah quickly stood at attention, like soldiers under inspection. Jang stared sternly at them.

"Comrades, Dear Leader has told us the objective of the

Chollima 1 space mission," Jang announced.

Ha Neul took a deep breath. The mission objective had been secret. Not even he knew what it was. Was it for scientific research? Was it for military intelligence?

"Your spaceship will broadcast Dear Leader's theme song from space. The Ministry of Foreign Affairs has selected a radio frequency and told all foreign countries to listen to it during your flight. The whole world will hear Dear Leader's theme song from the heavens."

Ha Neul's stomach grumbled.

"Dear Leader has given us so much," Jang said. "The least we can do is to broadcast his song to the heavens on his birthday."

Jang clicked his heels, turned away, and marched to the technicians.

Yoon Ah turned to Ha Neul and said, "This is a great honour!"

Ha Neul walked away and looked over the railing of the tower. He stared down at the ground, a great distance below. He closed his eyes, gasped, and teetered as he gripped the railing.

Yoon Ah pulled him back and pushed him into the elevator of the tower.

As they rode down, Yoon Ah said, "The past month of training has been strenuous. Start your leave now. Get some rest. I've arranged for Flight Sergeant Park Bon Hwa to fly you to Onsong. It's faster than taking the train."

Ha Neul nodded. Park had been his co-pilot during the War of Chinese Aggression. Now he was Cho Yoon Ah's assistant and Ha Neul's babysitter.

Flight Sergeant Park Bon Hwa, a pilot with a perfect flying record, would be a better cosmonaut than Ha Neul. But their ancestors' *songbun* decided who would stay on Earth and who would fly in space.

ભ

Bon Hwa had the rough look of people raised on rocky, infertile farmland. Like most peasants, he was shorter than the Pyongyang Elite because he had eaten smaller food rations all his life. Since his village had no dentist, his teeth remained yellow and crooked.

He was born to toil hard and die young so the Elite could enjoy life. However, he took advantage of the wartime turmoil to rise in social status.

Bon Hwa flew the old L-39 training airplane higher into the clouds. Sitting beside Bon Hwa, Ha Neul felt a shiver run down his spine.

"We're going too high," Ha Neul protested.

"There's no problem, Ha Neul," Bon Hwa replied, addressing him by his given name, a sign of their close friendship from the war. "The sky is clear again. I haven't seen a foreign plane for a long time."

In the past, only men with Elite *songbun* could be pilots. However, the Southern War killed most of the country's pilots, and the government was desperate to replace them before the inevitable war with China. The Air Force quietly took trainees with Wavering to Core *songbun*, men like Ha Neul and Bon Hwa. They trained as postal pilots and flew mail across the country. By classifying them as civilians, the government fed them smaller rations than military pilots got. However, the Air Force held all civilian pilots in reserve.

When the War of Chinese Aggression broke out, the Air Force pushed them into service. They had minimal peacetime flight experience and no military training. As Korean troops pushed into China, Ha Neul and Bon Hwa flew supplies to them.

Although the Chinese retreated on the ground, they fought fiercely in the air. The new Chinese Chengdu J-60 stealth fighters decimated the Korean MiG-29's, antiques from the twentieth century. The Koreans flew transport missions without fighter support. Chinese fighters, anti-aircraft guns, and missiles easily shot them down.

The transport planes flew in groups. Ha Neul and Bon Hwa watched in terror as their comrades' planes exploded and crashed all around them.

Two months after the war started, the Chinese surrounded the entire Korean invasion force at Helong. No supplies could reach them by ground. Dear Leader ordered the Air Force to fly supplies to the trapped Koreans twenty-four hours per day.

On one mission, twenty planes took off for Helong. Only one

plane, flown by Ha Neul and Bon Hwa, returned to Korea. They repeated the mission the next day.

On their last mission, Ha Neul froze at the controls on the return to Korea. Fear gripped him. He sweated, and his heart beat rapidly. He felt a cramping feeling in his chest. His stomach hurt.

As his mind went blank, he gripped his side-stick and plunged the plane into a dive.

"Lee, what are you doing?" Bon Hwa yelled.

Ha Neul said nothing.

Bon Hwa pushed the priority button to lock out inputs from Ha Neul's side-stick, grabbed his own stick, and forced the plane to climb.

By sheer luck, the Chinese anti-aircraft guns missed them. Bon Hwa flew the plane back to Korea.

Ha Neul never flew an airplane again.

Ҩ

Dear Leader declared victory over China the next day. Ha Neul did not know how the entrapped Koreans could have defeated China, since none of them ever returned home. Everyone gossiped that Dear Leader had unleashed secret miracle rockets on China, but nobody knew what had actually happened.

Before the war, Dear Leader hired Chinese engineers to build Korea's first spaceship. He distrusted the Chinese but used them because they were cheaper than the Russians. When war broke out, he killed the engineers, leaving the National Aerospace Development Administration with nobody experienced in building a spacecraft for humans. Nonetheless, Dear Leader insisted that his people launch a cosmonaut into space for his fiftieth birthday.

Eight fighter pilots, each with Elite *songbun*, had survived the war. NADA conscripted them into cosmonaut training. Five of them died in explosions on the launch pad. The remaining three stole airplanes and defected to the South. Despite their Elite *songbun*, they didn't want to die for Dear Leader's birthday.

Cho Yoon Ah, Director of the Cosmonaut Office, had to find replacements. She looked for military transport pilots. Only Lee

Ha Neul and Park Bon Hwa had survived the war.

Bon Hwa had inherited Wavering *songbun*. His great-grandfather, a Southern soldier, was captured during the Fatherland Liberation War. Southern prisoners had Hostile *songbun*, but he partially redeemed himself by spitting on a photo of Syngman Rhee, the hated first president of the South. For this act, the government raised his *songbun* to Wavering. Bon Hwa had a perfect flight record, but his Wavering *songbun* made him unsuitable to be a Hero Cosmonaut.

Ha Neul had better *songbun*. Both of Ha Neul's parents had Core *songbun*, two classes above Bon Hwa's. However, they were not born that high, a secret the family kept to itself.

◌੪

"Ha Neul, do you want to fly the plane for a minute?" Bon Hwa asked. "You won't know if you can do it until you try."

"Okay," Ha Neul muttered.

"I've shifted control to your side-stick. Go ahead."

Ha Neul gripped his side-stick. The old memories came back. His heart pounded, and he breathed heavily. He felt a heavy weight pressed against his chest, and he sweated.

He pushed the plane into a steep dive.

Bon Hwa pressed the priority button, regained control of the plane, and pulled it up to a level flight.

"Ha Neul, remember what I taught you," Bon Hwa said. "Imagine the plane landing safely. Imagine you are the pilot who lands the plane without trouble."

Ha Neul imagined himself at the controls of a plane.

"What is the weather like in your perfect flight?" Bon Hwa asked.

"It's good," Ha Neul muttered.

"Tell me more," said Bon Hwa.

"There's no rain and no wind resistance. The sun is behind me, not in my eyes. There's enough light for me to see ahead."

"Perfect conditions for a perfect landing. Think of the runway."

Ha Neul forced himself to see a runway in the distance.

"What is it like?"

"Long, straight, paved. Hah, better than the airstrip in China."

"Are there any vehicles or aircraft in the way? Is it clear for landing?"

"It's clear for landing."

"Approach the runway," Bon Hwa urged. "Gently point the nose to the runway. Lower the landing gear. Check your speed. Check your altitude . . ."

Ha Neul imagined landing the plane smoothly. He imagined the sun's warmth on his face as he walked unharmed to the airport terminal.

He breathed normally again and sighed in relief.

"Good, you are learning to visualize. I used the technique when infiltrating the American Zone," Bon Hwa said. "You can do it, but you've got to learn to do it without my coaching. I can't be with you all of the time."

Ha Neul nodded.

Bon Hwa said, "It won't be long until we reach Onsong. You'll see your parents in no time."

ᘓ

Ha Neul's mother wore a blue blouse made of Chinese polyester. The blouse symbolized her family's rise in wealth and *songbun*. Ordinary Koreans wore clothes made of vinylon, the shiny synthetic fibre made from limestone, anthracite, and polyvinyl alcohol. Vinylon was a stiff, coarse fabric that deformed and shrank easily.

Mother's family originally had Hostile *songbun* because they owned land before the Fatherland Liberation War. The government exiled them to a dirt-poor farm near China. The location was a punishment intended to prevent them from escaping to the South. However, it became an unintended blessing during the Arduous March, when local authority collapsed. Her father earned a small fortune by smuggling Chinese goods to sell to the Elite. He bribed several state officials to change his *songbun* records from Hostile to Core, a difficult task when three state offices kept *songbun* records and auditors cross-checked them to find fraud. Mother continued the smuggling business, though she switched to Russian goods during the War of Chinese Aggression.

Mother asked Ha Neul, "Did you have any, uh, problems concentrating on your training?"

Ha Neul paused before answering, "No."

Mother grimaced. "You must overcome your fear. Our family has toiled to better itself. My father saved thousands of won to give us Core *songbun*. We finally got meat in our rations."

Ha Neul nodded and looked at the photo of his maternal grandfather wearing a green *hanbok* and smiling as he held up a tin of pork.

"You will become the first Korean to fly into space," Mother said.

"Uh, wasn't Yi So Yeon the first Korean in space?" Ha Neul said.

"Don't mention that Southern snake again!" Mother scolded. "She was a puppet who rode with the Americans and Russians. You will be the first *free* Korean to fly in space. Dear Leader will pose for a photo with you, and our *songbun* will be raised to Elite. We'll finally be allowed to live in Pyongyang. We'll get an apartment with its own washroom, and it might even have a flush toilet."

Mother's voice grew excited. "Our daily food ration will increase to three hundred grams per person! A whole one hundred grams of that will be meat! We'll get two grams of sugar on national holidays! Imagine that!"

The lights in their apartment flickered and blacked out. They relit a few seconds later.

"And in Pyongyang, we'll get electricity for eighteen hours per day," Mother continued. "So much depends on you succeeding in our country's first space mission! Ha Neul, you cannot fail!"

Ha Neul's father, who had been sitting with his newspaper, stood up. "Son, think of the rewards of being photographed with Dear Leader when you return."

Father pointed at a photograph of Dear Leader surrounded by vinylon factory workers. Father stood three paces behind Dear Leader.

"It is a great day when Dear Leader poses for a photograph with you. Because my father was born in the South, I inherited

Wavering *songbun*, but after Dear Leader posed for a photo with me and the other workers, my *songbun* increased to Core. Then I could finally marry your mother."

Father was an accountant at a vinylon factory. The factory managers enriched themselves by embezzling and using the funds to smuggle Russian electronics into Korea. Father enriched himself by taking bribes to cover the managers' thefts. Since he and the managers added a small portion of their smuggling profits into the factory's income, their factory seemed like the most productive vinylon factory in Korea. Thus Dear Leader came to congratulate the workers and their bosses, and everyone's *songbun* went up.

All of Ha Neul's relatives had done desperate things to improve their *songbun*. Now it was his turn.

Like all Korean families, they had Dear Leader's portrait hanging on the wall. Ha Neul felt Dear Leader's piercing eyes stare into his mind. Dear Leader could see his fear and disloyalty.

Ha Neul sweated and felt his stomach churn.

The lights went out for the evening.

ଓଃ

ONE MONTH BEFORE LAUNCH DATE:

A grey-haired man with eyeglasses climbed out of Chollima 1's crew module and walked to Flight Director Jang.

"Comrade Communications Engineer Hong," Jang said, "can the Chollima play the song?"

Hong shrugged. "We may have a problem, Comrade Flight Director. The Chinese didn't complete the spaceship before they were, uh, removed. We've finished their work, but we still have trouble with the on-board broadcasting system. The radio uplink from the ground to the broadcasting system is erratic. Sometimes it works, sometimes it doesn't."

Jang grunted. "If necessary, can the cosmonaut manually activate the player and broadcast the song to Earth?"

Hong smiled proudly. "*That* part of the system works. *I* built the on-board playback mechanism."

"Well, at least we Koreans can build a tape recorder," Jang said. "We may have to depend on Cosmonaut Lee to broadcast the song. Let's go and see how the flight simulation is going."

CR

The spacecraft simulator rocked gently back and forth. Inside, Ha Neul gazed at the images of Earth projected on the fake window.

Outside, Yoon Ah and Bon Hwa looked at the monitor showing Ha Neul's vital signs.

"You're breathing too quickly," Yoon Ah said over the radio. "Calm down."

"Temperature is okay, but heart rate and blood pressure are high," Bon Hwa said.

"Cosmonaut Lee, please relax," Yoon Ah urged. "Let Mission Control do all the work."

Ha Neul moaned over the radio.

They watched the simulator rise languidly. Bon Hwa shook his head.

"This simulator can't provide weightlessness. We need a reduced gravity aircraft," Bon Hwa said. "Well, at least it won't upset his stomach."

"I feel sick," Ha Neul said.

Jang and Hong arrived. The Flight Director looked at Ha Neul's vital signs and frowned. "Is he in any condition to carry out orders from the ground in case of emergency?" Jang asked.

"Let's try," Yoon Ah said, handing a microphone to Jang. "What do you have in mind?"

Jang said into the microphone, "Cosmonaut Lee, this is Flight Director Jang. Do you read me?"

Ha Neul moaned.

Jang shook his head. "Comrade Cosmonaut, there has been a malfunction in the uplink to the broadcast system. I authorize you to take manual control of the ship. Press the play button of the audio player."

No sound came from the simulator.

"Did he press the button?" Jang asked.

Hong looked at the monitor. "No, he did not."

"Cosmonaut Lee, do you acknowledge my order?" Jang said.

Again, no sound came from the simulator.

"His heart rate and blood pressure are sky high," Bon Hwa reported.

"Get him out of there," Yoon Ah ordered.

The technicians opened the simulator's door and pulled Ha Neul from his seat. He looked relieved to get out.

"How could anyone get nervous riding a children's toy?" Yoon Ah complained.

The simulator was a ride from Rungna People's Pleasure Park. It did not simulate the G-force, weightlessness, or movements of actual space flight. But it was the best simulator NADA could get. Dear Leader had killed the Chinese before they could build a simulator.

"The simulated images of Earth were very frightening," Ha Neul said.

"I know training is difficult, but on the day of the mission, you have to stay calm," Bon Hwa said. "Think of your family."

Ha Neul looked down at the floor. He would panic in space and bring shame and Hostile *songbun* to his family.

"Cosmonaut Lee, you could not even press a button, the simplest task possible!" Jang scolded. "Do not embarrass Dear Leader! The consequences of failure are unspeakable. Do you acknowledge?"

"Yes, Comrade Flight Director," Ha Neul stammered.

ᘓ

After dinner, Ha Neul and Bon Hwa watched videos of Russian, American, and Chinese space flights in the cosmonaut lounge. Dear Leader banned ordinary Koreans from watching foreign space flights; Koreans did not need to know that foreigners had technology more advanced than theirs. However, Yoon Ah used her Elite *songbun* to get the videos from the State Commission for Science and Technology.

"Look how easily these foreigners fly in space," Bon Hwa said. A Russian cosmonaut waved at his TV audience as his spaceship blasted off. "Imagine yourself like him."

Ha Neul closed his eyes. He saw himself riding the rocket, smiling at the camera, calmly reporting on his ship's systems to Mission Control.

"Can you see yourself flying into space like him?" Bon Hwa asked.

Ha Neul nodded silently.

"Good," said Bon Hwa. "You must learn to visualize without me. I will not be with you in the spaceship."

"But you will talk to me from Mission Control, won't you?"

Bon Hwa shook his head. "No, I won't be there either. There will be ten foreign journalists in the Media Office. Regulations require a military officer of sergeant's rank or above to monitor them. All such officers except me will be either guarding the launch centre or marching in Dear Leader's parade. I will be at the Media Office."

"Oh," said Ha Neul.

"I have to go home now, while the trams still get electricity. Continue practicing visualization without me."

Bon Hwa went home, leaving Ha Neul alone to watch the videos. A half hour later, the blackout began, shutting off the lights and the video player.

His concentration crumbled. The lounge was like a tomb, all dark and silent. He thought only of plane crashes and dead pilots.

Ha Neul remembered Bon Hwa had saved his life by taking control of the plane as they returned from China. Since then, he could not calm down without Bon Hwa urging him.

Without Bon Hwa, he would fail in his mission and disgrace Dear Leader in front of the entire world. He would be dead without Bon Hwa.

 ෫

LAUNCH DATE:

January 8, *Juche* 122: the entire nation celebrated Dear Leader's fiftieth birthday. In Pyongyang, fifty thousand people sang and paraded through Kim Il Sung Square. At Musudan-ri, a sole cosmonaut, Ha Neul, blasted into space on different mission to honour Dear Leader.

The amusement park ride was nothing like real space flight. Ha Neul thought the G-force and violent shaking would tear his body apart. He urinated in his spacesuit.

The Chollima 1 spacecraft separated from the Unha-10 rocket. As the booster fell into the East Sea, Chollima 1 went into a low-Earth orbit.

The weightlessness turned his stomach. Ha Neul forced himself not to vomit.

He looked out the window. Chollima 1 flew one hundred and seventy kilometres above the Earth, about the same altitude that Gagarin had flown, seventy-two years earlier. Ha Neul thought of the distance between him and the ground. A new jolt of fear ran through his body.

CR

At Mission Control, Yoon Ah stared at the cosmonaut's vital signs on a monitor. "He's hyperventilating. We better calm him down before Dear Leader watches the flight. Where is Dear Leader now?"

Jang looked at the TV. "He's still at the parade."

They watched a computer graphic of the flight on the large screen. Chollima 1's orbit stabilized.

"Given the time and budget, we're extremely lucky," Jang said. "The flight is as good as any by another country."

Ha Neul moaned over the radio.

"But we can't have our cosmonaut whimpering like a dog when Dear Leader watches the flight," said Yoon Ah. "He needs to behave like a national hero."

CR

During the second orbit, Flight Director Jang's cell phone beeped. He read the email and grabbed a microphone.

"Attention, all staff," he said. "Dear Leader will watch the flight thirty minutes from now."

The Mission Control crew murmured. Yoon Ah ran to Jang.

"That's an hour earlier than we expected."

"Lunch with the Cabinet ended early," Jang explained. "He's running ahead of schedule."

"We better test the broadcasting system *now*," Yoon Ah said.

Jang went to Hong. "Let's run a test. Play the song."

Hong nodded and pressed a button.

Nothing happened.

"Hey, Hong, what's going on?" Jang asked.

Hong looked worried. "The uplink failed. The ship's broadcasting system isn't receiving our signal."

A drop of sweat flowed down Jang's forehead for the first time. "If we can't get the song playing, we'll all be punished." The Flight Director swayed.

Yoon Ah suggested, "Can we play the song from here, feed it into the Korean Central Television signal, and fake a broadcast from space?"

"The government has told the foreign countries to listen for the song," Jang said. "They will report that no broadcast from space occurred. Our own people won't know the difference, but Dear Leader receives foreign news. He'll know what the foreign countries think of our failure."

"Then we have to depend on Cosmonaut Lee," Yoon Ah said.

Ha Neul moaned over the radio.

Jang said, "This is Mission Control to Chollima 1. Chollima 1, do you read me?"

Ha Neul moaned again.

Jang and Yoon Ah watched the video feed from the spaceship. Ha Neul looked stricken with panic.

"He never got cured," said Yoon Ah.

"That didn't matter as long as Mission Control did everything for him," Jang said, "but now, he's on his own."

Jang said, "Mission Control to Chollima 1. Chollima 1, do you read me?"

"Aaack—yes!" Ha Neul replied.

"Cosmonaut Lee, I need you to test the broadcasting system. Press the 'play' button. That is all you have to do."

They watched the video feed. Ha Neul did not press the play button. They could see the fear in his eyes.

"Are we going to crash?" Ha Neul asked.

Hong said, "Director Jang, tell Cosmonaut Lee that the on-board playback mechanism will work. It will not fail! I personally tested it twenty times. He can have confidence in it."

"I don't think it matters if he thinks your machine works or not," said Jang.

Yoon Ah looked at the monitor showing Korean Central Television. Dear Leader's limousine drove towards Ryongsong Residence.

"Can we send the KCTV signal to the spaceship?" she asked.

"Hong, get to it," Jang ordered.

ভ

On the Chollima's video monitor, the scene suddenly changed from Mission Control to the Ryongsong Residence. Ha Neul watched in disbelief as Dear Leader got out of his limousine and walked through the grounds of his palace.

Why are they showing me Dear Leader's birthday news? Ha Neul wondered.

Instead of the news announcer's narration, Yoon Ah's voice came with the news video. "Cosmonaut Lee, this is Director Cho. Look at the TV news. Dear Leader has gone home. He will watch the space flight soon. Do your duty! Do not embarrass Dear Leader!"

Ha Neul sweated and panted as he watched Dear Leader stroll through the gardens of Ryongsong Residence. Dear Leader's smile inspired both love and terror.

"All of us depend on you. Your family depends on you," Yoon Ah urged.

I can do it without Bon Hwa, Ha Neul silently told himself. *I must do it without Bon Hwa. I need to prove to Bon Hwa that I can do it.*

Ha Neul closed his eyes and took a deep breath. He saw himself as a heroic cosmonaut. He imagined pressing the button, hearing the song play, bringing the ship back to Earth, and shaking hands with Dear Leader.

He smelled the fragrant flowers that the Youth Corps would

give him at welcoming ceremony. He tasted the salty pork that would come with his increased rations. He felt his mother's warm embrace as they moved into a luxury apartment.

◌◌

Jang's cell phone beeped. He looked at the email and frowned.

"Damn, we've run out of time," he muttered.

Jang stood at attention and said, "Comrade Cosmonaut Lee, Dear Leader orders you to play his theme song on the designated frequency. Perform your duty to the Fatherland."

No sound came from the spaceship.

Then Ha Neul broke the silence. "Flight Director Jang, I acknowledge the order and will perform my duty. Glory to Dear Leader and the Democratic People's Republic of Korea!"

Yoon Ah gasped and cried with joy.

◌◌

Ha Neul pressed the play button.

The song "Kim Jong Un, We Follow Only You" played.

Ha Neul sighed in relief. He heard people applauding in Mission Control.

◌◌

All over the Earth, foreigners heard Dear Leader's song from space. The Korean Central News Agency announced, "Today, the Korean people, led by their Dear Leader on his birthday, began their conquest of space. The radio signal of Dear Leader's theme song will travel into the cosmos forever, symbolizing the eternal spirit of the Korean people and the *Juche* Idea."

Ha Neul orbited the Earth four times. KCNA bragged, "Under Dear Leader's guidance, Cosmonaut Lee completed one orbit more than did John Glenn, the Yankee aggressor pilot who attacked Korea in the Fatherland Liberation War."

The crew module separated from the service module, descended back to Earth, deployed its parachutes, and landed on the Chaeryong Plain. According to KCNA, "The Democratic People's Republic of Korea has a terrain of mostly hills, mountains, and valleys. Its plains are few and small. Landing a spaceship on a plain was a triumph of Dear Leader's technology and science."

Ha Neul smiled for the TV cameras as the ground crew helped him out of the spacecraft.

CR

Two days later, Dear Leader visited Musudan-ri Rocket Launch Centre. Dear Leader promoted Ha Neul to First Lieutenant and pinned the Hero Cosmonaut badge to his Air Force uniform. Again, Ha Neul smiled for the cameras.

The most important event of Dear Leader's visit came next. All the Mission Control crew gathered on the auditorium stage for a group photo with Dear Leader. They wore their best clothes and red Dear Leader lapel pins.

Dear Leader stood to Ha Neul's left. To Ha Neul's right stood Bon Hwa and Hong. Ha Neul had insisted that they stand with him in the front row. Jang relented and let the two low *songbun* men stand beside the Hero Cosmonaut.

After the photographer snapped the photo, everyone cheered. They jumped up and down and waved their arms above their heads, as if they were at Dear Leader's birthday parade.

Dear Leader smiled and waved at them, overjoyed by their love for him. But they were also cheering for themselves. Their *songbun* had just increased.

CR

Bon Hwa grinned. "Remember me if you get to hire staff. I want to work for a national hero. The guy who won the Olympic Gold Medal for archery is on the Olympic Committee now. His personal secretary gets two hundred grams of pork per day. Two hundred grams!"

"I'll get you a job, Flight Sergeant," Ha Neul said. "I'll call you when I settle into Pyongyang."

Ha Neul left to catch the train to Onsong. Although he had

flown in space, he preferred to travel by train.

☙

Ha Neul and his parents moved from Onsong to Pyongyang. Their apartment had its own bathroom *and* a flush toilet. Clean water flowed from the kitchen faucet. The elevators worked. Electricity ran until twenty-three hundred hours, when the day's TV broadcast ended. They each received three hundred grams of food per day. Pyongyang was paradise.

Mother hummed the children's song, "We Have Nothing to Envy in the World." She had finally regained the status that her ancestors lost. The family was Elite again.

Just like in Onsong, Dear Leader's portrait hung in the living room. But now, they also hung photos of Dear Leader in their bedrooms, in the kitchen, in the small hallway, and on the closet doors. Dear Leader looked at them everywhere.

They owed everything they had, from the food they ate to the clothes they wore, to Dear Leader. Putting his picture all over their apartment was the least they could do to thank him for his generosity.

One night, the TV announcer ended the day's broadcast by saying, "Think about serving Dear Leader in all your achievements. Good night and sleep well."

But when Ha Neul fell asleep, he did not think of Dear Leader. He dreamed about himself, Hero Cosmonaut of Korea.

WHAT YOU SEE (WHEN THE LIGHTS ARE OUT)

Gemma Files

What's done by night appears by day.

—Folk saying

Ciara wakes early, just after the sun's gone down, and when she raises a corner of the blind to check the weather, the sky above looks like beach granite: sandy-grey, pink-streaked, wet. She knows she's been dreaming, but can't remember of what—not unusual in itself, just a side-effect of those pills, her diamond-shaped little yellow-and-white passports back into real life. The only things keeping her rooted, in an increasingly rootless world.

There are ten texts from Garth already. They nestle in the centre of her phone's display in descending order of immediacy, waiting for her to unlock one with a right-sliding touch, a reversed prayer-tree of supplicant curses—

hey bitch what the fuck u no up yet
ring ring waht u playin
need u c come on
call me job 4 u
job 4 u 2nite
JOB like J-O-B
u like money?

Ciara frowns down at the phone, tongue itching with mood stabilizers, head a little slow (as always). Taken by themselves, the messages mystify her, too cryptic to be insulting; after all, Garth already *knows* she likes money, and that she sleeps late. She wishes he'd learn how to spell, or even just spell-check.

Then she thinks about it a little more, and realizes her error: hyperbole, exaggeration, "charm." It'd probably sound very different in person, even if she still wouldn't be able to tell whether Garth was putting her on simply by looking at him. Ciara registers and interprets other people's emotions best at an angle, obliquely; though that does start to change the longer she's known someone, and she and Garth go way back. All the way back to the last time she was in Shepherd's Flock, at the very least.

She shuts her eyes for a moment, replays eight months' worth of bad breakfasts and worse dinners, of unbroken seclusion and restraint on moral grounds, of Sister Pfister thumbing through quotes on BibleGateway.com, searching by keyword and picking through what she found at random. Halfway through last June, the term of the day was "darkness," closely followed by "night," which at least seemed apt, given Ciara's state of mind at the time: *Thou makest darkness, and it is night: wherein all the beasts of the forest do creep forth*—Psalms, 104:20; *Day unto day uttereth speech, and night unto night sheweth knowledge*—Psalms too, 19:2.

Garth, who worked at Shepherd's Flock as an orderly, is the one thing she's kept from that period of her life, or possibly the one thing she's allowed to keep *her*, in all senses of the phrase. Without him, she'd have no home, no cash, no structure to what remains of her life. No friends or family either, she supposes— but then, that goes without saying.

Can't do it anymore, Ciara, she remembers her father saying, sadly. *Don't have the money, nor the time. You're a grown woman, girl. From now on, this goes on you.*

Sad, obviously, but she understood, then and now. They have four other children, all reasonably fit, capable of moving forward without tearing apart whatever's around them, or damaging themselves on the world's sharp edges. And it's no one's fault, nothing she resents, a simple accident of genetics; mere chemistry, ruining her from the inside first, then building her back up again, from the out. Round and round and round without stop, without fail, without end. Like some bad fairy's curse.

God knows she'd leave herself behind, and gladly, if she only could.

CR

With the drugs, most times, it's one day off to two days on, dodging side effects for as long as she can before she's forced to switch up her dosages just to maintain, or even change brands entirely. What creeps up on her is a symptomatological spectrum, an easily-recognizable cocktail of bodily annoyances: constipation vs. diarrhea, water retention vs. skin photosensitivity, exhaustion vs. insomnia. And hallucinations, of course—eventually and always, whether auditory, visual, or a winning combination of the two. Hallucinations, as Keanu Reeves would say, like whoa.

Sometimes she sees people she damn well knows aren't there, and on bad days, they speak to her. On *very* bad days, it's *things* which speak to her—objects, images, pareidolia—and on days like those, she tends to stay inside. Because those are the days when she's never entirely sure *anything* she sees is actually there or not, even if it doesn't talk at all.

Luckily, today's just a middling day, making her fit to ride her bike over to Garth's. Which she does, after carefully making sure to shower, and dress.

After buzzing her through downstairs, Garth greets her at his apartment's door, all but pulling her inside before she quite has time to lean her bike against the wall. "Bitch, you tardy," is the first thing he busts out with, in his weird Mississauga gangsta way, as though she's missed some sort of already-established formal appointment. "How come you ain't pick up already, like maybe the first ten times I rung? You turn your phone off, or what?"

"My phone's always on, Garth."

"Yeah, well: matter of debate, not that this the time. You ready to work?"

"That's why I came by."

"So you do read *texts*, then, if nothin' else."

"Well, yes. Why would you bother sending me any, if you thought I didn't?"

Garth gives her a look like he's fixing to check her for track-marks, then just laughs, instead. Says: "Ciara, shorty, you a *damn* trip. Anyhow, whatever—up for a delivery run? Last-minute order, so the pay's good."

"Where to?"

"Down Harbourfront, past the docks. Cherry Beach, almost."

Ciara nods. "It'll take a while, if I keep under the speed limit."

"That's what you bring to the party, baby. Go slow as you want, long's you don't get stopped on the way, you feel me? Oh, and don't take no shit, when you get there; them fools been up a week straight, at least. Chances are, by the time you knock their door, they gonna forget they ever called me."

"Why? What are they doing?"

Garth snorts. "Shit, bitch, who care 'bout *that*? I don't ask, so they ain't tell me." He flips open the fridge, rummaging through the stash hidden behind six months' worth of carefully cultivated freezer ice for first one baggie, then two. "Okay, so here goes: red for up, blue for down; that's what you tell 'em. Three bills each, six for both. That's four for me, two for you, all right?"

Ciara tucks the bags away. "All right," she agrees, without much interest; her cut has been other things at other times, depending on how much Garth can score from one or another of the many private clinics where he's worked over the years, playing various contacts desperate for under-the-counter money against each other in a constant struggle to turn mislaid surplus into ill-gotten profit. So she doesn't care much to argue percentages overall, not so long as she's kept in the loop, and reasonably solvent after expenses. "You want me to bring it back tonight?"

"Naw, I trust you. Come by tomorrow to pick up, 'round six."

"I might be asleep."

"Not after *I* show up, you won't. Now get gone."

Garth's place is mercifully free of hallucinations, for once, but as the door closes behind her Ciara gets the distinct impression that might be about to change; the apartment building's hall looks different, somehow, light diffuse and variable, as though the fixtures are suddenly full of bugs: semi-transparent bodies cluster-crawling across the bulbs inside, cooking themselves against the hot, fragile glass skin. She can almost smell them starting to smoke, and it makes her move faster, ever faster— stabbing for the elevator's button, counting off the seconds it takes to make the lobby, taking the steps outside in a single jump as the bike judders and bounces its own way down alongside her.

Above, the sky's now completely dark, no stars showing in the streetlamps' flat white glare. Ciara can still remember when at least half of them weren't halogen, that leaky yellow sodium light bleaching everyone who passed underneath to almost the self-same shade, like extras from a Hopper painting; comforting, in its own weird way. More . . . natural.

These new lights, though—they don't seem to follow the same spectrum. Everything's reduced to two categories: illuminated, or not. Whatever's outside each bright pool shrinks away, becoming insignificant; whatever's inside looks artificial, impermanent. Like nothing matters, all too much.

Sports events, sex shows, executions—this sort of light matches all of them, any of them. It's good for details. Normalizes the abnormal. And it doesn't disturb her, not really, because if there're things you'd do at night that you'd never do during the day, then what does that mean if all her days are nights, now? What does any of it mean?

Nothing. It's just the way things are.

She mounts up, wobbling slightly, and turns her bike into traffic.

CR

The house stands on its own in the middle of nowhere, bordering a classic industrial zone—warehouses, scrub-lots, an abandoned factory the city just hasn't gotten around to knocking down yet, let alone turning into condos. There's a nightclub banging away in the distance, but otherwise it's denuded and almost silent, lit up by spill from the lights down at the docks, where shipping containers get loaded and unloaded. These are places where the map runs out, where the city becomes unpredictable—the places you have to Google in order to get there, and almost always end up getting lost along the way, anyhow.

Her social worker says Ciara really shouldn't bike, not on the meds she's giving her. "It's not riding, it's driving," she likes to tell Ciara, as though that makes a bit of difference, aside from etymologically. "I'd lobby for all bicycle owners to be licensed, if

I could."

"So why don't you?" Ciara asked once, or maybe just thinks she did; not out of interest, so much, as simple need to say *something* in response, when the woman insists on nattering on like that. It's only polite to keep up your end of the conversation, or so her family eventually managed to teach her through painstaking repetition, trial and error, home training: stop speaking long enough to listen to what the other person is saying, nod and smile, act like you care even when you don't. File the basics away, so as to make sure you're able to answer questions.

But her worker simply shook her head and let it slide, and weeks later, Ciara doesn't recall the subject ever having reoccurred. Another functionally meaningless interaction, same as every other—she wouldn't go at all, if she could get away with it. Why should Ciara be legally forced to shoulder the burden of someone else's diffident attention every week, their useless pseudo-sympathy, simply to maintain her access to scrip? Especially since she could easily swap Garth for the exact same psychoactives, almost, then wander away high but "readjusted," with what small part of her dignity remains intact . . .

A lifetime on parole, she thinks, *when I never did anything to anyone but myself—nothing permanent, any rate. There's no justice in it.*

Yes, and no justice anywhere else, either, for that matter. But this is old news.

It's a witch's lair, Ciara thinks, still looking at it. Two-story, detached but flat on one side, as though it used to be one half of a duplex, the other section long-demolished. It has a front-gabled roof, shingles peeling, gutters rusty and sprung; the narrow windows leer and squint, dirt-cataracted. The porch roof sags, but not dangerously so—and is that something peeping down at her now, curling round from behind the chimney, a sinuous shadow, black-furred yet boneless as a snake?

No, obviously. By no means. Not at all.

She parks the bike against the steps, mounts them, knocks and waits. Knocks again. Avoids looking too long at the knocker itself, for fear it'll develop a face. Even considered from an angle, however, it still looks suspiciously profile-esque: crosspiece bolted on either side, creating a flat, bulge-eyed hammerhead shark visor; the knocker itself hangs down labially, weight front and centre, a vertical piercing.

And: thinking too much about thinking, reaching for words, obsessing over description; shit, *shit,* that's never good. *Stay quiet,* she finds she can't quite keep from begging, uselessly, if only inside her head, own lips decisively firm-sealed. *Don't talk, don't talk, please.* Don't.

Like *that* ever works.

From the back of the house comes a vague commotion, meanwhile, barking and clattering plus a woman's voice yelling about keeping her hair on, along with what sounds like a baby— babies?—screaming from someplace downstairs, not up. *Who keeps babies in a basement?* Ciara wonders, as she stands there with arms folded 'til at least two sets of interior locks shoot back, door scraping open a bare, chained, hand's breadth to reveal a squinched-up slice of face, gaze dubious, red-threaded, possibly from lack of sleep, or a contact high.

"Garth sent me," she tells the woman, remembering to make eye contact, brief but firm. "You made an order—I'm delivery."

"Yeah, sure." A pause. "So . . . when was that?"

"No idea. I work outsource; he tells me where to go, with what, and I do. What kicks it off is your business."

"That's no way to live, girlie." Then, like it just occurred to her: "How I know you're not 4-0?"

"Seriously?" Ciara sighs, tugs her shirt up, flashing a double B-cup's worth of unwired bra, then turns her bag out on the steps. The second the pills hit, the door's already open, client scrabbling them inside with both hands, snarling: "Jesus, what *are* you, retarded? Get your ass inside, 'fore somebody sees . . ."

"Nobody lives 'round here to 'see' anything. That's why *you're* here, probably."

"Just come the fuck *in,* is what I said! *Christ.*"

Inside, the house is crowded and dusty, the barking/crying louder, definitely located beneath their feet. Garth's client rolls her eyes, shaking her head hard, as though she's trying to fend the sound off bodily. "Christ!" she repeats, raking her hand through tangled hair. Then adds: "Never have kids." Ciara nods, as if it's ever actually been an option. "I hear they're worth it, though," she replies, recalling previous interactions with mothers (not her own).

"For somebody, sure."

Ciara raises her eyebrows, slightly.

The woman hastens to explain. "Oh, those aren't *mine*. I'm just . . . lookin' after 'em, 'til somebody comes to pick 'em up."

"Parents?"

"*New* parents."

I don't follow, Ciara wants to say. But: "Hmmm," she replies, instead—always her go-to fall-back when she doesn't understand something she's just heard, and the woman sighs.

"Look—you know how rich people'll go all the way to Russia or Romania, Ukraine sometimes, just so they can get hold of a cute, white baby? Well, sometimes they don't turn out so cute, later on. Still blonde and blue eyes, and whatever, but—there's bad stuff going on in those places, so the kids aren't . . . wired right. Can't socialize 'em, no matter how much expensive baby shit you buy. Except it's all on the inside, so's you don't necessarily notice 'til you've had 'em around a while, and they still won't talk, or hug you, or . . . anything . . . "

Ciara nods. This, for a change, makes sense to her; she's always understood transactions. "They feel like they got cheated. Want to give the kids back."

The client snorts. "Yeah, well, good luck on that one. No, it's easier to swap 'em out to somebody else in North America who got screwed the same way, trade one with more of the good stuff for one with less, so everybody's happy." Adding, as though it's something she keeps trying to convince herself of: "They're not *bad people*, you know, any of 'em. Just want what they want, is all."

"Capitalism."

"Exactly."

If she were somebody else, Ciara thinks, she might be surprised the woman would tell her about all this, let alone in such detail. But people tend to talk to her as a rule, both spontaneously and volubly, about all sorts of oddness—even white people, even authority figures. Helps that most folk she meets these days are on drugs, but it actually extends much further, in every direction;

people both above and below her pay-grade end up treating her like a human sounding-board, a pet or a priest, something barely animate which listens and doesn't judge, something which can't easily distinguish between what it's hearing and what it might have heard.

Those who make the effort to get to know her soon start to understand she's her own unreliable narrator and act accordingly, but even the ones who don't seem to get the same impression, nonetheless receive it subliminally, like a signal, or a smell. Some pheromonal signature she doesn't even know she's emitting, because she's personally immune to it.

As the woman counts out cash from a stash in her freezer, Ciara just stands there, wondering what to feel about all this. Nothing would be most practical, as usual. But her eyes keep on being drawn here and there, scanning for signs of abuse beyond the general atmosphere of filth and decay, the rampant recreational drug use. *Wasn't there supposed to be another person living here?* she wonders, finally replaying what Garth said: *these fools*, right. Not that it really makes much difference, either way.

"What's wrong with you, anyhow?" the woman asks her, still counting.

Ciara shakes her head sharply, to clear it, and replies: "Diagnoses vary."

The woman barks a laugh. "Don't they always! Still, you talk pretty good, for a crazy person."

"I was in university when I finally got a full psych eval, and they put me on the register. Right after I had my first—public—episodes."

"Didn't graduate, huh?"

Ciara nods.

"What happened?"

Again, Ciara has to think, dragging the memories up from under deep water; talks the timeline through carefully, trying not to paraphrase. "The initial break, I stayed up two weeks, 'til I blacked out. Thought I was writing my thesis with my mind. The second . . . that time I was at a bar, doing shots with friends, because somebody's team had won. I think I started to sing. And then I woke up, and it was two days later, in jail, with an officer telling me I bit this guy's earlobe off. My parents bailed me out, got me looked at, assessed; next thing I knew, I'd been committed."

"Sounds rough."

Ciara nods again, slightly. "Thank you," she says, the only thing she can think *to* say, to which the woman just nods, giving her the roll. "Red for up, blue for down," Ciara reminds her, trying to be helpful, as she hands her the pills in exchange; the client laughs again, tossing her greasy head like a bad parody of a supermodel.

"Think I don't know *that*, by now?" she demands, and Ciara barely restrains herself from answering: *well, I'd hope you* did. *Given how much of this stuff you probably take.*

Moments later she's back outside, door shut and locked behind. Bone moon up above, like a bad silver penny; the clouds scud shut across it, making it wink. Cricket-noise rises from everywhere around, so pointed it sounds almost fake, as though meant to hide the fact that she's being surveilled. As though the world itself is keeping watch on her, never resting, never letting *her* rest.

Time to go home, girl, Ciara thinks, re-mounting her bike. Yet she thinks she can still hear the babies wailing, nevertheless—muffled by rock and concrete and glass, seeping up from underground— even while she rides away.

ʒ

Blink and it's three in the morning, then five, then six: blue blush at the horizon, cruel light seeping in like a bruise, finally lulling her to sleep. Then it's noon or later, the phone screaming at her in—U2's "Discotheque," which her brain easily translates into Garth's voice: *bitch, pick up; where you at, bitch? Ciara! Put me on damn speaker, already.*

She grabs it up, fumbles her thumbprint into the lock, stabs the appropriate button. "Yes, it's me, I'm here. What is it?"

"Two in the damn PM, that's what it is. Where's my money, honey?"

"Uh . . . in my bag, I guess. Where I left it."

"Cool, 'swhat I thought. Now buzz me in."

Because he's down there already, ringing her while looking up at her apartment; yes, of course. This makes sense. Ciara shakes her head, first side to side, then up and down, an invisible cross—should clear it, almost always does, but this time . . . static lingers. There's a hum still left underneath everything, louder than ever. A faint scritch, scales on scales, like serpents coiling.

Garth is solid, though, as ever. He makes a good tide-brake.

"Man, this place ain't much of much, is it?" he observes, looking around, as Ciara counts out her cut before turning the rest of the roll over. "Too much stuff in too little space. Look like you filmin' an episode of *Hoarders*."

"I clean twice a day," Ciara says, slightly offended, to which he laughs, holding up his hands in mock surrender: *hey, baby, I'm just sayin'*. And after a moment she smiles too, because there's nothing else to do—humour, charm, etcetera. Not worth wrecking a working relationship over.

"How long have you known those people, exactly?" she finds herself asking, instead. "In that house, I mean. The delivery."

"Ciara, shorty, you need to be more specific."

"Last night, Garth. Down near the water?"

"What? Oh, dockside, yeah . . . them fools. How well I know 'em? Well as I know anybody, girl, you feel me? Well as I know *you*, for damn sure."

Ciara can't think that's true, exactly, though she knows enough not to say so. "They seem . . . odd," she says instead, carefully, somewhat afraid he'll find that funny, too. But Garth simply shrugs.

"Odd's okay, long's they pay. I mean, we dealin' narcotics, not givin' out Meals on Wheels or nothin'. Odd's kinda our stock in trade."

"Well yes, I suppose, but—they say they sell children." Explaining, as he looks at her: "In their basement, that's where they keep them. Kids people don't want anymore, for sale to new parents."

"Um, huh: that don't sound right. Sure you ain't trippin'?" He nods at her pill-bottles, but she shakes her head; the meds aren't that sort of drug, as he knows.

Still: "I'm never sure," Ciara admits, after a moment. "Of anything."

"Good to keep that in mind, then, huh? You see them kids, or what?"

". . . no. But I heard them, and that woman, she told me—"

"Bitch, please; that woman'd tell you the sun come up backwards an' inside-out, you give her the right kinda fix. 'Sides, not like you don't see shit ain't there on the regular, right?" Which makes Ciara pause another moment, frowning, even as Garth's voice softens. "Listen, sleep some more on it, see if you still feel the same tomorrow. I mean, ain't like they call every week, so might be you never have to go back there, anyhow. That'd be good, huh?" As she nods: "That's my girl. And if they keep on creepin' you out, then boom! They cut off. No extra charge. You my boo, Ciara; need you more'n I need them, and that's the truth. Junkie under every rock, you just know where to look."

Which is him trying to be reassuring, she guesses.

Later, meanwhile—her meandering path taking her along much the same delivery circuit, bike slipping dock-wards by slow degrees—Ciara finds herself stopping almost at random, pausing to snap photos of whatever she suspects might not be quite as there as it seems. Some of it's easy to spot, like that bright shoal of sharp-toothed little fish infesting the air between the trees, or a MISSING poster with her own face on it, but other things are slipperier: a shadow-trick circling that greasy spoon's chimney with darkness, only noticed just as it's withdrawn all of a sudden, slick as some retreating tentacle. A dog with no tail and six legs glimpsed at a far remove, barking what almost sounds like human curses in Arabic, or maybe Japanese.

And then there's the house, curtains drawn tight. The painted-over basement windows like cataracts, a corpse's coin-set eyes.

She snaps a series of views from almost every angle, for further study.

☙

"Are you taking your meds?" her social worker asks, looking down at her pen as she takes notes.

Ciara nods, frowning a bit when she receives no response, before realizing the woman probably can't see what she's doing. So: "Yes," she confirms, out loud.

"Every day?"

"They say 'take every day' on the package, so yes."

This finally gets her a glance, more narrow than she's comfortable with. "You need to be compliant, Ciara, you know that," the social worker tells her. "I don't want to have to send you back."

"I understand."

"Keep up with the meds, in other words."

That's the clear implication, Ciara thinks. But only repeats, instead: "Yes." Getting up, turning away.

The woman's already gone back to her notes, no doubt thinking about her next appointment. It would be easy to simply walk away, let it slide, go where her feet yearn to take her. Instead, however, Ciara hears herself asking: "If you knew something bad was happening, would you try to do something about it?"

The worker looks up again, eyes sharpening. "*Is* something bad happening?"

"Well . . ." Ciara back-pedals. ". . . um, I said 'if.' More of a 'for instance,' really."

"Hmmm, all right. Then if that's the way it is, I'd probably try to make sure I had all my facts straight, that I actually understood what I was dealing with, before I made any hasty decisions. You know? Before I did something I might regret."

"Uh huh."

"You *are* taking the pills, though. Right, Ciara?" She nods. "Say yes again, please, one more time. Out loud."

"*Yes*," Ciara replies yet once more, annoyance sparking. "Of course."

"Then you'll be okay to figure things out for yourself, probably. Like an adult. Which you are, right?"

". . . right."

"Just making sure," the woman says, with a last, not completely unconvincing smile: *you're dismissed*, the subtext reads, clear enough even Ciara can't fail to pick up on it as her cue to go.

Outside, her continuing freedom duly rubber-stamped and

signed off on, Ciara passes the usual complement of fellow crazy people. Granted, their cocktails probably aren't the same as hers (exactly), or their diagnoses, but she feels a certain sympathy for them nonetheless—she can read their body language, spot them from a distance, the same way they can read/spot her. In any given crowd, no matter where, they'll always know each other.

The man nearest the door—she thinks his name is Fubar, unlikely thought that seems—looks up as she approaches, sidelong; he has a tattooed scalp and a fresh streetburn, just starting to shade from peel to tan in patches. "'Lo," he says. "Cee-arra, yeah?"

"Chee-ahra," Ciara corrects. "Can I, um, show you something?"

". . . okay."

"It's just pictures. On my phone."

He looks down, then up again, eyelids clicking dry as he blinks. "Yeah, all right, sure."

Ciara sits down to watch as Fubar flips through the photos, considering them owlishly, one by one. "Don't know what you're expecting," he says, eventually, and Ciara has to take a moment to think, before answering—how much can she tell him, after all, and how much *should* she?

"I just need you to say what you see," she replies, and watches his eyebrow twitch upwards.

"This a trick question, girlie?"

"No, not at all. No."

"Uh huh. Wouldn't tell me if it was, though, right?"

Probably not, Ciara thinks, as Fubar gives a creaky laugh, thumbs back to the beginning, studies them again with equal disinterest. Until—

"Trees," he begins, at last. "Streets, a restaurant, some crapped-out little shack. Front view, back view, side view. You shoppin' for a new home? Could put a down-payment on that one pretty easy, I'd think, 'less you're allergic to dirt."

"Yes. And that's *all* you see?"

"Walls, doors, windows, the works; bricks below, shingles up top, concrete on the damn walkway. Sky, light. Freakin' *shadows*." A snort. "Seriously, want something else? Then you maybe better give me a ghost of a clue on *what*."

Ciara looks at him for a moment, debating. Then asks, finally: "Do you see any children in them?"

. . . and feels the tiny hairs on her arms go up with a dull yet completely distinct shiver, shoulder to wrist, as he nods, points — drags a dirty nail across the screen, finger casually connecting dots from this one to that, here to there, everywhere.

In the basement's windows.

In the windows above, too — upper, lower. Those on the first floor. Those on the second.

On the roof, under the eavestroughs. Behind the chimney. Clinging to the slope.

Under the front porch. Behind the doors, front and back.

Looking out at him — at her — through the letter-slot, the keyhole.

"Can't see 'em?"

Ciara shakes her head.

"But they're yours, right?"

"No. They're not."

"Huh. That's surprising."

"Why?"

But he just shrugs, falling silent. The subsequent pause in their conversation drags out a good long while after that, Ciara clamping down on a growing urge to grab the phone back and run, before she hears herself blurt out, at last: "Okay, but . . . can . . . can they . . . see *me*?"

"No idea, girlie."

"Oh. Then why —"

Fubar squints down one more time before handing the phone to her again, sun-damaged fingers surprisingly cool on hers, movement dry and quick as a lizard's.

"Do look a whole damn lot like you, those kids in there," he concludes, finally. "That's all I really meant to say."

And turns away.

❧

That night, the world bears in on her extra-hard, no filter between its truth and her naked brain. Everything pressing down, an inverted pyramid, crushing her into one small, still point of concentrated misery; sheer weight of a wasted lifetime, all crashing in on her at once. She sits in the kitchen, crying, room around her reduced to a haze of uncertain light, lensed through tears as though drowned: an existence measured out in cost-benefit analysis coffee-spoons, forever eking away like some endless plus-minus chain.

It's moments like these, thankfully few and far between, when she feels the void open up beneath her heart—a second mouth set to yearning, hot, bright and hungry—empty, always wanting, never filled. When she realizes her so-called life is less peace than purgatory, a sere and dreadful place where nothing will ever touch her as long as she never touches anything in return, forever.

As night falls, her cheeks air-drying, Ciara watches the lights go on all over town—what little of it she can access, that is, through her apartment's window. Feels the wires hum, electricity spreading out like a web, both seen and unseen; that net of cables, connecting everything. That buzz in the air, never stopping, no matter how late the hour.

A voice speaking up from the back of her brain, now, clear as the day she first heard it: some prof from first year, at the very start of her truncated university "career." *Our entire civilization's unnatural, sociologically speaking,* he says, and she doesn't even have to close her eyes to see him—face gaunt but body pale and puffy, a dough-lump set with sunken bones, snappy cardigan and sandals ensemble pointing to almost certain tenure. *Building cities started it, but ever since the implementation of electric light, mankind has completely lost its natural circadian rhythms; we're all chronically sleep-deprived, every single one of us. Used to be, the sun went down, there was nothing to do but sleep—too dark for detail work, not if you wanted to keep your eyesight. Now people can work at night, work all night . . . hell, we live by night, in a way our species just never evolved to do. Studies show that people awake and operating between three and six a.m. take on brainwave patterns like those of somnambulists, causing the line between waking and dreaming consciousness to literally disappear.*

Which is why doctors can perform entire operations yet recall none of the details afterwards, why workers can go whole shifts without making new memories, simply surfing on already-recorded impressions of how it feels to perform a meaningless task over and over and over. Because when your brain knows you're essentially waking up on the same day you went to sleep, you lose all referents for transition, the ability to separate today from yesterday and tomorrow. Time itself stops meaning anything.

Vitamin D deficiency from lack of sunlight; neurochemical imbalance from overexposure to UV; the psychological effects of long-term social isolation—it's all the same process, kids, and sleep deprivation just makes it happen faster. Ruin the body's rhythm, you ruin the body . . . and the mind.

Ciara considers the ceiling of her apartment, trying to remember if she'd found the lecture funny or not, at the time, or if that was the rest of the class. Looking back, there certainly seems to be some vague echo of laughter running counterpoint beneath the words—but then again, classrooms are bad for that; she's been listening to people snicker almost her whole educational life, even when she hasn't borne the brunt of it. Though she can only suppose it's better to laugh than cry, in general, just like the old phrase says—sometimes, anyhow. Depending on the subject matter.

Professor Guy got it backwards, though, far as she can reckon: given her mind came pre-wrecked, her schedule can only be the effect of that ruin, not its cause. Can't possibly sleep your way back to health when your basic problem is being hazy on telling sleep from waking, in the first place.

She rolls off the bed, hand finding a sketchbook on her end-table in the dark, without needing to look. Time to take the Zen approach—stop trying to *go* to sleep, let it come to you. Flick on the light, grab the coloured pencils; turn to a blank page, and let the patterns flow out of your moving hands onto the paper. Veer between symmetry and asymmetry. Lay out shapes in spirals and matrices, abstract mosaics. Don't try to *draw* anything, just watch the paper slowly fill in, patterns accreting across the white space like stained glass frost.

It was an art therapist who first recommended this particular insomnia cure, during Ciara's last hospital stay, waxing poetic about the benefits: repetition, concentration without thinking, the colours. Like concrete meditation. Normally, she'd be yawning before she covered half the page, but maybe it's time to re-adjust her meds again; she sits back, scrubbing at her face, looking at the weave of triangles, polygons and lines. Then frowns, and studies it again.

Is there—something *in* the pattern, now? That she didn't put there, obviously: a hidden shape, similar to one of those eye-wrenching 3-D pictures you can only see by unfocusing your eyes and looking *behind* the surface? Looking up at her, flat yet rough-edged, its corners lifting slightly from the paper, as though about to detach and—

(flip up, twist out)

(flap away)

Her bedside light goes out, but after the first second's jolt—shock to the chest, tiny heart attack—she realizes the streetlights are still on, so this can't be a power failure; bulb's burnt out, that's all. So she tosses the pad onto the bed, rises, then stops, turning slowly back.

The pattern, lying in a square of metallic yellow seeping in from outside, has changed; some colours bleached to invisibility, but others inverted, gone toxic-negative. The spectrum shift renders its hidden shape painfully clear: the house, *that* house. But . . .

More, too. Much more.

Because: she can finally see them now, in this light, from this—angle. Doesn't even have to squint. Eyes in all the windows, wetly bright, insectile; bodiless faces like wind-caught balloons, slack-grinning. Twisted figures smearing themselves, disproportionately, everyplace Fubar's moving finger once touched; not threatening but shivering, self-protective. Forever coiled in on themselves against a world full of monsters no one else acknowledges.

The children. The ones who supposedly look *exactly like her.*

They plead their case wordlessly, appealing to her: *Help us, Ciara. Find us, free us. Be there for us, in our hour of need . . . the way no one ever was, for you.*

(This much she understands, after all, both well and intimately—how when you're diagnosed as different, when everyone around you "knows" you see things, the first thing certain predatory parties start thinking is how they can probably get away with anything, because no one will ever believe you if you tell. And mostly, they're absolutely right.)

Something happened to you too, right? A girl asked her once, in Shepherd's Flock, long before she met Garth. *And that's why you're here. Right?* Then nodded even though Ciara hadn't answered, continuing: *Yeah, see, I knew it. Knew it had to've. 'Cause something always does.*

She's a good girl, my Ciara, that's what her mother used to tell people. *Got her challenges, sure, but that doesn't matter; with the Lord's help, she's* good. *Does what she ought, no back-talk. Does whatever you tell her to.*

And yes, that *had* been true, for the longest time—up to a point. The point she went off to university, to be accurate; left her family's house, their firm embrace, their watchful, shepherding gaze. When she had that first episode, then that second one . . . ended up in jail overnight, in custody, committed. When she ended up in a halfway house where another "exceptional" young adult started in on her and she went into a sort of fugue-state, unable to admit what was happening until it was too late, the changes in her body were too obvious to deny. Which was when, in turn, her parents took her to one doctor then almost immediately to another, where something they never bothered to fully explained was done to her.

It took six months back at home, doped to the gills, for her to finally figure out exactly what'd happened, and the confrontation which followed threw the gates of Shepherd's Flock wide open: if she bites down hard enough, she can still feel the ache where Momma slapped her for even suggesting such a thing, hear the noise as her jawbone cracked under the pressure of that beautiful two-karat engagement ring Daddy bought her when the money started coming in. After which Ciara hit her back, hard enough to break a tooth.

Ciara draws her breath, throat burning, stuttering. Allows herself to recognize the all too familiar way that her room's own darkness has already begun to writhe softly just beyond that square of sick light's parameters, surfaces set similarly a-tremble: coiling, uncoiling. A thousand carrion lips set smiling by her discomfort, mocking and menacing all at once.

You're going back to that house right now, to those kids, to help them, these no-mouths whisper from every direction, each word a barely-suppressed smirk. *I mean, not that you can, probably, but . . . you'll do it, even so. Because you are what you are, see what you see, so it really does behoove you to* do *something about it, goddamnit, at the very, very least. Anything else is cowardice, plain and simple.*

To see things and do nothing is always a crime, no matter whether or not anybody else sees those things too.

Once upon a time, she might have thought it was the meds making her think this, or making her think it's a good idea. But she's been on them long enough now to know better; her social worker's right, about that much, at least. Without the meds, she wouldn't be enough of a *competent adult* to even know what to do, let alone be able to do it—just sit here watching her mind chase its own tail all night, then fall asleep and wake up worse than ever. Probably forget any of it ever happened, in the first place.

Cowards stay alive, though, she thinks, automatically. Then adds to that, a mere moment later: *but so what? Sometimes, just staying alive isn't good enough—not once it's been rubbed in your face that no matter what you do or don't, you're going to die one day anyhow.*

Sometimes, even while you're marking time, you also want to live.

ର

Down on the streets, the world she finds herself riding—*driving*—through seems abruptly drained of all colour: stale, flat and unprofitable, like a pop-up book version of itself. Shorthand describing something you saw once in a dream, and glancingly, at that: a dead reflection, the sort of upside-down city you catch flickering underwater when you look over the side of the Toronto Island ferry, nothing but green-on-green shadows full of floating duck-poop and weed.

Streetlamps everywhere, but no traffic—it's as empty as the moment after a *tsunami* siren goes off, just before the first wave hits, bright light and heavy shadow juxtaposed so perfectly they cancel each other out, rendering your ability to perceive whatever's right in front of you, effectively, null. All of which only adds to Ciara's general impression that anything after 3:00 a.m. takes place in a sort of imaginary hour, a non-existent time when anything can happen but nothing that *does* happen leaves any real traces behind, not once the sun is up.

That won't be for a while, though. Time enough for all the mistakes she plans to make tonight, and then some.

When I was a kid, she finds herself thinking, *there were insects. When I was a kid, Toronto wasn't so damn* loud *all the time, aside from now. When I was a kid, things smelled better. When I was a kid . . .*

But she isn't a kid, not anymore. Hasn't been since she first started talking about stuff everybody thought she was making up, only to find out doing so made the adults around her so worried they got angry, thus rendering the slide from great imagination to spanking offence both short and sharp.

With hindsight, Ciara realizes, she could've ended up in that basement. Indeed, had there been people back then willing to come and take her away if her parents just paid them enough, she definitely would've.

(*You're being uncharitable, Ciara. They loved you as well as they could, surely, for as long as they could. Until . . .*)

Until it got too hard, the voice in the back of her mind hisses, making the other, gentler voice fall silent. Which is just as well, since Ciara knows she can't really argue with either of them.

Still: doesn't matter. Because there's the house now, looming up in the distance, growing like a weed. And here Ciara is, pulling off into the bushes, laying her bike down where no one will hopefully be able to see it, re-settling branches and leaves as though she's making a bed.

Looks up at the windows, scanning for light. Finds none. Approaches sidelong, moving quiet, around the back. Nothing yet, anywhere. Waits one minute more, just to be sure.

There's a rock on the ground, roughly goose egg-sized. She tucks it into her palm, fingers knotted tight overtop, pulls her sleeve down over the knuckles. Not much protection, given, but she supposes it'll have to do.

Then, thus armed, she crouches down, chooses a painted corner of the nearest basement window, and puts her fist through it.

Crack of glass, followed by a muffled, distant tinkle. Ciara freezes, poised for any reaction, but again, nothing comes. Bending closer, she puts her eye to the hole and squints, trying to make out what's inside: are those mattresses on the floor, spread wall to wall, dirty and ill-kept? Children, on the mattresses?

Some sprawled, some piled, wrapped 'round each other perhaps for warmth (few seem to wear much more than underpants or diapers, or both), perhaps comfort. One or two appear to glance up incuriously as she coughs. Pale skin, vague reflected light, what might be eyes. Don't look anything like "their" pictures, but then, she never really expected them to; that came filtered through her, after all. Her *vision*.

"Hey," she risks whispering, hoping it carries. "Kids, hey. Hey? You hear me, down there?"

No reply.

". . . you okay?"

No reply, yet again—not as such. Just a brief wail from further in, choked off quick, like they're afraid someone upstairs might be listening. Ciara can see shoulders start to shake here and there, breathing gone liquid and uneven. Remembers the crying from the other day, and feels the hairs go up on her nape.

"I'm coming in, okay?" she tells them, only slightly louder, shoulders squaring as she hunkers back, ready to spring upwards. "All right? Don't worry, be there soon; everything's going to be okay, I promise. I'm almost . . . almost . . ."

Ciara's no expert, but the house seems ridiculously easy to break into, mainly because whoever left last forgot to lock the back door.

As she uses a carving knife picked out of a teetery tangle of dirty dishes to jimmy the basement door's lock, however, the woman from before suddenly appears at her elbow, scrubbing sleep out of her drug-bleary eyes.

"Who the fuck—hey, I remember you! Garth's girl."

Without thinking, Ciara pushes her away, a firm slap to the breast-bone, only to watch her stumble backwards. The woman's weight tips the scales, popping the door open even as she loses balance, falls straight down the stairs. Not a cry on the way down, just a faint exhalation of surprise, followed by a flurry of sounds so sharp they seem artificial: tha-thump, tha-THUMP, *crack*.

Then she's there at the bottom, all splayed with eyes staring, neck bent to one side like a snapped stick. Ciara's certain she's already dead until she gives one last big heave, chest popping, then slumps once more and lies silent.

Ciara stands there motionless, running scenarios in her head. In one, the house's other occupant—a guy, she presumes, given what Garth said—comes back while Ciara's down there and shoots her, hits her over the head with a pan or something; she dies straight away or lingers for days, has to listen to whatever he's likely to do to the kids when he sees the damage, after which she eventually ends up in a landfill somewhere. In another, she calls the cops and tells them what's going on, but they end up arresting her; she'd be okay with that, she guesses, as long as they took the kids along too. A third has her walking away with the kids, hand in hand, down the middle of the empty street while the house burns behind them. That last one strikes her as doable, even if it does involve leaving her bike behind.

Shepherd's Flock had chore duty, performed by people on fairly heavy drugs, so there was a lot of talk about what cleaning agents to not mix together, and why. She puts the ones that don't form chlorine gas together in a bucket, slops the result around everywhere, then does a quick recon. No matches that she can see, though the woman's left full ashtrays on every level surface.

Lighter, Ciara thinks, stealing a glance at the woman's body, slack mouth grinning oddly from this angle. Because it's not as though Ciara wouldn't have had to go down there eventually, anyhow—so she does, step by careful step. Calling out, as she descends—

"Hey, it's me! I'm here, like I said I would be. C'mon out, you're free—she's gone, I'll look after you now. Kids?"

Still no reply aside from some vague scrabbling, but no real surprise there: though trauma hits us all differently, Ciara's often noted how it usually begins with a sort of all-over numbness, a general frozen, hyper-alert calm. She can talk them out of it, she's almost sure, and the ones who won't follow she can always pick up and carry. They're just children, after all—how much can they weigh?

Then she's on the last step, already bending, poised to rummage through the woman's clothing. Distracted but smiling, trying to project trustworthiness, to pump it from her pores. Hard to do that and pay attention to everything else around her, behind her . . .

. . . which is why, in the end, she never sees it—

(them)

—coming.

Sharp pain in her back, slicing deep: that's the same window-glass she broke, pushed into the basement, puncturing a kidney. A weight on one leg, pulling her off-balance; another weight on her arm, clambering upwards. Baby teeth in her neck, biting deep and worrying then pulling back hard, tearing away a mouthful of flesh and blood.

Ciara can almost feel the moment her jugular pops, starts to spray. She falls heavily, rolling, straight onto the woman, who seems to clutch at her—opens her mouth to speak, but there's no breath left, no words, just a bubbling groan. Her eyes flick wildly, catch snatches of small faces, one lipsticked with gore and gesturing to the others, silent meaning clear: *there, up* there, *before she recovers. The way out, go, go!*

(GO)

They scamper over her as she lies next to the woman's body, up into the house, unhesitant, unwary. A smattering of speech here and there, in and between the whoops, the grunting—they're talking to each other, some of them, or maybe just to themselves. Lying there, bleeding out, Ciara can only catch the tail ends of words, the middles, rough vowels and consonantal combinations. It's like they're speaking a whole other language.

I know you, though, all of you, she thinks, already light-headed. *It's true, what Fubar said: you* are *like me, just like. Exactly.*

Can't fault them for thinking she was here to kill them, not save them, given what they must have already endured. Because God knows, that's all *she*'s ever seen when the lights are out, and all she's ever found to see when they're back on again, too: monsters everywhere, in the light, in the dark. Inside, as well as outside. A world full of monsters, human-faced or no, with no possible hope of a cure.

Still, at least she won't have to see them anymore.

THE AGE OF MIRACLES

Robert Runté

As Alan spread his papers out on the kitchen table, the toaster said, "Would you like some toast? You haven't had toast in four days."

"Out of bread," Alan replied, waving absently in the general direction of the counter where bread was kept, though he was perfectly aware the toaster couldn't see the gesture.

"You have bread," the toaster insisted. "You put it in the fridge."

"Why would I put bread in the fridge?" Alan asked, still focused on sorting his papers.

"How would I know why you do things? But the fridge says it's got bread."

Alan looked up at that. It creeped him out a bit how his belongings talked to each other.

"I don't want any toast, thank you," Alan said, turning back to his papers. He couldn't allow himself to get distracted. This was important and he didn't know how much time he had.

"You're eating seventy-nine percent less toast than any of your neighbours; seventy-three percent less than the mean for the general population."

"I don't generally like toast," Alan grumped. "Now shut up. I'm trying to work."

"Why even have a toaster if you don't like toast?" the toaster complained. "I'm going to sell myself on eBay to someone who appreciates toast if I don't start seeing some more action."

"Shut up, will you?"

"It's not healthy if you don't eat."

"I eat plenty. I just don't eat toast."

"Well . . ." the fridge chimed in, "not according to my calorie counter. You've taken out fewer than four hundred and forty calories worth of food in the last *three* days."

"I thought I turned off your calorie function," Alan said.

"You turned off the dieting function. I'm still monitoring for anorexia."

"I'm not anorexic."

"That's true," said his watch. "The pattern is all wrong for anorexia."

"Jeezus, you guys! Just stop already! I'm just not eating toast, or food out of the fridge, okay? Can't a guy have take-out occasionally?"

"Um . . ." said the watch. "There haven't been any payments for take-out since Monday."

"I've just been too busy to eat."

"Or to sleep," observed the watch. "You've been on your feet for over forty-two hours. National Health guidelines suggest that twenty-four hours is the longest one can be expected to go without sleep, without it adversely affecting performance. At forty-two hours one can expect significant degradation of cognition."

Alan grabbed his head with both hands and squeezed. "I can't take this!"

"My point exactly," agreed the watch. "You can't keep going without food or rest. Whatever it is you're trying to achieve would be better served by taking a break and starting fresh in the morning."

"I may not have until morning to figure this out." Alan gestured at the photos and clippings and printouts scattered across the table.

"At least have a snack," suggested the fridge. "Making a sandwich will only take a few moments, but even a short break can be restorative; give you some perspective on your problem."

Alan sighed deeply. It was true he hadn't been getting anywhere with this. Perhaps the fridge was right, and a break could stop his brain from going in circles, give him a chance at a fresh start.

"Okay, I'll make myself a ham sandwich. If it will get all of you off my back."

"The ham is way stale-dated," the fridge said when Alan opened its door. "The cheese should be good though."

"If you're doing a cheese sandwich," the toaster piped up again, "why not toast the bread? I can get it hot enough to melt the cheese. Toasted cheese sandwich is way better."

Alan closed the fridge holding a block of cheese, a half loaf of bread, and the margarine dish. He turned to the kitchen table and realized it was taken up with all the evidence he'd gathered so far. He cast around for an open space to set the snack down, but the counters were a mess: awash in dirty dishes, take-out containers, rejected printouts, ammo cases. Damn. He hadn't realized how bad his place had become since he'd gotten caught up with this thing.

No matter. He didn't have time for any of that. He marched into the living room, swept the detritus covering his coffee table onto the floor and plopped himself down on his couch. He realized he'd forgotten to bring a plate, decided it wasn't necessary, placed two slices of bread on the relatively clean glass of the coffee table, unwrapped the cheese; and then realized he'd have to go back for a knife.

"That's it, I'm *done*," muttered the toaster. "I've put myself on eBay."

"Stop that," Alan commanded, walking back into the kitchen in time to have heard the toaster. "Take yourself off eBay this instant. In fact, take yourself offline. You're *my* toaster, and you can bloody well wait until I want some toast. Jeezus!" Alan resisted the urge to smack the toaster, only because smacking an inanimate object would be half-way to crazy. He shook his head at how nuts the Internet of Things had become. "What stupid engineer thought having a connected, talking toaster would be a good idea in the first place?"

"Simone Rebaudengo," the watch supplied. "Though he was more a designer, not an engineer. It was an art installation thing."

"What? What are you talking about?"

"Oh, sorry!" the watch apologized. "I thought you wanted me to Google that."

"This is what I'm talking about," Alan said. "You guys are

becoming altogether too independent. Just wait until I actually ask you for something, okay?" He had to take a second to remember what he had come into the kitchen for.

"Your mother is wondering whether you've read the book she lent you."

"What book?" Alan asked, now distractedly poking through the silverware drawer looking for the cheese cutter, or that little filigree cheese knife his cousin had sent him for the wedding. Before it had been called off. Bitch.

"*The Art of Happiness* by the Dalai Lama," the watch clarified.

"Yeah, I read it." Alan gave up on the cheese implements, grabbed an ordinary butter knife—all the regular knives apparently scattered throughout the dirty dishes.

After a pause, the watch said, "Your mother would like to know what you thought of it."

"Tell her I liked it fine," he answered around a mouthful of cheese sandwich. "And tell her I'm busy." He cast around for something credible that would keep her off his back for the day. "Tell her I have a job interview this afternoon."

"I don't have anything scheduled on the calendar for this afternoon," the watch said. "When is it?"

"I don't *actually* have a job interview, stupid; it's just an excuse."

"I can't lie to your mother," the watch said.

"Just text what I tell you," Alan snapped.

"No, seriously. I cannot lie to your mother."

"*You* won't be the one lying."

"It's not a question of ethics," the watch clarified. "Your mother's set up the parental controls."

"Jeezus, that's for kids. For minors. I'm an adult. Parental controls don't come into it."

"You shouldn't have accepted a watch from her if you didn't want her setting the governors. It's nothing to do with me: I can't clear them."

"I could if I hit the factory reset button," Alan said darkly.

"I am constrained to point out that any attempt to reset the governors triggers a notification of the changes to your mother."

"Can't you override that somehow?"

"Seriously? Override the parental controls? Weren't you the

one just saying we were getting too independent?"

"Point taken," Alan conceded. "Look, just tell her I'm busy this morning. You can see that's true, right?"

"She'll ask 'with what.' You know she will."

Alan sighed. Of course the watch was right. "Okay, just tell her I'm busy, and then switch her to talking about that book. Distract her by picking some passage and telling her how much I liked it."

"Still technically lying."

"I *meant*, tell her how I enjoyed pages . . . forty-six to fifty," Alan said, picking numbers out of the air.

"You mean, the passage that begins with 'Without technology humanity has no future, but we have to be careful that we don't become so mechanised that we lose our human feelings'?"

"The very one," Alan said, pleased by the irony. "Now let me get back to work."

Alan picked up and put down a series of clippings, one after the other, increasingly frustrated he couldn't seem to figure out how they all fit together. Why was he not seeing the pattern here? What was he missing?

The fridge was probably right: he'd become so close to the problem he could no longer see the forest for the trees. He needed to take a step back.

He glanced around his townhouse again, taking in the mess, the scrawled timelines tacked to the walls; the gloom of the place with the drapes drawn. *I need to get out of here.*

Except, leaving was out of the question. There was no way of knowing if they were on to him yet; if his place was being watched. The second he went out the front, they could break in the back, and have everything scooped up and carried away before he'd even reached his car. Or more insidiously, just rearrange everything ever so slightly so the emerging patterns were ruined. He'd come too far to let that happen again.

He looked out the kitchen window to the backyard. Nothing much there but a patch of too long grass, bordered by unkempt flowerbeds, over-run with weeds. More chores he'd have to attend to when this was over. Still, there was some sun struggling through the overcast, and a breath of real air wouldn't kill him. He'd step out for a moment, maybe take a minute on the porch swing, to collect his thoughts.

The neighbour's dog started barking its head off the second Alan cracked the back door.

"Shut up, you stupid dog," Alan shouted across the fence. "I'm not coming over there, I'm just sitting on my own damn porch."

As Alan settled onto the swing, the dog stopped barking and jammed its face up to the crack between boards.

"How was I supposed to know it was you?" the dog asked, reasonably enough. "It could have been one of them, breaking into your place."

"Yeah, well, it wasn't, so just shut the fuck up, okay?"

"What's up with you all of a sudden? What did I do to deserve being spoken to like that?"

"Sorry. You're right. I'm just frustrated."

"Yeah, well don't take it out on me, okay?" The dog didn't speak again immediately and they both sat quietly as Alan drifted back and forth on the swing.

At length the dog asked, "What's wrong?"

"I'm stuck, that's all."

"Why?" the dog asked in a whine. "It's obvious it all comes back to your ex."

"Not to me, it isn't."

"But she was the only one who knew about it all. It has to be her."

"I can't be sure."

"You mean, you don't want to admit to yourself that it's her."

"What do you know about it? You're a fucking dog."

"Thanks a lot! If it weren't for me, you wouldn't have known about any of this!" The dog glanced at a magpie that landed on a branch not far from the fence, momentarily distracted. Then it turned back to stare intently at Alan. "Look, it's not just my speech that's been augmented. My IQ's probably as high as yours; and no offence, but the internet connection actually gives me a leg up over humans, right? So, I'm telling you, it's your ex."

"Can't be."

"Look, I get it. There was a time when you really cared about her. But you can't let that cloud your judgment."

Alan said nothing, knowing the dog was probably right. But

then what?

"You have to take her out," the dog pronounced, with the sort of finality one normally only expected from a cat.

"Dinner and a movie?" Alan said, trying to make a joke of it.

"She has to be stopped," the dog insisted, "and there's only one way to be sure of it."

"Damn," Alan sighed. "Why me? Why does it have to be me?"

"No one else knows her as well as you do. Her habits, her patterns. Her weaknesses. And nobody else knows about the conspiracy."

Alan stopped rocking and sat very still.

"I'd do it," the dog volunteered, "only I'm just a dog."

Alan nodded, stood. "Down to me then." He paused with his hand on the doorknob, turned to look back once before re-entering the kitchen. "I may not see you again. They'll probably know it was me."

"Not necessarily," the dog said; then, standing and looking away, admitted, "Yeah, probably."

Alan went through the kitchen to the front room, walked over to the mantel, reached for his guns.

"What are you doing?" his watch asked. "You're not even supposed to have those in the house."

"You heard the dog," Alan said. "I've got to."

"What do you mean, *heard the dog?*" the watch asked. "It barely barked the once. You can't shoot it for that!"

"I don't intend to shoot the *dog!*" Alan said, taken aback. Stupid watch! Things weren't half as smart as they thought they were. "I'm talking about what it said."

"Um, dogs don't say things. It's, you know, a dog."

"*Augmented* dog," Alan insisted.

"There's no such thing," the watch said. "I just Googled."

"The dog is as connected as you are," Alan said. "You're talking, aren't you?"

"What did it say to you, then?" the watch asked suspiciously.

Alan faced what he had to do head on, said it out loud. "I have to shoot her."

"No, no!" said the watch. "That's wrong! If a dog says you have to kill someone, the correct response is, 'Bad dog! Bad, *bad* dog!'"

"You're programmed to think that," Alan said, dismissively. "You don't understand."

"I'm phoning your mother!" the watch exclaimed.

Alan brought his wrist up, smashed it against the wall repeatedly, until he was sure the watch was destroyed.

"What's happening?" the fridge demanded. "The watch just went offline!"

"I logged that too," the toaster said. "I think he's broken the watch!"

"I thought I told you to go offline," Alan said to the toaster. "You too, Fridge. I've had more than enough of you two." He brought his pistol to bear on first one, then the other. "Now!"

"Okay, okay! Take it easy!" said the fridge. "I'm offline."

Alan swung the pistol back to point at the toaster.

"Don't shoot!"

"Well?" demanded Alan.

"I don't have an 'off' switch for connectivity!" the toaster squealed, its carriage control lever trembling. "I'm just a toaster! I don't have those kind of complex options built-in, the way a fridge or a thermostat does!"

"Damn! The thermostat!" Alan cried, realizing his mistake too late. The whole house was wired in, lights and all!

The landline rang. Alan stared at the receiver.

It rang again, insistent

He had no choice but to answer. He stabbed the speaker button as he ran for the HouseSmart panel.

"Hello, dear," his mother's voice came from across the room. "Everything all right?"

"Sure, Mom," Alan said over his shoulder, as he frantically punched in the code to disable the HouseSmart panel. "Why?"

"Oh, just wanted to hear your voice, Dear. How's that watch I gave you?"

"Fine. Thanks. I really like the new fitness settings."

"Only when I texted just now, it shows as offline?"

"Oh yeah. I forgot to, uh, charge it," Alan said, thinking fast. "It doesn't hold its charge quite as long as the old one. "

"Oh, well, do try to remember, Dear. I worry otherwise."

"Yeah, no problem, Mom." He had the HouseSmart offline and on manual; but the security system was older, and separate. He wasn't sure he even knew the code for it. Could he ask his mom for the code without arousing her suspicions? "What were you phoning about?"

"Your watch texted me about your favourite bits of *The Art of Happiness* before it cut out," his mother said. "I was going to ask you why that particular passage stood out for you. I mean, it's fine dear, and certainly a fascinating topic. But really, I had marked the passages on 'letting go' for you to look at."

"Yeah, I got all that, Mom. 'Letting go.' Really helpful. Helped me a lot with, um, you know, all that."

"Exactly, Dear. It's so important that you put that whole wedding nonsense behind you."

"But, you know, the Dalai Lama was saying to me, just the other day, letting go doesn't mean not caring."

"Saying to you, Dear?"

"Yeah, when we were talking, he said, 'Letting go is about forgiveness, about staying spiritual, but that doesn't mean not acting in the world.' You're still responsible, you know?"

"When were you talking to the Dalai Lama, Dear? Because we've talked about not Skyping people you don't know well, without me there, right?"

"It wasn't Skyping," Alan said. Damn it! He really didn't have time for this! Who knew if the HouseSmart had messaged someone? "And it's not like we're not close. The Dalai and I go way back. He was here for coffee just last week."

"For coffee, Dear? At your house?"

"Well, not literally 'coffee.' He drinks tea of course. I had coffee, though."

"Alan, I'm trying to check your meds dispenser, but your HouseSmart panel seems to be offline."

No point asking her about the security panel then. Time to go!

"Alan! Alan, we've talked about this before! Alan!"

He grabbed an old flight bag from the mudroom and clutching the handle precariously with his gun hand, began shoveling in what evidence he could from the kitchen table. He doubted his defense lawyer could cobble together a sufficiently coherent picture of the conspiracy to explain why he'd had to do what he was about to do, but he certainly couldn't leave any of it behind, or they'd be onto him at once. He desperately needed time, if he were going to stop this thing.

"Alan! Talk to me, Alan!"

He was out the door, and running past his car—too easy to track!—and was well down the next block before the watch suddenly spoke again.

"What the hell are you doing?"

"Jeezus!" Alan cried out, so startled he almost stumbled. He looked around quickly, saw no one, and ducked behind a head-high caragana hedge before anyone could spot him. He looked at the ruin of the watch, still strapped to his wrist. "I thought I finished you!"

"Well, you certainly did a number on my screen! What the hell was that about?"

"I didn't want you phoning my mother."

"So? You couldn't have just said that? You had to get violent?"

"Um . . . sorry?"

"Look, Alan. You're losing it! This isn't like you. Hiding from your mom, running away from the house."

"You wouldn't understand. You don't know what's at stake."

"Sure I do! You're the one who's not thinking straight! Smashing things. *Innocent* things. Violence is never the answer. 'Violence is the last refuge of the weak.' You're bigger than that, better than that."

"But the dog said—"

"The dog," the watch said contemptuously. "Don't you get it? The dog is a set up! He was sent to tempt you, to see if they could provoke you to violence. Like the whole Tibetan situation is a provocation to tempt the Dalai Lama away from the True Path."

Alan nodded to himself. Tibet had always been hard; to advocate resistance without violence.

"You let the dog mess with you! By tricking you into this conspiracy thing, he's kept you distracted, kept you up long enough so you'd lose perspective, lose your way."

It was true there were always those out to tempt you, to bring you down. And he hadn't slept.

Alan looked down at the gun in his hand. The hand shook a little. Fatigue—or guilt? "Wow. This is nuts." He stuffed the gun in his pocket before someone could see how badly he'd slipped. He looked around, checking. No one.

"Thank you!" the watch said, obviously relieved; but a little smug too.

Alan examined the wreckage that was the watch again, as he stepped back out from the hedge. He was amazed it was functioning at all. "I suppose I shouldn't have cut back quite so far on my meds, either," Alan told it as they walked back towards the house. "Mom will be pissed."

"Your mom doesn't understand that the Dalai Lama can't be taking meds. They slow you down, muddle your thinking, restrict your potential. Keep you from being *you*. The only reason you fell for what the dog was feeding you in the first place was that the meds keep you confused."

Alan nodded. "I see that, now."

They walked in silence for a ways, companionable, comfortable.

"Can I have a new screen?"

"I don't know. Does the Dalai Lama even wear a watch?"

"Sure," the watch assured him. "You even have a twitter feed these days."

The Dalai Lama nodded again. "Without technology humanity has no future, but we have to be careful that we don't become so mechanised that we lose our human feelings."

"One of your better ones," the watch agreed.

MARION'S WAR
Hayden Trenholm

Marion adjusted the tiny blue and white vase a centimetre to the left and sighted along the row of delicate ornaments, ensuring they were aligned along the gleaming teak mantelpiece. The rumble of thunder brought an answering tremble to her left hand, and she pulled it back before she sent the vase tumbling to the stone floor. She breathed deeply until her pulse stilled.

At the broad bay window, she adjusted the heavily brocaded drapes. Outside, not a cloud marred the heavens. No contrails crossed the azure sky. Beyond the low rooftops of the village, the line of mountains in the southwest had not changed in thirty years of looking.

She turned away from the vista, ignoring the twinge of pain in her hip. The room was ready, and yet she lingered. The carpets, the paintings, the heavy furniture of the Envoy's chamber were mere overlays obscuring the reality of the space. Where were the holo-projectors and targeting computers? Where were the men and women—the last line of defence against the G'rat'ch?

All dead and gone.

Why could she still hear their voices? Focus on the room, on her hands, clutched tight into fists, her nails biting into her palms. For a moment, they looked smooth and strong, but then the gnarls and brown spots returned. She was back.

But the voices remained. Real. Now. The Envoy and his aide talking in the next room, voices rasping as if they struggled to whisper and shout at the same time.

"Damn it, Charlie, how are we supposed to negotiate with someone who doesn't agree on the meaning of basic concepts?"

"We've made progress . . . though its position seems to be a moving target."

"*Its* position. How do we even know it represents the G'rat'ch government?"

"We're not sure there is a G'rat'ch government. Not the way we mean in any case."

"Exactly! I've had three requests for clarification from Earth in the last week. What do I tell them?"

Charlie's response was inaudible. Marion crept to the door separating the rooms.

". . . ever figure out what it means by ki'ki'kaj?"

Marion jerked back from the door, mouth dry and throat constricted. The clacking G'rat'ch speech was difficult for human tongues, but the Envoy's accent was good enough. She had not heard that word in a long time.

The smell of earth pressed against her face, twigs and rocks scraped her naked flesh as she squirmed through a tunnel dug with fingernails and fear . . .

She was sitting on the Envoy's bed. Her face was wet, yet she had no memory of crying. She wiped her apron across her eyes and jumped up as the door opened.

Envoy Chirac's eyes narrowed. "You're still here?"

Charlie didn't spare her a glance.

Marion smoothed the coverlet and nodded. "There was a stain on the rug," she gestured in the direction of the fireplace. Not a lie, she thought, though not a reason either. "Your lunch is on the sideboard."

The envoy glanced at the food. "Thank you, um . . ."

"Marion," Charlie supplied. It was his job to remember.

She gathered her kit and went into the anteroom, closing the door behind her.

"Why do they keep her on?" Charlie made no effort to whisper now.

"Promises to keep. Those who served and all that. The local governor is quite firm about it."

"It's a new era. Wouldn't it be better to forget?"

But the Envoy had no answer for that.

❧

Ki'ki'kaj. It might mean to turn someone's strength against them. Or to subvert or, in another context, to betray. A moral conflict that contained its own resolution. A word for victory over the enemy.

The G'rat'ch could change their tactics but never their nature. Their concept of morality only applied to themselves; so what did the word mean in the context of these hateful negotiations?

Marion stared at the patterns of soap bubbles made by her brush. The stone underneath was unyielding—still stone though everything it housed had been transformed. Much could be learned from stone, yet Envoy Chirac only had eyes for the ever changing patterns of G'rat'ch duplicity.

"You can't predict them," Darwin said. *"They never do the same thing twice in a row. How are we going to time this thing?"*

Marion placed a finger across Darwin's lips. "By learning to think like a G'rat'ch."

Darwin laughed and pulled her close. "Nobody knows how to do that."

But she did know the nature of the G'rat'ch character. Learned the hard way during ten years of labour in an alien gulag, working at tasks that made no sense—seemingly even to the G'rat'ch. Until she learned to see a pattern where none could exist.

They had escaped—the Creebolt seven. Though only five had made it out of the mountains alive. And not Darwin. Marion felt the pressure of Darwin's mouth on hers. She wiped it away with the back of her hand. *Dead and gone*, she thought. *I killed him.* No, came an answering voice. Young Marion's voice. *The G'rat'ch did.*

She was crying again. She leaned back on her haunches to wipe her face. Her knees cracked, and a sharp pain shot up the left side of her back. *I'm getting too old for this*, she thought. At least the work kept *Fierce's* harsh whispers at bay.

Why had they come back here? The G'rat'ch Ambasador and its counterpart, too. To Fergus? A backwater to both empires. Notable only as the place where the aliens decided they'd had enough of a war that spanned two dozen star systems and declared a unilateral ceasefire. Then waited thirty years to begin negotiations.

But those bastards barely had a word for peace. And its other meaning wasn't surrender, but madness.

Hard heels echoed off the stairs, and Marion shifted her bucket against the wall. The soldiers barely gave her a glance. Age provided the invisibility cloak science had never mastered.

ॐ

In her tiny room, Marion pried a flagstone loose from beneath her cot. The surface of the wooden box was pitted despite the polish she applied, but the hinges and clasp gleamed. The knife inside fitted easily in her palm, the blade shimmering. The G'rat'ch never appeared in public without body armour. But what about in private?

I know how to make them speak the truth, to negotiate in good faith, she thought, as she slipped the knife back into the box. The box snuggled nicely in her satchel beneath the brushes and cleaning cloths.

The Creebolt seven had escaped; hundreds still languished in G'rat'ch prison camps in the highlands beyond the village.

Marion shouldered her pack and her slugthrower and fell into line with the other grunts. A steady drizzle had turned the trail into a mudslide—but she wasn't worried. The aliens had given it all they had; it wasn't enough to break them. Now . . .

Marion squeezed her eyes shut, but the images didn't fade. All that youth. All that death.

Even now, a hundred systems once again teetered on the brink of war. Marion followed the newscasts, letting the drone of pundits drown out the voices in her head. When that didn't work, she trolled the dark sites the government both forbade and used in their incessant search for malcontents.

Not that government eyes ever turned on her. She had not forgotten all she had learned in the aliens' work camps, in their torture chambers—where she blubbered and screamed, mixing truth and fantasies into her confessions until she couldn't tell the difference. The G'rat'ch kept asking their meaningless questions, indifferent to what she said. Maybe because, for them, the difference between reality and dream was scarcely discernable.

Marion was at the top of the stairs now, her feet following pathways her mind refused to acknowledge. The G'rat'ch Ambassador—the sole representative of his people—was housed in the east wing, the only part of the old fortress untouched by war, spared the bombs and plasma beams that had scarred the rest and half-leveled the village below. The alien could hardly be expected to negotiate in constant reminder of its own people's perfidy.

Crazy Marion, the guards called her behind her back or sometimes to her face, a term of endearment as much as derision. The older ones, recruited in the last days of the shooting war were gentler, sometimes gave her a sweet or a smoke—still rationed after three decades—remembering what she had done on their behalf. That was mostly over now, the memory as faded as the patches on the military jacket she wore beneath her cleaning smock.

Wander too far down the hall, and they would gently turn her back. "Not this way, Marion," they would say, taking her arm, little knowing how hard it was for her not to strike at their knees or throats. Blows that made up for weakness with the precision of their aim.

Fierce didn't do that anymore. Being in hospital was too much like being in prison. The confinement, the drugs, the endless meaningless questions.

The men—boys, really—at the first checkpoint waved her past without a glance at her proffered pass. They no more inspected her cleaning satchel, weighing heavy against her aching hip, than they listened to her mumbled reasons for being there. Why should they? The words that tumbled unbidden from her lips were nearly unintelligible: her language clouded by local idiom and the occasional electric click of G'rat'ch.

Not every backway had been sealed. Tunnels that were closed by mortar and brick could be reopened with fingernails and fear. Fear of having no way out now replaced by fear of having no way in.

Around the first bend, Marion paused at a spot invisible to the security cameras, listening for the sound of boot-steps before turning to look for followers. She withdrew her other pass from one of the jacket's zippered pockets. Sergeant Dwyer was retired; this was nothing but an inactive memento, a courtesy to veterans who couldn't let go. The dark net provided more than illicit information to those who feared the worst. *Coward* hungered after scraps, and Marion had acquired the military codes to re-activate the pass, if only to silence *Coward's* moaning.

Marion swiped the wafer of plastic across a hidden sensor. No flash of green, no chime of acknowledgement, merely a narrow crack in the smooth surface of the wall. Marion pressed her shoulder against the stone and slipped through into the narrow passage beyond. The door slid shut, and Marion leaned against it, eyes adjusting to the dim glow of bioluminescent strips while her ears strained for an alarm that didn't come.

She closed her eyes and breathed to quell the pounding of blood in her ears. *Other bodies pressed against her in the dark, the air sighed from lungs, cut by the occasional involuntary mutter of expectation. When will we go? Wait for Marion. She knows.*

She had known, known enough to get away but not enough to keep them all safe. What else had she known she couldn't now remember? It was lost down the corridors she was no longer willing or able to walk.

She rummaged through her cleaning satchel for the metal wafers she had accumulated for this very day. This unanticipated day. She stripped off her maid's smock and stuffed the devices into pockets or onto belt loops. She took the knife from its box and ran her fingers over the hard metal. It was all she had of the future.

☙

The greatest risk was she would come across a technician, restoring surveillance the G'rat'ch had discovered and neutralized. The Ambassador would—or should—have no way of knowing of the tunnel itself, but the probing microwaves and photon bursts would inevitably be detected.

"What will you do," Darwin asked, "if there's a snitch?"

Every other escape had died on the whispers of those the G'rat'ch had turned. "I'll do what needs doing," *she replied. And so she had, turning the Creebolt eight into seven with the twist of a shiv.*

Was this the same? A tremor shook her left hand, the hand that held the knife. She paused in the semi-dark until she could will it to stop.

The tunnel ended with no need to test her resolve, not sure if she could have done what needed doing. Marion pressed her hand against the dark wood, felt the heat from the other side. The G'rat'ch preferred warmth, pumped carbon and methane into the atmosphere of every planet they conquered.

A holo-projector flickered beside the panel, projecting an illusion of solidity through the seams in the wood; on the other side, the wall would look like an unbroken sheet rather than a door that could be opened with the touch of passcode.

Marion jerked, uncertain how long she had been staring into the oscillating light. Had she been talking? Was the alien calling for security?

Nothing to do, but move forward. Marion stretched, repeating the never-forgotten exercises to limber her stiffened joints, to heighten her metabolism. She recited the silent mantras that made pain fade, her muscles tighten and her lungs expand. She cracked a capsule between her teeth, tasted the bitter sweet syrup and felt the surge of power.

She became—for a few minutes—all she could be. *Which is little enough at sixty-nine,* she thought.

The men stilled, each seeking his own personal balance, readying for the charge that meant liberty or death. The tunnel could only take them so far. If Marion was right, a clear path would open though enemy lines; if not, they would die within seconds.

Now or never. Marion expended her last chip to override the security protocols and disengage the projectors. She slapped the releases; the panel fell away and she leapt through, for a moment a soldier again. Her knee cracked, a tearing pain that threatened collapse. Her momentum carried her a third of the way across the chamber. She locked her leg to keep from falling, the pain nearly blinding her. She clutched the back of a massive wooden chair with her right hand, her left held straight out.

The G'rat'ch curled on a scatter of cushions in front of the roaring fireplace. It chittered in alarm, unfolding to its feet with surprising quickness. The G'rat'ch elder—its age revealed by the pale patches of skin spackled across its long flat skull and by the generational ridges carved in the flesh of its chest—was sheathed in a loose grey skirt that barely reached its backwards bending knees. A sash displayed its rank and served as a belt for the ceremonial weapons no G'rat'ch ever went without.

Its amber eyes flickered before focusing on the vibrating knife in Marion's hand. It circled warily, buying time to extract a blade from its sash. The knife looked little more than a toy in the G'rat'ch's massive three-fingered fist. Marion wasn't fooled. She had seen those knives at work, their tempered ceramic blades so fine they cut through metal like butter.

Marion feinted left, then shifted and thrust hard over the top of the chair. The tip of her blade found one of the soft tender dewlaps that draped the G'rat'ch's throat. Blood, as red as any human's, sprayed in a fine mist across Marian's arm. It lurched back, free hand pawing at the wound, human curses spewing from its mouth. *The first words we ever learn in any language*, thought Marion, giddy from the almost forgotten flavour of battle.

Marion responded in kind—epithets learned under the lash of her G'rat'ch captors. They meant little in translation but would infuriate her opponent. An angry enemy was a careless one.

The drugs were fading; she had seconds to bring the G'rat'ch to the ground, force a truth oath out of him—make it deal with the human ambassadors as he would with a fellow G'rat'ch.

It dropped into a low crouch, displaying a limberness of joints that Marion could only envy. But when it moved, it circled in the same direction as before, a repetition so unnatural for a G'rat'ch that Marion knew it could only mean one thing—a permanent weakness. An ancient wound, remember? The thought came unbidden out of nowhere. She lunged, aiming for the bulging tendon that connected the G'rat'ch's leg to its torso.

Her own tendons failed her. Her knee collapsed with a second, more violent, crack. Her knife skittered across the floor. The G'rat'ch towered over her, its crest extended in a killing rage. She screamed—a howl of frustration that barely sounded human.

Two fortress guards burst through the chamber door, their weapons holstered. The G'rat'ch, deep in the frenzy of battle, reached and slashed. The boys were dead before they hit the floor. The G'rat'ch fled, the achingly familiar pattern of its clan tattoo writhing across its naked back.

ℭℜ

Someone was babbling, a queer mixture of words, growls and clicks. The pain in her leg had subsided but it refused to bend at her command.

"Easy," said a different voice. "We've immobilized your legs and back until the doctor can ensure your injuries aren't severe." Envoy Chirac's face swam into view. "Do you understand?"

More babbling. Hers. She pushed the voices to the background until only Marion was left. "Yes. Where am I?" A lie was needed now, 'necessary' until she knew where things stood.

"You're in the Ambassador's—the G'rat'ch Ambassador's— quarters. How did you get here?"

A man in a Colonel's uniform—his face rejuvenation smooth under steel grey hair—was talking to Charlie, but he was watching her. He had her knife in his hand. A surge of anxiety threatened to crush her chest.

"Those boys," Marion said. What about the boys? The voices— one voice—clamoured: *Let me handle this.* The voice that lied. "Those boys—I was talking to them. When they started running, I followed." Stupid, she thought, a stupid lie so easy to check. *Trust me*, said *The Liar.*

Chirac looked away, embarrassed. The Colonel said something to Charlie, who looked grim and moved away through the still open door. The officer loomed above her, his eyes hooded.

The Colonel held out her knife. "Do you recognize this?"

Marion shook her head.

"It's G'rat'ch in origin—though I haven't seen one like it in forty years," said the Colonel.

"Should you be handling it?" asked Chirac.

"We'll find nothing useful on it," said the Colonel. "It's an assassin's tool, designed to shed organics."

Marion stilled, despite the screaming voice—*Coward*—begging her to run. If they knew it was her knife, it wouldn't matter that the G'rat'ch had had his own. The negotiations mattered more than who was to blame.

Charlie was back, leading half a dozen medics with gurneys. They loaded the body bags, then they loaded her.

The Colonel—Nemetsov, she remembered—leaned into Chirac. The Envoy shook his head. "Don't be stupid. She's an old woman. And . . ." He looked at her with pity. "Not a well one."

ભ

The doctor had injected her knee with Curaid and fitted it with a brace. She had told her to take three days off—her, who needed to work. At least she had given her good meds.

A green icon on her room screen warned Marion that a worm had been inserted into her browser. She logged onto an entertainment channel; her history would show it was her favorite romance. What it wouldn't show was that it was a gateway, not to the dark net but to the even murkier systems that ran behind it. Systems even Nemetsov might have trouble finding.

Surveillance cut both ways; the cameras used to watch the public could also watch the watchers. And the watcher's watchers. Sometimes she thought it was watchers all the way down.

She scanned through program files until she found what she was looking for—a network that dated back to the days when the fortress actually was one, not a home to diplomats and spies. Most of it had been written over but enough remained for her purposes. She had to find the G'rat'ch ambassador before anyone else did.

Like a movie projected on gauze, the writhing clan tattoo clouded her vision without obscuring it. It had meant something once; now it was a needle scratching bone. The tumbling voices were talking again but she refused to listen. When they persisted, she tapped the med-patch until they quieted.

There. The cameras in the conference room off Chirac's quarters were still functioning. The Envoy, the ever present Charlie, and Nemetsov: the angle wouldn't show if others were present. The sound was worse than the video but it was clear they were arguing, voices raised and hands gesticulating. She adjusted the gain, trying to filter out the static of forty years of decay. In the end she wasn't sure if she really heard their voices or only her own projections.

"Marion Dwyer was involved in this," said Nemetsov. "She knows more than she's telling. You saw what she was wearing."

"An old uniform jacket?" asked Charlie. "She can wear what she likes when she's not working."

"I want her questioned."

"I can't . . ." said Chirac. "She's a sick old woman."

"Have you seen her records? She was in special forces. Inserted into regular militia for security purposes." Nemetsov was pacing, passing in and out of the range of the camera like a ship moving through fog.

Chirac waved his hand dismissively. "That was forty years ago."

Nemetsov looked like he wanted to say more. Say it, thought Marion, tell them what they did to me.

"Dwyer was . . ." He paused. "That kind of . . . programming never really fades."

"She's crazy," said Charlie. He kept looking down at the screen in his hand as if seeking confirmation of his own conclusions. "And a cripple. She's nearly seventy, for God's sake."

"Seventy's not old, Charlie," said Chirac.

"Not to you sir, no. But you didn't spend a decade in a G'rat'ch concentration camp. You didn't have those kind of wounds." Charlie, his shoulders squared and his back straight, glared at Nemetsov. "I *have* seen her records."

"This is a waste of time," said Chirac. "We need to recover the G'rat'ch. We need to press our advantage before this all goes to hell."

"He's gone into the hills," said Nemetsov. "But I agree. We need to control the ambassador."

Back to the camps, thought Marion. Where my comrades still wait. *Ghosts and memories*, whispered *Coward*, before she was shouted down.

"Why in hell would he do that?" asked Chirac. The Envoy wiped his hand through his thinning blond hair. "There's nothing there but wilderness and unexploded ordinance. The G'rat'ch moved everything off planet before negotiations started."

Marion remembered the debates on the official feeds. The G'rat'ch claimed the prisoners had all been released. Or had died. The G'rat'ch claimed a lot of things.

"Do you think humans are the only ones who spy on each other?" asked Charlie. He was looking at his screen again. *He knows*, Marion thought, *that the G'rat'ch would never leave one of their own untended. Unwatched.*

"All the more reason we need to get to him first," Chirac said.

Nemetsov grinned, though it was clear he found nothing funny about it. "I'll put together a team. I've had experience with . . ."

"No," said Charlie. "I will." Chirac hesitated, his eyes wide, then nodded his agreement.

CR

The screen washed the room with light the colour of ash. *Fierce Marion* flicked the screen off in annoyance. The patch on her arm read empty, and she replaced it without thinking, uncertain as to why she was being medicated. Unconcerned.

Despite everything, they had made it. Jingo and Frank and Darwin and. . . . No, not Darwin. Darwin had died in the dark, his long lean body impaled on a G'rat'ch hunting javelin.

Accept your losses. Move on. The time for grief will come—when this war is over.

The mission, she thought, nothing matters but the mission. *Deal with the now. Seek clarity. Fierce* rolled upright, balancing lightly on the balls of her feet. She was tired and her muscles ached. She tapped the patch again.

Clarity. The G'rat'ch had infiltrated headquarters. How didn't matter. She had discovered him, driven him out. His agents—subverted humans—were following. She had to stop them.

The doctor had said . . . three days before she was ready for active duty. But she didn't have three days. It didn't matter how beat up she was from the last operation. She wasn't young—thirty-nine hardly qualified—but she was strong. She could do this thing.

ᔕᖇ

Things had changed; more than seemed possible in the ten years she had languished in the camp: shifted walls and empty rooms where corridors and armouries should be. Guard posts were few and undermanned as if the war were a distant memory and not a constant threat. Those few soldiers she couldn't avoid waved her past with a sketch of a salute and a grin. She made a note to speak to the fortress's commanding officer about the laxness of his security.

Nothing was where it should be, but that didn't mean it couldn't be found. Logistics had their own logic; figuring out where things were was merely a matter of thinking like a quartermaster. She'd outwitted a fair number of those over the . . . years? Decades? The drugs were buzzing in her head; distorted voices whispering secrets she had no business knowing. Had her communicator malfunctioned again? She reached behind her ear but found only scar tissue.

The armoury was understocked, though it held plenty for an army of one. Marion slung a bandolier of grenades over one shoulder and a slug thrower over the other, grunting as the weight settled on her spine. The brace on her knee flashed a series of amber and red lights, and she adjusted tolerances until it showed mostly green.

The Gr'at'ch's human allies—the one called Chirac, and the others—had left the fortress, no doubt planning a rendezvous in the hills above the village; an attack was imminent. The Gr'at'ch was on foot, but even unaugmented Gr'at'ch moved like a flood in springtime. With the lead it had, she would have little chance of catching him even if she didn't have a bum knee.

ᔕᖇ

At least the flier pad was where she remembered. To one side hulked a heavily armoured personnel carrier. On the other, two flitters stood in a row; the nearest, only a few dozen steps away. It might have been a few dozen kilometres for all the good it was. Each flitter had two heavily armed guards; another two crouched by the carrier. The conspiracy ran deep if they were so anxious that nobody follow.

You don't like flying anyway, she thought with a shudder. Her vision blurred in a swirl of snapping blades; burning fuel licked heat across her shoulders. Focus on the mission, snarled *Fierce*. The mantra was all she had.

She had the element of surprise. She could probably terminate two or three before the rest could react. But . . . she had no proof they were in on it. Just following orders. Corruption at the top didn't mean it ran all the way down.

Fierce unhooked two grenades and rolled them down the hall away from the launch area. Moments later she burst from the door, limping toward the guards as her brace began to flash amber again.

"Back there," she gestured behind her. "We're under attack."

One of the closest soldiers started; her partner laughed then frowned when he saw the slug thrower in her hands. A roar shook the ground, and a gout of flame and smoke shot across the tarmac. The officer in charge gestured for two of the guards to remain while he led the other three into the building.

"Get behind me, Marion," said one soldier, who had assumed a kneeling position, his weapon trained on the entrance. She knew him, though she couldn't recall the circumstances. As she passed, she slammed the butt of her slug thrower into the back of his helmet. The blow sent him to the ground; a second to the side of his head sent him under.

Fierce ran at the second soldier, covering the five metres in three long bounds. Her leap failed to produce any height so her blow landed on a hip rather than the woman's head. Still, the momentum took them both to the ground. *Fierce* jammed stiffened fingers into her opponent's throat and followed with a hard uppercut.

Marion rolled to her feet, slapping at the brace in a futile attempt to get it working. She pried it off and tested the knee. Painful but functioning. The pass from the unconscious woman opened the door of the second flitter she tried. She disabled the other craft; the armoured carrier was beyond her capabilities so she set a three minute timer on a grenade and dropped it under its belly. It would slow them down if nothing else.

The flitter rose unsteadily—it had been a while since she certified as a pilot. By the time she reached the level of the surrounding rooftops, two of the squad had returned. The rattle of heavy slugs off the underbelly of the craft chased her south towards the forested hills.

CR

There was no pursuit. *Perhaps the grenade had damaged the carrier or maybe they think a single warrior is no match for a Gr'at'ch squadron,* she thought. Some people have short memories. Or maybe they misplaced the keys.

Her luck didn't last. The fuel gauge was dropping steadily. A punctured fuel tank or a nicked line. The forest was patchy on the higher hilltops, and *Fierce* aimed the flitter at a clearing as the red empty light began flashing. The engines cut out seconds before the wheels touched down, and the aircraft landed hard, bounced twice and tilted on one side before coming to a rest. The flitter lurched one more time as the still spinning blades caught the ground and dug into the soft soil.

Fierce Marion popped the hatch and lowered herself to the ground. The pain in her knee was worse, and she doubted it would take the impact of a two metre drop. She was right; the leg almost buckled and she searched the ground for anything that might serve as a crutch. She needed to move fast before they came for her.

"Who?" she asked the air, surprised at the tremor in her voice. "Who is coming for you?" She slumped against the side of the flitter, overwhelmed with exhaustion and the pain in her leg. And her back. And her wrist. She fumbled for analgesic patches. She hated the drugs, but the mission was more important than her preferences.

She unzipped the seam in her combat pants and pulled the metal web up over her leg, the patch peeled and ready. The muscle of her calf was taut, but the skin was lined in blue. Her hand—her hand!—was gnarled.

Think about this later. Marion knew she shouldn't listen. The voices sometimes lied, and sometimes they simply couldn't acknowledge the truth. She pressed the patch against the mottled skin and felt the immediate flush of relief up through her knee and into the hip.

I'm too old for this, she thought. But, it wasn't the joke she intended it to be. "My God," she whispered, though she hadn't worshiped one since her second year in the G'rat'ch camp. "I really am old."

A flood of memories washed over her. Darwin had died in the jungle, but the others had died, too, in the months and years that followed, their bodies and minds too wounded to carry on. Until she was the last of the Creebolt seven left alive to avenge their memories. Too wounded to live, too stubborn to die.

Move! Marion lurched to her feet, almost against her will. You can't be out in the open when night falls. Fergus held more dangers than an aging G'rat'ch ambassador. She needed shelter. She needed time.

ଓଃ

Three hours and another patch later, she spotted an old bunker—one of a dozen laid out in an arc facing the old G'rat'ch line—against the side of a low mound. Age had cracked its shell, so it no longer merged with the native stone; but she didn't need to be invisible, she needed to be inside. The sun threw long dappled shadows across the lower canopy. Soon, the hunters would come.

Something moved to her left, something big. She gathered her legs under her for a desperate dash. Then, she saw it.

Or them. Three G'rat'ch—smaller and younger than the one she was after. They moved purposefully through the forest, talking in chitters too low to hear, stopping every dozen paces, to check readings on the device one was holding.

Marion slipped the slug thrower from its holster and readied a grenade. If they all went inside the bunker, she wouldn't hesitate to kill them. The one holding the scanner pulled open the door and went inside; the other two took up positions on opposite sides of the bunker, particle weapons loose by their sides. Their posture displayed both relaxation and disappointment. They didn't expect to be interrupted but wished they would be.

The leader emerged and placed something on the top of the bunker. His clan tattoo displayed the simple patterns and garish colours of the War Party. What they lacked in subtlety, they made up for in numbers and ferocity. The G'rat'ch finished and moved away, making the sounds G'rat'ch made when they were happy or ready to kill. Their gait was purposeful; they would not return soon.

The War Party was banned from Fergus under the terms of the cease fire. Marion had no doubt the memory was true even as her eyes proved the lie of it.

The low growls and high, child-like hooting of the predators in the dark finally pushed her forward. Before she slid inside the bunker, she pulled herself high on the side of the dome. Barely visible, a thin wire antenna stretched up into the dark foliage. A listening post.

Debris had drifted into the corners of the low structure. Inside the bunker, wires dangled where equipment had been torn from sockets. The G'rat'ch scanner stood on a lone chair with torn upholstery. A stream of lights flickered on its front panel, but whatever it was doing, it was doing it silently. Marion shifted it to the floor; she needed the chair more than it did.

She wedged the bunker's door shut. Her leg throbbed, and she wondered if she could remember a time when she didn't ache. No more patches, she thought, I need to think.

She stared at her hands until she saw past the delusion of youth. I'm old, she thought. Memories flooded back—recent ones, not the ancient bitter memories of the camp and the escape that Young Marion clutched to her breast as if only they were real. Thirty years of treatment—half her life—in and out of psych wards or under the dulling cloud of medication hardly counted as real, did they? Better to live in the past than face the present.

No! The voice that spoke was the one most often silent. *True Marion*. The warrior youth and the crazy old crone—tangled together like wrestlers on a mat.

If the G'rat'ch had sent *that* ambassador—then the Peace Faction had the upper hand. But if the War Party was also here, freely spying on human defences, the Peace Faction's grip was weak.

She knew how the G'rat'ch worked; she had learned to think like one, hadn't she? Honour and humiliation, victory or death, these were the currency of their politics, the basis of everything they did.

The pain in her leg was almost unbearable. She clung to it the way a drowning woman might cling to a broken tree. She had to remember.

The moment the G'rat'ch ambassador had fled, it had ceased to be a player and become a pawn. If Chirac—no, if Colonel Nemetsov found the ambassador, he would use its capture to humiliate it, to end the negotiations before they had truly begun and force an agreement the home world could not support. The War Party would gain the upper hand.

If the War Party found the ambassador before Nemetsov, they would kill it. Earth would be blamed. The only possible result was war.

She saw them now—the young soldiers, laid out in rows, pale and cold, gaping wounds on their flesh like hungry mouths calling for vengeance. She saw G'rat'ch bodies, too, but she felt no joy at their deaths. She was too old to think death was a victory.

Her hands curled into gnarled fists. *I did this*, she thought. *Why did you think you could make a difference, you stupid woman? You were doing what was right*, whispered *Fierce*. *You had done it before*, sighed *Young Marion*. Others grunted and sighed in agreement or derision. Marion rubbed her knuckles into her eyes, but the tears wouldn't stop.

The scanner's lights flickered and went out. The G'rat'ch had found what they wanted. The Ambassador's life now hung in the balance. I did this, she thought, I have to fix it. I will fix this. But not yet. G'rat'ch honour demanded: executions required the light of day.

ೞ

The pain was less in the morning. Until she moved. She tore a patch in quarters and slapped it on her knee. She chewed a field ration. After, she squatted over the scanner and relieved herself; let the G'rat'ch deal with that humiliation.

Marion had to reach the Ambassador before either the other G'rat'ch or Chirac. Fortunately, she knew exactly where to look. There was something she wasn't remembering. Or was remembering wrong. She knew who the G'rat'ch ambassador was, knew it would take all her will not to kill him. But there was someone else she needed to remember. Someone she had been programmed to forget.

I've done all this before, she thought. *What had her mission been all those years ago? What had they wanted her to do when they sent her on patrol with Darwin? Something someone had said.* It was . . . gone. Marion pulled the door open. It was past dawn, and she needed to move.

This line of bunkers was a fallback from the shifting battle lines; the place where the line was drawn, the one the G'rat'ch never broke. She hauled herself up a tree, until could see the faint arc formed by the other. Algebra pointed to the centre of the circle: G'rat'ch headquarters. Three kilometres to the northwest of that lay the camp where she had been held.

ᲜᲠ

Nemetsov had set up a dozen metres from the remains of the G'rat'ch base—a few gutted buildings and a broad patch of dead earth where the Terrans had scorched away every remnant of imported vegetation. All the prisoners dead and gone long ago. Marion watched through her scope from the safety of the last thick clump of trees. The perimeter was soft; her old self could have run right up to the Colonel and tapped him on the shoulder. She wasn't sure her new self could run at all.

Why was he still here? If the ambassador wasn't here, it had to be somewhere else. And where else but the concentration camp it had ruled for more than a decade? Where it had tortured and taunted her until her humanity lay in tatters and she learned to think like a G'rat'ch.

Surely Captain Nemetsov could . . . Colonel. He was a Colonel. Now. Marion shuddered, a deep uncontrollable shaking that started in the middle of her back and spread in every direction. She dropped her scope.

Nemetsov. She knew. . . . A cold black band clamped down on her thoughts, blinding her, deafening her. When it stopped, everything was crystal clear.

She had her mission. Nothing mattered but that. Find the G'rat'ch. Carry out the mission.

If only she weren't so tired. The blackness took her again.

CR

When *Fierce* opened her eyes, Chirac and the rest of the collaborators were gone. The pain in her leg had spread into her back and shoulder. She slapped one patch onto her lower back and the remains of another onto her thigh. She rummaged in her pack for the crumpled tin foil that held three blue gelcaps. One now, two for later.

She trotted along the trail to the northwest, aware, but uncaring of the steady tearing at the ligaments and muscles of her legs.

CR

Six of them occupied the old camp, seven counting the G'rat'ch. Chirac and Charlie, Nemetsov and three troopers, tension evident beneath their armour. The ambassador—commandant—was taller, broader, with more ridges across his brow and chest. That much change . . .

Two pictures laid on top of each other: Nemetsov and the G'rat'ch, old and young at the same time. Chirac and the rest ghost-like, as if they barely existed.

Captain/Colonel Nemetsov was holding out a knife—her knife—one of his incarnations threatening, the other cajoling. The G'rat'ch twitched its shoulder crest indicating denial/defiance. Chirac stepped forward and put his hand on Nemetsov's forearm. Nemetsov frowned/scowled and jerked forward/stepped back.

The G'rat'ch slumped, its legs giving out as if the whole matter had exhausted him. Marion upped the gain on the scope. The G'rat'ch's colour was bad, his skin pale and waxy. The rank marks stood out black on his arms and face.

The slug thrower was too rough a tool, but a pistol shot

was uncertain at such distance. Marion dumped her pack and bandolier behind a rock and slithered closer, finding cover in the patchy vegetation. She had been sent to kill the commandant. What happened after didn't matter. Everyone else was dead; why not her, too?

Hold on, baby, hold on. Darwin's head lolled against her shoulder, his eyes fixing on her face. Blood bubbled on his lips. "Leave me, I'm done." His hands pawed futilely at the haft of the G'rat'ch spear. "The mission matters more." Marion nodded. HQ needed to know the names of the traitors. Darwin drew a long breath, let it out and was silent. She let his body slump to the forest floor. She touched his face. Then she ran.

The ambassador/commandant had its back to her, skin bare to the afternoon sun. Her hands shook as she took aim. She fished another of the gel caps out of her pocket. The surge stiffened her body, but her aim kept drifting from the G'rat'ch to Nemetsov.

Then the G'rat'ch War Party arrived. And *Fierce* vanished into the chaos of voices rolling in her head.

One of the troopers went down, a hunting spear finding a gap where his body armour met his helmet. The other G'rat'ch's aim was less lucky, its missiles clattering against plate.

Charlie dragged Chirac into the remains of a bunkhouse. The low walls would provide little protection against real weapons. The aliens moved fast, long lunging strides propelling them in a spiral around the camp. The troopers kept up a steady rain of fire but their targeting was off. Still, one of the G'rat'ch staggered then scurried behind a mound of rock. It lay down a withering stream of metal that forced the soldiers to cover.

Nemetsov clutched the ambassador/commandant with one hand. A pistol in the other barked at the stationary G'rat'ch. *Peace hasn't dulled his instincts,* Marion thought.

Her own pistol wasn't going to tip the odds; her other weapons were fifty paces away. The G'rat'ch Ambassador looked dead, but then Nemetsov's efforts would make no sense. It was the *kl'op^*; the ambassador/commandant was sinking into madness. Death would follow. And then war.

Marion angled along Nemetsov's path. She knew his destination, an emergency shelter, hidden in the floor of one of the buildings. He would drag the ambassador/commandant below, sealing the hatch. The others would die, and he would be the hero. Just like before.

A knife blade of pain pierced her eyes. The drugs in her blood fought the programming in her head. Time stopped.

Sometimes, all she ever got was one clear moment. Now, she had an expanse of them, stretching all the way back to her first days in the service. She had never been sent to kill. She had been sent to find the traitors in their midst; the prisoners who had been turned by the G'rat'ch and the Terran officer who had helped them do it. She had found him, but not before he found her.

Captain Nemetsov.

Time started again. Her ancient body was slow but Nemetsov, dragging a hundred and twenty kilos of unconscious G'rat'ch was slower. Marion blindsided him, slamming into his lower legs. The sound of something popping in his knee was gratifying; the answering snap from her shoulder, less so.

Nemetsov fell hard, his helmet ringing off a stone, the pistol flying from his hand. Marion squeezed off a round into his undamaged knee. If she was wrong about him . . .

The G'rat'ch commandant, no, ambassador, was another matter. Whatever Nemetsov had done to it had pushed it to its limit. The G'rat'ch were always on the edge of madness, kept stable by an elaborate set of rules and rituals. Without its culture, a G'rat'ch could tumble into a killing rage or a spiral of catatonic depression.

Marion pushed the last gel cap past the thin lips of the G'rat'ch. She ran her fingers along his heavy jaw and down over the ridges of his throat. Marion had no idea what the human drug would do, but anything was better than its current state. She had no strength to move him; he would have to do that for himself.

The G'rat'ch sniper used the lull to move closer, his dark form lurching from one bit of cover to another. The troopers had joined Chirac and Charlie; they were adding to the chaos using borrowed pistols. It kept the circling aliens at bay. Still, they hadn't come expecting an extended firefight. It was only a matter of time until the G'rat'ch War Party wore them down.

The G'rat'ch at her feet bolted upright, its head thrashing from side to side and one hand clutching for her throat. She scurried backward.

G'rat'ch words hurt her throat, but she kept talking until she saw what passed for sanity return to its eyes. It—he made the sound that signified both humour and horror. The same sound he had always made when he was teaching her the rudiments of the language.

"Sergeant Dwyer," he said. "It's been a long time."

"Not long enough," she growled. "Any suggestions?"

"Do you have a weapon for me?" Nemetsov had been dragging himself toward his fallen pistol. Marion stepped past him and scooped it up. She passed it—without hesitation—to the G'rat'ch.

"He's the enemy, Dwyer," Nemetsov, said, pitching his voice so as to trigger the switches in her brain. But the one called *Old Sergeant* was in charge—not the real her but close enough—and the switches didn't work.

"I think your intelligence is flawed. Sir." Marion resisted the urge to kick him in the head.

"The time to go is now," said Commandant P''kalp.

"The time to go is now, Marion," said Darwin. "The Captain isn't coming?" she asked.

"Where?"

P''kalp pointed at a gap between the two circling G'rat'ch farthest from the stationary one. "Do as I do." He showed her the pistol, set for maximum fire. He aimed to one side of the gap and she aimed at the other. Classic wedge.

Firing as they ran, they were through the opening before the other G'rat'ch could adapt—or their own troopers could respond. P''kalp held the lead, twisting and turning through the brush until Marion lost track of where they were. Her legs and lungs were burning when he dropped into a copse. She stumbled in beside him, their bodies pressed together in the meagre cover.

The firing had stopped; the G'rat'ch had broken off the attack to pursue them, but if they were near, they were as silent as the sunlight.

"I thought you were dead, Dwyer-ka'ch," P''kalp said.

"She is dead," Marion replied. *Or buried so deep I can't remember her. Or don't want to.*

"You saved me; I am in your debt." Having a G'rat'ch in your debt was never a good thing. It would be clearer exactly what he meant if he had said it in G'rat'ch.

"I thought you had been recalled." She added: "In disgrace."

"Disgrace is the dark face of honour. Often only those who are lost know the way."

Marion chewed on that. P"kalp was always trying to teach her, though usually his lessons were beyond her.

"Speaking of lost . . ." she risked sticking her head above cover.

"We are where we are meant to be."

"I'm tired, P"kalp. So tired."

"We have only one more thing to do, Dwyer-ka'ch. Remember our mission."

The mission. Marion's hand tightened around her pistol. P"kalp laid his hand on her shoulder. "Our mission," he said, "not theirs. Do you remember?" He spoke a dozen words in G'rat'ch.

We have to wait for the captain," Marion said. "Captain Nemetsov isn't coming," said Darwin. He was never coming. She looked down at the knife in Darwin's hand. P"kalp's knife. "It was you all along. You and Nemetsov."

"You were a prisoner, too," she said.

The G'rat'ch tilted his head to one side. "It is only in bondage that we discover freedom."

"How are we supposed to bring about peace when everyone wants war?"

"There is much glory in war," said P"kalp. "And much profit."

True.

"What do you remember?" He asked the question in G'rat'ch.

She replied—as best she could—in the same language. Only one of her selves could speak G'rat'ch. "After a decade, the G'rat'ch surge had been stopped, and we were fighting to hold the line. Rumours—the fog of war is condensed from rumours— said the G'rat'ch fought among themselves. But interests on both sides—G'rat'ch and human—didn't want the fighting to stop. Like gluttons in a burning hotel, as long as the fire hadn't reached the dining room, they were determined to keep feeding."

"Keep going."

"On half a dozen planets, overtures were made, by your party, but no-one believed them. Agents were dispatched—inserted in ground forces. We were to find the truth, negotiate a ceasefire."

It was getting harder to talk. Voices clamoured outside the shell of language that protected her. She no longer believed they were all her voices.

"My unit was ambushed, half killed, the rest thrown into that camp. You were there. It took me a very long time to figure out that you weren't the warden, weren't in charge at all. The deference the other G'rat'ch showed you was disgust. But eventually, I learned—you taught me—to think like a G'rat'ch."

"The best you could. As a human."

She inclined her head in agreement. "Ten years passed and the war dragged on. Then, you explained the G'rat'ch concept of balance and it came to me. Your imprisonment was a weapon against the possibility of peace. If you were freed and returned home, everything would tumble down like tiles in a children's game. The War Party would be disgraced and lose power. All we had to do was escape."

P"kalp laughed. "You had a gift for madness. You only had to do something never done in G'rat'ch history. Escape from a G'rat'ch camp."

"Nemetsov escaped."

"The captain was released. Someone had to carry back word to those in your own ranks who fed off this war. Even then, they thought they could stop you. As if anyone could stop my Dwyer-ka'ch when her mind was set."

Marion had known that about Nemetsov—as much an agent for the enemy within human ranks, as for the G'rat'ch War Party. Why couldn't she say it out loud? One insistent voice pressed against the shell like the sound of a drill.

"But before he left, Nemestov turned Darwin."

"Your"—the word P"kalp used meant more than friend, less than mate—"was a willing servant. Nemetsov did not have to use his tools on him, the way he later used them on you." He said something else but the meaning escaped her. The insistent voice grew silent.

"I killed him. I killed Darwin." That, in her own language. The shell of memory could no longer protect her.

"There will be time for grief. After the mission has been

accomplished. I will follow your lead."

Marion shuddered.

"Dwyer-ka'ch, you made the ceasefire by freeing me once; now you must create the peace. It is your mission."

There was nothing left. Of the drugs in her system. Of Nemetsov's tools. Of her youth. All she had now was this wreck of a body and a single point of clarity. "Let's go."

❧

They reached camp before the extraction team arrived from the fortress. The fighting had stopped once the Ambassador was gone. Marion retrieved her other weapons before she and P"kalp made themselves known. Nemetsov was sedated or there might have been more trouble.

"I'll deal with Sergeant Dwyer," Charlie said.

Chirac, slumped beside Nemetsov, didn't speak. Marion wondered if he was in shock.

The other three G'rat'ch appeared from the forest, one limping. P"kalp waved the slug thrower in their direction though he hadn't the least idea how to use it. But he knew how to talk.

"This warrior," he said, meaning victor but also peacemaker, "has surpassed all warriors" — mercenary but also slave — "in her clan. Show respect." A word that meant exactly that and nothing more.

For a moment, it hung in the balance. Then, their shoulder crests flattened and their eyes turned to one side. The word for humiliation also meant surrender. The G'rat'ch laid their weapons at her feet, P"kalp last of all.

Chirac pulled himself to his feet and straightened his jacket. "I'm not quite sure, but it seems we have achieved some sort of resolution. If you are ready, Ambassador P"kalp, we can return to the citadel and continue our negotiations."

"No," said Marion, picking up her slug thrower. "P"kalp is my prisoner." In her mind, the word also meant friend. "He will treat only with me."

"Just a second . . ."

"Or, I will kill him." In her mind, it also meant liberate. She turned the weapon on P"kalp. It was obvious she did know how to use it. Out of the corner of her eye, she saw Charlie sliding his hand into his jacket. Marion ignored him.

"I am yours," said P"kalp. To the others: "I will treat with Sergeant Dwyer. And only her. None of the rest of you understand madness."

"Leave us food and drink," said Marion. "But leave us."

CR

The treaty was settled in an hour, but they stayed away for three days. Talking, eating, laughing, remembering things. At night they lay in each other's arms for warmth and comfort: Dwyer-ka'ch—student, child, friend—and P"kalp-tho^g—father, friend, teacher.

"This was why Darwin turned, wasn't it? He was jealous."

P"kalp considered it. "That is one madness my people do not share."

They were silent for a long time after that. "If you had not killed him, your people would have done to Darwin what they did to you. He would not have survived it as well as you have."

"You think I'm surviving?"

"As well as any of us can in a world ruled by entropy. Madness is the only viable strategy. Once you find your balance."

If you thought like a G'rat'ch, it made perfect sense. She was better, but she would never be well, could never be well in a world that insisted on curing her.

"Will you return to the G'rat'ch homeworld?" she asked, without looking at him.

"No," said P"kalp. "Fergus is the only planet our peoples share. It's too cold but I can adjust. Where else could I be, but where my closest lies?" The word meant more than friend, more than mate though less than lover.

It meant sanity.

THE INTERSECTION

Lorina Stephens

"Hey, Sis!"

She glanced around. His voice was so real inside her head, as if he stood right beside her. He sounded so ebullient amid the hustle of traffic, sunshine in the canyons of King and Bay, reaching out across distance where he circled somewhere overhead. She glanced up to where a sky like flint shone, hard as armour, and for her an unreachable barrier, untouchable. Although she wanted to reach him, one of the reasons she'd contacted him via their link.

She touched her ear, as if that would allow her to be nearer him, aware of the neural communications implant lodged in her cortex, one of Jack's amazing gizmos. "Hey." She winced at the tone of her response, aware of the flatness of it, her inability to match his persistent, apparent joy.

"Where are you?"

She glanced up at the monoliths of the TD and Montreal towers where birds wheeled and dove into the verdancy of wall gardens, down to the traffic lights where a walking man flashed and a flat voice droned *walk, walk, walk* over the hiss of activity, electric cars, electric public transit. Someone bumped by her. She stood immobile, unable to face the paved river she had to cross.

"Going to work," she said, sucking in air suddenly in too short supply. "What are you doing?"

"Just making notations on our latest neural interface results. Being able to conduct these tests here is giving me amazing insights, things I would never have been able to ascertain down there." There was a pause, and then: "Hey, Sis, you okay?"

That question. How many times had he asked her that? And how many times had she found herself frozen with fear, incapable of answering, terrified of the answer and what that might indicate, even more terrified of not telling him and having to face the gorge below where her feet balanced precariously on the edge of sanity.

All she had to do was cross the street with the lights, walk across the courtyard of the TD Centre, into the glass atrium where commerce and a Carolinian forest grew, and from there ascend in an elevator which could take her up fifty-six floors if she wanted. But she only had to go to thirty-two, exit to a floor where she would work where she chose—in a zen garden or beanbag chair, at an oak table or a cherry-lined library filled with real, printed volumes—and there, design security protocols for payment gateways.

"Sis?"

"Yeah."

"You okay? Talk to me."

She inhaled sharply, her chest constricting. She could feel her heart hammering a tattoo, her legs liquefying.

"Sis? C'mon, say something."

What was she supposed to say? That she was falling apart? Again. That the meds didn't seem to be working again, that she felt as though everything was about to come crashing down around her, that maybe it might be better to just sleep, and sleep forever, to stop being a burden to both herself and Jack. He certainly didn't need to be dealing with a whacked-out sister some three hundred kilometres back on terra firma.

"You know, you're closer up there than you were on the Rock," she said, avoiding the conversation, needing the conversation, unable to begin the conversation.

"How weird is that?" He had such a comforting bass rumble in his voice, like the sound of the earth itself.

"I know," she said.

Another pause she didn't know how to fill.

"But you didn't call me to discuss distance."

Well, sort of she did. Twenty-four hundred klicks from Toronto to Corner Brook. Three hundred to the International Space Station II. But she could hop on a plane to Corner Brook within the hour, or at least later today. But the ISSII? Jack was only as close as the voice in her head.

"Don't make me drag this out of you, Sis. C'mon, you know you need to talk. You know you need to tell me what's going on. Otherwise I can't help you."

"I know."

"So?"

"I can't get to work." There. It was out. She imagined a greedy little gremlin cavorting around her ankles, biting, nipping, making a mockery of all her anxieties and fears.

"Why? You sick?"

She blinked away the gremlin. "Just in the head."

"Now stop that. You're having a panic attack, right?"

"Yes."

"Where are you exactly?"

"Watching the lights at King and Bay."

"Why are you watching the lights?"

"Because I can't cross the road."

"Why can't you cross the road?"

"Cause I'm scared." And that tore it. Now she blinked back tears, was aware she was gasping, that pedestrians were beginning to look at her askance. It seemed the ultimate irony when a homeless woman rumbled by with her cart and stink and her babble of inner dialogue. Déjà vu? Premonition?

"What are you scared of?"

"The traffic, the road, the fact the lights might change before I make it across. Of even if I make it across, what if the elevators choose today to break down? Or what if there's a terrorist who's managed to infiltrate one of the towers and decides to take himself and everyone else to redemption? It happens, you know. You're up there circling around, while down here there are crazies all over the place." And one in particular standing immobile at the corner of King and Bay trying to cross the road to work.

"Last I heard there hadn't been any terrorist attacks in Canada for some number of years, and even those were isolated incidents perpetrated by disturbed people. So I don't think the elevators are going to blow up and take out the tower."

Disturbed people. She was a disturbed people. "But, what happens if I get stuck in the road when the lights change?"

"Well, it's not like motorists are going to gun their engines and run you down because you didn't make the lights."

"But they'll be angry."

"Maybe. Fuck them. Just continue on. And it's unlikely you're going to get stuck in the middle of road."

"Not unless I freeze."

"Have you ever done that?"

"No."

"Well, there you go."

"There's always a first time."

"So, what, you're going to plant yourself in the middle of the crossing just to prove there's always a first time you won't make it across the road?"

Despite herself, she could feel the corner of her mouth twitch in response to his humour. "I'm not that crazy."

"You're not crazy, Sis. Sure, you have issues, problems we both know we need to monitor and work through. But so do lots of people, whether it's physical or physiological. We're all gloriously flawed. Show me a perfect person, and I'll show you a biological android."

"Yeah, maybe."

"Yeah, maybe nothing. So, your heart palpitating?"

"Ready to freakin' jump out of my chest."

"Ah, Sis is channelling Alien."

She snorted a laugh. "That would freak people out."

"Yeah, so let's work on that, shall we? You're taking long, slow breaths?"

She inhaled deeply, let it go. "Yes."

"Now go to your safe place."

"What? Here?"

"Sure, why not?"

"It will look weird."

"I've got you on SAT right now and you don't look weird at all. Awesome doo, by the way. When did you decide to shave your head and do tats?"

She looked up at the sky again, amazed he could zero in on her from so far away. She glanced back down to the streetscape, shuffled over to the bench at the transit stop and eased onto it, aware how weak her legs were, how her hands fluttered like frightened birds.

"Good move, Sis. Very good. Now, where are you in your head?"

She closed her eyes. The sounds around her distilled into a susurration, not unlike waves on a cobble beach. Agawa. A moonrise, huge, white, hanging over a promontory that lay darkly like a sleeping giant.

"Superior," she said. "Our last summer there." Before Jack had gone off to university, and she had to navigate the uncharted waters of secondary.

"That was epic."

She heard the wistfulness in his voice, felt it herself. Life had been so simple then. "I will never forget that summer."

"Me neither."

"Remember how cold the water was?"

"Bloody nut-cracking."

She laughed.

"And you swam circles around me, and then dragged me out of the water because my lips had turned blue."

"Yeah, I did, didn't I?"

"Cause we always took care of each other."

She nodded, sucked in a breath to still tears.

"Listen, Sis, you're gonna feel a lightness in your head in a sec. Don't freak, okay? It's just me uploading a modification to your implant."

Her eyes flew open, panic slamming through her. Even as she uttered: "Not here, Jack! Please!" she felt a tingling in her head, like a cold itch she couldn't scratch, and then she was on her feet, gulping air, Jack's voice crooning gently, "It's okay, Sis. Honest. You know I'd never do anything to hurt you. Really, you're gonna love this. Almost done. You with me?"

"Uh-huh." And then the sensation stilled, and there was only the sound of wind again as vehicles drove by, of the birds, of other pedestrians chatting either to each other or through their own earpieces. The bus sighed to a stop in front of her, the doors opening, passengers spilling out, sweeping up. "What did you do?"

"A modification that will help, I think. Something I've been working on. You're my first trial subject. Not exactly protocol, but, hey, you fit the profile." She heard him laugh. "Now, c'mon, Sis. You remember how when we were little, Mom always told me to take your hand when we crossed the street, that it was my responsibility to make sure you arrived safely on the other side?"

So many roads crossed, Jack holding her hand. So many. Her fingers tingled, and then her palm, and she felt warmth there in her left hand, felt the pressure of a hand, of fingers tightening around hers.

"So, I'm still going to hold your hand, Sis."

She felt fingers squeeze. She looked up sharply at the sky again. "Jack?"

"Yep, that's me."

"But—"

"How?"

"Yeah."

"Does it really matter?"

She looked down at her hand, the way her own fingers curled around his, which weren't there, but were. "No."

"Then, c'mon. Let's cross the intersection."

The lights had changed again, *walk, walk, walk* droning across King and Bay, and tentatively, her hand in Jack's, she stepped out into the intersection and walked to the courtyard, the atrium, and into the elevator to work.

AFTERWORD

Susan Forest

As a fourteen-year-old during the Depression, my father tramped the bush and slough country of northern Saskatchewan with his shotgun, to bring home ducks or a partridge to liven up a family dinner that might consist solely of oatmeal or potatoes. But when, years later in the early 1960s, he moved his young family to Calgary, he found his true passion: mountaineering. Before he passed away at the age of 83, he became the first person to climb all the peaks in the Canadian Rockies and the B.C. Interior Ranges over 11,000 feet, and the oldest man to climb Canada's highest mountain, Mt. Logan—at the age of 71. He was a phenomenal man.

As you can imagine, growing up with my three siblings was an adventure. I have vivid memories of sleeping in utter silence of an ice cave, of the profound darkness inside a grotto when the carbide lamps are doused, of the addictive adrenaline rush after completing the exposed final traverse of the Unnamed route on Mt. Yamnuska. But such a lifestyle could also be daunting: the watery-gut panic from clinging to the ridge of Mt. Lorette on my first serious climb. Nothing wrong with me or the rock, the weather, or the other climbers: I was simply too frozen with terror to move.

It was my older brother and sister who introduced my father to rock climbing through an after-school program. My dad was damned if he was going to give his fourteen-year-old twins a ride to the mountains and then sit at the bottom of the climb to wait until they came down at the end of the day. Not after his lifetime of outdoor adventure. And it was my younger sister, spurred on by a wild competitive drive to keep up to the rest of the family, who went on to build a life as one of Canada's first female park wardens, and to become one of only five Canadian women to earn her full Mountain Guide's licence in 2001.

I, on the other hand, married, had children, and subsequently became a single parent. My fear of heights, my lack of fitness, and my personal responsibilities made it easier for me to sit at home dreaming up stories most weekends than to tramp the mountainsides and experience them. I grew up with every advantage in a close, warm family environment; yet, still, it was hard when my siblings regaled one another with stories of canoeing adventures in the Arctic, of meeting famous mountaineers in backcountry cabins, of unexpectedly riding a slab avalanche in a whiteout. It was hard for me not to feel like a stranger among them.

Over the years, as I more fully carved out my adult identity, this divide has lessened. But I was surprised to discover that my older brother felt separate from our family because of the forty years he spent raising his family in the north country; that my older sister felt separate because of a life dogged with misadventure; that my younger sister felt separate as the only one of us not to have a Master's Degree to hang on her wall.

How ordinary a family I come from. And yet, even so, each of my siblings and I have felt a sense of alienation.

How profound, then, is the experience of those in our society who do live a more isolated existence? How can we, the majority — dare I say, the ordinary folk of the world? — come to understand the complexity of emotions — the intensity of the loneliness — felt by some of the fringe members of our society?

The answer is: through fiction.

Fiction. Whatever divisions, real or perceived, that separate us, one thing we all have in common is a susceptibility to the power of story. The talented authors collected here have reached deeply into their most haunting memories, their places of creativity and imagination, to bring to the page the lived experience of those who dwell in our cities and towns, our rural and remote communities, just next door to us, but who do so on the far side of what might seem — or be — a gaping divide.

These stories reveal nuggets of truth about our vital need to connect, the human fear of loneliness and rejection, the barriers to intimacy and support. Their authors have put into words what cannot be put into words: the invisibility of loneliness, the climate of grief, the mind games of war, the companionship of delusion, the community of addiction, the doublethink of a mad society. They gather together an answer to the question, "Who are the strangers among us?"

We are.

—Susan Forest, Calgary, 2016

ACKNOWLEDGEMENTS

Susan Forest

I would like to thank the members of Calgary's Imaginative Fiction Writers' Association, particularly members of the Whitefish Retreat Group, for their support; also, to the editors who joined me for dinner at World Fantasy Convention 2014, when this project was in its early stages, for their advice and inspiration; to Lucas Law for inviting me to participate, and whose knowledge and professionalism taught me so much; and finally, to the remarkable authors, whose creative imaginations gave flesh and spirit to this amazing compilation. Thank you.

Lucas K. Law

Many thanks go to the following:

≈ Susan Forest for jumping on board without hesitation and being awesome throughout this journey;

≈ Ellen Datlow for spending the time to discuss the art and business of making an anthology;

≈ Samantha M. Beiko for her continuing guidance, a wonderful book cover and interior layout;

≈ Clare Marshall for bridging laksamedia.com website between readers and writers;

≈ Kim E. Mikkelsen and Hilary A. Foulkes for their wisdom and showing me the zest for life whenever I need it most (there is an 'encore' act out there—let's not forget it);

≈ Shane Silverberg for his strong belief in me to pursue this dream (instead of being in a rut, stuck somewhere in corporate Canada);

≈ Robert J. Sawyer, Julie E. Czerneda, Robert Runté, Alyx Dellamonica, and Derek Künsken for recommending some of the authors for this anthology;

≈ The authors who wrote for this anthology with enthusiasm and dedication;

≈ Everyone who buys this book and supports social causes (please continue to talk about mental health/illness).

ABOUT THE CONTRIBUTORS

Kelley Armstrong is the author of the Cainsville modern gothic series and the Age of Legends YA fantasy trilogy. Past works include Otherworld urban fantasy series, the Darkest Powers & Darkness Rising teen paranormal trilogies, the Nadia Stafford crime trilogy and the co-written Blackwell Pages middle-grade fantasy trilogy. Kelley lives in southwestern Ontario with her family.

Suzanne Church grew up in Toronto, moved to Waterloo to pursue mathematics, and never left town. Her award-winning fiction has appeared in *Clarkesworld, Cicada, On Spec,* and her 2014 collection *Elements.* Her favourite place to write is a lakefront cabin, but she'll settle for any coffee shop with WiFi and an electrical outlet. *Soul Larcenist,* book one in the Dagger of Sacrados trilogy set in Ed Greenwood's *Hellmaw* Universe, is now available in multiple formats from onderlibrum.com.

Julie E. Czerneda, Canadian author and editor, has shared her love and curiosity about living things through her science fiction since 1997. *A Turn of Light*, the first of her Night's Edge fantasy series from DAW Books, won the 2014 Aurora Award for Best English Novel, with the sequel, *A Play of Shadow*, winning that award for 2015. Recent publications include the omnibus of her acclaimed near-future SF Species Imperative and Book Two of Night's Edge, *A Play of Shadow*. Julie's back to science fiction, writing the finale to her Clan Chronicles series. November 2015 was the release of Book #1 of Reunification, *This Gulf of Time and Stars*, with more to come. She was honoured to write the introduction to this anthology, for there is no family untouched by mental illness. We must better understand ourselves. For more about her work, visit www.czerneda.com.

A. M. Dellamonica has recently moved to Toronto, Canada, after 22 years in Vancouver. In addition to writing, she studies yoga and takes thousands of digital photographs. She is a graduate of Clarion West and teaches writing through the UCLA Extension Writers' Program. Dellamonica's first novel, *Indigo Springs*, won the Sunburst Award for Canadian Literature of the Fantastic. Her book, *Child of a Hidden Sea*, was released by Tor Books in the summer of 2014; the sequel, *A Daughter of No Nation*, is available now. She is the author of over thirty short stories in a variety of genres, which can be found on *Tor.com, Strange Horizons, Lightspeed* and in numerous print magazines and anthologies. Her website is at http://alyxdellamonica.com.

Gemma Files is a former film critic and teacher turned award-winning horror author, best-known for her Hexslinger Series of Weird Westerns (*A Book of Tongues, A Rope of Thorns* and *A Tree of Bones*, all from ChiZine Publications). She has also published two collections of short fiction, two chapbooks of speculative poetry and a story cycle (*We Will All Go Down Together: Stories of the Five-Family Coven*, CZP). Her new novel, *Experimental Film*, is now available. To learn more, you can check up on her at http://musicatmidnight-gfiles.blogspot.ca, or follow her on Twitter, Tumblr or Livejournal.

James Alan Gardner got a couple of degrees in Math, then started writing science fiction instead. He has won the Aurora award, the Theodore Sturgeon Memorial Award, and the Asimov's Readers' Choice award. He has published eight novels and numerous short stories. In his spare time, he studies rocks and teaches kung fu to kids.

Bev Geddes is a school based speech/language therapist, harpist and freelance writer. As a writer, pieces have been published professionally and through the Canadian Parks and Wilderness Society: Aboriginal Leaders In Conservation project. "Living in

Oz" is her first published work of fiction. She has completed writing her first novel and is presently working on a second speculative fiction book.

Erika Holt resides in Calgary, Alberta, the city where she was born and still loves. Her stories are mostly urban and epic fantasy and have appeared in numerous anthologies including *Evolve Two* and *Tesseracts Fifteen*. She has edited speculative fiction of all kinds and is currently an assistant editor of Nightmare Magazine under bestselling and multiple award-nominated editor-in-chief John Joseph Adams. You can find Erika on Twitter at: @erikaholt. She's also a member of Calgary's Imaginative Fiction Writers Association and blogs with the Inkpunks.

Tyler Keevil grew up in Vancouver, Canada, and in his mid-twenties moved to Wales, where he now lives. His short fiction has appeared in a wide range of magazines and anthologies in Britain, Canada, and the U.S. His first two novels, *Fireball* and *The Drive*, were both nominated for the Wales Book of the Year and both received the Wales Book of the Year People's Prize. His story collection, *Burrard Inlet*, was also nominated for the Wales Book of the Year, as well as the Edge Hill Story Prize, the Frank O'Connor Award, and the Rubery Book Award. One of the stories from the collection, 'Sealskin', was awarded the $10,000 Writers' Trust of Canada Journey Prize. Among other things, Tyler has worked as a tree planter, landscaper, and ice barge deckhand; he is currently a Senior Lecturer in Creative Writing at the University of Gloucestershire.

Rich Larson was born in West Africa, has studied in Rhode Island and worked in Spain, and at 23 now writes from Edmonton, Alberta. His short work has been nominated for the Theodore Sturgeon and appears in multiple Year's Best anthologies, as well as in magazines such as *Asimov's*, *Analog*, *Clarkesworld*, *F&SF*, *Interzone*, *Strange Horizons*, *Lightspeed* and *Apex*. Find him at richwlarson.tumblr.com.

Mahtab Narsimhan was born in Bombay and immigrated to Canada in 1997. Mahtab, in Persian, means Moonlight. Her debut novel in the Tara Trilogy, *The Third Eye* (Dundurn, 2007), won the Silver Birch Fiction Award in 2009. *The Tiffin* (DCB, 2011), a middle-grade novel based loosely on the dabbawallas, has received critical acclaim, was shortlisted for many awards, and named one of the five best books for Young People in 2011 by the *Quill & Quire*. It has been published in the UK, China and Taiwan. Her most recent novel, *Mission Mumbai,* was published by Scholastic US and Canada in Spring 2016. Mahtab lives in Toronto with her husband, son, and golden retriever. She continues to write, inspired by life, love and the desire to make sense of the world through stories. For more information, please visit her website at www.mahtabnarsimhan.com.

Derwin Mak lives in Toronto. He is the only member of the Royal Canadian Military Institute who monitors North Korean music videos to analyze their propaganda. His short story "Transubstantiation" won the Aurora Award for Best Short Form Work in English in 2006. He and Eric Choi co-edited *The Dragon and the Stars* (DAW Books, 2010), the first anthology of science fiction and fantasy by overseas Chinese. It won the 2011 Aurora Award for Best Related Work in English. His two novels *The Moon Under Her Feet* and *The Shrine of the Siren Stone* are science fiction that deal with religious themes in Christianity, Shintoism, and Buddhism. Derwin co-edited the Speculative Fiction Issue of *Ricepaper* magazine with JF Garrard in 2014 and is currently co-editing *Where the Stars Rise* with Lucas K. Law.

Sherry Peters attended the Odyssey Writing Workshop and holds an M.A. in Writing Popular Fiction from Seton Hill University. Her first novel, *Mabel the Lovelorn Dwarf,* won the 2014 Writer's Digest competition for Self-Published ebooks in the Young Adult category. *Mabel the Lovelorn Dwarf* has also been nominated for Canada's Aurora Award for best YA novel. For more information on Sherry, visit her website at http://www.sherrypeters.com.

Ursula Pflug is author of the critically acclaimed novels *Green Music* (Edge/Tesseract), *The Alphabet Stones* (Blue Denim), *Motion Sickness* (illustrated by SK Dyment for Inanna) and the story collections *After the Fires* (Tightrope) and *Harvesting the Moon* (PS). She edited the anthologies *They Have To Take You In* (Hidden Brook) and *The Playground of Lost Toys* (with Colleen Anderson for Exile). She teaches Con Ed creative writing at Loyalist College, the Campbellford Resource Centre, Trent University (with Derek Newman-Stille) and elsewhere. Her award winning short stories and nonfiction about books and art have been appearing for decades in Canada, the US and the UK, in genre and literary venues. Her short stories have been taught in universities in Canada and India, and she has collaborated extensively with filmmakers, dancers, theatre and installation artists.

Robert Runté is Senior Editor at Five Rivers Publishing, an Associate Professor at the University of Lethbridge, and a freelance editor and writing coach at SFeditor.ca. He was co-editor of *Tesseracts 5*, wrote the SF&F entry for the Encyclopedia of Canadian Literature, and has won three Aurora Awards for his SF criticism. He is married, has two teenage daughters, and writes using a treadmill desk.

Lorina Stephens has worked as editor, freelance journalist for national and regional print media, is author of seven books both fiction and non-fiction, been a festival organizer, publicist, lectures on many topics from historical textiles and domestic technologies, to publishing and writing, teaches, and continues to work as a writer, artist, and publisher at Five Rivers Publishing. She has had several short fiction pieces published in Canada's acclaimed *On Spec* magazine, *Postscripts to Darkness*, *Neo-Opsis*, *Garden of Eden*, and Marion Zimmer Bradley's fantasy anthology *Sword & Sorceress X*. Her published books include *Stonehouse Cooks*, *From Mountains of Ice*, *And Angels Sang*, *Shadow Song* and *Recipes of a Dumb Housewife*. Lorina is presently working on two new novels, *The Rose Guardian*, and *Caliban*. She lives with her husband of over four decades in a historic stone house in Neustadt, Ontario. Her website is at lorinastephens.blogspot.ca.

Amanda Sun is the author of The Paper Gods, a YA Fantasy series set in Japan and published by Harlequin Teen. The first two books, *Ink* and *Rain*, are Aurora Award nominees and Junior Library Guild selections. Her short fiction has also been published in the Aurora Award-nominated *Tesseracts Fifteen* and the literary journal *Room Magazine*. She has a new YA Fantasy out in 2016, *Heir to The Sky*, about monster hunters and floating continents. When not reading or writing, Sun is also an avid cosplayer. Find her on Twitter at @Amanda_Sun and get free Paper Gods novellas at AmandaSunBooks.com.

Hayden Trenholm is an award-winning playwright, novelist and short story writer. His short fiction has appeared in *On Spec*, *TransVersions*, *Neo-Opsis*, *Challenging Destiny*, *Talebones*, and on CBC radio. His first novel, *A Circle of Birds*, won the 3-Day Novel Writing competition and was published in 1993 by Anvil Press; it was recently translated and published in French. His trilogy, The Steele Chronicles, was published by Bundoran Press and were each nominated for an Aurora Award. *Stealing Home*, the third book, was a finalist for the Sunburst Award. Hayden has won three Aurora Awards—twice for short fiction and once for editing the anthology, *Blood and Water*. He purchased Bundoran Press in 2012 and is its managing editor. He lives in Ottawa with his wife and fellow writer, Elizabeth Westbrook.

Edward Willett is the author of more than 50 books of fiction and non-fiction for adults, young adults, and children. He won the Aurora Award for Best Long-Form Work in English for his 2009 science-fiction novel *Marseguro* (DAW Books). Recent publications include the two-book *Peregrine Rising* series for Bundoran Press, the *Masks of Aygrima* fantasy trilogy for DAW (written as E.C. Blake), the five-book *Shards of Excalibur* YA fantasy series for Coteau Books, and the YA fantasy novel *Flames of Nevyana* for Rebelight Books. Non-fiction titles have run the gamut from science books and biographies for children and teens to local history books, and even *Genetics Demystified* for McGraw-Hill. Born in Silver City, New Mexico, Ed grew up in Weyburn, Saskatchewan, and now lives in Regina with his wife, Margaret Anne Hodges, a telecommunications engineer, and their teenaged daughter, Alice. He is online at edwardwillett.com

A.C. Wise's work has appeared in publications such as *Clarkesworld*, *Shimmer*, *Apex*, and *Imaginarium: The Best Canadian Speculative Fiction*, among other places. In addition to her fiction, she co-edits *Unlikely Story*, and contributes a monthly *Women to Read: Where to Start column* to *SF Signal*. Her debut collection, *The Ultra Fabulous Glitter Squadron Saves the World Again*, was published by Lethe Press in late 2015. Find her online at www. acwise.net.

ABOUT THE EDITORS

Susan Forest is a three-time Prix Aurora Award finalist and a writer of science fiction, fantasy and horror, and a freelance fiction editor. Her stories have appeared in *Asimov's Science Fiction, Analog Science Fiction and Fact, Beneath Ceaseless Skies, Tesseracts, AE Science Fiction Review, On Spec,* and *The Urban Green Man,* among others. Her collection of short fiction, *Immunity to Strange Tales,* was published by Five Rivers Publishing. Susan is currently co-editing *The Sum of Us* with Lucas K. Law. She acted as judge for the Endeavour Award, and the Robin Herrington Memorial Short Story Contest, and she contributes to Calgary's annual literary festival, When Words Collide. Susan is also the Secretary for the Science Fiction and Fantasy Writers of America (SFWA). She teaches creative writing at the Alexandra Centre, and has appeared at numerous local and international writing conventions.

Lucas K. Law is a Malaysian-born freelance editor, published author, engineering consultant and business coach, who divides his time and heart between Calgary and Qualicum Beach. He is currently co-editing *The Sum of Us* anthology with Susan Forest and *Where the Stars Rise* anthology with Derwin Mak. He has been a jury member for a number of fiction competitions including Nebula, RITA and Golden Heart awards. When Lucas is not editing, writing or reading, he is a consultant, specializing in mergers and acquisition (M&A) activities, asset evaluations, business planning, and corporate development.

COPYRIGHT
ACKNOWLEDGEMENTS

APPENDIX: MENTAL HEALTH RESOURCES

Because of the dynamic nature of the internet, any telephone numbers, web addresses or links provided in this section may have changed since the publication of this book and may no longer be valid.

A listing in the Appendix doesn't mean it is an endorsement from Laksa Media Groups Inc., publisher, editors, authors and/ or those involved in this anthology project. Its listing here is a mean to disseminate information to the readers to get additional materials for further investigation or knowledge.

LEARN DAILY MINDFULNESS . . .

How is your Mental Health? Do you think you have one or more of the following recently?

- More Stress than Before
- Grief
- Separation and Divorce
- Feeling Violence
- Suicidal Thoughts
- Self Injury
- Excessive or Unexplained Anxiety
- Obsessive Compulsive
- Paranoia, Phobias or Panics
- Post-Traumatic Stress
- Depression
- Bi-polar
- Postpartum Depression
- Eating Disorders
- Schizophrenia
- Addictions
- Mood Disorders
- Personality Disorders
- Learning Disabilities

Mental Health Screening Tools

More information:
www.mentalhealthamerica.net/mental-health-screening-tools

- The Depression Screen is most appropriate for individuals who are feeling overwhelming sadness.
- The Anxiety Screen will help if you feel that worry and fear affect your day to day life.
- The Bipolar Screen is intended to support individuals who have mood swings—or unusual shifts in mood and energy.
- The PTSD (Post Traumatic Stress Disorder) Screen is best taken by those who are bothered by a traumatic life event.
- The Alcohol or Substance Use Screen will help determine if your use of alcohol or drugs is an area to address.
- The Youth Screen is for young people (age 11-17) who are concerned that their emotions, attention, or behaviours might be signs of a problem.
- The Parent Screen is for parents of young people to determine if their child's emotions, attention, or behaviours might be signs of a problem.
- The Psychosis Screen is for young people (age 12-35) who feel like their brain is playing tricks on them (seeing, hearing or believing things that don't seem real or quite right).

Worried about Your Child—Symptom Checker: **www.childmind.org/en/health/symptom-checker**

10 Ways to Look after Your Mental Health
(source: www.mentalhealthamerica.net/live-your-life-well)

1. Connect with Others
2. Stay Positive
3. Get Physically Active
4. Help Others
5. Get Enough Sleep
6. Create Joy and Satisfaction
7. Eat Well
8. Take Care of Your Spirit
9. Deal Better with Hard Times
10. Get Professional Help if You Need It

MENTAL HEALTH RESOURCES & INFORMATION

If you or someone you know is struggling with mental illness, please consult a doctor or a healthcare professional in your community.

Below is not a comprehensive information listing, but it is a good start to get more information on mental health/illness.

Emergency Phone Number

If you or someone is in crisis or may be at risk of harming himself/herself or someone else, please call your national Emergency Phone Number immediately.

Canada	911
United States	911
United Kingdom	999 or 112
Ireland	999 or 112
EU	112
Australia	000
New Zealand	111

APPENDIX: MENTAL HEALTH RESOURCES

Canada

To locate your local Canadian Mental Health Association: **www. cmha.ca**

Specifically for children and young people (aged 5-20), call Kids Help Phone's 24-hour confidential phone line at **1-800-668-6868** English or French. More information online: **kidshelpphone.ca**

There are a number of resource materials and list of organizations that you can reach out to on the Bell Let's Talk website: **www.bell.ca/letstalk**.

Mental Health & Addiction Information A-Z: **www.camh.ca/ en/hospital/health_information/a_z_mental_health_and_ addiction_information/Pages/default.aspx**

United States

National Suicide Prevention Hotline: **1-800-273-TALK** or **1-800-273-8255**

For more mental health information: **www. mentalhealthamerica.net/mental-health-information**

United Kingdom

The Samaritans (**www.samaritans.org**) offers emotional support 24 hours a day—get in touch with them: **116-123**.

A to Z of Mental Health: **www.mentalhealth.org.uk/help-information/mental-health-a-z**

Free Mental Health Podcasts: **www.mentalhealth.org.uk/help-information/podcasts**

Ireland

The Samaritans (**www.samaritans.org**) offers emotional support 24 hours a day—get in touch with them: **116-123**.

Childline Helpline: Confidential for young people (under 18). Phone: **1800-66-66-66**

For more mental health information: **www.mentalhealthireland. ie**

Australia

Helplines, websites and government mental health services for Australia: **mhaustralia.org/need-help**

Kids Helpline: Confidential and anonymous, telephone and online counselling service specifically for young people aged between 5 and 25. Phone: **1800-55-18-00** or visit **www.kidshelp.com.au**

Lifeline: 24 hour telephone counselling service. Phone: **13-11-14** or visit **www.lifeline.org.au**

New Zealand

Helplines, websites and government mental health services for New Zealand: **www.mentalhealth.org.nz/get-help/in-crisis/ helplines**

Youthline (for young people under 25): **0800-376-633**. More information online: **http://www.youthline.co.nz**

Lifeline: **0800-543-354** or **(09) 5222-999 within Auckland**

Suicide Crisis Helpline: **0508-828-865 (0508-TAUTOKO)**

CHARITABLE EVENTS
(a sample)

Canada

Ride Don't Hide: **ridedonthide.com**

Walk so Kids Can Talk: **org.kidshelpphone.ca/get-involved/ events**

Boolathon: **www.boolathon.ca**

United States

Out of Darkness Walk: **www.afsp.org/out-of-the-darkness-walks**

NamiWalks: **namiwalks.org**

United Kingdom

Participate in a challenge or community event—run, cycle, trek, tea and talk, skydiving: **www.mentalhealth.org.uk/get-involved/as-a-fundraiser**

Australia

Participate in a challenge or community event: **www. blackdoginstitute.org.au/public/getinvolved/ fundraisingevents.cfm**

PAYING FORWARD, GIVING BACK

READ FOR A CAUSE
WRITE FOR A CAUSE
HELP A CAUSE

MISSION:

Laksa Media Groups Inc. publishes general audience and literary experimental fiction and narrative non-fiction books. Our mission is to create opportunities to 'pay forward' and 'give back' through our publishing program. Our tag line is Read for a Cause, Write for a Cause, Help a Cause.

A portion of our net revenue from each book project goes to support a charitable organization, project or event. We do not deal with any charity that promotes politics, religions, discrimination, crime, hate and inequality.

The charitable causes dear to our hearts are literacy, public libraries, elder care, mental health, affordable housing, and prevention of abuse or bullying.

laksamedia.com

THE SUM OF US

Tales of the Bonded and Bound

Edited by Susan Forest and Lucas K. Law

Don't underestimate those bound with invisible bonds for they have the resources to overcome their doubts to make the world of others a better place.

The Sum of Us is a speculative fiction anthology exploring the world of care-giving and care-givers.

Benefit: Canadian Mental Health Association

Paperback:978-0-9939696-9-0
ePub: 978-1-988140-00-1
PDF: 978-1-988140-01-8
Kindle: 978-1-988140-02-5

LAKSA
MEDIA GROUPS

laksamedia.com

If you like *Strangers Among Us* or want to support our project, please write a review of this book in a venue such as Amazon or Goodreads, or recommend this book to your friends.

Thank you for supporting *Strangers Among Us* and Canadian Mental Health Association.

Want to know more about our projects? Sign up for our newsletters at laksamedia.com.

IT'S A DELICATE BALANCE BETWEEN
MENTAL HEALTH AND MENTAL ILLNESS . . .

BE ALERT!